Various Pets Alive and Dead

Various Pets Alive and Dead

MARINA LEWYCKA

FIG TREE
an imprint of
PENGUIN BOOKS

FIG TREE

Published by the Penguin Group
Penguin Books Ltd, 80 Strand, London WC2R ORL, England
Penguin Group (USA) Inc., 375 Hudson Street, New York, New York 10014, USA
Penguin Group (Canada), 90 Eglinton Avenue East, Suite 700, Toronto, Ontario, Canada M4P 2Y3
(a division of Pearson Penguin Canada Inc.)
Penguin Ireland, 25 St Stephen's Green, Dublin 2, Ireland
(a division of Penguin Books Ltd)
Penguin Group (Australia), 250 Camberwell Road,
Camberwell, Victoria 3124, Australia (a division of Pearson Australia Group Pty Ltd)
Penguin Books India Pvt Ltd, 11 Community Centre,
Panchsheel Park, New Delhi – 110 017, India
Penguin Group (NZ), 67 Apollo Drive, Rosedale, Auckland 0632, New Zealand
(a division of Pearson New Zealand Ltd)
Penguin Books (South Africa) (Pty) Ltd, 24 Sturdee Avenue,
Rosebank, Johannesburg 2196, South Africa

Penguin Books Ltd, Registered Offices: 80 Strand, London WC2R ORL, England

www.penguin.com

First published 2012
1

Copyright © Marina Lewycka, 2012

Set in 12/14.75 pt Dante MT Std
Typeset by Jouve (UK), Milton Keynes
Printed in Great Britain by Clays Ltd, St Ives plc

A CIP catalogue record for this book is available from the British Library

HARDBACK ISBN: 978–1–905–49055–4
TRADE PAPERBACK ISBN: 978–1–905–49091–2

www.greenpenguin.co.uk

MIX
Paper from
responsible sources
FSC™ C018179

Penguin Books is committed to a sustainable
future for our business, our readers and our
planet. This book is made from paper certified
by the Forest Stewardship Council.

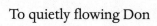

To quietly flowing Don

We live in new times – the age of the hero
is past – now is the time of the non-virtuous man.

Nikolai Gogol, *Dead Souls*, 1842

PART ONE

Various Pets

SERGE: The mill

The whole world is deranged, though most people haven't noticed yet. Everything still looks normal, but when he breathes in Serge can detect it, a faint whiff of madness in the air. It's 8 a.m. on Monday 1st September 2008, the London Stock Exchange has just opened and, all around him, the traders are already getting stuck in.

The trading floor at Finance and Trading Consolidated Alliance resembles a vast money-mill where profits are turned on an industrial scale. The cavernous hall, with its six long face-to-face rows of desks, seats some hundred people, and on each desk a bank of flickering monitors registers minute by minute the restless surge and fall of the markets. The windows are darkened, so that sunlight never bleaches out the monitors, and the ceiling is high enough to absorb the industrious hum of talking and keyboards clicking as trades are made. But in spite of this the air inside has a dead quality, a scorched sulphurous taint of hot plastic from hardware that has been running non-stop ever since it was installed, because to pause or switch off even for a moment would be a moment in which you weren't making money.

Along two sides of the floor are several glass-walled offices for the team leaders. The corner office at the far end of the north side is used by the quants who service the Securitisation desk, reflecting their importance within the corporate hierarchy. The quantitative analysts are the six guys and one girl who are supposed to be able to take the riskiness out of risk with the wizardry of mathematics.

The one girl is Maroushka. From his desk, Serge can see her through the open door, swinging back in the swivel chair, feet up on the table, mobile phone pressed to her ear. No shoes. No tights. Her toenails bling-bling like rubies. She's talking in that outlandish bubbly language of hers, and he finds himself listening when he should be concentrating on the data on his screens. He's never composed poetry before, but then he's never felt so inspired.

> *Princess Maroushka!*
> *Hear the song of Serge!*
> *Let our destinies converge*
> *On this . . . something-something . . .*
> *Green and sunny? Dark satanic . . . verge.*

'Hey, Sergei!' She sees him watching and wiggles four fingers in his direction.

He leans in the doorway. 'Hey, beautiful princess from Zh –' Where did she say she comes from? 'Did you enjoy your birthday on Friday?'

'Very good, thank you. You okay? I think you have been very much drunk. You have fallen on floor.'

'Yeah. I got a bit wasted. But it was worth it to see you dancing on the table.'

'It was folk dance of my country. In Zhytomyr is normal behaviour on birthday.' She blows a kiss and turns away to re-engage with her phone call.

'You should put that thing away. You'll get into trouble if Timo sees you.'

'Why for?'

Her legs are smooth and creamy pale, crossed at the ankles, the calves swelling where they touch, the curved contour of her knees blurring into shadow under the hem of her pale-apricot skirt. D&G? Versace? The perfume she wears is earthy, musky, slightly feral – it borders on the repellent but is in fact incredibly arousing.

'You're not supposed to use your personal mobile in here.'

'Not suppose?' She arches an eyebrow. 'In my country is normal, everybody is doing it.'

'It's a security thing? Because they have to keep a record of all phone calls. Insider trading and all that?' He leans in the doorway, his hands casually in his pockets. Does she realise how cool he is, beneath his ironically geekish exterior?

4

'I no trading. I calling my poor mother in Zhytomyr. She has breast operation.'

'Oh, I'm sorry.'

'Why you sorry?' She wrinkles her delectable brow.

'I mean, most people make a good recovery.' Serge burbles on, 'The success rate has improved dramatically . . .' He's struggling to sound wise and reassuring on the basis of zero knowledge. 'But still, it must be a worrying time for her . . . for you both . . . waiting to see if it'll recur –'

'No recur. Too expensive,' she pouts. Her cute little button nose tilts up.

'You don't have free medical treatment in . . . your country?'

'Ofcoss we have it. But only not for breast operation.'

Timo Jääskeläinen is moving towards them between the rows of desks, humming quietly to himself. Serge winks a warning and she slips the phone back in her bag. Timo Jääskeläinen is the Securitisation desk Vice-Principal, a softly spoken Finn with a big nose, perfect teeth, and a hundred grand's worth of Porsche in the basement car park. He sings tenor in an a cappella quartet on Saturdays, and goes back to Helsinki once a month to visit his mother. They call him Tim the Finn.

'Having problems?' He looms in the office doorway, baring his teeth, though he's obviously not smiling. He's wearing some strong kind of aftershave that smells of aniseed and benzene lighter fuel. 'Did I see you using your mobile phone, Maroushka?'

'She's phoning her mother in . . . er . . .' Serge says quickly. 'She's got breast cancer.'

'Ah. Okay.' He tries to look sympathetic, but it doesn't come naturally to him. 'Next time, you do it outside the building, please. Not in here. If people start to use their personal mobile phones, the trading floor integrity is compromised. You understand?'

Timo sidles off towards the loos. Rumour has it that he has prostate trouble. Maroushka takes the phone out of her bag again and turns towards Serge.

'Why for you talking like this, Serge? Cancer! What cancer? You have too nihilistic view on life.'

'I thought you said she'd had a breast operation.'
'Yes, make nice big breast. Men like it.'
'Oh, I see.'

Serge too spoke to his mother on the phone recently, though not about breast enlargement. She called him on his mobile as he was rushing for the tube, to say could they meet up because she had something important to tell him? So he had to think on his feet.

'Sorry, Mum. I'm going to be in London for a while, working on . . . er . . . a special project with . . . er . . . some guys from Imperial College.'

'How fascinating. You must tell me more when we meet. I'm at a bit of a loose end now Oolie-Anna's got a job. It'll be a lovely excuse for a trip down to London.'

The thing is, his parents think he's still living in Cambridge. He hasn't yet dared to inform them about his new job. Most normal parents, you'd think, would be pleased to have a son not yet thirty and earning ninety grand a year. But not Doro and Marcus. They'd consider it the ultimate betrayal of his ideals, meaning *their* ideals, because Serge doesn't claim to have any ideals – apart from a vague general sense of goodwill towards mankind. And womankind. Especially Maroushka.

Zoom in for close-up: Maroushka Malko, just turned twenty-eight years old, beautiful, cherished only daughter of distinguished academics (yes, they've already swapped some personal information but, as yet, no body fluids), graduate cum laude from the prestigious European university of Zh – . . . wherever. Enrolled for a PhD in maths at University College London, paying her way through her course. Started working for an office cleaning agency, until someone at FATCA discovered her mathematical talent, and she was given a temporary place among the quants.

Pan out to: Serge Free, almost twenty-nine years old, Cambridge educated, handsome . . . well, attractive . . . well, attractive if you're attracted to small skinny men with Buddy Holly glasses and a wonky smile (which she hopefully soon will be). Neglected son of hippy lefties, survivor of Solidarity Hall, the commune in South Yorkshire where he grew up with a floating population of adults, children and various pets alive and dead.

Despite these superficial differences, when you think about it (as he regularly does), he and Maroushka have quite a lot in common. They both joined FATCA just over a year ago. They're both mathematicians, they both work on risk-based derivatives, they're both clever. So it stands to reason they should hit it off. When you think about it, not many couples could share the Fibonacci code or the Gaussian copula for pillow talk. Of course there are some things about his past he will never be able to tell her: how the morning clothes scramble at Solidarity Hall kick-started his passion for fashion; how his early exposure to unpredictability primed his addiction to risk. Though maybe Maroushka would understand because, for all the quants at FATCA, risk is their raison d'être, their ambrosia, their drug of choice.

Since last year's credit crunch and the collapse of Northern Rock, a new level of uncertainty has underpinned their game. You can't turn on the TV without seeing panicky politicians advising the public not to panic, and jumped-up experts, wise after the event, explaining that formerly staid building societies had reinvented themselves as casino PLCs and started lending wildly to the wrong kind of people – people who didn't have a job, or who lied about their income, or who were already up to their ears in debt. People who shouldn't have been offered mortgages in the first place, except that the banks were awash with money, and it had to go somewhere.

And if you bundled together the middle-aged schoolteachers and strictly private dentists with the unemployed single parents and moonlighting plasterers, then sliced the bundles into high-, medium- and low-risk tranches, you could persuade the credit rating agencies like Fitch, Moody's and Standard & Poor's to award the top tranches a triple A. After all, even though the risk is pretty high that there'll be one or two defaults on those NINJA mortgages (No Income No Job No Assets – what the hell did they expect?) they're not *all* going to default, are they?

He smiles. It's at times like this that you need a sense of irony.

People are so stupid. They don't understand about risk. They let themselves be dazzled by returns of 7 per cent, 8 per cent, 9 per cent. Whoever is going to pay you that kind of money unless there's a reason? Then the Government started laying down the law, saying it wasn't their job to bail out reckless gamblers. Too right. But they bailed them out anyway, because they realised they had no choice. As Chicken so brilliantly put it, 'If I owe the bank £10,000, I've got problems. But if I owe it £10 million, the bank's got problems. Ha ha.'

What happens now? Nobody knows, and that's why everybody's so jittery. He sees the fear in his colleagues' eyes each morning as they huddle together for a meeting in their offices at the side of the trading floor, trying to analyse the threats, like rabbits bunching together in their cage while the fox is on the prowl. Are the markets on a bender? Should they be selling short or buying long? What will happen to their compensation? Even Maroushka's rattled, though she doesn't let it show.

The thing is, Maroushka thinks she's cleverer than him. In fact, she thinks she's cleverer than virtually everybody. Last year, her comp was bigger, it's true. But that's because she was working with the CDO team on that lucky deal with Paribas. Most of the time they're neck and neck, pitted against each other and against every quant in every deregulated bank in the financialised world, in an escalating race to find the definitive whiz-bang algorithm for the ultimate whiz-bang risk-free investment to yield infinite wealth, the magic philosopher's stone of our monetised age: unlimited upside.

When she was new, the guys on the floor – especially those who'd known her in the office-cleaner days – used to make comments about her tits, tried to grab, generally horsed about, but she floated above it all on a cloud of disdain. Rumours went around that she was a self-educated mathematical genius, that she'd arrived in London not speaking a word of English and taught herself by reading

Sherlock Holmes, that she was an underwear model, that she was a spy. She even went out with a couple of the traders once or twice, but there was never any of the usual gossip afterwards about what she was like, what she did in bed, what lurked beneath those skin-skimming designer outfits. Not a peep. Silence.

Seeing her let her hair down on Friday night at her birthday party was a revelation. They were all in a restaurant in the West End, a classy little joint off Haymarket with antique furniture, an incomprehensible menu and a wine list that started at £50 and ended at £3,000. She was the only girl there, of the seven of them; she must be used to that by now. She could certainly hold her own when it came to eating and drinking. It was incredible to watch someone so skinny putting away such quantities – where did it all go? They were in a private room and, once they'd got past dessert, the cognac and vodka started to flow. All of a sudden she kicked her shoes off and jumped up on the table and started spinning round in her bare feet, red toenails flashing on the white tablecloth, carefully stepping between the plates and glasses, clapping her hands and singing, or more like chanting, in her strange deep-throat language. Then the two French guys on their team got up and joined in, an old Carla Bruni number, and soon they were all dancing and singing and smashing glasses over their shoulders. Maybe a bit of other damage too. Unfortunately, as he started showing off his moonwalk moves, he put his foot on an empty bottle that was rolling on the floor and slid backwards, putting his head through an oil painting on the wall as he went down. When he came to, everyone else had left, apart from a couple of worried-looking waitresses, who bundled him into a taxi as soon as he could stand up.

What happened next? He's forgotten.

It was one of those unforgettable nights.

He catches her eye through the glass wall and blows her a kiss; she looks away, but he gets a quick glimpse of a smile. What would it be like, he wonders, to take her back to Doncaster, to introduce her to his parents, Marcus and Doro? Hm. Possibly a bit awkward at first.

He'll have to prepare the ground carefully. One slight problem is that he hasn't actually told his parents yet that he's packed in his maths PhD at Cambridge, and is working as a quantitative analyst for the UK branch of an international investment bank. And earning . . . well, quite a lot more than they ever did. When he meets up with Doro tomorrow, he'll tell her.

Yes, he'll definitely do it tomorrow.

CLARA: *Vandalism, pee and the Doncaster climate*

On the first day of term, 1st September 2008, Clara Free turns into a drab crescent of red-brick semis in Doncaster, eases her little Ford Ka into reverse, and lines up the school entrance in her wing mirrors. She looks over her right shoulder. She gives it a bit of gas. The car nudges backwards and scrapes the gate: *crunch*. Drat!

Getting out to inspect the damage, she enjoys a moment of smugness. Someone else, probably Miss Historical Postlethwaite, aka Miss Hippo, has done an even bigger crunch. The school sign is leaning over crookedly against the ugly chain-link fence with its frill of barbed wire: *eenhills Primary Schoo* (the 'Gr' and 'l' disappeared years ago) curved round a rural landscape of green hills folding into each other, although in fact the school is bang in the middle of a Doncaster council estate.

Parking is not her strong point, and this morning she's been particularly distracted. In fact, she's lucky to still be alive, given that the crunch could have happened while she was on the motorway, trying to drive and simultaneously read the letter from her mother that came in the post this morning.

> *I wanted to tell you our very exciting news. Marcus and I are thinking of getting married.*

Hey, what's going on, parents? After nearly forty years – why not leave well alone?

Her classroom with its lingering scent of bleach and beeswax polish breathes quietly, waiting for the children to arrive. She pulls her mother's crumpled letter out of her bag, wondering – why did she write a letter and put a second-class stamp on it? Why not just phone? Probably a sign of general dottiness.

We'll have a reunion, get all the old commune gang together, remember old times . . .

Can it be nostalgia for the lentil sludge? The green-painted floor-boards? The cheesecloth kaftans? The rotas?

. . . celebrate our lives together . . .

Cooking rota. Housework rota. Laundry rota. Childcare rota. Sex rota. All the rotas were pinned up on the noticeboard in the kitchen beside the shopping list.

We'd love you to be there, you and Serge and Oolie-Anna. But don't tell Oolie just yet.

Ha! It must be something to do with Oolie-Anna. At the end of the letter, squashed up in smaller handwriting, is a postscript.

And maybe you could contact the other commune kids and invite them too? I'd love to see how they've all grown up.

See, her mother believes she has oodles of spare time. Unlike her brother Serge – who, being a genius, is excused family obligations on the pretext that he's writing up his PhD. This has been going on for years. 'Oh, Serge is so clever – just give him time,' Doro says. For heaven's sake, how long does a PhD take?

Squeezed between her brother's genius and her sister's disability, she's carved out a space for herself as the sensible one, the organiser, the one everyone can lean on. Which is all very well, except sometimes it would be nice to have someone to lean on herself.

She stuffs the letter back in her bag, switches on her phone to call Doro, changes her mind, and texts Serge's number instead.

Call me, Soz. Our parents are up to something.

Then she heads off to the staffroom to greet her colleagues.

★

There's a fizzy new-term atmosphere; everyone's showing off their suntans and holiday snaps, and swapping information about their new classes with the teachers who taught them last year. From Mr Kenny, she learns that Jason Taylor is a sneak-thief and an endless source of trouble, Dana Kuciak, the Polish girl, is the class swot, and Robbie Lewis masturbates under the desk. Poor Mr Kenny, with his forty-year forty-a-day habit, is a victim of the new head's 'no smoking on the premises' policy, and his hands are shaking uncontrollably as he speaks. Still, she wishes he hadn't told her about her new kids – sometimes it's better to make your own judgements.

At ten minutes to nine, the bell rings in the playground. With a blast of shrill voices, 6F hurtles in, and her day begins.

They spend the morning finding out about each other, and the undifferentiated mass of children gradually separates into thirty-two individuals, with idiosyncrasies, challenges, complicated home circumstances and mystery gifts. It's at times like this that she thinks she has both the best and the hardest job in the world.

By midday, the sun has swung round, making the classroom hot and stuffy. The kids are fidgety after their six weeks' holiday, itching to get outdoors while the weather is still warm. She's about to disappear off to the staffroom for a quick coffee before playground duty when Jason Taylor sidles up to her desk. He's a pale, scrawny kid with dark rings around his eyes and a thin stubble of mousy hair.

'Please, miss, I forgot my dinner money. Me mam says can you lend me some while tomorrow?'

Close up, the smell of him hits her nostrils – cigarette smoke, stale chip fat and wee. She conjures up an instant stereotype of his mother: neglectful, obese and slightly unclean, the sort of woman who goes to the shop in her pyjamas (*Benefit Mum Spent Kids' Dinner Money on Fags and Booze*).

'I'm sorry, Jason. You know I can't do that.'

'Ple-e-ease, miss.'

'Don't you get free school meals?'

'No, miss, because me mam's working up Edenthorpe's.'

So her stereotype of Mrs Taylor has already taken a knock.

'What's up, miss? Don' you trust me?' he whines.

He's persistent, this one.

When she arrived at the school three years ago, she was brimming with ideas about the contribution she would make to this poor community, how she would light the small spark that would fire these kids up and propel them onwards, upwards, out of this drab, cramped barbed-wire-and-chain-link little world. At the end of her first week, she planted a fast-growing Russian Vine, hoping it would clamber up and cover the ugly fence in the car park, but even this rampant weed has now more or less given up its struggle against vandalism, pee and the Doncaster climate. And like the Russian Vine, she's finding the local conditions a challenge to her stamina. She opens her plastic lunch box and extracts a chocolate bar to give her a sugar fix that'll tide her over until her lunch. She snaps it in half, and gives half to Jason. Despite what Mr Kenny told her, Jason is one of those kids whose hopelessness tugs at the heart.

'Don't tell anyone I did that. Now, go away.'

Jason pockets it reluctantly. Then as she's about to close the box, quick as a cat, he dips in and snatches a raw carrot, carved to look like a rocket.

'What's this, miss?'

Before she can get her answer out, he's wolfed down the rocket carrot in three bites. At least he's still got his own teeth.

'It's a carrot, Jason. Vegetable.'

He clasps his stomach and makes vomiting sounds. 'Oah noah! I'm gonner die of vegetable poisoning!'

Despite herself, she laughs.

'If I die, miss, it'll be your fault.'

'You're more likely to die from *not* eating vegetables.'

'Mam says if I eat carrots all t' birds'll fancy me.' He gives her a leery bad-tooth grin. 'Do you fancy me, miss? Cos I reyt fancy you.'

Of all the no-hope kids in her class, there's always one that gets under her skin.

★

On the way home, there's been an accident on the M1 and the traffic is almost at a standstill. It's six o'clock before the bottleneck has cleared and she swoops down into Sheffield, skimming the Parkway roundabout under the curving tram tracks and the water chute from the leisure centre. Compared with the drab bricky thickets of Doncaster, Sheffield seems like a gleaming metropolis pulsing with culture and glamour. She parks her car in her space, turns the key in her door and kicks off her school shoes, like shedding an old skin. Then she puts the kettle on, lights her only cigarette of the day, and looks down from her plant-filled window at the people strolling in the square and the lights twinkling in the water, thinking about the kids in her new class.

When you're a kid, you assume the world you inhabit is the only world there is; you don't realise how temporary, how provisional everything is. How quickly things can change. She wishes she could take Jason Taylor aside and tell him that. 'Don't worry,' she'd say, 'you can escape. Look, I don't live in a commune now. I live in a lovely modern flat in the centre of Sheffield with a clean bathroom all to myself and tall windows full of plants overlooking a square with cafés and fountains. One day you'll grow up, then you can choose your own life.'

But she's not sure how true that really is.

SERGE: Cappuccino

One, one, two, three, five, eight, thirteen . . . The ghost rabbits are still there, crouching on his bed, as Serge struggles out of his dream. They watch, ears pricked up, noses twitching, sniffing the air, as if to forewarn him of danger. He rehearses – walk, tube, walk, office, hello team, hello Maroushka, work, work, work, quick lunch break. Then he remembers – he's supposed to be meeting Doro this afternoon.

Normally, he'd welcome the chance to have a break from the computer and spend an afternoon with his mother – but the trouble is, his two worlds, his past and his present, are so different, so inimical, that like the collision of two subatomic particles, the blast could totally annihilate him.

How to face this threat? He pulls the duvet over his head and goes back to sleep.

The rabbits have disappeared, and he finds himself wandering in the crumbly rambly maze of his childhood home, Solidarity Hall. It's early morning, they're getting ready for school, their clothes are in a heap on the attic floor. They grab and tussle. If he loses out, he'll have to go to school wearing something too small, too girly, or just ridiculously naff. His pulses are pounding. He ends up with the crochet rainbow waistcoat. His guts ache with shame and terror. His head feels full of concrete.

Now the dream shifts, it's afternoon, and they're waiting at the school gate. It's getting late. No one's turned up to walk them home, so Clara takes charge. 'Come on! Follow me!' She strides out into the dusk, singing the slumbering starlings song. The lane is long and winding, overshadowed by gloomy conifers. Clara starts to run and he runs to keep up. His heart is thumping: boom, boom, boom! His breath is quick and shallow. The house is in darkness when they get back, and the man from the electricity board is in the hall, telling them they've been cut off. Somebody's aunty is weeping at the foot of the stairs. All the Groans have disappeared. Then he opens the door of the sitting room, and everyone is in there, lying on the floor, dead. He lets out a howl, and Doro sits up, smiling.

'We're just acting dead, darling. The Dutch Situationists are here.'

They all get up and start chattering and laughing.

He rubs his eyes. Was it a dream, or did it really happen?

Shower, coffee, walk, tube, walk, office, hello team, hello Maroushka.

An hour later, he's sitting in the morning meeting with the six other quants. His head now feels full of polystyrene instead of concrete, so things are looking up.

At midday, Maroushka leans over his desk. She's wearing a yellow jacket with a very short ivory linen dress and slingback shoes you could stab kittens with.

'You coming for lunch soon, Sergei?'

'Yes. No. Sorry, Maroushka, I have to . . . go to the dentist.'

'Oyoyò! Gut luck!'

His mother doesn't realise the sacrifice she's asking of him. In fact, she doesn't realise that even sneaking away from the office for a couple of hours to have a coffee with her could be awkward. The FATCA building is a self-contained world where employees not only work, but can also socialise, exercise in the gym, get their hair done, buy essentials and small expensive gifts, eat in the cafeteria or, more often nowadays, wolf down a sandwich at their desks – in other words, there is really no reason for anyone to leave the building at all during the day.

Serge and Doro rendezvous in the Café Rouge opposite St Paul's on the first Tuesday in September 2008, because Doro refuses to go into Starbucks, which she says is an outpost of American imperialism. He doesn't mention that the Café Rouge is a wholly owned subsidiary of Whitbread Plc, or they could be wandering around all afternoon looking for somewhere suitable.

The weather is still hot, and the square around St Paul's is full of tourists wearing terrible clothes, bumping into each other as they shuffle around peering through their viewfinders at the great gilded Wren dome, glistening up there in the sky-blue sky. They don't realise it's an illusion – in reality two domes, supported in the middle by a sturdy brick cone. If he told her, Doro would probably say it's like the gilded edifice of capitalism supported by the invisible toil of the masses.

Doro, alas, is also wearing terrible clothes, which is a shame, because she's a nice-looking woman – tall, still slim, dark wavy hair lightly streaked with grey, and good skin. But no one over forty should wear a sequinned denim gipsy-flounce skirt – in fact, no one of any age. And that green linen jacket might have been okay in its heyday, but that was some twenty years ago. He has nothing against retro-chic so long as it's worn ironically, but he fears his mum really means it.

'I've got some exciting news, Serge.' She leans across the table, accidentally dipping the sleeve of the jacket into the froth on her cappuccino, then rubs her sleeve with a tissue, spreading the chocolate powder into a brown smudge. 'Marcus and I are thinking of getting married.'

'So what's all this about, Mum?'

Obviously it's not love at first sight, as she and Marcus have been living together since well before he and Clara were born. But Doro likes her little dramas, so he raises his eyebrows and leans forward.

'Tell me more!'

She dips a finger in the cappuccino foam and licks it. Thank God they're not in Franco's, where someone from work might see them.

'We thought it would be nice to make our love official, after all these years.'

Although he's quite an expert on unpredictability, his mother's changes of direction still leave him baffled. Throughout the commune years, marriage was reviled as an oppressive patriarchal institution. Now here she is, getting all dewy-eyed.

'Congratulations, Mum. You've caught the old goat at last! Ha ha.'

For God's sake, they're in their sixties! Can his dad still get it up?

'Yes, we've got plenty to celebrate. Me and Marcus going legit. Clara's promotion to Head of Science. Oolie's first job. The fortieth anniversary of Solidarity Hall. And soon your PhD.'

Uh-uh. We're getting on to dangerous territory here.

'Lovely jacket, Mum. Is it a designer label?' He plays for time, wondering how to break his news.

'Jaeger . . .' Doro hesitates. 'Recycled, of course.'

She means Oxfam. 'You and your recycling! The thing is, Mum –'

'We must all learn to live with less, Serge. Less waste! Less greed! Less mindless consumption!'

Doro has a long list of things she disapproves of, including consumerism, racism, war, Botox, Jeremy Clarkson and trans-fatty acids. Maybe bankers have been added already; if not, it can only be a matter of time.

'It doesn't work like that, Mum. The economy depends on people borrowing and spending – that's what creates wealth.'

He knows this shocking truth must seem counterintuitive to a person of her generation. For them, capitalism was the big no-no.

'That's ridiculous. How can being in debt create wealth?' she snorts. 'People who say that have obviously never been to Doncaster.'

This is going to be harder than he thought.

'Recycling may be good for the environment, Mum, but the economy needs growth.'

'Nonsense. We can't keep squandering the planet's resources on needless junk, creating mountains of waste alongside mountains of debt.'

She has this embarrassing way of raising her voice in public, as if trying to rouse the slumbering starlings. Ranting is probably one of the few pleasures left at her age. In the slanting light of the window, the little puckers on her upper lip look like crinkled paper, with deeper creases where the corners of her nose and mouth meet. Definitely sub-prime. Her last birthday was the big six-oh. Poor Doro. Age doesn't suit her. Well, it doesn't really suit anybody, does it?

'If everyone was like you, Mum, the system would collapse.'

'But that's what we want. Isn't it?'

'Yes, but . . .' He smiles indulgently. There's something particularly baffling about Doro's brand of illogic.

'So how's the PhD going?' She changes the subject, recycling a couple of spare sugar sachets into her handbag. 'Just remind me again, darling. What is it about?'

'The Hausdorff–Besicovitch dimension, Mum.'

Doro nods blankly. They have this conversation almost every time. She never seems to get it.

'Chaos theory. You know, the butterfly effect? How small events can have huge unforeseen consequences? Like the beat of a butterfly's wing in Mozambique can result in a typhoon miles away in Thailand. You've heard of Poincaré?'

'The rabbit man?'

'That was Fibonacci.'

'Ah yes. I always knew you were a genius, darling. One day they'll name a theorem after you.'

When he was a kid, Doro used to tell him he was brilliant, and she said it with such conviction he almost came to believe it, though deep down he thought these mathematical tricks were so obvious that anyone could do them. This thing he has with numbers, this knack of seeing patterns everywhere, sometimes seems more like a disability – the way some people are extra sensitive to pollens or soap powder.

'So this research of yours, Serge, does it have any practical applications?'

'It's a tool for predicting things which are usually considered unpredictable –'

'Like winning the lottery?'

'That sort of thing. Though it's more generally epidemics, earthquakes, hurricanes –'

'I expect one day you'll be fabulously rich,' she remarks innocently.

'If I ever am, I'll take you on the shopping spree of a lifetime.' He smiles to himself. It could be closer than she imagines. 'And not in Oxfam, either, Mum.'

'What's wrong with Oxfam?'

'Nothing. I just thought you might like –'

She leans forward across the table and looks at him critically. 'What's that flashy suit you're wearing? I bet that wasn't from Oxfam.'

When he got his first pay cheque, he went on a splurge in a boutique sale in Shoreditch.

'Ermenegildo Zegna, Mum, but I got it in the sale. It was less than half price.'

Her mouth puckers as if she can't decide whether to be cross about the label or pleased about the bargain.

'And why are you wearing those heavy glasses, darling? They don't suit you. They make you look like Buddy Holly.'

'That's the idea.'

'But he was tall and handsome, darling.'

'Mum . . .'

'Sorry. I didn't mean you're *not* tall and handsome. Not *not* handsome, anyway, but what I meant was –'

'Don't go there, Mum.'

'But the glasses make you look –'

'They're ironic.'

'How can glasses be ironic?'

'They can. Trust me.'

Doro leans back in her chair and laughs, a deep middle-aged chuckle. He laughs too, realising how much he loves Doro, with her bad clothes, wrinkles and merriment. He wouldn't have her any other way – well, perhaps he would change a few things. But he knows at heart he's Mummy's boy.

Clara, on the other hand, takes after Dad. Whenever he thinks about his sister, he hears the faint sound of a door slamming in the back of his mind. Although she's only three years older than him, she's constantly lecturing him about what he should be doing with his life. She never misses a chance to put him right about whatever she thinks he's doing wrong. Example: 'Maths is so abstract, Serge. You should engage with the real world.'

By 'the real world' she means the deindustrialised North. She believes she's a cuddly right-on human being bringing learning to those no-hope kids, when it's all an ego trip to make her feel morally superior, make other people feel bad about their life choices, and give her an excuse to pontificate about stuff she knows nothing about, such as global warming, fashion and capitalism. God knows what she'll say when she finds out about his job.

She's not bad looking – tall and slim like Doro, with Marcus's curly hair and amazing blue eyes – but men don't go near her because they're scared of her bite. Apparently she dumped her last boyfriend, a perfectly okay guy called Josh, a civil engineer, because he always agreed with everything she said. As far as Serge knows, she's been on her own for the past year – no wonder.

Clara's probably like this because she was the first baby of the commune. She was born in 1976 and named after Clara Zetkin, a German proto-feminist who invented International Women's Day. This was a day when the food at Solidarity Hall was always particularly horrible because the pre-'new men' took over the cooking, furiously boiling up random combinations of dried beans, lentils and veggies, while the women sat around moaning about 'women's impression', according to nine-year-old Clara, who was allowed to join in. When he was born in 1979, they named him after Victor Serge, a Belgian-Russian revolutionary with 'librarian tendencies'.

Their parents lived through a time of excitement and adventure in the late sixties and seventies, when they threw off the shackles of convention and freed themselves to experiment with completely new ways of living, cool music and stupid clothes – which can't be that different from the excitement of creating completely new formulae for managing risk, setting money free to roam the world in search of undreamed-of returns.

He just wishes he could explain the thrill of it to Doro.

'Like I was saying, Mum, storms, clouds, galaxies. All the great forces of nature . . .'

But she's not listening any more. Her attention has been caught by a woman with a large brown poodle on a lead, which is crapping on the pavement outside. She raps on the window. The woman looks. Their eyes meet.

'. . . they all follow certain hidden rules.'

Doro raps again. The dog is still straining away.

'And not just nature. For example, the stock market –'

'It's just a giant lottery, isn't it?' she says.

'Exactly, Mum. But if you study it over time –'

'Darling, people who study the stock market usually contribute nothing useful to society and sponge off the honest work of others.'

Her eyes have that manic gleam. This confession is going to be harder than he thought.

'I know. But *if* you do, you can see trends and patterns emerging . . .'

The woman, who is wearing pink leggings tucked into black boots, gives the dog's lead a little tug to encourage it.

'. . . so you can apply the same theory to the markets . . .'

His mother's eyes are fixed on the scenario outside the window. Maybe this isn't the right time to tell her.

'Look!' she snaps. 'Treating a public space as a lavatory. No thought for anyone else.'

The woman tugs harder, but the dog braces itself and carries on straining. He can feel himself getting hooked on this mini-drama too, but he tries to press on with his confession.

'You remember Fibonacci, Mum? The rabbit man? Well, some people use the Fibonacci code . . .'

His mother pinches her nose theatrically between her finger and thumb. The dog gives one last heave – and behold! A golden mound appears on the pavement beneath its bottom.

'. . . to predict when they're going to turn . . .'

A look of satisfaction lights up the poor mutt's face. Doro is still rapping on the window, holding her nose with the other hand. She may be right, but normal people wouldn't do that, would they?

'. . . though of course the irony about predicting the markets . . .'

The pink-leggings lady looks upset. The dog is sniffing happily at its steaming pile of gold. She tugs the lead and starts to walk away.

'. . . is that if there was foolproof prediction, there'd be no market!'

'Stop!' Doro leaps from her chair and dashes out into the street, yelling at the top of her voice. 'Someone could step in that! A child!'

People stare. The pink-leggings lady yanks the lead but the poodle drags back, not yet ready to be separated from its product. Doro is gesticulating wildly. Still, you have to admire her guts. At last, the dog lets itself be dragged away, and Doro comes back into the café and plonks herself down in front of her lukewarm cappuccino.

'The whole world's gone mad. It's all me, me, me! No one has any sense of social responsibility!'

'Calm down, Mum.'

As people drift away, he notices a woman in a yellow jacket staring straight at the window where they're sitting. Maroushka! What's she doing out on the loose?

'*And* someone should take her aside and tell her she's too old for pink leggings!'

CLARA: Hamlet, Fizzy

The new head teacher at Greenhills is called Mr Gorst. Mr Alan Gorst. He looks too young for a head, with round pink cheeks and black spiked-up hair. When he took over the headship at the end of last term, he announced that the traditional summer sports day (too many losers) would be replaced with an autumn Community Day (everybody a winner), to welcome new parents and encourage involvement between the school and the community. The way he said it, with a dark twinkle in his eye, made the staff (especially the female staff) feel as though they'd made a supremely fulfilling career choice.

Not everyone was pleased.

'They're already involved with the police and the Benefits Agency,' grumbled fag-deprived Mr Kenny. 'What more chuffin' involvement do they need?'

But Clara supports his approach. 'A Greener Greenhills' is her chosen theme for 6F's Community Day stall. If she can only get the kids to cherish their own immediate environment, it will make them more aware of the beauty and fragility of our planet, she tells a twinkling Mr Gorst. (Dare she call him Alan? It seems too intimate.) Mr Gorst / Alan says it's inspirational.

Their stall will feature potted tree seedlings – rowan, poplar, hawthorn and cherry – from which the streets of the estate are named. The parents will plant them in front of their houses, hopefully in the appropriate streets (otherwise there could be confusion in twenty years' time). There will also be petitions to save dolphins, cut carbon emissions and ban kids from playing football on Rowan Green (this suggestion came from Mrs Salmon, whose mother lives nearby). There will be a paper recycling bin and plastic recycling crates where parents can put their used plastic bottles. Kids from 6F wearing wellies will jump up and down on them (Miss! Please! Me!

Miss! Me! Me!). At the end of the day, it will all be collected for recycling by a local firm called Syrec (South Yorkshire Recycling) based out at Askern. This is the tricky part.

It took her two hours of dialling through the Yellow Pages to find a firm willing to collect the waste. The man at Syrec, when she got through to him, sounded like a nineteen-year-old on speed or a call-centre salesman flogging a dodgy mortgage. He agreed to take it all away for twenty quid, and she wasn't in a position to argue, but she's not managed to contact him since to confirm, and according to Mr Kenny, whose wife works in the Council, they've just been awarded a big regional development grant, so maybe that's why.

In the corridor after lunch she bumps into Miss Historical Postlethwaite hauling two big display boards towards the hall. She's wearing Roman centurion-type sandals with high wedge heels, a cowgirl blouse and a medieval-style chain belt around her middle. (Really, you can take history too far.)

'Hello, Heidi. Is that your Community Day display?'

'I'm giving the folks on the estate a little peek into their history,' she breathes, jingling her faux-Victorian ear-danglers. 'They're so deprived of any connection with the past.'

Clara looks at the boards, covered with neatly mounted photocopies of black and white photographs and spidery handwritten memoirs. According to Historical Heidi's display, the Greenhills Estate was built in the 1930s, to replace the slums of red-brick terraces that sprawled around Doncaster, and they named the streets after trees to give it the feel of a little corner of rural England.

'Fascinating!'

She and 6F spend the afternoon mounting their own idealised version of the estate, the kids' wonky drawings of their streets and homes floating on a leafy crêpe-paper sea. After they've gone, she tidies up her classroom and sorts her things for tomorrow, when there's a knock on the door and in comes Mr Philpott, the caretaker, wearing his brown button-up overalls. He advances, grinning mysteriously, holding out a large package wrapped in brown paper.

'Ta-daah!'

'Is it for me?'

She tears off the paper. Inside is a clear plastic box with air holes in which a ball of gingery fluff is curled up asleep. A rush of emotion colours her cheeks.

'Why . . .?'

'To teach the little villains kindness and responsibility. Remember what the Head said? You can keep it in the classroom. I'll look after it at weekends.'

She remembers vaguely that Mr Gorst/Alan mentioned something in a staff meeting, and she'd immediately dismissed the idea as not for her (*Dead Hamster Debacle – Teacher Arrested*).

'I . . . I don't think I can keep it.' Her heart is beating so hard she's sure he must be able to hear. 'I've had some bad experiences with pets.'

Mr Philpott looks crestfallen. 'I thought you'd like it, duck.'

The ball of ginger fluff stirs. Tiny pink paws rub trembling whiskers. Two bright button eyes blink open. It is heartbreakingly adorable. Well-meaning people like Mr Philpott and Mr Gorst/Alan think caring for pets will teach children kindness and responsibility, but she knows that what you really learn is the precariousness of life, the inevitability of death.

'I do . . . only . . . Has it got a name?'

''Amlet the 'Amster.'

'That's a great name. But . . . Hamlet died young!'

''E 'ad personal problems, din't 'e? But this one just sleeps all the time.'

The little creature has curled up again and gone to sleep.

'For in that sleep what dreams may come when we have shuffled off this 'amster coil.'

'He's talking about death.'

'You know, I wondered what the 'eck 'e were on about. I saw t' play at t' Civic Theatre. Watched it twice, and I were none the wiser. I even bought t' boowk.'

'Your boiler room is a sanctuary of erudition and culture in a barbarous world, Mr Philpott.'

'Aye, if I had my time over again, I could've been an intellectual, like you.'

After he's gone, she puts the hamster box on the window sill, takes her phone out of her bag, and scrolls down to Serge's number. The little curled-up ginger creature has jolted her memory.

Serge is often mysteriously unavailable for weeks, but this time he answers on the first ring.

'Serge Free.'

'I know it's you, you little troll. Have you been avoiding me?'

'Claz! Why would I do that?'

'Has Doro talked to you about these proposed parental nuptials?'

'Yeah, she came down to London today.'

Which is strange, since Serge is still at Cambridge finishing his PhD. He mumbles something about collaboration with a maths team at University College, then starts on about an argument concerning doggy-doo with some woman wearing pink leggings. Her mother seems to be getting more and more eccentric in her old age.

'Poor you. Was it embarrassing? Did people stare?'

'Just a bit.'

'D'you remember that time you fell over in the park and came home covered in it? You even got it in your hair. Doro went ballistic.'

Serge was always uncannily accident-prone as a kid. Doro used to call him dyspraxic.

'Yeah, I remember. Wasn't it Freud who said shit is a dream-metaphor for money?'

'How Doggy-Doo Can Make You Rich! Billionaire Secrets Revealed!'

'There could be something in it.'

'Get a grip, Soz.' He's almost as mad as Doro. 'Anyway, she wants us to track down the kids from the commune. But I've got my hands full trying to organise a stall for the school's Community Day. I can't get hold of the recycling company.'

She talks about her problems with Syrec, and Doro's strange letter. He makes occasional supporting grunts down the phone.

'I've looked on Facebook, but none of the Solidarity Hall kids seem to be signed up,' she says.

'Tosser and Kollon aren't really Facebook types. I last saw Tosser . . . ooh . . . two years ago?'

'I last saw Star on TV. In a police raid on a climate camp. She was still wearing that rainbow crochet top and raggedy velvet skirt. I thought social networking was the big thing among that lot.'

'Mm. Maybe.'

He sounds distant and distracted. She can feel her irritation rising. How did it happen that holding the family together became her job?

'And it's strange Otto isn't on Facebook, given his obsession with all things technical.'

'Otto? I dunno. Maybe he's changed his online name. Isn't this more your sort of scene, Claz?' he mutters.

'Why's it always me that has to do everything?'

'You're good at it. You have the organiser's touch.'

'Like you have the touch of death.'

'Sheesh! You're not still going on about that icky hamster! Get over it!'

'It's not the hamster, Soz. It's your total refusal to accept responsibility for . . . Oh!'

She jabs her phone off, and takes several deep calming breaths.

Whatever they start off talking about, it always seems to come back to Fizzy. Thinking of him (or her) makes her choke up with remorse, even after all these years, and she doesn't know whether to feel more upset at Serge for killing him, or at her parents for letting it happen.

Fizzy was her class's pet hamster when she was at primary school in Campsall. He (or possibly she) lived in a cage on the nature table. Fizzy was named after Bucks Fizz, then number one in the hit parade. He was unbelievably cute, like Hamlet, with ginger fur and a white tummy, pink paws, and a little black spot that looked like an ink splodge on the tip of his nose. On Fridays the kids took turns to take Fizzy home and look after him for the weekend. Clara was the lucky one who got to have him for a whole week at spring half term. Doro collected her from school, helped her carry the cage home, and set it in a corner of the sitting room.

Fizzy was a champion carrot-chomper; he whizzed round on his hamster wheel like a boy racer; and when she took him out of the cage, he sat in the palm of her hand twitching his whiskers and looking around with bright beady eyes. Serge, who hadn't started school yet, was mad with envy.

'I want a go!' He made a grab.

'Gerroff! He's mine!' Clara closed her hand around the hamster, feeling its little frame squirming between her fingers.

'I just want to hold it!'

'You can't, so there!'

'Don't grab, Serge,' said Marcus, who was sitting on the sofa trying to read a newspaper.

'Darling, just let him hold it for a moment,' said Doro.

'No,' said Clara.

'Doro says I can.'

'You can't because you're too little and you'll kill it.'

'I'm not little. I just want to hold it.'

'Clara, don't be selfish,' said Doro.

'You can't make me,' said Clara, squeezing him tight.

'Yes, I can.' Serge lunged and prised the little creature out of her hands. He held it up in the air like a plane and ran around the room yelling, 'Ner-ner! Ner-ner!'

'Give it back!'

Clara ran after him and grappled it out of his hand, pressing it against her chest. Then she noticed something odd. Actually, it wasn't just odd, it was horrible. The hamster wasn't squirming any more.

'Aaaaw! He's dead!'

She opened her hands and stared at the limp furry scrap. One of its eyeballs seemed to have popped out.

'Put it back in its cage,' said Doro. 'It's probably just frightened.'

They put Fizzy back in his cage, and Clara poked him every few minutes. But he didn't move.

'He killed 'im!' she sobbed.

Marcus looked up from his newspaper. 'That's what happens when you fight over possessions. Now go and play outside! Scarper!'

'What'll I say, when I have to take 'im back to school?' Clara wailed.

'We'll find another one,' said Doro.

On Saturday, Nick Holliday drove them into Doncaster to scour the pet shops. There were only two, so it was a quick scour. The first shop had one hamster, an albino, fat and white with pink eyes. The other shop had four hamsters, very cute, with brown-grey stripes, but they obviously weren't Fizzy. Clara started to sob again.

'There might be a pet shop in Rotherham,' said Nick.

But the Rotherham hamsters were only babies.

Undeterred, they set out for Sheffield, Clara and Serge squabbling on the back seat of the car, with the empty hamster cage between them. She wanted Serge to admit he'd killed Fizzy and apologise, but he wouldn't even admit the hamster was dead. He kept reaching across and hitting her, so she had to hit him back.

At one point Nick, who was generally an even-tempered kind of guy, pulled over in a lay-by and screamed, 'If you don't stop this minute, you can both get out and walk home!'

In Sheffield, they eventually found a hamster which was the same gingery colour as Fizzy, even the same size, with the same white fur on its tummy. Only it didn't have a black splodge on its nose.

'It's no good!' she howled, stamping her feet.

Nick said, 'Nobody'll notice the difference. You'll see.'

Fizzy was buried in a paper bag in the garden.

When no one was looking, Clara went and dug him up – to check whether he'd gone to heaven yet. She'd learned at school that you went to heaven if you'd been good. But he was still there.

This made her howl even more.

On the Monday after half term, she took the new hamster in its cage back to school, and handed it to the teacher, who put it on the nature table with barely a glance. None of the kids seemed interested. She breathed a sigh of relief. Then the girl who had preceded her on the hamster rota put her hand up.

'Please, miss, it's t' wrong 'amster.'

She was a skinny freckled girl from an extended family of loud-mouth aunties, tough uncles and mean-looking cousins who all lived in the Prospects, a warren of crumbling terraces not far from the school.

'No it in't!' Clara retorted. 'You can't even tell the difference.'

'Yes I can, cos t'other one were a bit black on't nose,' said the girl.

Next day, three of the girl's cousins were lying in wait for Clara after school. They called her a murderer, thumped her about, pulled her hair, and stole her red star hairclips that Moira had made for her. Jen, who was late picking them up from school, didn't see a thing. Next morning the girl turned up in class with her mousy hair pinned back in the red star hairclips, instead of her usual pink daisy hairclips. Clara spotted them immediately, but didn't tell.

No one else noticed.

SERGE: Chicken

'Who is old woman you meeting today, Sergei?' asks Maroushka, sidling up to his desk.

'What old woman?'

'In Café Rouge. I have seen you!'

'That was . . . just a friend . . . a friendly dentist.' (Sorry, Mum!)

'Hey, you know wired people.'

'Yeah. What were *you* doing out there, anyway, babe? Let me guess – an assignation with your secret lover?'

'You have very amusing idea, Sergei. Ssh! Here comes Chicken!'

She raises a scarlet-tipped finger and, turning to follow the direction of her eyes, he sees that their boss has just appeared in the entrance to the trading floor.

Despite his nickname, FATCA's senior partner Ken Porter is a handsome, muscular man who looks more like a Dobermann than a chicken, a mature hunting dog with sharp white teeth, glossy black hair and quick shiny eyes. Although at fiftyish he must be past his prime, he still exudes a sort of testosterone-charged animal vigour which, according to the gossip, makes him irresistible to women. His office is a leather-and-mahogany shrine of golfing trophies, shag-pile rugs and investment art, in the style of a nineteenth-century gentlemen's club, up on the top floor of the steel-and-glass FATCA tower, where the senior partners entertain clients so important they're only referred to by their initials or an account number.

Serge has only been up there once, the day he was interviewed for his job. It was more a seduction than an interview: Chicken's offer – 'cutting-edge research; opportunity to apply your skills in a dynamic international environment; money, lots of it, more than you'll know what to do with' – against the lonely satisfaction of his still-unfinished PhD, the monk-like cell in a medieval college, the miserable £9k bursary.

While he hesitated, Chicken had jabbed his finger at the FATCA logo on a company report – a globe encircled with the words AUDACES FORTUNA IUVAT.

'You're a scholar, Free. Know what that means? Fortune favours the bold.'

Then he'd reached out, gripped Serge's hand, and shaken it up and down like a killer dog trying to break the neck of some little creature it's just caught.

Most days Chicken takes a stroll along the trading floor, walking with a slight wide-legged roll, like he's got a permanent hard-on. Or he drops into the morning meetings, just to spread a bit more testosterone around. You can smell it on the air, or maybe it's just his aftershave, a pungent musky smell that brings up in Serge's mind a faint whiff of his childhood.

He pauses by Serge's desk, leaning to examine his screens. 'All right, Freebie?'

'All good, Chief Ken.'

'Freebie' is Serge's nickname at FATCA. Everyone here has a nickname (apart from Maroushka, which is already a nickname for something ordinary, like Mary). It's meant to foster an informal and creative atmosphere. Ken Porter thinks his own nickname is Chief Ken, but it didn't take long for some wag on the trading floor to abbreviate it to Chi-Ken, and from thence to Chicken. Despite his nickname, he's undoubtedly the top dog in the pack, and you have to feel some admiration for a guy who's made it so big-time, and wears the suits to prove it.

'I see your ABS fund is coming in at just over two million, Freebie.'

The ABS is an algorithm-based investment strategy which Serge created in March to capitalise on the downward spiral in the US housing market, when the whole international banking system was thrown into turmoil by the uncertainty surrounding their multibillion investments in US sub-prime. But where there's uncertainty, there's risk: and risk is the godfather of serious money. And this year he's been making it in shedloads for FATCA.

'That's what we want; the best and brightest of your generation working for us.' Chicken grasps his hand and pumps up and down.

Serge glows, winces and tries to maintain eye contact, all at the same time. Out of the hundreds of employees at FATCA, it's kind of cool that Chicken has noticed his contribution. Suddenly Chicken drops his hand. The smile freezes over, the teeth are still bared.

'I need to know how you got your information, Freebie.'

'I didn't have information.' A rush of alarm. 'I . . . er . . . worked out a better way of hedging the risk so we could boost the yield. It's . . . it's an extension of Itō's Lemma.' He is gratified to see a glimmer of respect light up in the bright doggy eyes.

'The Lemma, eh?'

Chicken, he guesses, is somewhat out of his depth with the new maths. He belongs to the previous generation of bankers – the barrow boys, as they were called – hard, hungry men who were recruited in droves into City jobs in the late 1980s to replace the bowler-hatted toffs whose gentlemanly protocol was thought to be too fuzzy for the post-Big Bang trading conditions. What you needed to make money in that newly deregulated environment were aggression and cunning, and Chief Ken has bucketloads of those. But nowadays, the newest intake to the City tend to be geeky people, maths and physics nerds like himself, who were initially a tad uncomfortable in the purlieus of money, though it's surprising how quickly you can get used to eighty plus k a year.

'Risk-free risk. Limited downside. That's what we pay you for, Freebie. Have you shared it with the team?'

He thinks there's a whiz-bang numerical trick to take the risk out of investment, like a key-code à la Dan Brown that will unlock the steel-reinforced door leading to a glittering chamber of infinite wealth.

'It's complex, Chief Ken.'

'Good. The more complex the better – harder for some other sneak-geek to steal or copy. '

Chicken smiles, and Serge feels the radiance light on him like sunshine. He could add that it also makes it much harder for anybody to keep track of what was in the original investment bundle, so in the end nobody knows what anyone is worth, apart from the quants like himself who put the packages together. And they've mostly forgotten, or got bored and moved on to something else.

But that's not what Chicken wants to hear, so he says, 'I'll bring it up in the quants' meeting tomorrow, Ken.'

'Good man. I'll go and tell Maroushka.'

He advances towards Maroushka's desk, the gym-toned muscles flexing beneath the expensive cloth of his bespoke suit. One day, the thought slips into Serge's head, I'll wear a suit like that.

DORO: Groucho Marxist

'I really shouldn't have shouted at that pink-legged woman. It achieved nothing, embarrassed Serge and left me in a foul mood,' thinks Doro, watching her reflection in the train window floating across the mile after mile of dispiriting countryside as she heads back north on Tuesday evening. London is less than an hour and a half away from Doncaster, yet it seems like a different country in a different era. She can't understand how anyone can put up with it – such a crush of traffic, the streets filthy, the people ignorant. It was just the same when she and Marcus lived there, forty years ago. She's glad to get away.

Glad to get away from Serge too, who seemed not himself today – tense and manic, rattling on about incomprehensible things. Just listening to him is exhausting. If only he'd settle down and finish off his PhD, which has been hanging over him for aeons. Clara too seems preoccupied with the minutiae of her job. She wishes she could talk to her children in a friendly, open way; she wishes they wouldn't always patronise her and humour her, treating her like some relic whose life is in the past. The bold, radical and outrageous values of her generation are regarded by her children as quaint lifestyle whims on a par with tie-dyes and loon pants, which make them keel over with laughter.

She's tried to explain about solidarity and class consciousness, but the words have no meaning for them. The language itself has changed. 'Revolutionary' is what you call the latest mobile phone technology. 'Struggle' is trying to get home on the bus with your bags of shopping. They think listening to indie music is what makes you a rebel. They think they invented sex. She was the same at their age, of course, and that's the worst thing about it – they make her feel old.

She remembers her own parents with a mixture of fondness and guilt: how she'd loved their non-judgemental Quaker kindness, and appreciated their cash bailouts when times were hard; how she'd mocked their bourgeois conformity and outdated sexual hang-ups as she'd plunged headlong into the student movement of 1968.

'A young woman really should wear a brassiere,' her mother had admonished (she pronounced it 'brazeer') when Doro had binned her bra, whose tight cotton straps (those were the pre-Lycra days) cut red welts into her shoulders.

'It's a symbol of patriarchy, Mother.'

'I'm sure if the patriarchs had had bosoms, they wouldn't have let them bounce around, Dorothy.'

She has never quite forgiven her mother for christening her Dorothy.

'Why should women constrict themselves in bras in order to please men?' she'd sneered. 'It's false consciousness. Adopting the values and beliefs of the oppressor.'

Bras and false consciousness had been a subject of intense discussion in her women's consciousness-raising group in 1968, when she and six women from university, including Moira Lafferty (then still Moira McLeod), had met every Wednesday evening to pour out their feelings about their bodies, their boyfriends, their families and their hopes for themselves. That was when she'd dumped Dorothy, along with her bra, and started calling herself Doro, which sounded interesting and powerful. Moira, who was both Doro's oldest friend and her most long-standing rival, was a bit flaky on the ideological front and prone to false consciousness, even then. Moira was the one who argued that since men screw around, women would become liberated by doing the same, and the others nodded, lacking the confidence to dispute something about which they knew so little. Moira was the one who clung on to her bra when the rest of them binned theirs in solidarity with their sisters in the USA, chortling about the myth of bra-burning.

Now Oolie hates to have her overgenerous bouncy breasts restrained, and Doro's the one who insists.

'Which oppressor?' her mother had scoffed.

'Well, Daddy, I suppose.'

Which made them both laugh, for it was hard to imagine anyone less suited to the role of oppressor than her gentle, diffident historian father.

'Don't be silly, darling. It's not about men, it's about gravity.'

Doro shared a flat in Islington with two other girls from her course, Moira McLeod and Julia Chance. Julia, a thin Celtic beauty from Wallasey, was engaged to Pete Lafferty, her childhood sweetheart, who spent most weekends at their flat. Within six months, Julia and Pete had split up and Julia had gone back to Merseyside with a broken heart and a fistful of Moira's auburn hair.

Observing this, Doro was reluctant at first to bring Marcus Lerner back to the flat. She'd met him only a few months ago, when he'd pulled her out of a hedge in Grosvenor Square where she was cowering, terrified by a rearing police horse, on an anti-Vietnam War demo in March 1968. Out of the turmoil of flailing batons and horses' hooves, he reached out his hand and gripped hers.

'You all right, sister?' He had blazing blue eyes and wild curly brown hair; he wore a black leather jacket and a red bandana around his forehead like a real revolutionary.

'Fine, thanks, comrade,' she said, dreading the moment he would realise she was just a third-year sociology student, and not a revolutionary at all.

'Let's get you out of here.'

He sat her on the back of his scooter, and she thought he was going to take her home, but instead he whisked her off to his room in a house near Hampstead Heath. It was a small attic room with a mattress on the floor, bookshelves made out of old floorboards supported by bricks, and a wooden door balanced on four columns of bricks for a desk, on which were spread the handwritten notes of Marcus's PhD. The curtain was an unwashed pink sheet with a lung-shaped stain in the centre. Doro found it all deliciously romantic. When he told her in a deep serious voice about the revolutionary movement in Paris, from whence he'd just returned, and the struggle of the masses for freedom and dignity, she eagerly offered up her virginity to the cause.

Afterwards, they lay watching the candlelight flickering across the damp-stained eaves, and listening to the scurrying of mice and the thud-thud-thud from the room below, which Doro thought was an insomniac DIY enthusiast but turned out to be another PhD student called Fred Baxendale, who was writing his dissertation – something obscure about Karl Marx's *Critique of the Gotha Programme* – on an ancient manual typewriter.

She bumped into him the next day coming out of the mouldy bathroom on the first floor, wrapped in a small towel. To her surprise, he was a pale, skinny man wearing a knitted cap pulled down over his ears, under which wisps of mud-coloured hair protruded. From the way he'd been banging at that typewriter, she'd expected a muscle-bound Titan.

'Hi, I'm Fred.' He extended a hand, gripping the edges of the towel together with his other hand.

'Hi, I'm Doro,' she said, averting her eyes, fearing the towel might drop.

Fred the Red, as he was known, played classical guitar and had an occasional sleep-in girlfriend who was also thin and pale with close-cropped mud-coloured hair. Marcus said they were both Althusserians, and Doro nodded, having no idea what he was talking about but imagining something to do with mould or mud. Whichever, Doro was in love – not just with Marcus, but with the whole muddy mouldy set-up, the stained sheets, the roll-up cigarettes, weak tea and burned toast, the hours of conversation which slipped seamlessly into sex and back into conversation again.

When Marcus discovered she was not a revolutionary but a sociology student, he didn't seem to mind. A few months later, when she'd graduated and started her first job as a part-time liberal studies teacher, she moved into his room, leaving the Islington flat to Pete Lafferty and Moira, who got married and separated all within six months. Single again, Moira moved into the house in Hampstead, temporarily occupying the first-floor room next to Fred's, which belonged to a student who was spending the year at the Sorbonne. The house itself was owned by a Brazilian academic who had returned home in 1963 without making any arrangements for the payment of rent. So it was free for them to live there, but the house was sliding into dereliction. None of the windows closed properly, the ceiling in Fred's room was bowing under the weight of Marcus's bricks and books, and the black mould in the bathroom, having colonised the grout between the tiles and around the bath and basin, was starting to creep across the ceiling. Moira, who spent hours in the bathroom with herbal shampoos and conditioners, did her best to control the mould with an old toothbrush dipped in bleach, but it was a losing battle.

Because the house was rent free, no one ever moved out, but more and more people moved in. When the student whose room Moira inhabited returned with his French girlfriend, there was an accommodation crisis which turned into a fight. Moira refused to leave. The other couple put a mattress on the floor and moved in alongside her, probably thinking they would drive her out with their full-volume love-making. Doro tried to persuade her to find some-where else, but Moira's objective was to get off with the student and replace the French girl. When this failed (and Doro suspected she also tried to get off with Fred and Marcus) Moira resorted to recruiting a succession of volunteers to out-love them. The queues for the bathroom were swelled by a succession of naked bewildered guys who couldn't quite figure out why they were there, but sensed there was an agenda other than sex. The Brazilians on the ground floor, friends of friends of the original Brazilian, also seemed to multiply in numbers and volume. The lavatory now had to be flushed with a bucket because the ball-valve lever was broken from all the action it was getting.

One night, shortly after eleven, when everyone was in bed, and the whole house reverberated with cries, shrieks, groans, gasps, thuds, thumps, guitar music, expletives and bossa nova, Doro became aware of another sound, a subtle creaking that seemed to be com-ing from the floor in the corner of their attic room. Marcus was sleeping off a particularly animated half-hour of sex. She went over to investigate. As she stepped out gingerly with her bare foot, she noticed that the floorboards beneath the lino seemed to yield a bit.

The sensation was odd enough to make her pause. Then the creak turned into a groan, and suddenly the floor started to slip away. She clung on to the door frame to stop herself sliding too, and watched in horror as a great crack opened up between the wall and the floor, through which a ton of bricks, books and floorboards thundered down into the room below.

'What the f—!' she heard Fred's cry, and a muffled squeak from the Althusserian girl. Then silence.

Marcus, now fully awake, reached out a hand to pull Doro away from the hole in the floor, and they raced downstairs to find Fred and the girl writhing under a heap of mud-coloured bedclothes covered in books (the bricks and floorboards had mercifully mostly fallen against the far wall), showing flashes of pale naked limbs and tousled mud-coloured hair as they tried to work out what had happened. The girl discovered a huge gash on her shin, and started to cry. Doro sat on the edge of the bed and put her arm around her.

'It's nothing compared to what'll happen in the revolution, sister.'

After the collapse of Fred's ceiling/Marcus's floor, the accommodation crisis became acute. Marcus and Doro dragged their mattress downstairs to the damp basement kitchen, which was the only available room, and were woken each morning by everyone else stepping over them as they congregated to make breakfast. Over cups of tea, burned toast and lumpy porridge around the kitchen table, a vision emerged of a place where they could all live together in a non-bourgeois non-private non-nuclear non-monogamous community, where they could put theory into practice and reach out to the masses; a community based on Marxism, vegetarianism, non-violence, non-competitiveness, creativity, communal ownership, home-grown vegetables, free love, Althusserian ideas (optional) and rejection of stereotypical gender roles (i.e. no housework); a place adorned with Capiz shell lampshades and macramé flowerpot holders, where everything would be shared from each according to his ability, to each according to his need.

★

Doro sighs. It was an adventure and, given the chance, she'd probably do it all again. But with fewer lentils.

As dusk falls, the train pulls into Doncaster station, and there's Marcus waiting for her on the platform. His brown curls are now white, but he still stands tall, his eyes are as blue as ever, and he's wearing that red T-shirt she bought for him many years ago with the slogan '*I am a Marxist Groucho tendency*'.

SERGE: *The mermaid*

Long long ago, before Serge and Clara were born, their previously normal parents were suddenly overwhelmed by insane ideas. This is what Clara told him. They decided pirates' property was robbery and family life was impressive, she said, and they abandoned their house and hamster and went to live in a commune. As the oldest of the commune kids, Clara's role was to interpret the Groans' baffling pronouncements, though being slightly deaf at the time, she sometimes invented things.

The trouble is, although her hearing's okay now, Clara's still bossy, and still makes things up. Like she's convinced he was entirely to blame for that hamster debacle, and even though he's almost twenty-nine now, she treats him like an Asbo. Which is why he doesn't always tell her stuff.

For example, he lied to her yesterday about not being in contact with Otto. In fact, a year after Otto was taken away from Solidarity Hall, following the fire, they bumped into each other at Glastonbury, and have kept in touch. At Cambridge they linked up again. Although he was two years ahead of Otto, and in a different college, and couldn't understand why Otto had chosen computer science, which seemed pedestrian compared with maths or physics, they sometimes went out and got wasted together, and had intense conversations which neither could remember afterwards. The thing is, he was well within his rights to withhold this information, because he knows Otto won't want to come to any saddo reunion. And because even if he did, he can't be trusted not to blab to Clara about Serge's career change – not out of malice or envy, but because he's a blabby kind of guy.

As it happens, Otto phoned last night, and ended up blabbing about a tricky situation he's got himself into with regards to his girlfriend, who is pregnant, and his flat, which is about to be repossessed.

44

The two things are connected, because Molly Mackie – a pretty red-haired girl whom Serge dated once – is a dancer in a small grant-funded troupe. Her income, combined with Otto's meagre postgrad studentship, enabled them to secure a mortgage on a two-roomed flat above a hairdresser's in Mill Road. But now Molly's pregnant she's had to quit just as their mortgage interest rates have gone up, and they find themselves facing homelessness.

'Jeez, I should have known better than to get involved with these money dudes,' said Otto, in the quasi-Californian accent which he'd acquired during his gap year and never shaken off.

And Serge had said, foolishly as it turned out, 'Don't stress, kid. I'm solvent. I can tide you over.'

The thing is, he got his bank statement this morning, and what he can't understand is how the seven of them managed to run up a bill of £13,107.01 on Maroushka's birthday bash. And what he also can't understand is why it all came off *his* credit card. He remembers volunteering his card at the beginning of the evening, in fact he was quite insistent. She was watching, with that indecipherable half-smile, and yes, okay, it's a bit sad to equate dick size with bank balance, and probably she wasn't thinking that at all, but the trouble is you can never be sure what women are thinking when they look at you that way. Anyway it's a convention, surely, that the guys share the cost at the end of the evening? He vaguely remembers there was a flurry of cards and banknotes at some point, and some banknotes came his way and he stuffed them in his trouser pockets. He remembers the maître d' was a bit unfriendly. Something about broken crystals, for God's sake. He remembers he banged his head and blacked out. He remembers throwing up in the toilets. He remembers also throwing up in the taxi. The taxi driver was a bit unfriendly too, understandably, so he had to tip him well. Today he checked his trouser pockets after the bank statement came; there was the credit card receipt but no itemised bill, and all the cash he found was four screwed-up fifties.

On the ninth floor of the FATCA tower, he lets himself out of the lift, wondering how he's going to broach this delicate subject. Most of the quants are at their desks. Tim the Finn has disappeared somewhere, but he must have been in already because the potent smell of his aftershave still lingers around the Securitisation area. The two French guys, grads of the École des Hautes Études Commerciales, were knocking it back that night. Now they're in conference with a futures analyst, trying to cobble together a cocoa deal that'll assign the main risk of any downturn to the farmers. He'll catch them later. Joachim Dietzel (everyone calls him the Hamburger, because he comes from Hamburg – subtle, eh?) is sitting at his desk poring over a martingale representation. Lucian Barton and Toby O'Toole (nicknamed Lucie and Tootie), the two ex-UCL physicists and the biggest boozers on the desk, are staring into their monitors. Lucie is pink and freckled, with an awful ginger mullet, which he obviously thinks is cool. Tootie has pale-grey eyes with strangely enlarged pupils, an unpleasant nasal voice and acne scars.

'You remember that bash for Maroushka's birthday?' Serge leans casually against Lucie's desk. 'Did you know the bill came to more than thirteen k?'

Lucie shrugs. 'Maybe they made a mistake at the restaurant.'

Tootie's lip curls. 'Don't tell me you're feeling monetarily challenged, Freebie.'

'I just wondered, since there were seven of us . . .'

'Why don't you ask *her*? She's the one who ordered the Château d'Yquem.'

Tootie nods towards the door, which opens at that moment to let Maroushka in. She's wearing pale green today, with a string of silver baubles around her neck. She slinks past them on her way to the glass-walled office, pausing for a minute by his desk to ask, 'Everything normal?'

Should he ask her about the Château d'Yquem? No, that would be the ultimate loss of face. He'll sort it out with the restaurant, or ask the guys to chip in.

He can't phone the restaurant until he gets the chance to nip out of the building at lunchtime. Unless . . . The disabled loo is the only room on the floor which you can lock from the inside, and is rumoured to be a den of illicit sex and prohibited phone contacts with headhunters. He slips away from his desk and loiters until the coast is clear, then sneaks in, locks the door behind him and whips his phone out. It's hot and airless in there, and stinks of chlorine, pee and . . . what *is* that smell? A familiar odour pricks his nostrils, a familiar odour that belongs to a different context. He focuses on its distinctive components. Benzene. Aniseed.

The restaurant doesn't seem to have a website, so he has to call Directory Enquiries. When he finally phones the number it rings and rings, and he's just about to click off when an angry female voice answers, 'Yes?'

He asks to speak to the manager.

The woman says, 'If it's La Poire d'Or you want this is the wrong fucking number, and it's the fourth today, and just between you and me I wouldn't bother because the food's crap and they rip you off.'

'I'm sorry, miss. But you don't have to be so shouty.'

'Fuck off!'

The phone goes dead.

He looks again at the receipt in his hand. There's something about the number that seems odd – £13,107.01. That 1p at the end – where did it come from? There was nothing on the menu that ended in 1p, in fact everything was in multiples of £20, even the water. Nor could it be a percentage added as a service charge. It's more like a number pulled out of thin air, with a few pence stuck on at the end to make it seem precise. No, he's seen that number somewhere before. He stares: 131071. Isn't it the sixth Mersenne prime? $M_p = 2p - 1$, where p is a prime, in this case 17? Yes! A coincidence? A pattern?

Back in the trading hall the buzz has stepped up a notch as the traders get into gear. All around him, money is being made at a phenomenal rate – in fact, he's helped to make quite a chunk of it himself. These guys aren't any brighter than he is, they probably couldn't even recognise a Mersenne prime, yet they're making shed-loads of money. Most quants don't trade, though some VPs, like Timo Jääskeläinen, straddle both roles. He's often sat at Timo's elbow and watched the dance of the data, as they've tried to pin it down in an algorithm. Timo is an able guy, but a bit of a plodder.

The rumour is that it was Timo who 'discovered' Maroushka, when he was fretting over an algorithm one night while she was hoovering around his desk. She pointed out the mistake, then carried on hoovering. Surely if Timo can make money trading, then he could do the same. He could avoid all this hassle by paying the bill off himself, then claiming it back off the other guys if the restaurant doesn't cough up.

This isn't the first time he's thought of doing a bit of personal trading. When he was first buying his flat and needed a deposit, he started investigating some of the engineering companies around Doncaster, partly out of sentiment and partly because he thought his local knowledge would give him an edge. But then his broker offered him a 110 per cent mortgage, so he put the idea on the back burner. Now this sticky patch with the bill and Otto's cash-flow problem gives him a reason to follow it up sooner rather than later. He'll play it careful, set himself tight limits. He won't go mad, like he's seen other guys do.

He sits back and takes the time to study the FTSE Fledgling, Small Cap and AIM markets. He's noticed some interesting recent activity here. There's a tremor that ripples upwards then draws back down. The same tremor is there in Small Cap, where his target shares are located, though you wouldn't notice unless you knew what you were looking for. The pattern's familiar, the usual ebb and flow of the market – what's unusual is the retracement, which has slipped back below the previous pivot point. Something similar happened last week and again yesterday, but by the time trading closed it had righted itself. Today it's happened again, and this time the retracement is 38.4 per cent – that's 0.2 per cent lower than it should be according to the Fibonacci code. Is this a variant within the normal range of Fibonacci retracement, or the start of a market reversal? His heartbeat has stepped up a gear. He brings the charts up on his monitor.

The thing about predicting the markets is that it's as much about psychology as science. The more people predict something, the more likely it is to happen – the stampede effect. Fibonacci allows for this human factor, it's an intuitive system which has quite a following among traders, thanks in part of course to Dan Brown. There are all sorts of crude adaptations of the golden ratio out there, but the real secret of making money is simple – you have to get in there first.

'There's money to be made in falling markets if you're bold enough to seize the moment, and smart enough to know when the moment is.'

He remembers the exact words Chicken had spoken during his interview a year ago. Serge had been sitting on a leather swivel chair, sweating with nerves, half strangled in that same borrowed Queens' tie he's wearing today (the difference now is that it's ironic), knees clamped together and anchoring both feet on the ground in order to resist the temptation to swivel.

When he was offered the job and they initiated him into this game, it seemed incredible that you could borrow stocks and then sell them on straight away, before you'd even paid for them, then wait until the price drops and buy them back for less than you sold them for, and return them to the original lender, pocketing the difference. At FATCA, the traders do it every day. Some of them don't even borrow the stocks – they just sell them on the intention of later buying them back. It's called naked short selling, all perfectly legal, and it's the sort of thing that would send his mum and dad apoplectic if they knew.

Given the millions he makes for FATCA, is it so very wrong to want to make a little extra for himself – just to get himself out of this fix and help out a childhood friend? Strictly speaking, it is a bit wrong – City boys like him aren't supposed to trade for themselves in working time. Their bonuses are supposed to reward that selfish impulse, which is a natural part of human nature, in spite of what Doro says. But many do have personal accounts registered with the Compliance Officer, who checks they're not breaking the rules. And some people also have unregistered personal accounts, he knows, where the possibilities are greater. Although all their calls are recorded and their emails logged, it's largely reactive monitoring – nobody actually listens or looks through them unless there's a reason.

It's not easy to open an anonymous bank account in these days of money-laundering regs. But the thing is, he does already have access to a semi-dormant club bank account in the name of Dr Black, which is kept ticking over by a few people who forgot to cancel their subs – it's a hang-over from his undergraduate days when he was treasurer of the short-lived Queens' College Cluedo Society. And he'll have twelve k left in his savings account, even after bailing out Otto. If only that annoying restaurant bill hadn't popped up he wouldn't even be thinking of trading on his own account.

So where to start?

In his day job, he works on synthetic Collateralised Debt Obligations (CDOs), where the big money is made, but no way is he going to put his own hard-earned cash into this mishmash of dodgy mortgages, retail credit and unsecured car loans, hedged up with a bit of high-end borrowing, all rolled up like an apple strudel, chopped into slices and wrapped and sold and sold again, until everyone has lost track of what was in the original mixture. They call it securitisation; what a joke. It's hard to imagine anything less secure. He knows – everybody knows – it can only be a matter of time before it goes crashing down again.

At least with old-fashioned stocks and shares you know what you're getting; you can be reasonably sure what's in the package you buy. The easy money nowadays is made by trading big volumes on small variations in price, but you need the capital to start with, and he isn't in that league. To get where he wants quickly, he'll have to take risks.

He scrolls the Companies House register for details of South Yorkshire firms, where his local knowledge and contacts could give him an edge and minimise the risk. Here's one, based in Askern. Syrec: South Yorkshire Recycling. The name rings a bell. Wasn't Clara going on about some big regional development grant? Askern Villa, the team he's followed since childhood, has been slipping calamitously down the league; but the Syrec story is more upside. Syrec isn't listed on the Stock Exchange, but the parent company, South Yorkshire Consolidated, is listed on the Alternative Investment Market. SYC is a portfolio company with interests in waste reclamation, finance, building development, sheltered housing, residential homes and retail parks. Ten minutes' research reveals they have a good folder of northern local-authority contracts, but this new development grant doesn't seem to have made it into the national media, for there's been no immediate price spike. That's the advantage of local knowledge. The major shareholder of SYC is another company, called DASYS Ltd, which is registered in Luxembourg. Why Luxembourg? Not easy to trace the ownership there; but the company's prospects look good.

Edenthorpe Engineering, listed on the Small Cap market, is another familiar name: a traditional Yorkshire family firm, which has been making machine tools since 1957, and a big employer in the Doncaster area. He once had a work experience placement in their offices, not far from Clara's school, and he has certain affectionate memories of that summer, and of a receptionist called Tiffany, who had the most amazing tits. But Edenthorpe's last return looks shaky and, as the bankers' mantra goes, there's no room for sentiment in the markets.

Endon (Enterprise Doncaster – ha ha) and Wymad (West Yorkshire Media Advertising – slightly out of his area, but what a stupid name – they're bound to crash) also attract his attention and, looking at the figures, he can discern the same incipient pattern of a market on the turn from bull to bear. This could be his moment.

People like Doro think that making wealth is just a matter of buying shares and waiting for the value to go up, powered by the noble sweat of workers' brows. They don't realise that banks can make money when the market falls, by borrowing and selling shares they don't actually own, then buying them back when their price has dropped. The problem is when the price rises instead, and you have to buy them back at a loss.

Doro nearly had a hissy fit when he mentioned this once. 'It's utterly immoral to make a lottery of people's livelihoods!' she shrieked, rather missing the point.

It's not going to be easy getting her to accept his new career, but that's not what's on his mind right now.

He goes back to the disabled toilet, locks himself in and phones a brokerage firm that advertises in the Sunday papers. He places his trades, two k each for a short position on the three different Small Cap shares, using up almost half his kitty, and as an afterthought takes a long punt on SYC on the AIM with the rest. It all takes less than ten minutes, but his tension has built up to such a pitch that it feels like an hour. He breaks out into a sweat as the broker confirms his details. There's that smell again – aniseed and benzene – cloying in the close atmosphere. Yes, Tim the Finn must have been in here nursing his troubled prostate, poor guy.

When all the transactions are confirmed, he lets himself out into the corridor carefully and returns to his desk. The retracement is still there, shimmering through the skein of graphs on the monitor like a mermaid tangled in a fisherman's net against an ebbing tide – there for the taking. If the markets are really set to fall, this could be the big one, the once-in-a-lifetime opportunity to scoop in his thousands as they plunge. He watches the shimmering pattern of numbers resolve and fade and remake themselves, and whispers under his breath: 'Bring it on!'

DORO: *Under the watchful eye of Che Guevara*

It's quite odd, thinks Doro, dibbing holes in the vegetable bed, that neither Serge nor Clara expressed any great enthusiasm for their parents getting married. Odd too that Marcus suggested it, in the context of adopting Oolie. She hasn't discussed it with Oolie yet. It would mean explaining that she and Marcus aren't her real parents, and she's not ready to start digging up heartaches which go back to the commune days.

This morning, on the way back from the nursery where she'd bought the seedlings, she drove past the lane that led to Solidarity Hall, and was struck with a pang of nostalgia so intense it was hard to tell whether it was sweet or bitter. In those days, she never seemed to worry about anything. Everything was more vivid, the days longer, the colours brighter, the music better, the people more amusing. She smiles, remembering – and knowing this is a sign she's getting old, but indulging herself anyway.

The dry soil crumbles under her hands as she prepares the rows and wonders whether it's too early for planting out the spring cabbage. She sticks the seedlings in the holes, pressing them in with her fingers. In a way, her children are *her* cabbage seedlings, sown in the friable soil of the seventies, nourished by a rich compost of well-rotted ideas through which they'd all tunnelled like curious worms in search of adventure and a freer, fairer society – whatever that might mean. Like so much else, it seemed clearer, brighter in those days. Now her seedlings have been planted out in a much harsher world. She worries. Will they survive and thrive?

She thought it was the garden she missed more than anything – that near-wild quarter-acre she'd tamed and cultivated – the sunflowers, the tomatoes, even the bloody rabbits. After the fire in 1994, when they moved to their house in Doncaster, with its hand-kerchief square of lawn, she put her name down for an allotment. It took her seven years to reach the top of the queue, but now here she is, in this sunny forgotten corner on the edge of the city, planting out her spring cabbage. And realising that what she really misses is not the garden after all, but her own prime of life, and the childhood of her children.

They had arrived at Askern in November 1969, through one of those leaps of imagination typical of the post-68 ferment. At that time it was deeply uncool to admit to having been to public school, or being upper class or having money. So it came as a surprise when they discovered that Fred the Red, despite his woolly hat and cockney drawl, had access to a family fund. Fired with enthusiasm by their conversations, he went out one day and bought the former coal owner's mansion at Askern for £1,300 at an auction of Coal Board property, without actually ever having seen it. He announced the news as they were sitting around the table in the Hampstead kitchen.

'We will move from theoretical practice to practice in itself,' he declared.

She had no idea what he meant, but it sounded inspirational.

'We'll use our education to enrich society, not just ourselves,' added Marcus, in his thoughtful rumbly voice that sent tingles through her, 'bearing in mind that the economy is determinant, but only in the last instance.'

'We'll build a society where everyone has a chance to fulfil their human potential?' she said hesitantly, afraid they might laugh at her naivety.

'Because the personal is political,' simpered Moira, in that breathless way she had of stating the totally obvious.

When the five of them – Fred and a friend called Nick Holliday, and Marcus and Doro and Moira – made the journey up to South Yorkshire in Nick's orange VW Beetle, they could barely conceal their disappointment that it wasn't right beside the coal mine, but set apart on a country lane towards Campsall village half a mile from Askern colliery, whose gaunt twin winding wheels dominated the flat landscape of square fields stitched together by ragged hedges, as far as the eye could see.

Solidarity Hall, as they named their new home, was a huge draughty red-brick Gothic mansion, a sort of scaled-down St Pancras Station, halfway between Pontefract and Doncaster. It had been built for a pit owner in 1890, close to the small pretty town of Askern, once famous only for its spa, and it reflected the grandiose ambitions of its age – when Britannia ruled the waves, and the great Yorkshire coalfield fuelled the nation's manufacturing boom and powered the trains and ships that carried trade to every corner of the empire. In 1946, in the fervour of post-war nationalisation, it had been taken over by the National Coal Board for offices, and an annexe built for the manager to live in. But then functional new offices had been built near the colliery, and the latest pit manager had long since decamped to a cosy modern bungalow in Askern, so the building had been empty for several years before the commune moved in.

It smelled of damp, the narrow Gothic windows let in little light, and the puke-green decor had last been renewed in the 1950s; but it was in better condition than the house in Hampstead, with six chilly bedrooms, plus four in the attic eaves where the kids would one day have their domain. They removed the plywood office partitions to reveal two cold cavernous reception rooms and a vast draughty kitchen full of crusty Formica and chipped enamel. And there was the pit manager's annexe, which Moira said would be a perfect art studio, while Marcus and Fred immediately earmarked it as a Marxism Study Centre for the local community. Doro was entranced by the half-acre of straggly garden with its lilac and apple trees, overgrown vegetable plot and runaway vines leaping through the hedges.

The Althusserian girl was furious at the proposed move and, accusing Fred of dilettantism and interpellation of function by ideology, stormed off, slamming the door of the Hampstead house so hard that a shower of glass from the window above tinkled down on to the footpath. And so Nick, a small, intense maths postgrad, not part of the original collective but owner of the orange VW, was invited to move in. When Doro admitted to Moira that she found him quite attractive in a geeky kind of way, with his big brown eyes and thick curly eyelashes blinking behind black-framed spectacles, Moira made a point of bedding him at once. She was like that.

Nick also had an occasional girlfriend called Jen with noisy high-drama ways, who claimed that feminism was descended from witchcraft and tried to persuade the women to dance naked around a bonfire in the garden on midsummer's night (they were saved by the Yorkshire weather). It was hard to imagine what Nick saw in her, apart from the attraction of opposites. She went off to live with a guy in a Reichian therapy commune where they practised rebirth and primal screaming, and Doro felt a guilty twinge of relief when she departed.

Askern was on the edge of the Yorkshire coalfield, and Marcus applied for work at the coalface to be alongside the proletariat, but was deemed overqualified and offered a job in the new Coal Board offices instead. He was their first ever PhD. Fred, whose PhD was still unfinished, got a job underground at South Kirby, but only lasted a month before he decided to devote his energies to setting up the Marxism Study Centre in a bedroom of the annexe. Nick taught maths at a Doncaster comprehensive, and was possibly the most highly qualified teacher they'd ever had. Moira worked two days a week as an art therapist at a centre for people with head injuries in Rotherham, and later got a stall on the Saturday market in Pontefract where she sold paintings, lampshades, coloured-paper mobiles and glass-bead jewellery, which she made at the kitchen table in the annexe. 'To beautify the lives of the masses,' she said. Doro worked part-time at the Tech, teaching liberal studies to Coal Board apprentice electricians and fitters, which left her with enough time to start taming the garden.

In the evenings, they sat around the long yellow-painted table in the kitchen, smoking pot under the watchful eye of the Che Guevara poster on the wall and discussing the progress they'd made in advancing the revolution.

She still has the poster somewhere, rolled up in the back of a cupboard.

CLARA: *The slowness of plants*

Roll on, three thirty! The kids have been playing Clara up all afternoon. They're at their worst when the weather's warm and humid, like today. She's been explaining about the tree seedlings on the window sill. The thing about plants is their slowness – they take time to settle into their environment; they adapt to its demands. Some trees take thirteen thousand years to grow to their full size; these seedlings have hardly started, she tells the kids. They groan and yawn.

Before leaving for home, she checks on Hamlet. He's got entangled in his bedding. With a flutter of panic, she untangles him, tops up his water bottle and tickles his tummy. *Please don't die on me, Hamlet!* He throws her a grumpy look and retreats under a duvet of peed-on straw.

Mr Gorst/Alan's car is still there as she makes her way out with her bag full of marking slung over her shoulder. And here he comes, striding hunkily across the car park. She smiles; he smiles back. The door opens again and here comes someone else wiggling towards them, wearing a busty Regency frock with Roman centurion sandals and a Gladstone-style handbag. She climbs into the passenger seat of his car. Where's the prehistoric Fiat? Written off? Could Mr Gorst/Alan be attracted to Miss Historical Postlethwaite, her bad driving, her breathless enthusiasm and her history-themed wardrobe? They give Clara a friendly wave and drive off.

Yes, she knows her reaction is irrational, unkind and unwarranted, and for this reason she always makes sure to treat Miss Postlethwaite with absolute politeness. But she is one of those people who make Clara appreciate the company of plants.

It's almost six when she gets back to her flat. On the landing by the door, Ida Blessingman, who has the flat opposite, has spread the contents of her several shopping bags as she rummages for her keys, cursing softly and filthily under her breath. This is a fairly regular occurrence.

'So how was it?' Ida asks, finding the key at last and turning the lock, 'or should I say how was *he*?'

Clara has already told her about Mr Gorst/Alan. She sighs, describing his departure with Miss Hippo.

'Darling, there are men who wallow in banality,' says Ida, heaving her shopping bags into the flat. 'And they choose their women accordingly.'

'Trouble is, she's really quite nice.'

'Doesn't matter. Try thinking of her as a bitch.'

Ida is four years older than Clara and at least twenty pounds heavier, but wears the sort of expensive well-cut clothes that make her look shapely and stylish, and has thick black sheepy curls that always look interestingly unbrushed. She works as a lawyer in Paradise Square, has two divorces behind her and claims to prefer cheesecake to men.

'She lists her interests on Facebook as history and dressmaking,' says Clara.

'A killer combination,' says Ida. 'You need a stiff gin.'

SERGE: *The global elite*

The Poire d'Or restaurant, when Serge finally got through to them on Wednesday, didn't know anything about his bill, but promised to look into it. Since then, they've not returned his call, but he's not too worried because the shares he took a short on have been sliding steadily, and the Footsie closed on Thursday evening seventy points down. He calculates that if he was to buy them back now, he'd be nearly 20 per cent up on his initial outlay. Not bad for an hour's work. All he needs is steady nerves to hang on and maximise his return.

By Friday afternoon, to his amazement, he's made enough to pay off most of his credit card bill, if he chooses to, and still lend Otto another month's mortgage payment. It was ridiculously easy. Another run like this and he'll be back where he was. In fact, he'll be slightly up. He's pulled in his haul, and the Fibonacci retracements are still surging his way. Next time, he'll play with higher limits. His head is still spinning, and he needs to steady himself. He texts Otto to invite him for a celebratory drink, but gets no reply, so instead he approaches Princess Maroushka at her desk.

'Are you doing anything tonight, Venus?'

Leaning over her chair he breathes in her weird perfume.

'Yes,' she says. On her monitor there's a quick blink of a screen minimising.

'Tomorrow?'

'Yes also.'

'Sunday?'

'What you want, Sergei?'

She swivels round abruptly in her chair and their eyes meet. She has that disconcerting way of smiling and not smiling, which he finds irresistibly sexy.

'A drink? A meal? A film?'

This is at the very clean end of the range of things that he wants, but it's a start.

'Okay.' She turns back to her screen.

Maybe she's having her period. Women often get ratty at that time of the month. Babs, his last girlfriend, was like that – wouldn't let him near her. He'll try again, when she's had a chance to calm down.

But at six o'clock sharp, before he can finalise any arrangements for Sunday, she pulls on her jacket and heads towards the lifts at full speed. Why the hurry? Most people won't be leaving for another hour or so. He hangs around for a while, reluctant to go home just yet. The floor is humming with Friday night vibe, like the whole world is going out to celebrate the end of the working week. During the day English is spoken on the trading floor but, as everyone begins to relax, their talk breaks up into a babble of languages. The three blond Aussie guys have palled up with the two blonde American girls (let's hope they have a friend) and they're going out to get seriously wasted. The dapper-suited Japanese bond traders are laughing their heads off quietly in their corner. There are a couple of Singaporeans on that team too, but they tend to hang out with the Chinese, in their palaces of excess on Gerrard Street. Even the slightly stiff Indians on Currencies are heading off to a bar with Lubkov the long-haired Russian mathematician and Ishmail al-Ali the smiling Palestinian ex-aeronautics student who is reputed to have lost FATCA £5 million through a computational error. He doesn't look as if it bothers him.

Above the hubbub, Tim the Finn's voice warbles, 'I'm forever blowin' bubbles . . .' and one or two others join in.

Serge can't sing, but he feels the lightness bubbling up in him. He has something to celebrate too, and though he can't discuss it with anybody he decides to tag along with the two French guys, both in their late twenties and darkly good-looking in that louche Gallic way, and the older fairer Hamburger, who are all heading off to a bar to drink to the beauty of life, the Hamburger's baby daughter and Carla Bruni's smile.

'*. . . hyper mignonne . . . plutôt baisable. Qu'en pensent les Anglais?*'

'Like a . . . *Comme une gazelle?*' he volunteers.

They laugh and he laughs too, suddenly engulfed in a warm gloopy wave of at-oneness with this beautiful young high-flying free-floating no-baggage global elite, whose title is wealth, whose passport is brains, whose only nation is money.

CLARA: *The singing parent family*

On the car radio, they're playing Bob Marley – 'By The Rivers Of Babylon' – as Clara sits tapping her thumbs against the steering wheel in the Parkway traffic jam driving back into Sheffield on Friday night. It was her favourite song when they lived at Solidarity Hall, and it leads her thoughts back over the half-forgotten trails of her childhood.

. . . there we sat down, yea-ea, we wept . . .

After the death of Fizzy the hamster, and her pasting by those horrible boys, she withdrew into herself; she stopped putting her hand up for the teacher's questions; everything came to seem so muffled and far away, she just couldn't be bothered. As time passed, she began to stumble over her reading. She often had earaches and skipped school to stay at home at Solidarity Hall, where there was always something interesting going on.

'I want to go to a different school,' she told Doro one day.

'Why, darling?'

'I haven't got any friends.'

'We have to learn to make friends with all different kinds of people,' said Doro.

'Why?'

'Because we believe in cooperation.'

How come nobody had told her this before?

'Why?'

Doro shrugged and gave her a hug. 'Because it's the sort of people we are.'

. . . when we remembered Zion . . .

She sings along, remembering.

People at her junior school used to pity them – the commune kids – because they wore each other's clothes and wolfed down their free school dinners. Although they weren't actually hungry, she remembers how they yearned for meat and for puddings, which were seldom on the menu in Solidarity Hall. What the other kids didn't know, what they could never explain, was the advantage of having several parent-adults who looked after them in a benignly haphazard way, whom they could play off against each other. They didn't know the freedom they had in the commune playroom, which they called Thinlandia because it was the ex-isle of Lennie the Leader. And Clara was its queen.

. . . carried us away . . . captivity . . . required of us a song . . .

Once, when she was nearly eight, a couple of years after the hamster incident, she overheard Mrs Wiseman, her class teacher, telling the Head, 'They're all from singing parent families.' She said it in a whisper, hiding her thin lipsticky mouth behind the pages of the register, as though the phrase was too shocking to be uttered aloud, but to Clara it sounded magical.

Her confidence must have bounced back enough for her to put up her hand and ask, 'What's a singing parent family, miss?'

'I wasn't talking to you, Clara,' she replied.

That night, over dinner around the long yellow-painted table in the kitchen at Solidarity Hall, she asked, 'What's a singing parent family?'

As usual, there were several conversations going, and everyone was talking so loud it was hard to get a word in edgeways. She had to repeat her question a few times and bang her spoon on the table to get attention.

'Don't shout, Clara,' said Marcus. He and Fred the Red were discussing pirate property. (For some reason, they seemed to find this topic endlessly fascinating.)

It was Moira Lafferty's turn on the cooking rota, and she was a vegetarian who believed in balanced proteins, so beans and brown rice were on the menu again. Otto and Serge started flicking their bullet-hard beans at each other – they were bullet-hard, because no one ever remembered to presoak them. Serge ducked to avoid a flying bean and toppled backwards on his chair on to the floor. Everybody ignored him apart from Doro.

'Are you all right, Serge?' she said. 'You're always tumbling. Anyone would think you were dyspraxic.'

Clara banged her spoon again. 'Why doesn't anybody listen to *me*?'

'Speak out, Clara,' said Nick Holliday.

'What were you saying, darling?' asked Doro.

'The teacher said we're a singing parent family. So why don't you ever sing?'

'Arise ye starlings from your slumbers . . .!' Fred the Red's deep baritone rolled from the end of the table.

'Arise ye criminals who won't . . .!' Marcus joined in.

'It's not singing parent, it's single parent, Clara,' Nick Holliday explained in his quiet teachery way. 'It's when children have just a mother or just a father . . .'

She felt a small prick of loss at the dullness of it.

'The reason in the vault of thunder . . .!' thundered Fred, waving the ladle for attention and weighing into the discussion. 'I would say a family means whatever you want it to mean. Historically, it has taken a number of different forms, including –'

'Are we a single parent family?' squeaked Serge.

'Course not, pratt stick. We've got loads of parents.'

'Don't call me a pratt stick.'

'Doro says you're a pratt stick!'

'Clara, Serge, please . . .'

'She started it . . .'

'Oh, shut up!'

'Great dinner, Moira.' Marcus grabbed the ladle from Fred and helped himself to more stew, which apart from the beans contained only chopped onions, tinned tomatoes and several of Moira's long auburn hairs. 'Shouldn't one of you feminists explain to Clara that the family's a patriarchal construct to facilitate the subordination of women and enslave them within the domestic sphere?'

As he spoke, a light clicked on in Clara's brain. She stirred the words around in her head like a magic potion. She committed them to memory. She practised saying them out loud when she was on her own. They tasted of power.

Then, one day, she got her chance to use them.

'Now, I'd like you all to write a page about your family,' said the class teacher, Mrs Wiseman.

It was her habit to set some work, then leave them to it while she sneaked off to the staffroom to smoke a fag. The kids could see her through the staffroom window, puffing away.

Clara put her hand up. 'Miss, the family's a pastry ark construction to fascinate the sobbing nation of women in Domestos fear.'

Everyone stared at her in amazement. The teacher fixed her with a stony look.

'Those are very big words for a very little girl.'

Clara just smirked and lowered her eyes, letting the words work their magic.

There was a ripple of shuffles and whispers around the classroom. Sensing a rebellion, Mrs Wiseman ordered them to get their books out and disappeared into the staffroom for a fag and a sulk. She didn't return until just before lunch, by which time a full-scale riot had broken out and kids were running around the room yelling, 'Sodding nation!' while others were banging their desk lids and chanting, 'Pase-tree! Pase-tree!'

. . . how shall we sing the Lord's song in a strange land? . . .

From then on, the other kids, even the hamster girl, started to treat her with respect. They consulted her about spelling, sex, smoking and other essential information. She always answered their questions fully and freely, inventing the things she didn't know. At home, in front of the mirror, she practised the Look.

That's how she discovered the joy of teaching.

It was Nick Holliday who'd encouraged her to become a teacher, with his weird shouty partner Jen, Otto's mother, before she decamped to another commune where all the kids were called Wild. Sometimes she misses all her weird co-parents. Chris Howe and Fred the Red, who'd chosen Oolie-Anna's name, theorised about developing the socialist personality. Fred the Red wore the same dung-coloured jumper and a black knitted cap pulled over his ears year in year out, and smelled of cheese and drains, but he played the guitar and told thrilling bedtime stories about Lennie's adventures in Thinland. Chris Howe, plump and pink like an uncooked sausage, paraded around wearing just a T-shirt and made the kids giggle. Moira Lafferty with her lovely hair and Capiz shell jewellery showed them how to make masks and finger puppets. Chris Watt introduced vegetable carving into the commune in order to disguise the vegetableness of vegetables, so the kids who turned their noses up at anything green or crunchy could pretend they were something else (Clara finds the magic still works for her, and it obviously works for Jason too). And for a while there was Mystery Megan – that's what the kids called her, because she never said anything.

So many mums and dads to fuck you up with their good intentions. She sighs, remembering the grubby intimacy of the playroom at Solidarity Hall, with its sky-blue ceilings and rainbow walls and stacks of dusty books piled up in one corner, and the mad belief put about by the Groans that they were on a mission to change the world.

. . . yea-ea, we wept, when we remembered Zion . . .

Maybe Doro's right – maybe it would be fun to get everyone together again one more time. A few fat raindrops splat against the glass from a heavy purple cloud hanging over the city skyline. The air smells humid and close. She flicks the windscreen wipers on and prays it will clear up in time for Community Day tomorrow.

SERGE: High heels

There's rain in the air as Serge follows the flow pouring out of the office at home time; occasional drops splat on his head, but the breeze is warm and they dry quickly. He wonders where Maroushka has vanished to. The French guys and the Hamburger are up ahead, and he keeps a distance, ready to abandon them should she materialise.

Still trailing them, he crosses the square in front of St Paul's, heading towards a wine bar which according to the Hamburger stocks the ultimate burgundy. Then his eyes are caught by a flash of yellow in the milling Friday night throng. Yes, it's Maroushka. Strangely, she's in almost exactly the same place he saw her when he was having a coffee with Doro. A coincidence? A pattern?

He breaks away from his group and heads off in her direction. She's weaving in and out of the sweaty home-time throng and the tourists bunching around the cathedral. She disappears. Then he sees her again. It's easy to spot that yellow jacket. It draws him like a beacon. Poetry pulses in his veins.

> *Princess Maroushka!*
> *Hear the song of Serge!*
> *Don't you feel the urge*
> *To be with me beneath the starry skies?*
> *Faint Fibonacci spirals in far-off galaxies.*
> *We'll hold our breath*
> *Waiting for lightning strikes*
> *And run along the beach in our Nikes.*

Okay, not the Nikes.

Suddenly someone shoves past him, a thin tall woman with streaked blonde hair and a classic Vuitton over her arm.

'Steady on, lady,' he mutters, but she's already out of earshot, barging her way in Maroushka's direction. Seems like she's on her tail.

As she gets close, she lets out a long low wail, sort of halfway between a moan and a war cry. Maroushka hears, stops, turns, sees the woman and breaks into a run. The woman starts to run too. He follows, weaving through the crowd behind them, keeping them just in sight.

The blonde is shouting something that sounds like 'Iranian war!'

What the fuck's going on?

Maroushka turns her head for a second and yells, 'Go and piss yourself!' over her shoulder, then she speeds up her run – but her high heels are against her – she's wobbling all over the place, at risk of breaking an ankle.

The blonde, who is wearing flat pumps, is gaining ground.

Should he intervene? Something tells him that he should not.

All of a sudden, Maroushka stops dead in her tracks, steps out of her shoes and, leaving them standing there on the pavement, hitches her skirt halfway up her thighs (wow!) and breaks into a serious athletic sprint. In three seconds she's round a corner and out of sight.

The other woman stops at the corner and looks around.

He stops too.

The woman turns. Their eyes meet. He picks up the shoes, and slips them into the pockets of his jacket. She bursts into tears.

'Lady . . .'

'You're all the bloody same! Shaggy sex-crazed bloody goats!'

With a wrenching sob, she lurches back into the crowd and disappears.

He takes the shoes out of his pockets and sniffs them. They smell of fresh sweat and new leather. Already he is imagining one delicious scenario after another whereby he will return them to their owner. He strolls along Godliman Street towards the Thames, holding them close to his body, under his jacket. As he reaches the Embankment, the skies open; he lifts up his face and lets the rain pour down on him like kisses.

CLARA: *The carrot rocket*

Although the whole of Yorkshire has simmered in a late heatwave for a week, the weather breaks on Friday night. To Clara's dismay, it's chucking it down on Community Day. The stalls have to be shifted into the hall and the kids dash in and out, dragging in mud and towing disgruntled parents in their wake. There's a sickly sweet smell of damp poverty and a kind of soggy turbulence as the families swirl around barging into each other in the confined space. The windows are all steamed up; the noise is deafening.

Mr Philpott the caretaker has donned an ancient brown suit and a red bow tie, which gives him a look of faded gravitas. Mr Gorst/ Alan is looking dishy in chinos and a jacket. He's working his way around the stalls, shaking hands with parents, offering smiles of encouragement to the teachers, tousling the damp hair of kids in a way that is both earthy and godlike. Now he's with Miss Hippo at the next stall, congratulating her on her photographic display of *Historic Greenhills,* which has attracted a noisy crowd of finger-jabbing pensioners, while she jingles her Cleopatra-style earrings and wiggles her Regency-clad bum. He hasn't glanced in Clara's direction yet, but he will get to her next. (Be still, oh beating heart!)

Unfortunately only one seedling from her stall has so far been adopted, by a woman from Rowan Drive, who absolutely insisted on a cherry tree. The plastic-crushing has been cancelled due to the weather, and bags of newspapers and plastic bottles brought in by the parents are accumulating under the table and around the walls; they hand them over with a satisfied smile, pleased at their own generosity – 'There you are, duck' – as though they're for her personal gratification. The petition against football on Rowan Green is running at sixty signatures already. Some people have signed twice. Only two people have signed the carbon emissions petition. The dolphin petition has been folded up and wedged under the wonky leg of one of the tables.

She's beginning to feel dejected, when there's a ripple in the crowd and she sees Jason Taylor heading towards her. Behind him, holding on to his hand, is a stunningly pretty girl with a tumble of silky blonde curls falling across her face.

'That's 'er,' he whispers, nudging the girl. 'Miss, this is me mam.'

Mrs Taylor is not how Clara had imagined her. She'd expected someone plainer, fatter, grubbier.

'Hello, Mrs Taylor.' She shakes her hand, which is so heart-wrenchingly tiny and fragile it feels like crushing a snowdrop.

'Jason says you can make carrots into rockets, miss.'

She looks about seventeen, though this must be biologically impossible, and Clara guesses she's at least in her late twenties. She has the same intense grey eyes as Jason, and the same pale skin, but on her it looks not sickly but delicate, almost translucent.

A surge of protectiveness takes Clara by surprise. 'Please, call me Clara. My mum's going to do a vegetable-carving demonstration later.'

She smiles, peeping up through angel curls. 'Is the new headmaster here, miss? Jason says he's reyt nice.'

'He is. I'll point him out to you.'

Jason is watching with a look of tender anxiety. 'All right, Mam? All right, miss?'

'Mm. We're not having much luck with our plants, Jason,' she confides. 'We can't even give them away.'

'Nah, miss. Yer doin' it all wrong.'

He takes the sign reading 'GREENHILLS TREES – FREE TO GOOD HOMES!', turns it over and, using the petition-signing pen, he writes in big letters on the back.

SPESIAL OFFER
MINACHURE TREES ONLY £1
GRAT VALUE !!!!!!

Just then, out of the corner of her eye, she spots Mr Philpott waving an agitated brown-suited arm from the far side of the room. She gestures to him to come over. He shoulders his way through the crowd.

''Amlet . . .'

Then his eyes fall on Mrs Taylor.

'Fair nymph!' He straightens his bow tie. 'To be, or not to be, that is the question.'

Mrs Taylor blushes and her cheeks go all dimply. 'I couldn't agree more, sir. I hope Jason's not been too much trouble. If he is, just tell me, and I'll wallop 'im.'

'Mr Philpott . . .!' Clara whispers, but he's far away in Elsinore.

Suddenly there's a commotion at the back of the hall – then a single loud familiar voice. 'Come along, Oolie! This way!'

A tall figure is shoving her way forwards, gripping a small dumpy girl by the hand, moving with a sort of swaying sidestep, as though she's on the run from *Strictly Come Dancing*, a long silvery rain cape glittering behind her. Clara winces. What on earth's her mother wearing? At times like this, she wishes Doro was someone else's mum whose eccentricity she could enjoy at a distance.

Oolie is looking anxious and clinging on to Doro because she doesn't like crowds. When she catches sight of Clara, she runs up to hug her.

''Allo, Clarie. We pottied them plants, din't we, Mum?'

She pokes a finger into the compost and licks it.

'Yes, darling. Leave them alone now,' says Doro. 'Sorry we're late, Clara. I brought some vegetables for the carving demonstration, like you said.'

She flings off her silver rain cape, rolls up her sleeves and rummages in her carrier bag. Then she clambers up on to a chair and booms in a voice that carries right across the hall, 'Parents and pupils, please can I have your attention! I'm going to demonstrate some simple carving techniques.'

Even after nearly forty years in Yorkshire, her mother's vowels still bear the unmistakeable ring of the South. Oolie, by contrast, speaks with the accent of her Doncaster special school.

'What's she gooin' off about?'

'To grace your table with beautiful and appetising vegetable art!'

71

Grace your table! Clara recalls the grungy yellow table in Solidarity Hall, cluttered with unwashed plates, unemptied ashtrays overflowing with dog-ends of spliffs, and the dried-out remnants of vegetarian casseroles.

In a few deft strokes Doro cuts semicircular petals around the globe of a radish and with a flourish plops it into a jug of water, which Clara brought to water the seedlings.

'The secret is to soak them in cold water!'

The room falls silent; all eyes are focused on the tall middle-aged madwoman standing on a chair with a radish in one hand and a paring knife in the other.

'Soon, the petals will swell and open out!'

Clara feels herself redden as people jostle closer for a better view, while her mother repeats the whole embarrassing exercise on some more radishes. Then she brandishes a monster carrot.

'Now I'm going to carve a rocket!' She starts to chisel.

'Marvellous, innit?' murmurs Mrs Taylor.

Unobserved by Doro, Oolie is fishing the radishes out of the water with her fingers, and popping them in her mouth. Clara tries to catch her eye to warn her off, but Oolie ignores her. Jason has disappeared.

Then, she spots Mr Gorst/Alan at the next stall saying goodbye to Miss Hippo (about bloody time) and inching through the crowd towards her table, his eyes twinkling dangerously. Her heart quickens. Beside him is another man, a stranger, tall, suntanned, handsome in a greying foxy way, with gimlet eyes and steely hair.

'Let me introduce Councillor Malcolm Loxley, our Chair of Governors.'

'Can I interest you in a tree?' she says.

'You can interest me in anything, love. I'll have the cherry.' He hands over a pound with a rakish grin. Her eye falls on a small enamelled flag of St George pinned in his lapel. A football fan? A patriot? A Doncaster chauvinist?

'How about a carrot rocket, Councillor?' Doro calls, from the heights of her chair, where she's still chiselling away.

'Who . . .?' asks Mr Gorst/Alan in a whisper.

'My mother – she's demonstrating vegetable carving.'

'Oh, I see. Fascinating.' Then he notices Mrs Taylor. 'Who . . .?'

'Mrs Taylor, Jason's mother.' Clara introduces them. 'This is Councillor Loxley, the Chair of the Governors, and this is the new Head Teacher, Mr Gorst / A . . .'

Jason has reappeared, sitting under the table opening up the bags of plastic bottles. She gives him the Look, but he carries on regardless.

'Pleased to meet you, sir . . . sir.' Mrs Taylor's gaze moves between Councillor Loxley and the Head. Somehow, as if by psychic power, the top button of her blouse pops open. 'I thought it were 'im.' She gestures contemptuously towards Mr Philpott.

'I'm sorry, Mr Philpott . . . a misunderstanding,' Clara whispers, seeing his face darken.

But now another crisis strikes. Oolie has disappeared.

'Oolie! Oolie!' Doro peers down from her chair.

Clara starts searching. Her little sister will be getting panicky – she's so short she can easily vanish in a crowd.

Suddenly there's a shriek. 'Watch out!'

She looks up in time to see a rocket-shaped carrot whizzing through the air. Over on the far side of the room, Mrs Salmon yelps and staggers against the coffee stall. Scalding coffee sloshes into the tightly packed crowd. The convulsion spreads in a shock wave. Shoulders shove, bums bump, elbows and heads collide – whoops! There goes the history display! Miss Hippo lets out a genteel historical mew.

The floor is awash with coffee, rainwater, plastic bottles and darting children. Something catches Clara's foot, she tumbles and grabs out for the nearest thing, which seems to be Mr Gorst / Alan's upper leg. She feels . . . Before she can feel anything interesting, he reaches for her hand and pulls her to her feet so sharply that she knocks Doro's chair – 'Sorry, Mum!' – who teeters and topples – 'He-e-elp!' – bringing down the *Greener Greenhills* display and the councillor, who lands on top of Mrs Taylor, who lands on Clara. It's all getting very intimate and confusing. Mrs Taylor's blouse pops another couple of buttons. Out of the chaos, Mr Philpott surfaces from under the table, hauling Oolie-Anna by the hand. She lets out a loud radishy burp.

''Ere she is. C'mon, you little clown.'

Clara tries to throw him a warning look, but it's too late – Doro has gone berserk. 'Don't you ever dare call her that, you bumptious ignorant old man! She's not funny! She's perfect! Do you understand?'

'Mum, for goodness' sake!'

She's never seen Mr Philpott look so scared.

Oolie starts to wail. 'I *am* funny! I wanna be on TV! I wanna shag Russell Brand!'

Under the table, someone sniggers.

'Jason!' yells Mrs Taylor, also berserk. 'Gerrout o' there, you little fucker!'

Jason emerges, slyly exchanging grins with Oolie. Mrs Taylor, still half unbuttoned, snatches a plastic bottle from the floor, and whacks it down again and again and again on his skinny shoulders, until Clara intervenes.

'It's all right, Mrs Taylor. I'm sure he didn't mean any harm.'

'Like fuck 'e didn't!' says Mrs Taylor.

It isn't until she's halfway home on the motorway that she remembers she forgot to check on the hamster. And something else is bothering her. What happened to the tree seedlings? They have all disappeared without a trace.

DORO: *Pessimism of the intellect and optimism of the will*

Holding tight on to Oolie-Anna's hand as they struggle up the stairs of the moving bus, Doro thinks, 'I really shouldn't have shouted at that funny old man. He probably thought he was being kind.' She remembers now, with a flush of embarrassment, that she knows him slightly from allotment meetings. She also regrets shouting at Oolie, though her daughter's concept of naughtiness undoubtedly includes throwing things at people. Now she's sulking and saying she wants to go and live with Clarie, and Doro has to stop herself from saying, 'Clarie doesn't want you, Oolie. She's got her own life to live.'

'Look, Mum! Greggs! Let's stop!'

Oolie raps on the window of the bus as it lumbers through the town past the dismal straggle of cut-price shops and karaoke bars. Greggs bakery is one of Oolie's favourite haunts. Given her tendency to pile on plumpness, Doro has to be strict with her – especially as she's not averse to the occasional cream puff herself. That's another reason she feels Oolie isn't ready to move into a place of her own. She would eat all kinds of rubbish, and who would keep an eye on her?

'Ssh. We'll have lunch when we get home.'

That officious social worker with his clipboard and his patronising leaflets really got up her nose, trying to tell her that she was being overprotective and that Oolie-Anna must 'step outside her comfort zone' and 'connect with her personal dreams' and 'blossom into the fullness of her individuality'. For pity's sake. Who does he think invented individuality and personal dreams, back in the seventies?

'Hey! He's well fit!'

Oolie waves both hands at a traffic warden busily ticketing a row of cars by the shopping parade. Although she didn't mention this to the social worker, Oolie's uninhibited sexuality is also a worry. Would Oolie remember to take the pill every evening if there was no one to remind her?

'Come on, Oolie. We're there.'

Clinging on to the handrails they stagger down the stairs and out on to the pavement of Hardwick Avenue, where Oolie makes a bee-line for a puddle left by the recent rain and stamps in it with both feet.

Their inter-war semi is set back behind holly bushes in a quiet tree-lined street where their neighbours are dentists and accountants; it has three generous bedrooms and a small sunny garden – it's the sort of house they could never afford if they moved back to London now, they'd be lucky to get a one-bedroomed flat for the same price. It's because of the deindustrialisation of the North, Marcus explained. All the time they thought they were experimenting with revolutionary ways of living, the real revolution was slowly taking shape under their noses: the demise of manufacture, the triumph of finance.

Since he's retired from the Institute, Marcus has ensconced himself in Serge's old room, which he uses as a study. If Serge wanted to come home to finish writing up his PhD, they'd have to come to some arrangement. Goodness knows what Marcus gets up to in there. He says he's writing a history of the non-Communist non-Trotskyist left – the Fifth International, he calls it. It can't be good for him to spend so much time picking over the past, which only makes people unhappy. Yes, he's become much more withdrawn and grumpy recently.

She puts the kettle on and opens the fridge for milk.

'*Be the change you want to see.*' Mahatma Gandhi's words are fixed to the fridge door with a green frog magnet; they've taken the place of '*From each according to his ability, to each according to his need*', which hung on the fridge door at Solidarity Hall, held in place by a red flag magnet.

She takes a cup of tea upstairs and sets it down on Marcus's desk.

'How's it going, love?' She ruffles his hair with her fingers.

He starts and looks up at her, smiling, blinking owlishly behind round glasses, as though he's just woken up from a deep sleep.

'That Italian comrade who came over in 1984 – can you remember his name?'

'Bruno. Bruno Salpetti.'

Doro shuts her eyes for a moment, and finds she can remember not only his name but the rough-smooth texture of his cheeks where the stubbly bit ended and the baby-soft bit began, the clean smell of his soap, the fine black hairs on his forearms and belly, and the thicker mass of black curls below.

'That's it!' He scribbles it down. 'Was he in Potere Operaio?'

'Lotta Continua.'

Does Marcus know about her and Bruno? And, after all these years, would he mind?

'That was my first encounter with the politics of autonomy. Listen to this.' He leans forward and reads from the screen of his computer. ' "Although the workers have to sell their time to the capitalist who owns the workplace, their human needs and desires are opposed to those of the capitalist." '

'My most beautiful *compagna*,' Bruno had called her. It's a long time since Marcus said something like that. Yes, in those days she could still give Moira Lafferty a run for her money, despite her long auburn hair and DD boobs. The new men, it seemed, weren't that different from the old men.

' "Autonomy is the workers' struggle to assert their own personal and economic goals . . ." '

Even Fred the Red, who spent his days wandering in the wordy thickets of Marxist theory and his nights with a succession of tearful girlfriends from London, found time for Moira. In fact, he was probably the father of Star.

' ". . . in the face of the employer's relentless pursuit of profit . . ." '

The dictates of sisterhood meant you weren't supposed to feel angry or jealous towards other women, because we were all victims of sexism, and we had to solidarise. Beautiful women were oppressed because they were only sought after as sex objects, and plain women were oppressed because they weren't sought after at all.

We *were* sisters, Moira and I, she reflects. We stuck together like sisters, but we also squabbled and fought like sisters, especially over Bruno Salpetti.

★

Bruno arrived in Solidarity Hall from Modena in 1984, at the start of the miners' strike, declaring he wanted to share the straaggling of the proletaariat. He slept on a mattress on the floor of the Marxism Study Centre, which had long since been transformed into a play-room for the kids. His only luggage was a little backpack which contained a selection of readings from Gramsci's *Prison Notebooks*, a razor, and a pair of very small black underpants. (Moira, needless to say, found some pretext to investigate and whispered her findings to Doro.) The razor went unused – he grew a beard, which usually Doro didn't fancy on men, but on him it looked excitingly leonine. The underpants appeared on the washing line with pleasing regular-ity. He broke the monotony of their bean-grain diet with wonderful spaghetti dishes made with fresh tomatoes and olive oil; he main-tained that Gramsci had more to offer to the revolution than Trotsky; and he believed in, and practised, free love. He was only twenty-five, but what's a decade or so between friends?

Moira, as you would expect, was the first to get in there.

'He's got a dick like a gorilla!' she reported with characteristic refinement.

Doro felt a flush of annoyance. What does *she* know about bloody gorillas?

'Oh, really,' she said.

It was bad enough that Moira was bedding Bruno at any time of day or night, but she had to advertise what a good time she was hav-ing with little crescendos of shrieks and sighs that could be heard in every corner of the house. Although it was solidly built, there was something about the layout of Solidarity Hall which meant that sound percolated through stairwells and corridors. And whatever you were doing you had to stop and listen – there was no escape. Once it was the curly-haired milkman collecting his money; Doro was on the doorstep in her dressing gown, fumbling in her purse for some change, and suddenly his ears pricked up. Their eyes met. A little smile spread across his face and he looked at her enquiringly.

'She's got TB,' said Doro. 'She often coughs like that. I expect she'll die soon. It's quite tragic.' She slammed the door.

The kids naturally were curious, and Nick explained that it was a sign that Moira was very happy. This was confirmed for them one day when two women from Women Against Pit Closures came collecting for the soup kitchen which had just been set up in the village hall. Doro invited them in and offered them tea. They entered gingerly, stepping over the debris in the hall, looking curiously at the posters on the walls ('THE TEARS OF PHILISTINES ARE THE NECTAR OF THE GODS' was still there), sniffing the lentil-flavoured air. Sticking close together, they followed her down the long gloomy passage into the kitchen, where Clara and Serge were having an after-school snack of peanut butter and cornflakes at a table which hadn't been cleared since last night. As they sat down and Doro put the kettle on, the ceiling above started to creak, and the sounds of Moira's bliss were suddenly very audible.

'By 'eck, she sounds 'appy. Must've seen t' fairies at bottom o' t' garden,' said the younger one, who was called Janey.

'D'you rent 'im out?' asked the older one, called June, who had a smoker's voice and a sagging crinkled face.

'Yes,' said Doro, 'but there's a queue.'

They exchanged quick looks.

Janey said, 'D'you want to 'elp us in't kitchens?'

'Sure,' said Doro.

'Bring *'im* too,' said June, flashing two rows of incongruously pearly teeth.

Another time, it was a pair of Jehovah's Witnesses.

'It's a bad case of devil-possession, we're trying to exorcise . . .' Doro began, but they didn't hang around for an explanation.

Maybe it was the milkman, or June and Janey, or even the Witnesses, but somehow word got around the village, and they started to get a steady trickle of visitors, male and female, who would call on some pretext and stand on the doorstep trying to peer through the open door into the house. In those weeks of the miners' strike, there was always someone coming to their commune collecting for petrol-money for the pickets or donations for the soup kitchen where miners and their families could get at least one meal a day, and they were pleased and excited that they seemed at last to be making links with the local community, who had previously shown little interest in the Marxism Study Centre or the Anti-Colonialism Discussion Group.

Bruno was delighted when Doro conveyed the news that the women in the village had invited him to volunteer in the kitchen.

'They like to experience the Italian cuisine?'

'Er . . . I think so,' said Doro.

Moira was less pleased. She'd cut quite a figure on the picket line at Askern, with her flaming hair and interesting slogans ('Miners are the midwives of socialism!') which drew puzzled but admiring glances from the ranks of the pickets.

'I've been called all sorts,' declared Jimmy Darkins, Chairman of the National Union of Mineworkers' local branch, 'but never a midwife. I shall 'ave to give it a gooa.'

Moira obviously revelled in all that male attention. She and Bruno would regularly rush home exhilarated after picketing duty, fling themselves down on the mattress and make noisy love. It was awful.

Now she'd just have to choose between spending her time with a load of women doing boring domestic chores on an epic scale, or letting her lover loose in that hormone-heavy environment.

'The role of the women is absolutely crucial in this struggle, Bruno,' Doro said.

'But the picket line is where it's at, comrade,' urged Moira.

'Hm. However, as Gramsci says, is important to build the counter-hegemonic positions in all social institutions.' Bruno twirled his fork through the pasta.

'Exactly!' cried Doro.

Moira shrugged defeat, slurping in a mouthful of spaghetti alla Napoletana, letting the sauce dribble down her chin.

'Oh my!' said June, when Doro led Bruno into the Askern miners' welfare hall next day.

The room fell silent as twenty women stopped what they were doing and stared at the newcomer.

'Come on in, duck! Don't be shy! We're not gonner rip yer keks off. Not till after dinner, any rood.'

Bruno smiled innocently.

Janey whispered to Doro, 'Does 'e talk English, love?'

June whispered, 'Does 'e talk the language of love?'

Unfortunately Doro had a class that afternoon, so she had to leave. Bruno came home several hours later, hitching up his jeans as he lurched through the door, his face covered with reddish blotches.

'How was the cooking?' asked Moira sulkily.

'The ingredients were poor.' His voice sounded faint. 'It is a disaster the British masses have a diet of such impoverishment.'

'How did you get on with the miners' wives?' asked Doro.

'The proletarian women displayed extreme . . . how I should say . . .?' He fumbled for words, '. . . class consciousness.'

The problem of class consciousness dogged Doro for days. If that's the secret, there could be no hope for her, she fretted, drowning her disappointment in soapy water as she rinsed the breakfast clutter in the sink. For she couldn't help being thoroughly and undeniably middle class. But then so was Moira. So were all of them, in their thoughts, their habits, their tastes and preferences. The fact that they'd all just gone off picketing didn't alter that one iota. Did any of the women in the soup kitchen wear dungarees or read George Eliot or eat vegetarian mush? Although they'd lived up here on the fringes of this working-class community for fifteen years, they'd barely touched its inner life. Having finished the washing-up, she smoked a joint and brooded on the inherent unfairness of the class system, which suddenly seemed to cut her off from all possibility of happiness.

'Why are you sad, my most beautiful *compagna?*'

His arm was around her shoulder.

'Oh! I'm . . .' her eyes filled with tears, '. . . I'm just thinking of the unfairness . . .' a sob rose in her throat, '. . . of the class system.'

'Do not weep, my noble spirit. It is of course unjust. But this is why we are in straaggle, yes?'

His fuzzy cheek pressed against hers, his warm hands searching the opening of her blouse.

'Yes!'

'Pessimism of the intellect and optimism of the will?'

'Yes!'

Doro learned a great deal about class consciousness and struggle that day. And her pleasure was enhanced when she later bumped into Moira coming out of the bathroom with a mardy look on her face.

Sometimes Bruno slept with Doro (who also slept with Marcus, who didn't know), and sometimes he slept with Moira (who also slept with Nick Holliday and Fred the Red, who did know) and sometimes he got back from the soup kitchen too exhausted to do anything but sleep. Then one evening when he arrived back from the soup kitchen, there was a young woman with him.

'This is Megan.'

He introduced her to the group, repeating their names for her.

'Hi.'

She looked up from lowered eyes, not smiling, and stuck to Bruno like a shadow.

Doro didn't feel particularly threatened by Megan at first. She wasn't pretty – at least, not in a conventional way – she had a thin angular body with heavy breasts, a long curtain of dark hair, and grey-green watchful eyes. She moved silently, like a cat, and hardly spoke. In fact, she's not sure, even after so many years, who Megan really was, except that she'd been married to a strike-breaking miner, and was brought into the commune by Bruno. Doro can still remember that night. She shivers.

It was the dead of winter, the long bitter winter of 1984–5, and it was strange, Doro recalls, that Megan had no possessions with her, not even a coat. Bruno explained that she was running away from an abusive relationship. They welcomed her unquestioningly, made up a bed for her in the annexe in Moira's studio, and the women lent her the clothes she needed.

It turned out that Megan had a son, a sullen five-year-old called

Carl, who stayed with Megan's mother in Harworth during the week but often came to Solidarity Hall at weekends. He was a clingy insecure child who didn't mix with the other kids, and stole from the kitty. His nickname was Crunchy Carl from his habit of crunching insects – spiders, flies, butterflies, or whatever he could get hold of – between his fingers. Once when Chris Watt reprimanded him, he spat at her and called her a fat slag. His father was never talked about and, when Doro asked, Megan just shrugged and said, "'E took off, din't 'e?'

Chris and Doro tried to explain what the commune was about without sounding too preachy.

'See, we're trying to create a society based on common purpose and sharing what we have, and looking after each other.'

Megan stared for a long time. 'You mean, you don't have your own possessions?'

'We do have some possessions. But we share the money we earn, and everyday things like books and clothes.'

'In't nobody gonner share *my* clothes.'

Doro refrained from pointing out that actually she was sharing *their* clothes.

' "We have moved away from the post-war vision of a society based on shared prosperity, to a society based on grotesque accumulation of personal wealth on the one hand, and increasing insecurity on the other." '

Marcus, still reading from the computer screen, looks up to catch her eye.

'Drink your tea, love, before it gets cold.'

SERGE: *The rabbits*

Serge must have been nearly six when he first encountered Fibonacci, because he remembers the Groans at Solidarity Hall were all
preoccupied with the miners' strike that year, and the kids were
often left to their own devices. However, one day Nick Holliday and
that Italian guy built a wire-mesh rabbit cage in the back garden,
with two rabbits which were supposed to teach the kids responsibility, non-competitive play, and introduce them to non-patriarchal
social communities, i.e. there was supposed to be no Mr Rabbit.

Despite this, the kids came back after school one day to find five
baby rabbits snuggled up around their mother, still blind, almost
bald, and unbearably cute. They took them out one at a time and
passed them around. There was him, Clara, funny little Otto and
Star, who at that time was a toddler in permanently stinky nappies.
(Oolie-Anna hadn't been born.) Anyway, they kept passing the baby
rabbits around and stroking them and kissing them, maybe squeezing them a bit too much, especially Star, who wanted to make them
open their eyes, and when they put them back they realised they
weren't moving a lot. In fact, they weren't moving at all. In fact,
they were dead.

Clara, who was the oldest, and had already experienced pet-death
trauma, said they should bury them in the garden and not tell anybody. So they did. He didn't know where exactly they buried them,
but he recalls how hard and dry the ground was as they scraped
away with a trowel to make a big enough hole, and he remembers
being sick on the grave.

But amazingly, as if by magic, a few weeks later, more baby rabbits appeared. Five of them. Otto thought they'd come back from
the dead, and started to blub. His own fear, which he kept to himself, was that they'd never really been dead at all. Clara told Otto
not to be so stupid, and she said they should leave them alone this

time, and alert the Groans. Nick Holliday, who was Otto's dad and a school teacher, took the opportunity to give the kids a long lecture about sex and where babies come from. It sounded highly implausible.

Two of the new baby rabbits died within a week, but three survived. Then just as they were getting used to having six rabbits instead of three, six more babies appeared. This really freaked all the kids out. It seemed like the rabbits which kept on appearing so inexorably were in fact zombie-bunnies linked in some supernatural way with those little hairless corpses they'd buried. They started to burrow their way out of the cage; before long there were rabbits and rabbit holes all over the garden. Every month there seemed to be more.

'We planted them in the garden and they growed,' whispered Otto.

As the rabbits multiplied, all the flowers and vegetables in the garden were nibbled down to the roots, apart from the gooseberry bushes and the sunflowers, which were too tall or too tough. The herbs planted around the back door in plastic buckets and a cracked chamber pot disappeared. Only the rosemary bush, planted well off the ground in a disused toilet bowl, escaped. What had been the lawn was now bare earth with a few patches of grass and grotty bits of leftover vegetables scattered everywhere, because of course now the rabbits had to be fed. Little balls of rabbit pooh clung to everybody's shoes and got trodden into the already grungy carpet. Sometimes he noticed a strange sinister smell lingering in the garden.

'How many rabbits d'you think we'll get?' he asked Nick Holliday one bedtime.

Surely Nick would know when it was time for this scary torrent of zombie-rabbits to stop. He liked talking with Nick, because he always answered the kids' questions seriously, though he could sometimes get long-winded.

'It's a Fibonacci series,' Nick explained. 'It just goes on getting bigger.'

'Fibber who?'

'He was an Italian mathematician from the twelfth century. He discovered this series.'

Serge felt a great urge to confess the terrible secret of the buried rabbits. Nick was a gentle guy and he might be more forgiving than the other Groans. He was about to explain what had happened that afternoon, how it had all been a terrible mistake, when Nick reached for a sheet of paper, and started to draw.

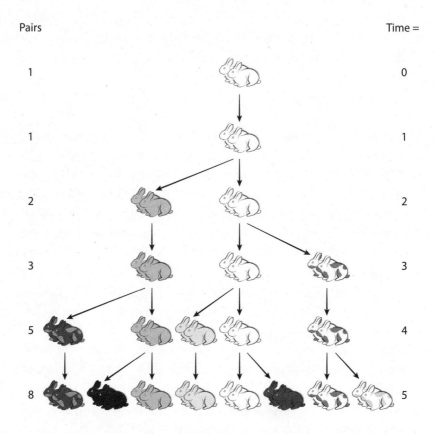

Pairs

Time =

1   0

1   1

2   2

3   3

5   4

8   5

When the number of rabbits in the garden reached twenty-six (fortunately some had died) the Groans convened a meeting to debate what should be done. Marcus suggested taking them to the miners' soup kitchen, up at Askern, but other members of the com-

mune who were vegetarian reacted with horror. Moira Lafferty
tried giving them to a pet shop, but they weren't pretty enough, and
the owner already had too many. Doro put a notice outside on the
gate saying 'LOVELY BABY RABBITS FREE TO GOOD HOMES' and one
day a bloke came in a van and took all the babies away.

'They'll go to poor children who haven't got any rabbits,' said Doro.

But next time he came Serge noticed the sign on the side of his
van: 'RANDY'S REPTILES'. He didn't say anything to Doro. To be
honest, he was getting spooked by the rabbits too. He'd pinned
Nick's diagram up on the wall by his bed, and he studied it nightly
as he drifted off to sleep. He realised the sequence could be extended.

$$1\ 1\ 2\ 3\ 5\ 8\ 13\ 21\ 34\ 55\ 89\ 144\ 233\ 377\dots$$

Three hundred and seventy-seven rabbits. He felt his chest tighten
with panic as he added the new numbers.

He and Otto shared a bedroom up in the attic, so they often talked
together, even though Otto wasn't yet four and talked a lot of rubbish, because of his mum, Jen, who didn't live with them any more
but took Otto away to her commune at weekends and holidays
where they practised primal screaming. Otto usually came back
with a sore throat.

'You sit in this William Right organ box,' he explained to Serge in
a croaky voice, 'then you scream and you get energy.'

'What does it feel like?' asked Serge.

'I dunno.' Otto sucked his thumb and twirled a finger in his hair,
which was white-blond and curly like an angel's. 'I think it's like the
rabbits. They get reborned.'

'But rabbits don't scream, Otto.'

'They screamed under the ground. We din't hear them.'

But one night, the rabbits did scream. The sound was terrible,
visceral, primal. It ripped through his dreams, making him jump
out of bed and rush to the window. The garden was in darkness, but
there was just enough moonlight to see a flicker of movement
down below, shadows chasing shadows.

'They're doing it,' said Otto, standing beside him on tiptoe with a multicoloured crocheted quilt wrapped around him, because he didn't have any pyjamas. 'That's how they make their babies.' His skinny shoulders were trembling.

Serge put his arm around him for comfort, then took it away quickly – although he was only six, he already knew that boys didn't do that sort of thing.

'We might see them in the morning,' Otto said.

'No, because . . .' He guessed Otto was wrong, but he couldn't explain why. Then there was another sound in the garden – human voices, yelling.

'Get away wi' you!' A woman's shriek, and then a man's voice shouting, 'Scarper!'

In the morning, there were no babies. A mess of fur fragments and mangled bunny limbs was spread out all over the garden. There was that strange smell, pungent and pissy. He realised now it was the smell of death. Not a single rabbit was left. Otto went very quiet. Star started to cry.

'It was only a fox. Let's get going,' Clara said in her usual bossy way.

It was her job to see them all safely to school.

When they got home at four o'clock, they found that there had in fact been two survivors of the rabbit massacre, who must have bolted underground when the fox attacked. Over the next few weeks he and Otto went back every day to check for babies, but none appeared.

'It's because they're both mummies,' he explained, but Otto maintained it was because they'd run out of energy and needed the organ box.

He didn't bother to argue, because something else Nick had told him was preoccupying his mind. The complex branching pattern of the rabbit couples in the diagram, Nick pointed out, was the same pattern you could see in the head of a sunflower, a pine cone, or in leaves, twigs and branches of a tree. It was there coiled in the shell of a snail or in the spiral of a galaxy spinning through space. You could find it in a violin string when you divide it to make a musical scale, or in the perfect proportions of classical building. He talked faster and faster, and his eyes shone the way Marcus's eyes would shine when he was on about socialism.

Serge started to collect snail shells and pine cones in an old shoe box that he kept under his bed, and every night he added a few more numbers to his sequence. When things got bad, he talked to the numbers almost as if they were his friends, and made up rhymes to help him remember.

Over the next few years, after Oolie-Anna was born, and Megan disappeared, and the fire happened, and the break-up of the commune, and all the Groans went mad, and Doro got into a fight with Moira Lafferty, and Jen came and took Otto away for the last time, and Nick Holliday left, and Clara went off to University, and the Chrises and their weird kids vanished into the night, he often went up and sat on his bed in the attic and arranged his snail shells and pine cones in a pattern, and dwelled on the mystery of the Fibonacci numbers, the way they seemed to unwind one after another in an infinite spiral of order and harmony which swirled everything up together like the stars in the sky.

1 1 2 3 5 8 13 21 34 55 89 144 233 377 610 987 1,597 2,584 4,181 6,765 10,946 17,711 28,657 46,368 . . .

PART TWO

Family Snaps

DORO: From each according to his ability, to each according to his need

Doro has been trying to get through to Serge, without success, so she phones Clara instead on Sunday evening, not about anything in particular, but because she wants to chat. However, what starts out as a perfectly friendly conversation about plants and trees suddenly turns into an attack upon her vegetable-carving demonstration. Why is Clara so prickly? Surely the hormones of adolescence must have calmed down by now. A bit embarrassing, she said. What's to be embarrassed about? She was just trying to be helpful.

'If just one family eats more vegetables as a result, it will have been worth it!' she shouts, and slams the phone down.

The post-argument silence reverberates in the kitchen. Upstairs, she can hear the clack-clack-clack of Marcus's keyboard. The sound makes her feel hollowed out and useless. It's as if all her energy has gone into external things – her relationships, her children and the daily life of the commune – leaving nothing but memories, certainly nothing she could write a book about.

'D'you want a cuppa?' she calls up the stairs.

Serge was more placid than Clara, even as a baby, engrossed in his own funny little world. Yes, if only he could install himself in his old bedroom with his computer, away from the distractions of student life, she's sure he'd soon polish off his PhD. This project at Imperial College London seems to be a pointless diversion. And she can't understand why Clara insists it's University College and not Imperial College – she must have got confused. If only she'd calm down, and stop trying to organise everybody, she'd soon find someone tolerant and good-natured to settle down with. It would be nice to be a grandmother. And if only the weather were better she could have gone up to the allotment with Oolie, but Oolie threw a tantrum and she didn't feel like going on her own.

If only . . .

She switches the kettle on and tries to find the news on the radio, but her ears are still ringing with Clara's invective.

Clara was the first of the babies in the commune, and everyone practised their parenting skills on her, so maybe that's why she turned out to be so cussed. Doro feels a pang of guilt about Clara's communal upbringing, though that can't be entirely to blame, for right from birth she was a grizzly and fretful little bundle. She learned to walk and shed her nappies early, and by the time she was three she could sustain a lengthy conversation, consisting of one word on her part – why? – and a detailed and ideologically correct response from the person who was supposed to be looking after her. Yes, there were occasional mishaps. Like that time she caught her brushing her teeth with a tube of Canestan, which one of the sisters had left in the bathroom. That's what happens when you have four or five intensely involved co-parents, all bringing their own experiences and agendas to the task of childcare, and no one in overall authority. It must have reinforced Clara's sense of self-importance. After all, she wasn't just a child, she was a prototype of a new kind of human being – the torch bearer of the non-bourgeois non-private non-nuclear non-monogamous non-competitive non-violent society they'd set out to create.

Poor kid.

By the time Serge came along, then Otto, Star and finally Oolie, the adults had got a bit bored with all that, and were content to play football or watch TV with the kids. Besides, the commune itself was undergoing so many changes that the idealistic principles they'd embarked with more than fifteen years ago were coming under strain.

The Chrises Watt (female) and Howe (male) had arrived at Solidarity Hall in 1985, after the acrimonious split in the Workers Revolutionary Party which some attributed to the defeat of the miners' strike, some to financial involvement with Libya and Iraq, and some to the sexual shenanigans of the Party's leader, Gerry Healy. (Chris Watt once confided in Doro that Gerry, though less handsome than Chris

Howe, was a tiger in bed, which made Doro shudder with double horror.) They arrived on a Friday afternoon with their two pale silent children, installed themselves in the room which Jen had vacated recently and, over the course of the weekend, glumly munched their way through the commune's entire supply of fruit, baked beans, beer, cheese and cornflakes while bemoaning the lack of meat and the historic defeat of the working class.

Everyone expected they would leave on Monday, but by lunchtime there was no sign of movement from their room. However, when Fred and Marcus returned from Tesco in the afternoon with replenished stocks they emerged and began eating again. The pale kids lolloped out into the garden and started kicking a ball around, trampling Doro's pea seedlings and decapitating the tallest sunflower. Doro went out to remonstrate with them, but seeing their eyes bright and cheeks flushed with colour, didn't have the heart to tell them to restrict their games to the rough patch behind the fruit trees set aside for the kids.

By Thursday, they'd run out of food again, and Doro, setting out on the supermarket run, asked Chris Howe whether they'd like to contribute.

Chris Howe looked shifty. 'What's your policy on sharing? I thought you worked it out according to ability and need.' He pointed at the slogan stuck up on the fridge.

'Yeah, we do,' said Doro. 'Everyone contributes according to how much they earn.'

'We don't earn nothing. We're on benefit.'

He said it with such finality that Doro just nodded and went out to the car.

She pushed the trolley around Tesco, seething with resentment, and heaped it up with white sliced bread (reduced), potatoes (reduced), baked beans (three for two), cornflakes (jumbo-size own brand), tea bags (ditto), margarine (cheap and nasty), cheese (mild cheddar, plastic-wrapped), powdered tomato soup (cheaper than tinned), lentils, dried split peas, red kidney beans, porridge (all own brand), tinned tomatoes (three for two) and a large bar of Cadbury's Dairy Milk which she ate in the car on her way home.

'Didn't you get no beer?' asked Chris Howe, helping her unpack.

He was wearing a baggy Che Guevara T-shirt and no trousers. And, she couldn't help noticing, no underpants.

'We can't afford it.'

As he was stowing the bread, potatoes and cornflakes in the larder, the etiolated children moseyed in from the garden, ripped open the pack of cornflakes, and started to cram dry handfuls into their mouths.

'Stop that!' snapped Doro.

They looked at her silently with sad eyes.

She retreated to her bedroom with a cup of tea, a bad conscience and a slight feeling of nausea from the chocolate. The book she was in the middle of, *Woman on the Edge of Time* by Marge Piercy, had disappeared from her bedside table and she had to make do with a two-year-old copy of the *New Left Review* from Marcus's side of the bed. The trouble with communal living was that everything drifted towards entropy. If Marge Piercy had ever come to Solidarity Hall, she might have envisioned a slightly more chaotic utopian future. Then there was a knock on the door, and Chris Watt sidled in with the book in her hand.

'I hope you don't mind. I borrowed this.'

Doro did mind, so she didn't say anything. She could see immediately that the bookmark she'd put in near the end had vanished, and been replaced by a cigarette paper stuck in near the beginning. Chris Watt perched herself on the foot of the bed, and surveyed the room. She was wearing a grubby cheesecloth blouse and no bra.

'Are you and Marcus a couple, like?' she asked.

'Mmm.' Doro tried to sound non-committal. Being part of a couple was, in some circles, considered worse than being a running dog of capitalism.

'Like Chris and me. We thought it was time we tried a . . . you know . . . less monogamous way of relating.'

Doro thought of Chris Howe, the limp pink sausage-like penis dangling below the T-shirt, and felt another wave of nausea.

Chris Watt picked up the copy of *New Left Review* which Doro had put down, and started flicking through it. Doro could smell her earthy, soapy and slightly herby smell from the foot of the bed. She must have borrowed Moira's shampoo.

'It's not me, it's *him* that wants to try non-monogamy,' Chris said after a while in a low voice, almost a whisper.

'But . . . don't you feel jealous?' asked Doro, remembering her own paroxysms of unvoiced jealousy, mainly relating to Moira.

'He says jealousy's a bourgeois emotion. He says it's about possession – like you feel you have the right to possess another person.'

'Men always say that,' Doro sniffed, suddenly emboldened by Chris's candour. 'But is it what *you* think?'

Chris shrugged. 'The kids like it here.' She was looking directly at Doro now. Her eyes were brown and cow-like, and a bit watery, as though she'd been crying. 'They asked me if we can stay.'

Doro felt her cheeks flush. 'But haven't you got . . . I dunno . . . a place of your own?'

She felt she was handling this very badly.

'You see, we were expelled . . .'

'From the WRP, I know. But where you live . . .'

'After the split we were living in Tufnell Park, sharing a house with some comrades from the Workers International Solidarity Collective. We held the meetings in the basement. Then there was a disagreement about the nature of the Soviet Union. The others said it was state capitalism, but Chris was heavily into Posadas and he insisted it was a partly regenerated deformed workers' state. I don't know exactly what the argument was, because I was in the sitting room, watching telly with the kids. Then Chris burst in and said we'd been expelled.'

'Oh, heck!'

The commune was still adjusting to Bruno's departure at the end of the strike, the silent spectre-like presence of Megan, now visibly pregnant, and the disruptive weekend forays of Crunchy Carl. Could they accommodate new members? In her heart, Doro would probably have preferred the two Chrises, despite their far-out politics and their lollopy ever-hungry children, to Megan and Carl. But asking Megan to leave was out of the question – she was Bruno's leaving gift.

When the small black underpants had disappeared from the washing line for the last time, Doro had felt an intense pang of loss. It was as if he'd left behind Megan to remind them the commune wasn't just about free love, it was about looking after each other, especially those who are most vulnerable and needy. However hard you try to set up the perfect self-contained world, there are always more needy people out there, desperate to come in. You can't turn them away without turning your back on your own better self. At the end of the day, you just have to be grateful that you're not one of the needy ones.

'So you're sort of homeless?'

'Sort of.'

Doro caught Chris's eye, and thought she noticed the glint of a tear.

'I don't know if Jen's coming back. I'll have to talk to the others.'

'Thanks, sister,' said Chris.

CLARA: *Down sin drum*

'Down sin drum. Downs in drum. Downs in drome.'

Whichever way nine-year-old Clara configured the words, they still didn't make any sense. She pressed her ear against the door and listened. She could hear the yowling of the new baby and the Groans talking in whispers. It was so different to how she remembered the night they brought baby Serge home, or newborn Star, when there were corks popping and laughter and people dropping in with bunches of flowers and second-hand Babygros. In the end, Doro opened the door. Megan was there, sitting in an armchair with one boob hanging out of her blouse. She looked exhausted and thin. Clara had never noticed before how many grey hairs she had.

'Come and meet your new sister, Clarie. She's a very special little girl.'

Doro took her hand and led her into the sitting room, where the baby was in a carrycot, fast asleep. It didn't look very special, though it was cuter than baby Serge, who was horribly puckered and yellow when he was born. She was secretly thinking that babies are very overrated.

'She's downs in drum.'

Clara stared blankly. Sometimes the words of the Groans were utterly baffling.

'She's got extra chrome zone,' said Nick Holliday, who was pouring out tea from the big brown pot. Marcus, Moira Lafferty and Chris Watt were there too, squashed together on the saggy red sofa. It was deadly cold in the room, despite the fire smouldering in the grate.

'Look, she's only got one line,' said Marcus, taking the baby's tiny hand and turning it up to show Clara the palm. 'It means she's going to need lots of help growing up.'

He slipped his arm around her and pulled her on to his knee. 'What d'you think, Clarie? Are you up for it, my special girl?'

She nodded. She couldn't see what having one line on your hand had to do with growing up, but she liked the feel of his warm body and the tobacco smell of his breath on her cheek. She wanted to be the one who was special, not this silent interloper.

'We've chosen a great name for her,' said Chris Howe, sticking his head in through the door. 'We're going to call her Oolie-Anna in honour of Lennie.'

It was a weird name, but nice. Clara knew all about Lennie the Leader from Fred, who'd shown the kids a picture of a wild man with a big coat and goatee beard, and told them the story of how Lennie had caught the train to the station in Thinland. Where Oolie-Anna came into it she had no idea. She hung around the cot for a while, hoping the baby would open its eyes or do something interesting, but it just lay there snuffling in its sleep.

She went to fetch Serge, who was in the annexe watching *Doctor Who* on TV with Fred.

'Come and see the new baby.'

He came and stood by the cot, trying to look interested. She saw him poke it with his finger when he thought no one was looking. It cried a bit, then went quiet again.

'It looks all right,' he said non-committally.

She went up to her room and made a card on folded paper with drawings of hearts and flowers and bows and a baby in the middle, and the words 'Happy Birthday Oolie-Anna' in big red letters. She gave it to Megan, who started to cry.

The arrival of Oolie-Anna (no one ever called her Ulyana) changed all their lives. As the adults adapted their routines to make time to look after her, Clara, who'd just turned ten, took on more responsibility for the other kids, seeing them to and from school, supervising their games and checking on their homework. It seemed only a small step up from being in charge of the pets – first the hamster, then the rabbits – though her track record here had not been fantastic.

She has only a hazy recollection of Megan, who tended to ignore all the kids, including Crunchy Carl and Oolie-Anna. Doro, on the other hand, threw herself totally into her new role as a co-parent of a Down's syndrome child, as if she could overcome the developmental effects of the spare chromosome through sheer willpower alone. She spent hours coaching Oolie's speech and movement to minimise the outward signs of her disability. She read books, badgered the health and social services endlessly, and campaigned against slights and petty discrimination. Helping Oolie-Anna to fulfil her potential became her new project; and although it was hard to feel actually jealous of Oolie, Clara sometimes resented all the attention she got.

A new Oolie rota was set up so everyone had a turn looking after her. Doro, who was still working as a liberal studies lecturer at the Tech, cut down her hours. Marcus swapped his Coal Board job for a part-time lectureship in economics at the Doncaster Institute, to spend more time at home. Chris Howe crossed the counter and started work in the Benefit Office. Fred the Red stayed at home doing something called 'theoretical practice', which seemed mainly to involve talking on the phone. There was now a bit more money coming in. Little luxuries started to appear – chocolate cake and ice cream, fish and chips once a week, beer and the occasional bottle of wine for the Groans. Nick Holliday, who wasn't into babies, spent more time with the older kids, and Clara learned there was more to teaching than just bossing people around. Megan, silent and catlike, watched all this from the sidelines. It was hard to tell what she made of it all.

Baby Oolie-Anna wore rainbow-coloured hand-me-downs, crocheted by Moira, and when she acquired teeth, Chris Watt carved vegetables into animals and flowers for her. Chris Howe made a flying-saucer mobile from painted cardboard, and Fred emerged from his room with his guitar and sang revolutionary songs involving plenty of clapping and chanting, in which Oolie participated with drooly enthusiasm. Marcus stuck a new sign on the kitchen noticeboard beside the rotas:

A society's greatness is measured by the way it treats its weakest members.

CLARA: Leviathan

As soon as Clara enters her classroom on Monday morning, she senses something has changed – a subtle alteration of smell or mood. The room is quiet, but the texture of the silence is different. Something's missing. Then she realises Hamlet's cage door is fastened – but the cage is empty. She forgot to check on Hamlet before she went home on Saturday. She has a vivid flashback to the chaotic scene on Community Day and, although 6F is due to arrive any minute, she rushes off to find Mr Philpott.

He's sitting in the boiler room reading a book, wearing two pairs of glasses, one on top of the other, because the light's dim and murky. The boiler is smouldering with a dry clinkery smell, and the air is opaque with heat and smoke. A fine layer of ash and coal dust coats every surface.

'What happened to Hamlet, Mr Philpott?'

'Alas, poor 'amster . . .'

She feels her stomach lurch. Could she have saved it, if she'd remembered to check on Saturday?

'But where's the body? He needs a proper burial.'

'What did you 'ave in mind? Christian? Muslim? 'Indu?'

'Er . . . what d'you suggest?'

He doesn't say anything, just cocks his head over to one side, and she realises he's indicating the boiler.

'You mean . . . Hamlet . . .?'

'Cremation. No muckin' around in't graveyard.'

Just then, there's a knock on the door and a pale knobbly scalp pokes in. It's Jason, his head newly shaved. It looks awful.

'I came to find you, miss. Please, miss, the kids are all waiting.'

'Oh – I'm sorry! Thank you, Jason!'

As she makes for the door, Jason shuffles up to Mr Philpott in his oversized trainers, and mumbles, 'Me mam says can you lend me some dinner money, sir?'

'Jason, you know Mr Philpott can't . . .'

But Mr Philpott is already fumbling in his wallet for a fiver.

Jason grabs the money, says, 'Ta very much, sir,' and disappears.

There's a near riot by the time she gets back to her classroom. They've been on their own without a teacher for all of five minutes, and already anarchy has set in.

'Miss, miss, what 'appened to t'amster?' Tracey Dawcey shrills, as she enters.

'I saw it Sat'day, miss. It were 'ung upside down on't wheel,' Robbie Lewis shouts. 'Its 'ead wor 'angin' reyt off! Blood were drippin' out!'

'Miss killed it, din't you, miss?' yells Jason.

It's what Hobbes called the war of all against all, and she has to be the Leviathan, a role she quite enjoys. She fixes them with the Look and t-a-l-k-s v-e-r-y s-l-o-w-l-y a-n-d f-i-r-m-l-y. It's such an obvious act, yet the kids fall for it every time.

They like strictness, it makes them feel secure.

She tries to have a word with Jason at lunchtime, but he's disappeared, and she spends the hour on the phone trying to track down the man from Syrec who – surprise, surprise! – has not turned up to collect the plastic bottles and newspapers as promised. All she gets is an answering-machine message referring her to a mobile number which plays a message directing her back to the first number.

At the end of the day, when all the kids grab their bags and scattered possessions and stampede for the exit, she collars Jason, and blocks his way by putting her arm across the door.

'Jason, I think you should give that money back to Mr Philpott.'

'Why, miss? 'E give it me.'

'I think he thought he was helping your mum out . . .'

She suspects the loan had nothing to do with Mrs Taylor, and was just a flash of opportunism on Jason's part. She hesitates, stuck for words. Jason puts her right.

'You mean 'e thinks 'e can shag 'er for five quid?'

'That's not what I meant.'

'Let me go, miss. I've got to meet my nana. Is it true, miss, you killed t'amster?'

'Of course not.'

But in the moment that she loses concentration, Jason ducks under her arm, wriggles past her, out through the door, and he's gone.

After tidying the classroom, she goes to find Mr Philpott. Her argument with Jason has upset her. At times like this, she feels like she's getting nowhere with these kids – like she's a fool for even trying. But Mr Philpott is in no mood to cheer her up. He's in the lobby, still cleaning up the debris from Community Day, swabbing down the floor with soapy water and Zoflora.

'All this muck!' He waves his brush towards the plastic bottles and newspaper mountain heaped untidily at one end of the hall. 'You should never 'ave encouraged 'em. Give 'em an excuse, an' they'll bring their dead grannies in for you to burry. Load of dicky dodgers around 'ere.'

'I'm sorry, Mr Philpott. I've been trying to contact the recycling firm. Let's put the rubbish in the boot of my car, a bit at a time, and I'll recycle it at the supermarket in Sheffield. Look –' she reaches inside her bag for a five-pound note '– I've come to give you this back.'

'What's that for?'

She had intended to lie, to tell him that Jason had given it back voluntarily. But an unexpected wave of truth captures her, and she finds herself saying, 'Mrs Taylor's very pretty, but I don't think she's right for you, Mr Philpott.'

'You think I'm too old?' He removes his glasses and gives them a polish.

'No, not too old. But . . . maybe she's too young.'

He folds the five-pound note and stows it in the breast pocket of his dungarees.

'You know, there's a lot a gentleman of my age can offer a beautiful young widow.' He winks. 'Don't be upset about t'amster, duck. I'll get you another one.'

★

At half past four, as she makes her way out to the car park, she notices Jason is still there, loitering by the school gates. A moment later a woman approaches – an older woman, smartly dressed – jacket, lipstick, high heels – quite different from the other mothers in their jeans and jumpers.

Jason runs up and hugs her. It must be his nana.

The woman, aware of being watched, looks up. For a moment their eyes meet and hold.

Clara feels a chill of something long buried.

Why does she seem familiar?

SERGE: Thunderstorms

Monday morning. Maroushka acknowledges Serge's greeting with her usual four-finger wiggle. He searches her face for a hint that she'd spotted him following her and the blonde woman on Friday night, but she is typically inscrutable.

'Gut veekend?'

'Yes, thanks, Student Princess.'

Does she wonder what happened to her shoes that are at this moment standing to attention on the bookshelf in his bedroom, getting ready for their big moment? He can't wait to see the look on her face when he gives them back. He must remember to ask her about the Iranian War.

At lunchtime he follows her as she leaves the trading floor, catches a crowded lift down to the atrium, and exits the building. Where the hell is she going? He walks along the pavement looking for her, but she's vanished.

> Student Princess Maroushka!
> Hear the song of Serge!
> My song of love,
> It's not a dirge . . .

Trouble is, not many things rhyme with Serge, and even fewer with Maroushka.

The air is warm and soggy. A distant barrel of thunder rolls out over the rooftops. At Pret A Manger he grabs a sandwich, which unfortunately turns out to be crayfish (they don't seem to have proper food around here), and heads back towards the office, quickening his pace, but he's still a couple of blocks away when the storm breaks. He ducks into a doorway with a crowd of damp strangers, pressed together watching a sheet of water pour down in front of them. The thunder rolls again, much closer now. Suddenly it crashes almost overhead. He feels a moment of sheer terror – and in a flash his mind leaps back to another terrifying storm, years ago.

He and Otto were kids, and Nick Holliday was putting them to bed, up in the attic at Solidarity Hall. He remembers cowering under the sheets from the terrible volleys of thunder, and the fierce rain drumming on the eaves. 'Maybe a butterfly flapped its wings somewhere,' Nick had said. Otto had flapped his arms and laughed nervously. But as Nick talked, Serge had lost his fear, captivated by the image of the butterfly beating its tiny wings and moving an imperceptible current of air, tipping some subtle balance, which, magnified a million times in motion, unleashed a hurricane that caused palm trees to bend double, and huge waves to lash a faraway coast.

Maybe Maroushka's like that – sensitive-dependent on initial input, the way a small variation at one point of a dynamic system can have magnified effects elsewhere. He just hasn't found the right trigger yet to release her typhoon of passion. While he stands waiting for the rain to clear, and pondering the mysteries of women, the phone rings in his pocket. He checks the number before answering, but it's only Otto, calling up for a blab, still effusive with thanks.

'Man, you saved our lives . . . I'll pay you back when I get a break . . . Molly says hi too.'

'No problem . . . yeah . . . say hi from me.' Serge lets Otto's words wash over him like rain. 'Funny – I was just thinking about you and Nick. Remember that storm? The time he told us about the butterfly effect?'

'Yeah, and Crunchy said we should pull the wings off all the butterflies. Weird kid. Bit of a psycho.'

Funny how memory works. He can remember Nick and Otto and himself up in the attic listening to the storm – he can't remember Crunchy being there at all.

'I've always had a worry about Crunchy Carl. You remember the big fire, when Oolie got trapped in the annexe?'

'But Crunchy'd already left by then.' Otto sounds sceptical.

'He could have come back, couldn't he? See, Doro found some pine cones in the annexe after the fire. And once, Crunchy nicked those pine cones I kept under my bed and lit a fire with them in the front room. Megan had to put it out.'

'Proves nothing, Soz.'

'No, except he knew about my pine cones. And another thing, he knew where the back-door key was hidden.'

'You should've told the police.'

'Yeah. But Doro told me not to.'

He remembers Doro telling him to keep quiet about the pine cones. But what he remembers most is being gripped by the chance congruence of so many unlikely events: Oolie getting dropped off early that day; the school chess club being cancelled; Doro being late back; Otto missing the bus. And something else – a person or people unknown – a malign initial input that was the catalyst. What was the probability of all that?

'Clara thought it was those lads from the Prospects,' says Otto. 'Because they always used to pick on Oolie. Remember when she lobbed bricks at them? How is she, by the way?'

'Fine, I think. Haven't seen her in a while.'

A stab of guilt – he must ring her back before long.

'D'you remember those stories she used to tell us? The slumbering starlings, and the sobbing nation of women?'

He wonders whether Otto and Clara had a fling sometime in the past. His sister's love life is a source of speculation which she annoyingly refuses to discuss with him.

'Doro came down last week,' he tells Otto. 'She announced she and Marcus are getting married.'

'Married? What the fuck for? Do people still *do* it at their age?'

'Dunno. I'm not sure if Marcus can even still get it up.'

'Maybe they're ready to settle down in the Domestos fear. Heh heh.'

'I tried to tell Doro I was working in the City, to slip it casually into conversation. But I just couldn't get it out. The way she was going on, I'd have sooner confessed to child murder.'

'Yeah. All that guilt we internalised. But you know what, Soz? I envy that lot – they had something they believed in.'

'I know. Values and stuff. It all seems a bit retro.'

They chuckle at the backwardness of their parents.

As he rings off, the rain thins to a fine shower and a half-rainbow glimmers in the sky above St Paul's dome. Wow! How can something so simple – something that doesn't even cost any money – be so ridiculously, unbelievably beautiful? He pulls the iPhone out of his pocket again and fumbles with the camera setting, but in a few seconds it's vanished.

Maroushka is already at her desk by the time he gets back. Where has she been? He flicks the rain from his hair, hoping it's not too obvious that he went out of the building. Chicken is on the prowl again, dispensing wisdom and testosterone around the trading hall.

'You know what wrecked the economy?'

He leans over Tootie, who says nothing, but raises his pale eyes like a worshipper about to receive communion.

'Politicians interfering in the free market. Look at that fool Clinton. Tried to make housing affordable to blacks, Latinos, other losers who couldn't afford it. Fannie Mae, Freddie Mac, massive US sub-prime mortgage players, widen home ownership, give mortgages to people too poor to pay them off – brilliant idea, so long as property prices kept rising. Then they collapsed . . . Moral is, trust the wisdom of the market.'

'Wisdom of the market. Brilliant way of putting it, Chief Ken.'

Tootie is a low-grade bum wipe.

Serge's eyes follow Chicken as he advances and perches one meaty buttock on Maroushka's desk, leaning so his sightline is directly above her cleavage. She's wearing a white broderie anglaise top which looks both virginal and irresistibly sexy.

'You know what's wrong with this country?'

Maroushka says nothing. Chicken pauses, enjoying his mastery, the fabric around his groin bulging visibly.

'Shall I tell you?'

She nods.

'Decline of religion. Think about it, Maroushka. People need something to tell them what's right and wrong. Values.'

Maroushka giggles through small white teeth. 'In my country, money have value. Religion is for babushkas.'

Chicken's smile wavers. She watches him coolly. How does she get away with it?

Meeting Serge's eye, she pulls a little flirty pout as if to say she's only humouring Chicken and she'd much rather, all things being equal, be flirting with him. But they're not equal, are they? Seeing himself through her eyes, he feels swallowed up by his own insignificance, a hamster on the wheel of capitalism, grinding out numbers to feed the fathomless appetite of the FATCA money mill. Girls like her – they're attracted to power and wealth. They can't help it, it's in their DNA. If he's to win her heart, he has to take his destiny into his own hands.

He's covered his loan to Otto. He's made enough to pay off his credit card by the end of the month – but why pay it back just yet? By the time the APR kicks in at 16 per cent, he could have made a few more grand at 20 per cent. So why stop now? Why not take the next step, build a financial reserve more quickly than he could just from his salary and bonus, and then get out?

He's heard the traders going on about spread betting. It's the way to make a lot of money quickly, cashing in on the spread between the high and low points of the market. It's simple, and it's tax free. It's riskier of course – you can lose a lot of money quickly too. You have to know when to stop. But he's proved to himself he has the gift. And he's not greedy. When he's made his million (or maybe two, because you can't do much with one million these days) he'll put this City world behind him. He'll go to Brazil, and live in a house by the beach, and devote himself to mathematics again.

The plan has been gelling in his head ever since he joined FATCA, the details gradually becoming clearer with each deal. He'll write a bestselling book giving the low-down on the tricks and scams of the City. He'll donate generously to progressive causes, to make things right with Marcus and Doro. He'll buy his mum a few decent outfits. He'll set up a prize for the delinquents in his sister's school. He'll write poetry. He'll marry Princess Maroushka, and whisk her away into the realms of pure mathematics to save her from this empty life of statistical prostitution. You could say the restaurant did him a favour with that dodgy bill (which they still haven't sorted, despite numerous phone calls) because that spurred him to look more creatively at his own options. And Otto with his mortgage problem – he was so pathetically grateful for the loan, Serge didn't have the heart to tell him he wasn't that bothered when he repaid.

He's noticed, in the year he's been here, a constant churning of people, faces that appear, smile, become friends for a while, or at least drinking companions, then vanish without a trace, blown away like jetsam by the winds of trade. What happens to the ones who disappear? Those who failed to make the grade, or got found out doing something they shouldn't, or who managed to break free – where are they now? There's an empty desk for a day or two, then a new face appears, scrubbed, blank, eager to learn and to earn, as he once was. They'll be here tomorrow, and the day after, until the end of the month, and the year, and how many years after that? He needs to start planning his exit now.

All around him the traders are going mad, placing deals in the peak hours before closing time. The noise comes in waves, like the ebb and flow of the sea. Focusing his eyes on the columns of data on the monitors, he seeks out the Fibonacci retracements. But they won't stay still. The graphs waver like strands of seaweed in the restless currents of global trade. The indices pulse like gorged molluscs. Profits surge and fall and surge again on the tides of the world's markets, into which the vast rivers of human endeavour ceaselessly pour: 61.8 forwards, 38.2 back. Phi. The Golden Mean.

CLARA: *Petrol*

Clara winds her way homewards through the mean suburbs of Doncaster, peering through a grey drizzle that smears her windscreen because her windscreen washer reservoir is empty and she doesn't know how to fill it. It isn't until she stops for petrol on the A6182 that she discovers her purse is missing from her bag. The guy at the petrol station, who has a deep tan and a gold chain around his neck, is not particularly sympathetic when she tells him she has no money and no card. He threatens to call the police.

'Go on, then, call them,' Clara snaps. 'It'll save me having to call them myself.'

'People around here've got no respect.'

'Respect for what?'

'Respect for private property. They're a load of benefit bums and dicky dodgers.'

'What's a dicky dodger?'

'Someone like you,' he says.

'Well, they used to be coal miners and steel workers, and whose fault is that?'

'Not mine,' says the petrol guy. 'I just work here.'

Then she sees on the forecourt, beside the rain-soaked sacks of firewood and the bucket of wilting carnations laughably labelled 'fresh flowers', a box of potted plants. Tree seedlings, to be precise. Some of them still have the labels stuck in, in Doro's handwriting. They're on sale at £5 each.

'Where did you get them from?'

'I dunno. So are you going to pay or what?'

'They're stolen property. You're handling stolen property!'

'Sod off.'

'I will!'

So she gets into her car, slams the door and drives off back to Sheffield.

'Yeah, yeah, don't worry, when I get my new credit card, I'll go in and pay what I owe,' she tells Ida Blessingman, who has invited her over for a porcini omelette. 'But it was satisfying.'

'D'you want to borrow fifty quid, to tide you over?' asks Ida.

'Thanks. Have you got a fag I can borrow, too?'

SERGE: The cockroach

Serge is finding that with the time he spends on his personal trades, he has to put in extra hours to keep on top of his day job. After his initial gains, the results have been mixed.

'I hear you've been at it all hours in here, Freebie,' says Chicken on Friday afternoon, resting his hands on Serge's desk. 'Are you winning?'

So who has reported his late nights to Chicken?

'Yes,' he grins disarmingly. 'I've been . . . you know . . . working . . .'

'Working on what?'

'I've been running a Monte Carlo simulation. Feeding through a few numbers to see how they perform,' he lies.

'A Monte Carlo?'

The bright doggy eyes blink uncertainly. Serge presses home his advantage.

'Yes, once you've started putting through a sequence, you can't really interrupt it.'

'So that's what's keeping you in the office all night?'

Could Chicken have found out about the private trades he's been placing? Could someone outside the door of the disabled loo have overheard his musty whispered conversations with his broker?

'We value our reputation here at FATCA.' Chicken lowers his voice and Serge notices his left eye twitches a bit as he leans forward. 'If you've been breaking any rules, I need to know. Regulators sniffing around. Last thing we want is an FSA investigation, at this moment in time.'

'No rule-breaking, Chief Ken. Just . . .' A small alarm bell tinkles in the recess of his mind. What's this about the Financial Services Authority? Why *at this moment in time*? '. . . just elegant number work . . .'

He's about to launch into an explanation of his six years studying maths at Cambridge, his unfinished PhD on fractals, but maybe Chicken is sensitive to being patronised about his amateurish grasp of maths.

'It's based on . . . er . . . an extension of chaos theory.'

'Chaos, eh?' Chicken looks satisfied. 'There's going to be a bit of that on the markets soon, with Lehman Brothers under pressure. Unless a buyer emerges. You've been following the news?'

Serge nods.

'Good man. Keep winning.'

Chicken's eyes have just fallen on Maroushka, whose yellow jacket blings through the glass wall of the corner office. Straightening himself up, he pulls in his belly. Serge can almost see the bulge of his hard-on silhouetted against the windows, beneath the supple silk-wool cloth of his charcoal-grey suit.

He can't hear what Chicken and Maroushka say to each other in the office, there's too much foreground noise, then Chicken moves away to continue his walkabout and Serge logs into his computer.

'Sergei?'

He looks up. Maroushka is standing behind him, leaning over his shoulder. He breathes in her perfume.

'How's things, Princess?' This is the moment to engage her interest. 'I've been reading an interesting book about the Iranian War.'

'You are interesting in politic?' The dark eyebrows arch.

'Oh yes. Really interested. I was hoping you could fill me in on the history –'

'My subject is mathematic, Sergei. History is for older persons.'

'Yes, but –'

'But you know, Sergei, I am here only with student visa. When study is finish I must go back to Zhytomyr. But Chicken is apply for permanent work visa for me. You understand, Sergei?'

'A visa? Maroushka, we could . . .'

But she's already slipped away to her own desk.

He opens up his screens. A ripple in the numbers on the AIM catches his eye. New data whirls and drops in columns – the glimmer of a new pattern emerging. He forces himself to focus on the screen. There's something going on here. He was right, the FTSE 100 is tumbling, and bank shares have taken a pounding since the news of Lehman Brothers' demise. But for some reason the Small Cap, where his shares of choice are traded, is inching the other way. Oh, shit! Even as he watches, all the profits he made on short selling those South Yorkshire shares last week are washed away. He is haemorrhaging money. He makes a beeline for the disabled loo, to place a stop order. But it's engaged. Oh, shit!

He waits, pacing up and down on the trading floor which, interestingly, is the same colour as the rabbit-pooh-trodden carpet of Solidarity Hall. Strange how these patterns repeat. A few people look up and nod, but they're all too fixed on their screens and keyboards to take much notice. It's only mid-afternoon, but through the tall east-facing window the new moon is bobbing about like a paper boat on a turmoil of clouds.

He has to decide, when he can get back in there, whether to stop his bets before they go any higher. Or should he hold, gambling on another fall? If he had the cash reserves, he could do what the big guys do – push them back downwards, with more focused short selling. Trouble is, he hasn't even got the money in his account to cover what he already owes.

But FATCA has. FATCA's vaults are overflowing, and all those hyped-up traders obsessed with their Profit and Loss statements are pouring in more by the minute – he too has added his trickle of piss to the ocean of wealth. Yes, if FATCA could just *lend* him the money until he's got himself out of this fix . . . If he could just *temporarily* charge his losses to FATCA . . .

He resumes his pacing. Stop. Hold. Stop. Hold. Suddenly his shoe crunches on something hard. He looks down. A small, shiny brown shard is pressed into the carpet in front of his desk where Chicken had been leaning. It looks like . . . can it be . . . a cockroach? He recoils in revulsion. How the fuck did that get in here? He looks again. Is it an avatar? He pokes it with his foot. No, it's not a cockroach – it's a tiny USB flash drive. It must be *his* flash drive. He stares at it for a few seconds, then he picks it up and slips it into his pocket.

DORO: *Be realistic –*
demand the impossible

Doro is filled with resentment as she trundles the vacuum cleaner around the house on Friday. Not only does she have to give up a fine afternoon on the allotment to talk to this bloody social worker about Oolie, but for some inexplicable reason she feels compelled to clean up the house before he comes. Her mother's generation of women were supposed to find fulfilment in cleaning, but in Solidarity Hall it was such a hopeless task that all such ambition was scrubbed out of her.

Marcus said he'd help, but he's still upstairs on the computer and, when she goes up to fetch him, she finds he isn't working at all but snoozing in his chair, his head lolling down on his chest, one hand still slumped on the keyboard. Seeing him like this she is struck by how much he has aged, how bowed his shoulders are, how grey his hair is and how thin on top. He must be almost seventy, a strange age to be talking about marriage. But kind of romantic. A wave of tenderness catches her off guard. He's a good man, she thinks. She's been lucky. She tiptoes away without disturbing him.

Oolie is at Edenthorpe's, where she will be until Edna the cafeteria manageress drops her off after five o'clock on her way home. She has a job in the cafeteria three days a week, collecting and washing the dirty dishes. The other two days she goes to college to learn literacy, numeracy and other survival skills with a peer group she has known almost all her life, and whom Doro knows too, because when they go on outings she often volunteers as an extra chaperone.

When the social worker had first suggested the job at Edenthorpe's cafeteria, Doro had smiled, remembering the last time she'd been up there, when she was handing out leaflets at the gate calling for a general strike. It must have been some thirty years ago, because Clara had been a baby, strapped on her back. The men had laughed and screwed up the leaflets, which she put down to false consciousness, and one of them had given Clara a toffee, which she'd snatched away, provoking a screaming fit. It was strange to think of Oolie working there, and outrageous that the pittance she was paid was subsidised by the Council.

She misses the afternoons they used to spend together working on the allotment, happy interludes of purposeful activity and bonding. Oolie loves gardening, she's in her element with her stubby little fingers stuck into the black compost and her cheeks rosy from the fresh air. But now, seeing Oolie come bouncing home at the end of each working day bubbling with stories about who said what and who's copping off with whom has softened her attitude. Oolie saves up her money in a coffee tin and has started fantasising about how she will spend it. She's got a collection of brochures of exotic places she plans to visit, her vocabulary has broadened to include previously unknown swear words, and she's learned to tell fibs.

The vacuum cleaner rasps and rattles as it picks up bits of invisible dirt from the carpet; if only it was so easy to suck up the debris and detritus that are clogging up her own life. It's not even the housework that she finds wearisome so much as the coddling, cajoling, comforting, minding, mediating, massaging of egos – all that emotional work which women do, which no one recognises as work. Unless you're a nurse or a social worker or a teacher, in which case your female socialisation has prepared you for a low-paid career in one of these undervalued professions. '*Be the change you want to see*' taunts her from the fridge door. It sounds so easy, but then Gandhi had an army of women to run around after him and coddle him, and nothing to worry about except grand ideas like World Peace.

She rummages in her drawer for a T-shirt with a suitable slogan, which she keeps for such occasions. Ah! This is the one for a social worker! '*Be realistic – demand the impossible.*' She slips it on over her head, and notices with regret that her breasts, which used to push out 'r' and 't' now hover above 'm' and 'h'. (Her mother had been right about the 'brazeer', as about so much else.) A quick comb-through of her hair, and she's already on her way downstairs when the doorbell rings.

★

Mr Clements is a young plain-spoken Yorkshireman with a pleasant ruddy face framed by thick fair hair that sticks straight up from his forehead and blond stubble around his chin, which may be destined for a beard. He looks a bit like Clara's previous boyfriend, Josh, who disappeared off the scene in circumstances which Clara refuses to discuss, and this causes Doro to feel a twinge of dissatisfaction with her daughter, who has not yet settled down with a suitable partner and shows no signs of producing the grandchildren that she yearns for.

'Hiya, Mrs Lerner. How's it going?'

'Fine.' She resents being called Mrs when she's not married, and Lerner, which is Marcus's name, instead of Marchmont, which is hers. 'Would you like a cup of tea?'

'Ta, duck. Milk but no sugar.'

He seats himself at the kitchen table and shrugs off his blue denim jacket. Just to show him she's not a person to be trifled with, she hands him his tea in a cracked and chipped 'BATTLE OF ORGREAVE 1984 VETERANS' mug, a relic of the miners' strike.

'Blimey, that was a long while ago.' He takes a long sip and studies it with interest. 'I was just a lad. I remember, my dad got arrested, and my mam thought it were the end of the world. But it spurred me on to do summat different with my life, instead of just going down the pit like everybody else.' He pulls a file out of his briefcase. 'So how's Oolie-Anna been getting on at Edenthorpe's?'

'Fine.'

Mr Clements nods, ticks a paper in his folder, and she's grateful that he resists pointing out that the job was his idea, which she had strongly opposed at the time.

'Yes, she's a right character. Edna says she has them all in stitches.'

'She enjoys the company,' Doro admits grudgingly. She still finds it disconcerting to think of Oolie having relationships outside the family.

'The next stage we have to think about is independent living, Mrs Lerner. A flat of her own.'

'She's not ready for it,' Doro snaps back.

Mr Clements shuffles the papers in his folder and takes another sip of tea.

'You're right to be concerned, Mrs Lerner. But in the long term it'll be better for everybody if Oolie-Anna can spread her wings and learn to fly. Don't you agree?'

His cheeriness is relentless. Doro knows she's being manoeuvred into saying yes.

'We all want what's best for her, Mr Clements, but we have different interpretations of her needs.'

'So can I take that as a yes?'

'No, you can't. I know Oolie-Anna a lot better than you do.'

She stares furiously across the table at the pink young face.

'We have to plan for the possibility of kiddies with Down's outliving their parents nowadays.' His tone is unwaveringly upbeat. 'We want to avoid the situation where they lose not just their parents but their familiar living environment at the same time. So we like to start the process of separation early –'

'You think Marcus and I are going to croak any minute now?' she interrupts, feeling the heat build up in her cheeks.

Mr Clements, unruffled, drives home his advantage. Dealing with client rage is all part of his training.

'That's not what I'm saying, Mrs Lerner. On the contrary, we need to plan as far in advance as possible so we're not caught out when . . . when you and your husband are no longer able to care.'

He doesn't raise his voice or deviate from his script. She wants to throttle him.

'It'll help if you can confront your fears, Mrs Lerner. If there's any particular worries you have, we can discuss them. It's natural for you and your hubby to feel concerned . . .'

What else does he know, she wonders? Do the social services files of 1994 cross-refer with the police records of the day?

'If it's because we're not married, we are actually planning –'

'Your ages are the main factor we have to think about, Mrs Lerner – though of course that's often the case with Down's kiddies.'

Doro resists the impulse to vomit all over his briefcase.

'Oolie-Anna is not a kiddy.'

'That's just my point, Mrs Lerner. So shall I book us another meeting for next week, when you and your hubby've had a chance to talk it over?'

He's persistent, this boy.

'No. That won't be necessary.'

She stands and frowns until he rises to his feet.

'Well, I'd better be getting along. Thanks for the tea, Mrs Lerner.'

He smiles, patient and confident. He thinks he's making progress.

After he's gone, she sits at the kitchen table for several minutes. For some reason she feels utterly drained. On the wall in front of her, a clock is ticking away above a faded group photograph of the Solidarity Hall commune, taken in the back garden. Megan is in the photo, with Oolie, so it must have been sometime between 1985 and 1988. They all look so ridiculously young, the women with long untidy hair, the men with fluffy sideburns and moustaches, the children scruffy and mischievous. Where have all the years gone? She wishes she hadn't been so aggressive with the young social worker – he didn't deserve it, he means well, and actually he's quite good at his job. She knows that her resistance to Oolie moving away must appear irrational to him, but she isn't ready to unpack the carefully put-away past.

Not yet.

Marcus comes down and slips an arm around her shoulder – he must have heard the front door click.

'Okay?'

'Okay. How's the book going?' she asks.

'Great. I've finished the analysis of the left and I'm just about to start on the role of the women's movement.' His eyes brighten.

'Mm.' She sits forward, trying to look interested, but her mind is still replaying the conversation with the social worker, snagging at the points at which she should have said something different.

'I'm coming to realise just how important feminism is in the history of our movement.' He glances up at Doro, and his eyes soften. 'Maybe *you* could write that chapter, love. From the woman's perspective.'

Doro tries to think about feminism, but all that comes to mind is an image from long ago of a handful of Moira Lafferty's auburn hair clutched in her fist. She reaches out and squeezes his hand, realising she's being offered a great honour, but the earlier feeling of exhaustion and resentment has congealed like cold porridge around her heart.

'You write it, dear. I'm sure you know much more about it.'

He wanders through into the kitchen to put the kettle on.

'So how d'you get on with the social worker?'

Doro gives the leg of the chair where Mr Clements was sitting a petulant kick.

'He's determined to get Oolie into that bloody sheltered housing scheme. He'll go on and on till he gets his way.'

'That might not be such a bad idea, you know, love.'

He fishes in his cup for the submerged tea bag, and squeezes it with his fingers.

'Have you forgotten the kids throwing bricks at her, Marcus? Have you forgotten the fire? She's too vulnerable. No.'

What she doesn't say is that out of all the chaos, fun and disappointment of the commune, Oolie is her surprise accomplishment, even more than Clara and Serge, the unsteady twinkling star who illuminates those years.

SERGE: *The Gaussian copula*

By the time Serge gets into the disabled loo to place his stop order, he's already £40,000 down.

Back at his desk, he starts to feel panicky about the scale of his losses. But the little brown cockroach that will see him right is nestling in his pocket. He'll copy it on to his hard drive when he gets home. The more he thinks of it, the more it seems like a sign: the Mersenne prime; the wanton tango of the market; the cockroach capsule of information. They must be linked together.

He doesn't believe in destiny or karma or any other mystical mumbo-jumbo – the commune inoculated him against all that – but he does believe in patterns. He's seen them with his own eyes, intricate beautiful patterns, configured out of apparently random events. He knows that chance is seldom as random as it seems – chance and its close cousin, risk.

What is the risk that Chicken will come back, looking for his lost memory stick? What is the risk he'll find out if Serge downloads his data? Will the risks be offset if he sets up a decoy, by dropping the stick next to someone else's desk? Or is it best to gamble that Chicken won't find out at all? Actually, there is a formula for figuring out these complex risks. It's the Gaussian copula, beloved of derivatives analysts.

$$\Pr[T_A < 1, T_B < 1] = \phi_2\left(\phi^{-1}(F_A(1)), \phi^{-1}(F_B(1)), \gamma\right)$$

Thinking about the copula brings to mind copulation, and his thoughts stray back to Maroushka. The chances of them ending up in bed together, he reckons, are about 50 per cent. If Maroushka ends up in bed with him, though, then the chance that he will end up in bed with her is 100 per cent. If Maroushka ends up in bed with Chicken, however, his chances are greatly reduced, but still not zero (there is, after all, the possibility of a threesome, though the thought of a threesome with Maroushka and Chicken is distinctly scary). The risk of two people in bed together being struck by lightning is infinitesimal. But if one is struck, the risk to the other person in the same bed jumps to, say, 99 per cent, while the risk to the person sleeping on their lonely own in a faraway bed is still almost zero. On the other hand, if one person has a heart attack in bed, the risk to the other person (or people) in the same bed is still much the same as it was before. A heart attack and a lightning strike are different kinds of risks, yet neither of them comes completely out of the blue.

Now let's jumble up these risks and repackage them. Let's put together a bundle which includes, say, the lightning strike, him and Maroushka in bed, and Chicken having a heart attack. The chances of them all happening are still pretty low, because of the lightning strike. But if you take out the lightning strike, what are you left with? Serge hasn't a clue – and the truth is, neither have most people who trade in risk-based derivatives.

Okay, so forget about lightning strikes and threesomes, and think mortgages, car loans, hire-purchase agreements – these are the sorts of risks that preoccupy the guys on the FATCA Securitisation desk. They're all hard at it, tapping at their keyboards, late on Friday afternoon. What's the risk that someone will notice he's not participating? He stares at his screens, and attempts to engage with the shifts and turns of the market, but his heart is hammering so much that he soon gives up and takes the lift up to the cafeteria for a calming cup of chamomile and ashwagandha tea.

Outside the cafeteria window a bank of cloud, electric blue, is massing over the city. A few heavy raindrops spatter against the pane like falling stars. Far below, people the size of ants are unfurling umbrellas, hurrying into cabs and buses, rushing to get home before the storm breaks. In an hour or so, he will be down there too, hurrying towards the tube with the mysterious contents of the cockroach capsule in his pocket. A rumble of thunder spreads and dissipates into the air. Somewhere, there has been a lightning strike.

CLARA: *Cheesecake*

It's raining in Sheffield too, as Clara stands at the checkout queue in Waitrose on Friday evening, piling her purchases on to the belt, wondering whether it's bad to have chocolate mousse *and* tarte au citron *and* cheesecake *and* two bottles of prosecco. No, it's not bad. Because I'm worth it. And because I need cheering up.

'Cash or card?' asks the girl.

She pulls one of Ida's twenties out of her pocket, and takes her feast back home.

The theft of her purse has soured her mood all week, like a bad taste in the mouth. In her mind, she's still replaying the scene where Jason knocked against her as he ducked under her arm to get away on Monday afternoon. That must have been when it happened. Talking to the class next day, she'd given Jason the Look, but he'd avoided her eye and kept his head down. Mr Kenny's description of Jason sticks like gum on the floor of her mind, filthy but stubborn.

When she asked Mr Philpott whether she'd dropped it in the boiler room, all he offered was, 'Who steals my purse gets trashed.'

Mr Gorst/Alan twinkled sympathetically, and asked if she wanted to call the police. She shook her head. It was her fault – she should have left it in her locker in the staffroom. She didn't blame the kids, she just said her purse had vanished from her bag, and she appealed to the kids' better nature.

'If anyone would like to return something to me, I won't say anything and I'll be very happy and grateful. You can just leave it in my desk drawer. If one of you knows what I'm talking about, you know the right thing to do.'

She kept checking the drawer. She was so confident the kids would do the right thing.

But they didn't.

'So did it turn up?'

Ida helps herself to a slab of cheesecake out of the box on Clara's kitchen table.

'No.' Clara pops the cork of the prosecco and sighs. 'I guess if you're going to end up on the dole anyway, or doing some dead-end job for five quid an hour, why not nick someone's purse and spend it while you can? Why bother to be better than that?'

'Here, you need some more of this.' Ida slaps a brick of cheese-cake down on Clara's plate. 'Before you start getting sentimental.'

She pours out two glasses of prosecco, and between them they polish off all the cheesecake, half the tarte au citron and most of the chocolate mousse. Because they're worth it.

SERGE: Passwords

Evidently Chicken has a sentimental streak. The cockroach memory stick, when Serge finally opens it up on his laptop at home, is full of snaps of the Porter family. Ken and Caroline with their kids William and Arabella, all happy smiley, waving from the deck of their yacht, lazing around the pool of their house in no-tax Monaco where they are domiciled, though as far as Serge knows they actually live in Holland Park. (He knows all this because Chicken cannot resist the occasional little brag on his morning walkabouts.) There he is in close-up, wearing a DJ, with a proprietorial arm around Caroline, a tall blonde with glittery jewellery, glossed lips and deep sad eyes. Why does she look vaguely familiar?

There he is dressed up in combat gear, brandishing a paint-ball gun in a rainy forest with some other guys from the top floor at FATCA – they're all grinning like psychos. There's a folder of golfing photos – his companion is a blond curly-haired Apollo type who stands a head taller than him and wears a yellow polo shirt with . . . what's that logo? He zooms in. Gant. Nice. There's a series of Chicken doing the grip 'n' grin with a guy with big ears and a cheesy smile. Serge stares. Jeez, it's Tony Blair!

There are some pictures of his kids posing with assorted high-maintenance teenage gear: cello, quad bike, golf clubs, pony. The girl has Chicken's dark good looks, dimples and little pointy teeth. The boy is smaller and plumper, his face is round – Serge stares – he has the same almond-shaped eyes, the same half-open mouth and slightly lost look as Oolie. A rush of empathy almost sweeps him off course. How can you rip off a man with a Down's syndrome kid? He pushes the image to the back of his mind, and opens the only non-photo folder, an old-style calendar application with anniversaries, birthdays (the kids' nicknames are cringe-making –

Willywonka and Jinglebell), including Maroushka's (hey?), and various other significant dates.

But where's the meat? Where's the file containing details of all the FATCA bank accounts? Passwords? Scams? There's nothing but a load of stupid snapshots. His spirits sink, and all the anticipation that was buzzing in his head dissolves into a dull mystified disappointment. The void made by the forty k he's just lost is still there, nearly half his annual salary, on which he'll soon be paying credit card interest at 16 per cent, as well as spread betting interest at 18 per cent. Shit! He pours himself another glass of Barolo and finishes off the burned crust of the pizza he picked up from Peppe's on the way home. He'll just have to remortgage his flat.

His penthouse flat is sparsely furnished and restful. The main room has a squashy sofa, an armchair and a low table – that's all. The kitchen is full of high-spec kit that he's never bothered to master. Why complicate life when Peppe's is just down the road? He has a low hardwood bed from which he can look straight out of the window and count the stars in the sky. There's a built-in wardrobe, some drawers and a bookshelf with his college books and Maroushka's shoes, still waiting for their owner.

While he's been browsing through the picture files, the storm has abated, and the night outside his window is clear and bright. He takes in the view of London – the movement of traffic between the stillness of buildings, whirling seething patterns of headlights slicing through darkness, and faint above the city lights the galaxies of stars spiralling out of nothingness, chaos and order, stretching in every direction as far as the eye can see. You could lose yourself down there in all that darkness and light; you could drift towards entropy yet still be shielded from the terror of infinity, safe from spinning out of control, as numbers sometimes do.

Maybe that Barolo wasn't such a good idea. The clash of strong wine against insoluble problems has left his brain feeling bruised, his chest bursting as though someone is pressing on his face with a pillow. On impulse, he grabs his raincoat, takes the lift down to the ground floor and lets himself out through the door into the empty street. The sky is clear, but the pavement is still treacherous with puddles. He steps around them carefully to keep his shoes dry. The storm-washed air smells of ozone and wet leaves. Intoxicated with the scent of it, he walks briskly in random directions, drawn sometimes by a brightly lit café, sometimes by a dark alley where cobbles shine in lamplight, until his breaths come deep and slow and the thrumming in his head eases into a dull background ache.

On the way home, he stops at the cashpoint on Cheapside to get some money for the weekend. As he keys in his four-digit PIN number 0248 – the month and year of Doro's birth – a stray thought crosses his mind. He knows it's not advisable to use birthdays for passwords, but everybody does, don't they? After all, there are so many possible permutations and combinations. Many – but computable. Suddenly the calendar file of birth and anniversary days he downloaded on to his laptop takes on a whole new significance. Here could be the key he needs. He hasn't got the skill or the patience to unlock it. But he knows a man who could.

Otto stayed on at Churchill College after he graduated, to study software systems at the far reaches of techno-geekery, cruising those way-out galaxies where maths, programing languages and technology collide. When he talks about what he's doing, it sounds like sci-fi to Serge. He goes to symposia on hypervisor encryption and cryptovirology but, like many cyber-heads, he's more interested in the technology than the ethics angle. Once, as an undergrad, he designed a packet sniffer to capture the questions on the final-year divinity exam papers, which he posted on all the college noticeboards: it was his idea of a joke.

'He's at a conference.' Molly's voice sounds faint and anxious down the phone. 'Is everything all right? I mean, about the money?'

'Sure,' says Serge. 'No stress. I'll ring on Monday.'

The thought of confiding in Otto – blabby, excitable, unreliable little Otto – is scary. But what choice does he have?

CLARA: *Grommets*

Clara dunks her head under the stream of warm water from the shower, and rubs the shampoo through her hair, wondering how come – despite all the feminist rhetoric at Solidarity Hall, and the fact that her A level grades were almost as good as Serge's – how come he's the one who got away to Cambridge and never comes back, geeking out with his nerdy friends in their medieval wonderland, while she's stuck here, half-in-half-out of Doncaster, still shackled to her crazy family, still trying to shepherd lost kids (who repay her by nicking her purse), still trying to be a Solidarity Hall kind of person. The thought 'not fair' bubbles to the surface of her mind, and she pricks it sharply. 'Not fair' is for losers and whingers, not for her.

The trouble is, as the oldest child of the commune, she was raised to several divergent blueprints. Feminism, Marxism, vegetarianism, autonomy, responsibility, spontaneity, courage, consideration, self-expression, self-confidence, unselfishness. There was always someone telling her eat up your vegetables, brush your teeth, read this book, go and play outside, help those who can't help themselves, be your own person and take no notice of what anyone tells you – it was as though half a dozen quarrelsome good fairies had got into a fight as they tried to shower their gifts over her.

She rinses out the warm coconut-scented foam and rubs her hair, carefully wiping her ears with a corner of the towel wrapped around her finger. Even after all these years, she's still careful about drying her ears. Yes, if Doro had looked after her properly, instead of having one eye out for Serge's genius and the other for Oolie's disability, she'd have realised that Clara's regular earaches after washing her hair were not normal, not caused by the shampoo, like stinging eyes. It wasn't Doro but Chris Watt, who'd once been a health visitor, who spotted the traces of blood and pus on the pillow one morning.

'Glue ear,' she pronounced, and Clara was dragged off to the doctor in Askern by Marcus, who held her hand in the shabby disinfectant-smelling waiting room and showed her the scar where he'd had his pin decks taken out. She ran her finger along the thin white line beneath the elastic of his underpants, wondering whether she too had pin decks, and whether it would hurt to have them removed.

The grommet operation when she was thirteen changed everything. She began to do better at school, and started taking part actively in lessons rather than lurking at the back with the bad kids. The world became much clearer, but also more mundane. In the pre-grommet days, conversations, though muted, were often intriguing, touched with magic, teasing the imagination to fill in the muffled syllables. It was having the grommets inserted in her ears, more than Oolie's birth or the start of her periods, that marked the end of her childhood.

After Megan left with Crunchy Carl, the atmosphere in the commune seemed to ease, and everybody relaxed. Serge spent hours geeking out with Nick Holliday, and Otto tagged along. Tosser and Kollon hung around Thinlandia with Star, doing weird drawings of Thinmen and Thinwomen, who had long spiky limbs and lived in tunnels. (Yes, newly grommeted Clara tried to tell them it was Fin, not Thin, but they came from London, and they said it was all the same.) She took to reading novels up in her room, avoiding Oolie-Anna because, although Oolie was cute, she was also quite demanding, and Clara didn't want to get roped in for hours of childcare while the Groans droned on in their endless meetings.

Then, one day, Oolie-Anna herself changed all that.

On their way to and from school, they used to cut through the Prospects, a maze of crumbling red-brick terraces which had been thrown up between the wars to accommodate miners at the Askern colliery. The front doors opened straight into the alley, and there was usually a little gang of wannabe-toughs hanging out by the derelict toilet blocks around the back, making remarks as they passed. That day, Clara was coming home from school, walking fast enough to leave the other kids trailing behind. Her ragtag entourage cramped her style, and their constant bickering got on her nerves, especially Tosser and Kollon with their scarecrow hair and ridiculous names. (They'd been christened Toussaint and Kollontai, but that was too much of a mouthful for the kids at school.) At fourteen you're sensitive to peer pressure.

She'd just turned the corner into Prospect Street when a small chubby kid in a yellow jumpsuit came hurtling towards her, hair sticking out, face scarlet with panting and terror, mouth open in a scream. It was Oolie-Anna. A couple of little yobs were behind her, chucking bits of broken brick at her legs, shouting, 'Run, freak! Run!'

She stumbled and flung herself at Clara's knees. Clara picked up a half-brick and hurled it back at the yobs. Blind fury guided her arm and she hit one of them smack on the nose. Blood spouted everywhere.

'Fuck off, you fucking retards!' she yelled. 'Fuck off, else I'll fucking kill you!'

The yobs stopped dead. They were smaller than her, but there were two of them. For a moment they just stared. Then they started swivelling round, looking for support from their usual weaselly cohorts. But they were on their own. She picked up another brick. 'I fucking mean it!'

They turned and ran, whooping over their shoulders, 'Freak! Freak! Freak!'

Oolie-Anna clung to her legs, wailing.

'It's all right,' Clara said. 'They're just morons. Let's go.'

When they got home, the front door was open and Moira Lafferty was in the sitting room yacking on the phone, her feet up on the sofa, silver rings on her purple-varnished toes, Capiz shell earrings jingling as she talked. She waved at the kids with her free hand, releasing a faint smell of patchouli and BO, and carried on yacking.

Clara usually liked Moira's benignly neglectful approach to childcare. Moira worked two days a week in a rehab centre for people who'd had brain injuries, and treated them all like they were a bit brain injured. She'd sit at the kitchen table crafting finger puppets or a Capiz shell necklace, letting the kids join in or raid the fridge – there wasn't usually much to raid – or just watch TV. But she'd recently got a new man in her life, and her concentration had dipped to a low point.

Doro went wild when the other kids told her what had happened. They thought it was a great joke, the yobs running back into the terraces leaving a trail of blood spots on the cobbles, but Doro didn't see the funny side. She screamed at Moira, who said she was sorry she hadn't realised the door was still open, but the phone had been ringing and blah, blah, blah . . . and anyway there was no need to stress because Oolie-Anna had been protected by good karma.

Then Doro flew at Moira, yanking her hair – 'I'll give you bloody karma-rama!' – and Moira sobbed a bit.

Next thing, they were holding and hugging each other, and Doro thanked Moira for giving up her afternoon to look after Oolie. Then they both started yelling at Oolie for running away.

This was too much.

'She'd be *dead* if it wasn't for *me*!' Clara stamped her feet, her eyes wet with tears. 'You're both *retards*!' (She knew not to say 'fucking' at home.)

'Don't use that word, Clara,' said Doro.

Seething with rage and self-pity, she stomped off up to her room and flung herself on the bed. A minute later, Oolie-Anna joined her. She was sniffling too. Clara hugged her and told her about the slumbering starlings.

After that, Oolie-Anna started tagging along behind her, saying, 'Tell me about them slummin' starlings. You my best sister, Clarie. I won't leave you ever.'

And somehow Oolie-Anna became her responsibility. She was never sure whether she'd chosen it, or whether it had been subtly dumped on her by the Groans.

Once, while she was trying to do her homework up in the attic with Oolie pestering her for a story, Doro poked her head round the door and said, 'We're just doing yoga, love. Can you keep an eye on your little sister for an hour?'

Clara turned on Doro furiously. 'Why does it always have to be me? Why don't you ever ask Serge, or one of the boys? Anyway, she's not my sister, is she? She's not my *real* sister!'

Doro went bright red. 'What nonsense! Of course she's your sister.'

She slammed the door and thumped off down the stairs. Oolie's lips puckered up, her tongue slipped out of the corner of her mouth and her little pixie eyes filled with tears.

'I'm sorry, Oolie, I didn't mean it.'

''S all right, Clarie, I still love you. You won't ever leave me, will you, Clarie?'

'Course not.'

She put her arms around her, and they stood like that, with Oolie's face pressed against her belly, locked together in a sticky compound of love and guilt, listening to the sounds of the Yoga Nidra tape and 'Addio Lugano Bella' and the Wailers and the theme tune of *Doctor Who*, mingling and drifting up into the attic along with the odour of patchouli, stale cabbage and spicy bean stew. After a while Oolie's shoulders stopped shaking, and Clara resigned herself to skipping her homework yet again.

Somehow, despite all the homework interruptions, her exam grades were good enough, and in the sixth form she started sending off applications to university. When Oolie got wind that she was going away, she set up a storm of weeping, and Doro had to intervene.

'It's all right. She still loves you, Oolie. But she's got her own life to live.'

Sheffield University was far enough away for her to be independent, yet near enough to come home at weekends. After graduating and doing her PGCE, she looked for jobs in the area but, despite Oolie's tearful pleading, she didn't move back to live in Doncaster. Her bright new flat with its shiny bathroom and tall plant-filled windows overlooking a square of cafés and fountains is her compromise between the pull of responsibility and the call of autonomy.

She clicks on the hairdryer, letting the warm current of air on her damp skin blow away the stress and anger of the day. The bathroom is steamy, and smells of coconut and cleanness. The bliss of living on her own, with central heating, unlimited hot water and nobody else's washing up in the sink, still sends a shiver of luxury through her.

Those little yobs who set upon Oolie were like the lost kids she teaches at school; the difference now is that she can see their vulnerability, their fear of the unfamiliar. Yes, she and Serge were the first kids from their school ever to go to university, they were lucky they had dedicated teachers who went out of their way to help them, and she wants to be like that. Though nowadays, dedication is seen as a bit sad, and money is the big incentive. Nowadays, the people running the show are the ones who have only ever helped themselves. No wonder the lost kids snatch out for whatever they can get. She wraps the towel around her and pads through to the kitchen to put the kettle on.

There was only about thirty quid in the purse anyway.

SERGE: *Dick Fuld*

On Monday morning, 15th September 2008, as soon as Serge gets into work, with the borrowed USB stick snug in his inner jacket pocket, he walks the few paces down the corridor to the men's washroom, and slips it under the basins. Then he goes to the trading floor.

Nobody notices him.

By lunchtime, news about the collapse of Lehman Brothers has already started to hit the screens, and in the ensuing turmoil no one gives him a glance when he goes out of the building into St Paul's Square to phone Otto.

'It's Serge. I think I'm in a bit of trouble, kid.'

'Yeah? Share.'

Otto sounds jumpy, like he's on speed or something.

'I had a flutter, and I lost.'

'Mhmm. Your money or theirs?'

'Mine. But I can't cover my debt.'

'What happened?'

There's a nervy edge to Otto's voice. He's used to being the one who needs advice, not the one who gives it.

'I took a spread bet on some equities. I thought I was on to something. The Fibonacci retracement. Remember those rabbits? I thought the shares were slipping. But then they changed direction. I lost forty k.' Serge chuckles drily, as though it's all a big joke.

Even if Otto were to pay him back every penny tomorrow, it would only make a small dent in the pile he owes.

'Forty k. Holy shit.' Otto sounds rattled. 'If you need the money back, man, I mean, I'm sure we could . . .' He trails off.

'It's not about the money I lent you. I made a mistake, that's all.'

'I thought you understood all that stuff. I thought you were the numbers dude.'

'Nobody really understands it. We use these formulae for managing risk, like the Fibonacci phi or the Gaussian copula. But you know how it is with any formula – you put bollocks in, you get bollocks out.' He keeps his voice calm and easy to show he's still in control.

'Man, is that what you do for a living?'

Serge can hear Molly's voice in the background, and faint strains of a Bach fugue. It all sounds so cosy and domestic. For the first time since he's known Otto, he feels a prick of envy.

'We work in securitisation. We turn mortgages and loans into securities. We bundle them together and sell them as investments.' Serge feels in no mood for chatting, but he wants to keep Otto engaged. 'Traditionally, when people take out a mortgage to buy a house, they repay with interest to the bank. But with securitisation, you borrow the money to buy your house, then the bank sells the debt to another bank, or to an investor, like a pension fund.'

There's a moment's silence.

'Isn't that a bit risky?' Otto croaks. 'I mean, if I lend someone ten quid, I make sure they pay me back. But if I can sell the debt on to some sucker, and I still get my money back . . . I'd lend ten quid to any old dossers, wouldn't I?'

'Yeah. But you need something that *looks* safe, if you're going to sell it on. Something with a triple A, like mortgage securities – safe as houses. Mind, you'd be surprised what the rating agencies will give a triple A to, these days. Of course if they don't, the banks can always take their business elsewhere.'

'So you get cosy with the rating agencies?'

'That's where the maths comes in. We massage the risk.'

Just articulating the words brings home to Serge the sheer madness of it. It's like watching an aeroplane in flight – what the hell keeps it up there? It takes a special kind of person to believe that such a great lump of metal will stay in the air. And yet it does – in the right hands it will take off and fly around the world. No wonder so many of these new City whizzes are physicists and engineers.

'And even if you take a big gamble and you lose, the Government has to bail you out. See, if the system ever stopped working, it'd be the end of capitalism.'

'Isn't that what the Groans went on about in the commune?'

'Exactly.' Serge chuckles, trying to sound chilled. 'Totally mad.'

'Man, I was amazed they gave us a mortgage. Me a student and Molly a dancer. And pregnant. But if we can't pay, they take the flat off us, right?'

'Right. Which they hope has meanwhile gone up in value, Cambridge being a hotspot. So you're probably in the medium-risk tranche.'

'They do say as safe as houses, don't they?'

'Yeah, so long as houses are safe. It's only when house prices started to fall . . .' He stops; better not to panic Otto just as he's committed to the housing market.

'But calculating the risks – that's your job, Soz, that's what you're good at, right?'

'Yeah, sure. Risk factor modelling. Teasing out the fat tails of the Gaussian curve.' He slips easily into older-brother mode. No need for Otto to know the exact nature of the risks he's been taking; it would only stress him even more. 'It usually comes right in the end. You know, the wisdom of the market? It's just the timeframe that's the problem. Like I need some cash right now?'

'I geddit, man. I'll talk to Molly about the loan . . .'

In the background the music has ended and he can hear Molly whispering, 'Who is it?' Her voice sounds croaky.

'No, I told you. It's not about that, kid. I just want to borrow some cash to tide me over – you know, unofficially? Strictly temporary? From another account at the firm? Then as soon as I've got myself out of this hole, I repay. Nobody finds out.'

It isn't until he hears himself saying it out loud that he recognises the plan that's already formed in the back of his mind.

There's a crackly silence, then Otto says, 'Just because you've had a run of losses, man, doesn't mean you'll win next time. Gambler's fallacy, remember?' His voice sounds spooked at this unexpected reversal of roles. 'Anyway, you'd need security clearance.'

One nice thing about Otto is that he's completely non-judgemental. It's a practical problem, not an ethical thing – his brain just doesn't register in that dimension.

'Passwords?'

'You've got the passwords?'

'Not exactly. But I've got birthdays. I found my boss's memory stick with a load of pictures, and there was a file of birthdays. If you could just help me . . .'

'Soz, you're mad.' Otto's voice is suddenly serious.

'Not mad. Just a bit desperate. It must be possible to hack in, right? Strictly temporary?'

Another silence. 'Mm. Did you say you've got the memory stick?'

'I did have. I'll check when I get back in.'

'Cos the easiest thing might be to plant a little rootkit on it. So when he puts it back in, you can access his files.'

Rootkit. 'Root', like vegetables, which are good for you. 'Kit', for making something constructive. The word sounds reassuringly wholesome.

Back at his desk, he watches the doors and chooses his moment when there's no one in the men's washroom to go and find the memory stick. He can still hear the faint buzz from the trading floor as he lets the door swing closed behind him. He looks under the basins where he left it, slightly out of view under the overhang of the unit. But it isn't there. He looks again. Maybe it got kicked under the small gap between the floor tiles and the splashboard that conceals the pipework. Getting down on his knees he puts his head to the floor, and sure enough now he can see it, a small shiny brown object resting a centimetre beyond his reach under the waste pipe. The gap is too small for his hand, but he has a comb in his pocket. Holding one end of the comb with his fingertips, he tries to swipe it underneath the splashboard. As he does so, he hears the door creak open, and a pair of polished brown Churches stride across the tiles towards the urinals.

'Having trouble, mate?' The voice has a nasal Aussie twang. It must be that new VP from the commodities team whose name Serge can't remember.

'Yeah, I've lost something.'

The Aussie finishes his slash, washes his hands, then gets down on the floor beside him, peering under the splashboard. Just at that moment the end of the comb connects with the USB stick, and he gives a hard flick. The USB stick is lighter than he expected. It spins towards them, towards the head of the Aussie pressed on the floor next to him. It flips over and comes to rest in his blond hair. The Aussie stands up, disentangles it and passes it to Serge. Only it's not a USB stick, it's a dead cockroach.

'Yours, is it?' he says. His eyes are very pale blue. His face looks a bit pale too.

Serge attempts a cryptic grin. 'My pet cockroach. He's called Dick Fuld.'

The Aussie throws back his head and laughs out loud, clinging to the rim of the basin to steady himself.

'Looks like he's real dead, mate.'

'Yeah. Bummer. Not enough . . . liquidity.'

While the rest of the trading floor is glued to the screens, watching the unfolding drama of the Lehman collapse, he sneaks to the disabled loo and phones Otto. There's no reply, so he sends a text.

Stick has gone.

Then he phones his bank and manages to arrange a loan secured against his apartment – an investment he could barely afford at the time, but which he hopes has rocketed in value. At least the interest rate will be lower than his credit card and spread betting account. The smarmy git at the end of the phone tells him with grovelling politeness that they can only lend him £200,000. There's something about his manner that reminds Serge of the dead cockroach in his pocket. When he tries to fish it out, he finds one of its wings has fallen off. He drops it in the toilet and flushes it away.

He's lost his confidence in spread betting, so he rings up his broker to place some regular trades, hedging carefully, going back to his familiar Yorkshire territory, which brought him luck before. After that, he passes the rest of Monday afternoon in a bewildered haze, pretending to be quantifying the Lehman meltdown whenever Tim the Finn hovers at his shoulder. Even the light brush of Maroushka's arm against his back as she passes on her way to the cafeteria doesn't arouse him.

It's not until the evening that Otto rings him back.

'What did you say you had in that file you copied, apart from photos, Soz?'

'Dates. Birthdays.'

'Perfect. Names?'

Serge breathes. Plan A, the rootkit, has fallen through, but Otto's obviously working on Plan B.

'Sure, I've got names. Even nicknames. I reckon it'll be the boss's wife or the daughter.'

'Cos he's a sentimental bastard?'

'Exactly.'

It's such an obvious lapse of security. Serge had always assumed other people were more careful than him, until he once saw Doro logging in with *his* birthday.

'There's a nice bit of software I've got that might crack it. Does he have a Hotmail address? It's an easy way to test out passwords. Or Gmail. Or BT.'

Serge can almost hear the tick-tick-tick of Otto's brain as he thinks aloud. He likes a technical challenge.

'So you're guessing he keeps the same passwords for all his transactions? Even his bank accounts?'

'Don't *you*?' says Otto.

'Yeah, but I can never remember passwords.'

'Nor me. I've got too much other useless crap in my brain. Heh heh.'

Otto's voice – confused, comic, cocky – does not inspire confidence. Underneath it all Serge can hear the same lost boy, shivering inside his crocheted blanket. Except that now he needs Otto to rescue him from the mess he's in.

'D'you remember what the Groans used to say, in the commune – private property is robbery?'

'Send me the file, Soz. I'll have a play around.'

CLARA: Horatio

Mr Philpott is as good as his word. Clara opens the door of her classroom to be greeted with the familiar whiff of foetid pee and a whirling rattling sound which takes her by surprise till she realises it's the sound of the hamster wheel spinning furiously. The new arrival in the hamster cage is a bit darker in colour than Hamlet, and much slimmer and livelier. He's already overturned his water bowl and flung his bedding all over the place (*Musclebound Hamster Champ Brings Terror to Local School*). But none of the kids notice that the hamster is different. They're too busy chattering about their week-end's exploits.

Jason Taylor and Robbie Lewis are sitting next to each other, passing something between them under the desk, nudging and grinning.

She mouths, 'Stop it!'

They shuffle shiftily, and she smiles inwardly as she gives them the Look. She hasn't forgotten her stolen purse. But in their child-ishness she sometimes catches a glimpse of the adults they will become – in and out of trouble, unemployed, hanging around the streets unless . . . That 'unless' is why she's still here.

At lunchtime she goes down to the boiler room to thank Mr Phil-pott.

'You like 'im, eh?' he beams. 'Better than t' last bugger.'

'Have you got a name for him?'

''Oratio. The philosopher.'

'Mm. That's good. What would hamster philosophy be like, d'you think?'

'If a 'amster could speak, we could not understand 'im.'

'Very profound. Shakespeare?'

'Wittgenstein.'

'Really?'

'I told you I should've been an intellectual.'

Come four o'clock, the quiet that fills the classroom is still framed by shrill voices outside in the playground, the slamming of car doors, the hum of engines gradually fading into distance. And this is when she notices that the silence is more intense than it should be. An unobtrusive noise that's been rattling away in the background all day is suddenly still. The hamster wheel has stopped. She's about to investigate when there's a knock on the door.

'Come in!'

She expects it'll be Jason or one of the other kids who's forgotten something, but the door opens and in comes Oolie-Anna.

'Oolie! What're you doing here? How did you get here?'

She runs up and gives Clara a hug. 'Edna dropped me off, din't she? I told her Mum and Dad was out, and you was looking after me.'

'You shouldn't have, Oolie. Mum'll be worried sick.' Clara puts on her Leviathan voice, which makes Oolie giggle.

'No, because you're gonner drop me off at five o'clock.'

'But why?'

'Cos I want to talk to you.'

Oolie starts wandering around the classroom, looking at the drawings on the walls and the display in the nature corner. She's wearing, for once, a short-sleeved blouse, and Clara notices with a shock the scars on her arms which are usually covered up.

'I wish you was my teacher, Clarie.'

'I'm glad I'm not. You'd be naughty all the time.'

This makes Oolie laugh, throwing up her little round chin and closing her eyes.

'No, I wouldn't.' She points. 'I like that picture.'

It's a drawing by the class swot, Dana Kuciak, of sunset over Doncaster Cathedral, copied from a photo.

'What d'you want to talk about, Oolie?'

'I want to go and live in my own flat.' She sits down opposite Clara with a sulky face, and starts fiddling with the coloured pencils. 'Mr Clemmins says it's all right. But Mum won't let me.'

144

'Who's Mr Clemmins?'

'He's the social worker in charge of me. Mum don't like him.'

Clara's eyes widen. This could be interesting.

'Why not?'

'She says he thinks he knows everything and he don't.'

'Hm. But why do you want to live on your own?'

'Cos Mum makes me work on the allotment and Dad farts all the time.'

'It's because they love you, Oolie.'

Oolie looks unconvinced. 'I don't want to work on the allotment. It's boring.'

'So what d'you want to do?'

'I want to watch filums but they won't let me.'

This is new. Can Oolie even follow a film?

'I'm sure they will.'

Unless Doro has dreamed up some new rule. Her behaviour has become so erratic recently. Surely it's not still the menopause. Or maybe incipient Alzheimer's.

'What d'you want to watch, Oolie?'

'Filums.'

'Like what?'

'*Girls at Play. Unin'abited*. This lad at work give 'em me.'

'Oh, you mean they're like DVDs?'

'Yeah. Filums.'

'Oolie, can't you talk about this with Mum yourself?'

'No. Cos soon as I start she goes on about you know what and she thinks it's going to happen again if I live on my own, but it in't, cos I'm older now, and not so daft.'

Clara has never heard her sister utter such a long sentence before. In fact, she can't recall ever having heard Oolie allude to the long-ago fire which almost killed her and blew the commune apart.

'What's going to happen again?' she prompts gently.

But Oolie shakes her head and clams up.

All of a sudden, a sound of rustling paper over by the book corner breaks the silence. A couple of books have slipped on to the floor, and an invisible hand is leafing through the pages. They stare.

A brown furry head peeps round the corner of a page, rips it off and stuffs it into its cheeks.

'Hey . . .' Clara whispers.

'Hey!' shrieks Oolie, and dashes off in pursuit.

But he's quick, this Horatio. Before Oolie can get there, he's already round the other side of the room. Clara tries to intercept him, but he slips between the cupboard and the wall, and re-emerges by the waste bin.

'Quick, Oolie! Over there!'

Oolie isn't so nimble. She stumbles over a chair, stubs her toe and squawks with pain. The hamster disappears. Clara tiptoes over to the spot where he disappeared and silently gets down on her hands and knees.

But Oolie doesn't do silent. 'There! There!' she yells. 'The little bugger!'

They're both down on their hands and knees now. The hamster is back in the book corner, staring at them through beady eyes. They crawl towards him. He watches, still busily chewing up *Horrid Henry* and tucking the shreds into his cheeks. When they're about a metre away, he vanishes again. This time Clara saw where he went. There's a space between the bottom of the bookcase and the floor. He scuttles along it, dives round a corner, then he's gone again. Oolie races after him, knocking chairs over in all directions. The hamster is heading towards the door, with both of them after him on hands and knees, when the door swings open and in walks Mr Philpott.

'What –?'

'Quick!' she shouts. 'Quick! He's run away!'

She races out into the corridor, just in time to glimpse a ginger blob slipping round the corner.

'This way! He's on the loose!'

The three of them break into a run, but the hamster is quicker.

At the end of the corridor, where it widens into the entrance hall, they stop and catch their breath. There's no sign of the hamster. Then the door of the school office opens and earthy-but-godlike Mr Gorst/Alan emerges.

'What's going on?'

''Amster on the run!' cries Mr Philpott.

'Call the coppers! Quick!' shrieks Oolie (she likes men in uniform).

Mr Gorst/Alan follows them out into the hall. They fan out in different directions.

'There 'e goes! Little bugger!'

Oolie hares off through the double doors towards the playground, running and shouting at the top of her voice. She comes back, pink-cheeked and breathless.

''E done a runner.'

The hamster has completely disappeared.

'You're quite a runner too,' says Mr Gorst/Alan.

She laughs. 'Not as fast as 'im. 'E were reyt quick!'

'I had a hamster once.' A dreamy look has come over him.

Clara gazes deep into his twinkly eyes, and hears herself putting on a low mellifluous tone to murmur, 'Really? Tell me about it, Alan.'

But no words come out of her mouth.

Oolie is full of excitement on the way back to Hardwick Avenue.

''E were nice, 'im.'

'Who?'

''Im what said 'e 'ad t'amster. I wish I could 'ave a 'amster.'

It's past five o'clock when she drops Oolie off. But something is snagging in her mind as she drives back towards Sheffield. Before the encounter with Mr Gorst/Alan, before the chase for the runaway hamster, there was something else Oolie had let slip.

'I'm older now, and not so daft.'

Clara's always assumed that Oolie never talks about the fire because she's forgotten. But obviously something's still there, buried in the storeroom of her mind, and if she's ready to talk, maybe it's time to exhume those old ghosts and lay them finally to rest.

DORO: *The cries of Catty Lizzie*

After Clara has left on Monday evening, Doro resists the temptation to reprimand Oolie for not coming straight home, and busies herself in the kitchen. Fish pie of cod, prawns and smoked haddock, topped with dauphinoise potatoes, is what she has in mind as she watches the brown coils of potato peel tumble into the sink under the blade of her peeler.

Marcus and Oolie are curled up together on the sofa in front of the television. She regards them fondly through the open door, observing how alike they are, despite Oolie's distinctive Down's physiognomy. There's a funny way they both have of wrinkling their noses when they laugh. She's never noticed that before. They say people can grow alike through spending time in each other's company, the way some people come to resemble their pets. Though Doro sometimes thinks she catches a trace of Bruno in Oolie's features, and wonders whether maybe that's why she finds it so easy to love her.

Where does biology end and nurture begin? In the commune days, they'd tried to escape the whole oppressive nuclear family set-up, drawing inspiration from the communal childcare on Israeli kibbutzim. After all, weren't shared beliefs and commitments a much more logical basis for love and parenting than a mere accident of biology? It's strange, but kind of nice, that after all these years Marcus wants to get married. They must get around to talking to Oolie about it. She's never questioned – why should she? – that she's just as much their child as Clara or Serge.

Does Marcus ever question where Serge's looks come from? She wonders. Neither she nor Marcus are small and dark, and his maths ability is not inherited from them, that's for sure. He was always a strange, moochy little kid, sneaking off up to the attic to play with his pine cones and snail shells. Clara and Marcus, on the other hand, are similar in looks and personality – serious, earnest, impractical.

Which is why she's in here peeling the potatoes and he's in there watching the Channel 4 news. To be fair, Marcus did ask whether there was anything he could do, but his way of peeling potatoes is to cut thick slabs off each side. You'd have thought someone who can manage the history of the Fifth International could master a potato peeler, but apparently not.

'Come and sit, Mum!' Oolie pats the space on the sofa beside her. 'Dad says it's about the cries of Catty Lizzie.' She tries to tickle Marcus. 'Catty Lizzie!'

'Ssh! I'm listening. Scarper!' He wriggles free and turns up the volume.

'I wanna watch telly with you!'

'Collapse of a major American bank,' he calls to Doro through the open door. 'Crisis in the world's financial markets. Just as we predicted. What a sight – look!'

She puts her head through the door and sees on the screen a procession of men in suits, carrying boxes.

'What's going on?'

'Staff at Lehman Brothers leaving the building carrying their possessions in cardboard boxes.'

'Why?'

'No one will do business with them. Their assets are all tied up in toxic loans. Capitalism eats its own children.'

'She never!' says Oolie.

'I'm sure they won't be the last. According to Kondratieff's theory, another slump was long overdue.'

'Mm.' Doro slices the potatoes, arranges them over the fish and puts it all in the oven. Then she joins them on the sofa.

Marcus is sipping in excited gulps from a bottle of lager. 'What I fear is that a depression will once more bring the ugly spectre of fascism to our streets.'

'Really?'

Doro tries to picture what fascism in Doncaster would look like. Gangs of blackshirts goose-stepping around the Frenchgate shopping centre? The idea seems a bit ludicrous.

'When people feel insecure, they look around for someone to blame – Jews, immigrants, gypsies. That's what happened in 1929 after the crash – governments everywhere slashed public spending. There was chaos. The Great Depression. Then Roosevelt came along with the New Deal in 1933. Spent millions on infrastructure. Created jobs for the unemployed. Turned the whole thing around.'

'But how could he spend, if they'd run out of money?'

'He borrowed. You have to borrow to invest. Keynes argued we should do the same in Britain, but they were saved by the Second World War. Of course war is the biggest public spending spree of all.'

Marcus is the only person she knows who talks in fully formed sentences, but his cleverness is sometimes a tad irritating. It's strange how someone so bright can be so unaware of this. Dear Marcus. The spark that used to flash between them has long since given way to a cosy glow, warm but not exactly incendiary. She finds her mind drifting back to the fish pie, whose delicious smell is stealing in through the open door.

'We were supposed to be the generation at the end of history,' he's saying. 'We were supposed to be on the threshold of a new era of accumulation of unlimited wealth. Now we see the truth behind this seductive facade.'

'Dad, you've just farted!'

'No, I haven't!'

'Quick! Open the window!'

Oolie fans the air with her hands. The bottle rolls on to the floor, dribbling lager into the carpet. I'll have to remember to wipe it up before it begins to smell, thinks Doro, wondering if she'll end up like her mother, her clever, witty mother, who surrendered to domesticity after the birth of her children.

What did Clara call it – trapped in the Domestos fear?

After the others have gone to bed, she scrapes the burned remnants of the fish pie out of the dish and remembers that Bruno Salpetti had once used the same phrase that Marcus used tonight: 'the seductive facade'.

SERGE: J1nglebell

Serge, too, feels trapped, squeezed in the lift, chin to chin with half a dozen vacant-eyed traders on Tuesday morning. Why is he here? What is the meaning of life? Is there a God? What is happening to property prices in Brazil? Such questions have been preoccupying him more and more recently. To judge from the look in their eyes, the other guys haven't got the answers either. Putting all your heart and skill into running round inside a spinning hamster wheel is fine for a while, if you're making money, but demoralising and exhausting when you're pushing flat out and getting nowhere. The collapse of Lehman has made everything around them seem shaky and insubstantial. Will FATCA be next?

Talking to Otto yesterday made him feel better, but Otto's quite a fantasist, so desperate to please that he'll make promises he can't deliver on. It was stupid to pin so much hope on that 'borrowed' memory stick. And even assuming Otto can get access to the FATCA bank accounts, it won't necessarily solve Serge's problem, and it could make things much worse. The trades he made with the cash from his remortgage are going nowhere, drifting up a bit, down a bit. He frets as he sits at his desk trying to squeeze numbers into a new formula which will take into account the hits that are already piling up in the sub-prime property market. Maroushka is at her desk, head down, doing the same thing.

At last, in the late afternoon, the message comes through from Otto. He feels it vibrate silently in his pocket. A one-word text.

J1nglebell

Duh! Alphanumerical. It's so obvious! Really, he could have worked it out for himself. He heads off towards the washrooms. As he turns into the corridor, the door of the disabled loo swings open, and Tim the Finn emerges in front of him. He has a strange expression on his face, a grimace of pain maybe, though Serge wonders whether, in the fleeting moment before it turned into a grimace, it wasn't actually a grin.

When the coast is clear, he sneaks into the disabled loo and rings Otto back.

'Did you get a user name?'

'There's two: k.porter1601 or Kenporter1601. 1601 is the girl's birthday.'

Just as he'd guessed. Ripples of relief radiate through his body. He takes a long breath, pulling the damp smelly air into his lungs.

'Hotmail?'

'Gmail. And I found a bank account. It's a private account, though, not FATCA, and obviously not his main account. He only seems to use it for trading. As far as I can see, it's not registered at FATCA at all.'

'Tut tut. You had a peep?'

'Yeah.'

'How much?'

'Just over seven hundred k. That should ease your problem, Soz. Strange thing is, there's been quite a lot of movement in the last few weeks.'

'Oh yeah?'

That's interesting – if it's an unregistered account the FATCA Compliance Officer doesn't know about, Chicken probably won't be in a hurry to draw attention to it. Maybe he'll hesitate to make a fuss over a few irregular transactions. So long as they're not *too* irregular. The mistake is always to be too greedy.

'By the way, there's a new remote desktop app that lets you trade online with an iPhone. I'll send you the link.'

'Perfect. Thanks, Otto. Hey, our little secret, right?'

'Right.'

The black panther of dread crouched above his heart yawns, stretches and, with a limber leap, vanishes through the tiled wall.

He throws open the door and makes his way lightly back to the trading floor.

Tim the Finn is there, jabbing away at his keyboard. He hasn't noticed Serge's absence. Maroushka is in the glass-walled office now, eating a muffin and flicking through some printout graphs. At the end of the row, the two Frenchies are discussing Sarko and Carla, and the troubles at AIG, in between furious bouts of number crunching. Across the trading floor, he can hear the voice of the Aussie VP joking about the need for a Government banks bailout plan. On the huge TV suspended from the ceiling Maria Bartiromo, the Bloomberg Money Honey, presides over her domain like a silent queen, mouthing her animated but soundless pronouncements on the day's exchanges. The facade of normality is intact. Everything is as it should be.

DORO: *The seductive facade*

'Beware the seductive facade of bourgeois feminism,' Bruno had warned, drawling out his vowels so-o-o seductively. 'Behind its revolting exterior is conceal the desolate hinterlands of neurosis and self-indulgency.'

But after Bruno returned to Modena in 1985, the women who had loved him – Megan Cromer (furtively), Moira Lafferty (noisily) and Dorothy Marchmont (guiltily), to name but three (though doubtless there were others) – instead of falling into a quagmire of jealousy and recrimination, decided that they should keep alive the flame of his memory and maintain the links they'd developed during the strike with the local miners' wives.

One day in March 1986, when Oolie was just a few months old, they ran off 200 copies of a leaflet entitled *Which Way for Women?* on the inky old Gestetner in the outside toilet (it had been moved there from the Marxism Study Centre, when it became the playroom) and distributed them through the letter boxes of the houses in the Prospects and nearby streets in Campsall, Norton and Askern, inviting women to a meeting in the front room of Solidarity Hall at 2 p.m. on the following Sunday, to discuss women's oppression.

In anticipation of the hordes who might attend, Chris Watt hoovered the threadbare carpet in the sitting room, Doro brought in the chairs from the kitchen and arranged a vase of dried flowers in the fireplace, to hide the heap of old newspapers, pamphlets and other stuff that accumulated there, and Moira Lafferty brought down three mirror-work patchouli-scented floor cushions from her bedroom, and lit a joss stick to cover the smell of damp and mice. Megan had gone away for the weekend, to stay with her mother and Crunchy Carl in Harworth, and although none of them actually said so, Doro was sure she wasn't the only one to feel relieved.

★

The front door had been left open, but all three of them jumped to their feet when the bell rang; someone tall and slim, with sun-brown skin, pool-green eyes and tight golden curls, hesitated for a moment in the doorway, then stepped forward into the room. The trouble was, it was a man.

'Er, this is a women's meeting,' Doro ventured hesitantly, because he really was very gorgeous, and also because there was something familiar about him – where had she seen him before?

'I got your leaflet. Which way for women? That's a question I often ask myself.' His voice was familiar too.

'We haven't worked out the answer yet, that's what we're here to discuss,' Moira breathed, flushing bright pink and moistening her lips with her tongue.

Their eyes locked.

'So I can join in?'

'Definitely not!' said Chris Watt.

'But . . . maybe it's okay,' said Moira with a helpless-little-girly lilt to her voice. 'I mean, men and women are sort of united, aren't we? I mean . . . in class struggle?'

The green eyes studied her with interest, resting on the auburn hair and flushed cheeks.

She really can't help it, thought Doro. She just can't talk to a man without flirting. The thought infuriated her. 'It's not okay. Not this particular meeting. But you can come to other meetings . . .' Doro looked into the dark-fringed pools of his eyes and crossed and uncrossed her legs, which were long, slim and bare. Moira Lafferty might have the boobs, but she had nice legs – and a good bum – in those days. '. . . such as anti-fascism, or Cuba solidarity.'

Still he stared at Moira, who exuded her usual smell of patchouli, cigarette smoke and bodily fluids, which presumably some men found irresistible.

'Or you could join the Marxism study group,' added Chris Watt. 'See, we're developing a new politics of the left, which is neither Communist nor Trotskyist, but based on the idea of workers' autonomy.'

An expression flashed across his face which to Doro did not look like unbounded enthusiasm.

Just then, the doorbell rang again. 'Eyup! Anybody in?' a woman's voice shrilled.

The person who followed the voice was definitely a woman, though it took Doro a few seconds to recognise June Cox, one of the Women Against Pit Closures who'd first visited them during the strike.

'Well?' June settled herself into the most comfortable armchair, and fished a packet of cigarettes out of her bag. 'What've you decided, girls?'

'This is a non-sm–' Chris Watt began, sniffing the smoke from June's cigarette that coiled up towards the blue-painted ceiling, but Doro kicked her shin. If proletarians wanted to smoke, who were they to stop them?

'They're still trying to decide if I can stay,' said the curly-haired man. 'Typical women. Can't make their minds up.'

Chris shifted her glare. 'Thank you for that manifestation of unreconstructed male chauvinism.'

'Show us what you've got inside yer trousers. Then we'll make us minds up.' June puffed, enveloping him in a cloud of smoke.

The man flashed his eyes and began toying with his zip. Moira looked as though she had to restrain herself from leaping forward to help him. Doro flinched – she'd caught a glimpse of something unappealingly grey and sweaty-looking which she hoped was just underpants.

'All right, lad! That's enough! Zip it up!' barked June, and turning to Doro she asked in a low voice, 'Is 'e 'ere? 'Im wi't spaghetti?'

Doro shook her head. June looked glum.

'We called this meeting to discuss the role of women,' Chris Watt interrupted. 'To share our experiences of oppression. Have you anything you'd like to share, June?'

'Experiences?' June flicked a long finger of ash into the fireplace, dusting the already dusty dried-flower arrangement. 'My 'usband Micky were an experience. Little Micky! A reyt love-cake! 'E worked down Bevercotes. We always 'ad us sex on Wednesdays and Saturdays, regular as a turd. 'E used to wear my frillies next to 'is skin under 'is vest and pants when 'e went down't pit. Liked the feel of my silk on 'is pecker while 'e were working underground, said it reminded 'im of me. And 'e were wearing them on't day 'e died!' She sighed, looking around the circle of eyes.

'Didn't you find that oppressive?' asked Chris Watt.

Doro gave her another kick.

'A rockfall pinned 'im on't ground.' She studied the hushed faces of her audience, then pulled a fresh cigarette out of the packet and lit it from the smouldering stub of the last one, which she tossed into the fireplace. 'When I seen 'im laid out on t'ospital trolley, my 'eart fumps like a fish and I flings myself on't trolley, an' 'e opens one eye and says, "Don't cry, Junie. They've got yer knicks. But thank Jesus I weren't wearing t' bra." Them were t' last words 'e ever said.'

There was a long silence, broken by a suppressed giggle – Doro couldn't tell whether it was from Moira or the man.

'Thank you, June, for sharing that with us,' Chris Watt said. 'Maybe we should open our discussion by challenging received stereotypes of male and female sexuality.'

You really have to admire someone who's so gifted with the kiss of death.

'She's a reyt gobshite,' whispered the man to Moira, loud enough for them all to hear. ''Er Micky's still alive and living up Castleford wi' Dot O'Sullivan.'

'Shut yer gob and get back on yer milk cart,' June growled.

Doro stared at him again. Yes, it was the lovelorn milkman.

'Why don't you just piss off?' Chris Watt snapped at the milk-man, sniffing the air.

Doro found herself sniffing the air too. An acrid cloud of smoke had drifted into the room – not cigarette smoke, but bluer and more pungent. It was billowing from the fireplace; a moment later, a burst of flame swallowed up the dried-flower arrangement.

'Help! Help!' shrieked Moira, looking around in all directions but mainly at the milkman, who was fiddling with his fly again.

Doro started batting at the flames with a cushion, like it says you're supposed to in the home safety guides. Smouldering sparks, fanned by the chimney draught, had already ignited the pile of newspapers.

'I'll fetch some water!' Chris Watt dashed out to the kitchen, but by the time she came back with a jug, the milkman had already unzipped himself and was spraying the fire with a golden stream of piss.

'Oh, wow! That's so amazing!' Moira murmured.

Doro grabbed the jug from Chris's hands and flung the contents over Moira.

After the others had gone, Doro and Chris Watt stayed to clear up the mess of cigarette butts and soggy newspaper, and ended up arguing about whether allowing June Cox to smoke was colluding with the exploiters (said Chris Watt) or respecting her freedom of choice (Doro's position).

SERGE: *The markets*

Is he colluding with Chicken's wrongdoing by using his unauthorised account, or simply exercising his freedom to make money in any way that's not strictly illegal? Serge wonders, as he brings up the Jinglebell log-in on his laptop. Otto was right – it looks like a personal account with the private client branch of a rival investment bank. There's £751,224.34 in there – with the mortgage he's raised, it'll give him a decent pool of capital to trade with. Once, this would have seemed like a massive amount of money; now, in the distorting mirror of City incomes, it seems paltry, just about enough to buy a two-bedroomed flat in his apartment block.

Most of the transactions in Chicken's account are with a couple of online brokerage firms, one in London and one in New York. Once Serge has got the hang of the patterns used in setting up the passwords, a trawl through variants quickly opens the sites and lets him in. Tomorrow, when trading starts again, he reckons he'll quickly repair the black hole in his finances. Although the Nikkei and Hang Seng are already open, the Eastern markets are notoriously volatile, and he doesn't trust himself in that unfamiliar environment. He can't afford any more losses; he'll say goodbye to spread betting, stick to companies whose form he knows, and wait for the London Stock Exchange to open.

From the windows of his penthouse (he still can't quite believe he really owns this sleek abode – or at least, he owns the quarter of it that the bank doesn't own) he looks out towards the City with its tall blocks of lights blazing in the night, quite eclipsing the humble little stars and the pale washed-out moon, money stamping its presence across the sky. He can't pick out the FATCA tower, but he knows it's there, his hamster wheel, waiting for him.

Next day, when he gets into work, he chooses his moment to lock himself in the disabled lavatory with his iPhone, and uses Otto's remote desktop app quickly and carefully to place his trades. He was right about the Fibonacci retracement – he should have held his nerve. The markets are plunging again, but erratically. He holds SYC, which has recently acquired an interest in a chain of sheltered housing and residential care homes in the North of England, and opens another short position on Edenthorpe Engineering. The company reports show Edenthorpe was floated on the Stock Exchange in 2004 to raise capital for a new plant at Barnsley. Although it's a well-run firm with a skilled workforce and a healthy balance sheet – not to mention Tiffany's tits – heavy engineering in his opinion is doomed. Who needs all that old rusty machinery and its crumbling Gothic infrastructure when there's so much profit to be made in the gleaming money-mills of the City? In the current economic climate, this is an ideal candidate for short selling. He can now trade with confidence because, if he wins, Dr Black is in the money, and every time he loses, Kenporter1601 picks up the bill.

The biggest gamble he takes of course is that he'll get away with it. He knows that any police investigation would quickly reveal the real identity of Dr Black, but it would also reveal that Ken Porter has an unauthorised personal account, has been trading in breach of FATCA rules, and who knows what other illegal practices. The very existence of the 1601 account is suspicious. It's like he and Chicken are locked together in a murderous embrace, each with a knife to the other's throat. So long as Serge replaces what he borrows, he reckons Chicken will not push for a bank enquiry. He'll find out that *someone* has accessed the account easily enough, but he won't readily find out *who* – not without revealing his own game. And if the money is replaced, his incentive to find out will be so much less. After all, Serge isn't actually stealing, but simply borrowing (strictly temporary) the proceeds of someone else's crime.

Besides, Chicken has other things to worry about this week. After a lethargic summer, markets all over the world are in panic. The Footsie has dropped below 5,000; the Russian Stock Exchange is suspended; gold is at an all-time high; and governments everywhere are getting into a mega-flap. Dour Darling urges calm. Grumpy

Gordon promises discipline. Lloyds takes over ailing HBOS and immediately £2 billion is wiped off its value. Rumours abound.

'They're going to blame short selling,' clucks Chicken on his morning walkabout, though most of the traders must have already worked this out for themselves. 'They'll say we're causing the crash by shorting equities, when any dickhead can see we're shorting because equities are crashing. A rational response to market conditions. Now they're talking about banning short selling.'

Serge can hear his voice from the next aisle, bubbling with suppressed rage.

'You know what's wrong with this country? Nanny-state noddies interfering with market freedom. Get your positions open, before they slam the door on us.'

Maybe because of all the stress, Tim the Finn is having a particularly troubled time with his prostate, and this is a problem, from Serge's point of view, because while he is slowly emptying his bladder in the disabled loo, Serge is unable to get in there to place his trades. Nevertheless, he chooses his moments, and trades quickly and accurately, observing and predicting the turns of the market. Luck is with him. By the end of the week, when the Financial Services Authority puts a temporary ban on short selling the shares of twenty-nine key companies, he's made up his losses, and is twenty k up. When he's not trading, he now opens up furtive online property searches in Brazil.

On Friday, he decides he needs a bit of escapism, so he looks around on the net for a film to see and chooses *Iron Man*. Its blend of subtle comic-book irony and retro sci-fi heroism matches his mood, and the redemptive message about peace and good triumphing over evil is almost spiritual.

CLARA: Iron Man

Clara regrets having wasted her Saturday night watching *Iron Man* at Meadowhall. The film was a childish male fantasy, and the guy she went with, a partner in Ida Blessingman's firm of lawyers, had a thin black moustache and cold rubbery hands that kept on finding their way into her bra.

'He's just broken up with his girlfriend,' Ida had said. 'It'll do him good to go on a blind date.' She probably thought she was doing Clara a favour too.

He spent the evening trying to operate her nipples like a PlayStation, until she dug him sharply in the diaphragm with her elbow and heard a satisfying wheeze.

'What's the matter?' he gasped.

'Good luck keeping up,' she said.

At the end of the film, he dropped her off in his Audi, they pecked each other on the cheeks, but she didn't invite him to come in. It's not as though *Iron Man* was even her choice. That's the trouble with men – they confuse fantasy and reality. No wonder Ida prefers cheesecake.

She pours water over a chamomile tea bag and watches it expand, releasing its depressing pond-watery smell, and finds herself thinking about Josh, guessing that he would probably have chosen *Iron Man* too, though the groping might have been less desperate. It wasn't exactly Oolie's fault that they'd split up, but the fact that she told him, last time they met, 'Clarie says you ent got no onions of your own,' can't have helped.

Before going to bed, she checks on her Facebook friends, mostly people from her student days who stayed on in Sheffield because, like her, they enjoy the Peak District – walking, cycling, rock climbing and other energetic pursuits. Recently they've started to pair up and post pictures of their bald indistinguishable babies. She posts enthusiastic greetings to each new member of the species, wondering how she's ever going to be able to get to that stage herself. As Doro keeps reminding her none too subtly, her biological clock is ticking away.

'So how d'it go?'

Ida invites herself in for a coffee on Sunday morning. She's still in her dressing gown, a turquoise silk kimono with gold embroidered dragons that curve around her boobs. She must be at least a size eighteen, but the way she looks and moves makes Clara feel gauche and bony.

'We didn't hit it off.' Clara stirs the cafetière. 'I think it was his weird moustache. Like a serial killer.'

'But rather special, no? And absolutely loaded, by the way.'

'Ha! If I'd known, I wouldn't have poked him in the ribs,' she says, lying, because Ida seems annoyed.

'Why did you do that?'

'Wandering hands.'

'You'd rather be groped by that boring headmaster? Hey, you're blushing!'

Clara laughs.

What would it be like, going to see a film with Mr Gorst/Alan? She wonders, slipping some croissants under the grill. It wouldn't be *Iron Man*, that's for sure. It would be something deep and inspirational. Would they hold hands? Would they grope? Or would love creep up on them, twinkling like dawn in the east?

The way he had talked to Oolie the other day was so kind and easy.

On the way home Oolie had said, ''E were reyt nice. I bet you want to shag 'im, don't you, Clarie?'

Oolie is sometimes startlingly perceptive.

SERGE: Girls

Despite the ban on short selling, Royal Bank of Scotland shares have lost a fifth of their value. The Bradford and Bingley is in deep shit, and looks like it will soon follow in the footsteps of Northern Rock. LIBOR has gone through the roof. Although everyone around him is manic with panic, Serge feels immersed in calm, like a deep-sea diver who has descended below the turmoil of surface currents. With UK new mortgage approvals at a new low, the work pressure is temporarily off him, and he finds he has time on his hands. He starts arriving later in the mornings and leaving earlier in the evenings. No one appears to notice.

Day and night meld into one blue rectangle of online hours. When he's not riffling Chicken's bank account, he sometimes browses his emails (remembering to 'mark as unread' each letter after he closes it), enjoying the sense of intimacy from peeping through Windows into his boss's soul. Like an apprentice Chicken studying the calling that will one day be his, he's begun to acquire an arm's-length expertise regarding expensive whisky, cut-price art and hand-crafted humidors from Chicken's online shopping forays. (Unfortunately, clothes hardly feature – Chicken goes bespoke.) What would Doro and Marcus make of all this gear? Actually, he knows exactly what they'd make of it.

Marcus would say, 'That useless humidor costs more than your average worker in Doncaster earns in a month.'

Doro would add, 'And they had one just like it in Oxfam last week for £2.99.'

Sometimes he wonders whether they're really his parents at all, or whether some trick of fate whisked him away at birth from his real (much wealthier) family, and deposited him in Solidarity Hall.

He smiles. Dear Marcus and Doro, despite their grey hair, have never quite entered the grown-up world, have they? They're still in that innocent pre-consumer age, like when he kept that box of Fibonacci snail shells and pine cones under his bed – his childhood treasures, which opened up his eyes to the timeless beauty of mathematics. A lump rises in his throat.

Those hyped-up FATCA traders don't give a frog's fart about anything apart from their Profit and Loss statements and where to get a snort. You can hear them, in between bouts of trading, going on about what they'll spend their bonus on, sprinkling brand names like holy water. What's he doing here, caged up with them in this hamster wheel? He's different. He won't let himself get seduced into that life of aimless consumption, fetishisation of high-value objects, partying to oblivion, life ruled by P&L, body rhythms ruled by uppers and downers. He wants money not to acquire stuff, but to buy freedom – the escape to the modest beach house in Brazil. Philosophy. Maths. Poetry. Dusk-to-dawn sex. Maroushka. Okay, so he might also have a nice suit or two.

Apart from the online shopping sprees, Chicken's inbox hosts a steamy correspondence with various women, which Serge felt bad about peeping into at first, but the intriguing subject lines soon overcame his scruples. Back in May there was Gabriella, a tall, regal babe on Fixed Incomes with heels that made her tower above most of the male staff at FATCA, who gave 'my kuddly Kenny' a fake leopard-skin posing pouch on his birthday. 'I want to taste your kum' was the subject line of her last email. (Babs never said anything like that!)

Before Gabriella there was someone called Chrissie in Treasury, whose subject line was 'Spanky and spunky'. Serge can't picture her at all, which isn't surprising, because contact between front-office staff (traders, arbitrageurs, fund managers and the like) and back-office staff (the more lowly paid boys and girls who collate the trading data, manage accounts and service the money-making elite) is frowned upon. Collusion between front and back office is one of the main avenues of fraud in the City. So Chicken is a rule-breaking risk-taker, cheating on FATCA as well as on his wife. Still, top corporate guys like him are under a lot of pressure and, if this is how Chicken chooses to relax, Serge isn't going to get judgemental.

Chrissie subjected Ken to a bit of mild chastisement, but nothing compared to Juliette – no apparent connection to FATCA – who beats Chicken up fortnightly on Friday afternoons in an apartment in Clerkenwell.

'You naughty boy, you,' she writes. 'I will see you 6 p.m. Friday and do not forget to bring those special boots size 8 [size eight – rather large for a woman, isn't it?] and if I find you of been up to any naughty tricks with other ladys I will Velcro you up and make you beg for it and whack you with my whip and you know what I will do next.'

He tries to picture Chicken, tied up and begging for it at Juliette's size-eight feet, flinching under the crack of a Ben-Hur-style whip. The image has a certain appeal.

Reading about Chicken's sexual exploits inflames Serge with a mixture of disapproval and envy that he finds oddly arousing. Or maybe not so odd, since he hasn't slept with anyone since . . . crumbs, it's more than a year since he split up with Babs, his girl-friend at Queens'. Though there's a lot to be said for wanking: it's cheap, it's safe, and the courtship is more straightforward. Still, the memory of Babs pricks at his conscience. He must ask Otto how she's getting on.

Babs was a postgrad botany student, a plump jolly girl with freckles, thick dark hair that swung across her face, and thick pale legs that swung beneath unflatteringly short skirts. She wasn't exactly his type, but the girls he coveted were out of his league. The thing is, achieving the grades he needed to get to Cambridge from his comprehensive school in Doncaster was as nothing compared to the hurdle of mastering the social rules once he got there. Not the arcane dining rituals – the commune's yellow table, with its bean-flicking, spoon-banging etiquette, had left him well prepared for the college dining hall (though the abundance of cutlery was puzzling at first). Not the exclusive college societies – he avoided them and hung out with the other fractals freaks. Not the tutors – they were generally kind and encouraging. No, it was the girls, the terrifyingly glossy self-possessed posh-school princesses. How the fuck did one get into their knickers?

They laughed at his jokes, they drank his coffee, they ate his food, they even allowed him to comfort their exam fears and boyfriend sorrows with a platonic arm around their gazelle shoulders. But that's as far as he ever got. There were guys in his college, blond six-foot rower types from minor public schools, who when they crossed the quad, it was like a phalanx of girls would race towards them, throwing their knickers over their shoulders as they ran. But that never happened to him. In his second year, an American scholarship boy called Oliver had the room above him, and the staircase was clogged with weeping girls – if Serge just opened his door, he could reach out his arm and haul one in, but all they would do was eat his toast and talk about Oliver.

So he was grateful to Babs, a teachers' daughter from Manchester whom he met during his final year, who approached the sex thing with down-to-earth cheeriness. They met in the bar after lectures, sometimes went to see a film on Saturdays, or ate pizza and listened to Martha Wainwright together. After three months of this, Babs suddenly stripped off her clothes one night and climbed into his bed. Her body was creamy and plump, with pendulous soft breasts, and her uninhibited vocalisation overrode his own nervousness. He was never quite sure he'd correctly located her clitoris, as advised by *Men's Health*, but after making love she clung to him squeaking and whimpering in a way he found quite endearing. He held her close and murmured sweet love words, which he hoped she wouldn't take too literally.

Babs was undemanding at first, and left his head free for maths. He was even unfaithful to her a few times on the side. But when she let slip, some three years into the relationship, that she longed for a baby, he panicked. He was only twenty-six at the time. Babies are cute – he has nothing against them – but the combination of Babs and baby filled him with the kind of hopelessness a prisoner must feel when he hears the cell door slam.

Desperate for an escape route, he wandered into a graduate

recruitment fair where a guy he'd known at college three years ago, whom everyone had regarded as an utter no-mark, was swanning around in a Dries Van Noten suit, spouting about careers in finance. Serge took down his details and sent in a couple of applications for City jobs without telling Babs, just to see what was out there. He hadn't expected to get a job offer so soon. The salary he was offered at FATCA was mind-boggling, especially after all those years on a PhD bursary. He hesitated, but not for long.

He felt terrible of course. But not as bad as he reckons he would have felt if they'd stayed together. It wasn't just the baby thing that had panicked him; it was the thought of a lifetime buried in Babs's pudgy soft embrace. He wasn't ready for it yet. He wasn't ready to abandon his dream of a faraway freewheeling life, shared with the girl of his dreams, who was not needy and noisy, as Babs had recently become, but distant and disdainful like the posh-school princesses. Dream girl, with whom he had already developed an intense one-handed sexual relationship, was slender and beautiful and, though the specifics of her appearance were vague, he knew he'd recognise her instantly when she would glide past him one day, self-absorbed, barely noticing him except to register a glimmer of amusement.

Someone like Maroushka, in fact.

Logging out of Chicken's emails and into the Kenporter1601 bank account, he's alarmed to find there's been a flurry of trading activity, tens of thousands flying in and out of the account all day. What's been going on? Browsing through the transactions history, he finds that Chicken has recently been trading in many of the same Yorkshire-based shares as he has. How come? Does Chicken have a special interest in the area? Is it a coincidence? Or part of a pattern? Edenthorpe Engineering, Wymad and Endon are all there. South Yorkshire Consolidated, parent company of Syrec, the Askern-based recycling firm; there's been some recent buying here. He knows they've just been awarded a substantial regional development grant, which could account for the jump in value of their shares. But how did Chicken get wind of this?

While SYC seems to be shooting up, Edenthorpe Engineering is on its way down. And Dr Black's account is swelling.

On Tuesday, he puts another £250,000 into SYC, going long, and joins Maroushka for a cafeteria lunch, instead of taking a sandwich to his desk as usual.

She's in a chatty mood.

'You been following creases in UK housing, Sergei?' she asks, munching her way through a steak sandwich with coleslaw and chips. The amount she can eat is astonishing – she always seems hungry. 'Things look very dodging in market. Same scenario like US sub-prime. High level of defaulting is becoming regular. Assumed continued rising of property value which underpin lending show sign of weakling. What you thinking, Sergei?'

Serge finds it difficult to focus on hedging and housing while she's sitting opposite him wearing a frost-white jacket over a blue polka-dot dress, absently running a bare foot up and down her leg as she dips a chip in her mayonnaise.

Princess Maroushka!
Hear the song of Serge!
Our passion will emerge,
In a faraway auberge . . .

When you're lumbered with a name like Serge, you have to be creative. There are so many things he wants to say, but before he can get any words out she starts skimming the room with her eyes, looking for someone more amusing to gaze upon. She fixes on a point behind Serge's left shoulder and, turning his head, he sees that Chicken has just entered.

He's with a couple of tall guys whom Serge hasn't seen before. They stroll between the tables, surveying their domain like Masters of the Universe, Chicken making introductions as they pass.

'Craig Hampton and Max Vearling from New York Head Office.'

They are sleek, smooth, and fragrant with musky aftershave, their smiles bleached like tooth-whitening ads. Maroushka looks up, flirting with her eyes. The visitors linger a moment then move on to the next table, smiling blandly, offering corporate handshakes. Craig Hampton and Max Vearling – who the fuck are they?

Next day, Wednesday, Maroushka comes in late wearing a new pair of spectacularly high calfskin ankle-strap platforms, tosses him a cursory hello, and gets straight on to her screens. He keeps an eye on her, thinking to follow if she should sneak out of the building, but she remains in her seat, head down, tapping away at the keys. When Timo Jääskeläinen goes off to the loo, she whips out her phone and goes to the glass-walled office for a quick yack, but apart from that she doesn't move from her place until lunchtime, when she takes a quick coffee break.

At about three in the afternoon, she strolls up to Serge's desk and leans over him to whisper in his ear, letting her hair brush against his cheek and her complex scent fill his nostrils, so he can't tell which is her perfume and which is the smell of her body.

'Sergei, we must re-examine Gaussian copula. Build in random systematic factor loadings. Big money opportunity.'

Then she slides away into the office to make another phone call while Timo is off the scene.

Serge too is puzzled by the way the markets are behaving, but Maroushka's behaviour bothers him more. She's taking a risk, using her mobile so openly. Timo could return any minute, and anyway one of almost a hundred traders could make a complaint. Surely she's not still phoning her mother in Zh – . . . wherever? He feels like warning her, but she already knows she's breaking the rules, so he opens up a new algorithm and concentrates on how to make gains in the new market conditions. If it works out, he reckons his bonus should be up on last year, despite the gyrations of the market. Dr Black's toilet trades are showing a handsome profit too.

But that evening, when he gets home and logs on, he discovers that Kenporter1601 is completely empty. Drained of every last penny. That can only mean one thing: Chicken has realised that someone has been tampering with the account. It was bound to happen sooner or later of course; in fact, he's surprised it took Chicken so long to cotton on. His stomach lurches as he wonders what'll happen next. This is the moment when Chicken will decide whether to call in the law, or to stay on the outside of it.

He plays over one scary scenario after another, and it's three in the morning before he finally drifts off to sleep, to dream of rabbits squeezed tight in dark burrows.

PART THREE

Paradise

DORO: *Trouble on the allotment*

Although Doro misses the wild rabbity garden of Solidarity Hall, she's transferred her passion to her allotment, a pocket-sized Eden where her crop of beans, peas, potatoes, tomatoes, beetroot, berries, apples and plums is ripening nicely. But all is not well.

'Summat's gooin' off,' says Reggie Hicks, the next-door plot holder and unofficial chairman of GAGA (Greenhills Allotments Gardeners Association), who has got wind of a dastardly plan on the part of the Council to flog off the land to a developer.

A meeting has been convened on the grassy space under the plum tree at the side of the communal water tap. Relaxing over a strong brew of tea on an assortment of canvas deckchairs, old kitchen stools and a stolen church pew, Doro joins the GAGA members to bask in the late Friday afternoon sun and consider their options. Reggie Hicks, eighty-four years old, an ex-miner from Rossington and winner of the biggest leek competition six years on the trot, is for an immediate all-out strike; Ada Fellowes, seventy-six, church warden, points out that this would just be playing into *their* hands. Danny Fellowes, also seventy-six, argues for negotiation and a softly, softly approach. Jim Smith, even older than Reggie and also a former leek laureate, launches into a long speech which nobody can understand, though Brussels sprouts are somehow involved. Helen Smith agrees and adds that *they* should be strung up by their gizzards. Winston Robinson, sixty-six, from Trinidad, all-time pumpkin champion, suggests a petition.

Ernest Philpott, sixty-four years old and caretaker at Greenhills Primary School, says, 'Fie on 'em, 'tis an unweeded garden gone to seed,' and calls for an immediate occupation.

Doro, at sixty, is the baby of the group. She says, 'Couldn't we change our name to something which has a less unfortunate acronym?'

'What's an acro-gnome?' says Danny Fellowes.

'What's wrong wi' being gaga?' says Jim Smith.

Meanwhile, nearby, the real baby of the allotments, Oolie-Anna Free, aged twenty-three, is pottering around the raised vegetable beds, watched over benignly by several pairs of eyes. She digs her hands into the compost heap, scoops out the rotting vegetable matter and crumbles it through her fingers on to the tomato seedlings. She's wearing a short-sleeved T-shirt, so the scars on her arms are visible. Watching, Doro's heart squeezes with a love so intense it almost feels like pain.

Doro often sees her life divided neatly into two parts: pre-Oolie and post-Oolie. The pre-Oolie Doro was slim, pretty, sexy, experimental, committed. The post-Oolie Doro is plumper, older, often too tired for sex, predictable, over-committed. Most of the time, she doesn't remember what it felt like to be the pre-Oolie Doro. We all build our lives around the immutables – the things we can't change – and she's built her life around Oolie. The allotment has been a big part of their life together, a shared enthusiasm, a place of safety, a calm haven in Oolie's stormy adolescence. To have all this threatened by remote stony-faced bureaucrats in league with money-grubbing developers is intolerable.

The first thing to remember in any offensive is that you need allies.

She leans across and whispers to Mr Philpott, 'I'm sorry I shouted at you the other day.'

Through the leaves of the plum tree, the September sun stipples a quivering pattern of light and shade on the grass, and on the gardeners sipping tea and passing around a slightly damp packet of digestives. High up in the blue, swallows are swooping and weaving for their gnatty suppers. Bees hum among the fruit bushes and, beyond that, the faint buzz of traffic from the A630 seems a part of the natural landscape too, though according to Reggie, it's the allotments' easy accessibility from major roads which has made them a target for developers.

'Some bugger wi' sticky 'ands is gonner make a ruddy mint out of this.'

'Pavin' over paradise,' says Winston Robinson.

'And building a multi-storey car park,' adds Doro.

As they sip their way through a third pot of tea, a plan of action emerges. Reggie, Danny and Jim will mobilise the other GAGAs. Ada Fellowes will contact the vicar: 'It's time 'e got a bit o' blood on 'is 'ands.' Doro, who's already met the local councillor, will invite him on a tour of the allotments and try to winkle out the full facts about the development. Helen will bribe him with jars of her world-famous-in-Doncaster blackcurrant jam. Winston Robinson will draft a petition. Mr Philpott will draw up a list of demands.

Not since the days of Solidarity Hall has Doro felt the thrill of participating in militant action.

'When are we going home, Mum?' Oolie whines.

'Soon.' Doro gives her a hug. 'We're just making a plan to save the allotment. You wouldn't want them to build houses here, would you?'

'I don't care.'

She pulls a bored face. She's been so grumpy recently. The only time she's her old bubbly self is when she's talking about Edenthorpe's cafeteria or winding Clara up.

'Look, Oolie, look at the swallows!' Doro points up into the sky, but Oolie shrugs.

'They're only bleedin' birds.'

When they get home, Doro puts the kettle on out of habit – though she's already had three cups and at her age she has to mind her bladder – and logs on to the internet. She goes to the council website, and makes a note of Councillor Malcolm Loxley's number. An answering machine picks up her call and, caught off guard, she leaves a confused, rambling message.

'You may remember . . . we . . . er . . . bumped into each other at Greenhills Primary School . . . ringing to ask for your help on an urgent matter . . .'

The radio is on in the background as she prepares the spaghetti in the kitchen – something about an American bank being seized.

Serve them bloody well right. No doubt Marcus will have a thing or two to say over dinner. But just as the pasta reaches the critical al dente moment, the telephone rings. Oh, heck! She juggles with the phone in one hand and the saucepan in the other, straining the pasta water into the sink – no hand left for the pan lid.

'Hello? Doro Marchmont.'

'Malcolm Loxley. Returning your call.'

The voice is deep, smooth, confident. A powerful voice, with a hard Yorkshire clip in the vowels.

'What can I do for you?'

'I was calling on behalf of the Greenhills Allotment Gardeners Association. We've learned that there's a proposal from property developers in collusion with backward elements within the Council to redevelop the allotments, and we're asking you to support our campaign [she can feel herself acquiring momentum as she goes along] to throw out these despicable profiteers and secure for the workers . . . I mean, secure for the allotment gardeners the full . . . oh, heck! . . .'

Unchecked, the mass of steaming pasta slides from the saucepan and slurps into the sink, twining itself in and around the unwashed washing-up like pale consumptive worms.

'. . . the full fruits of their veggies.'

'I see.'

'So . . .?'

'Can I ring you back on this?'

SERGE: *The $700 billion bailout*

'Can I ring you back on this?' Serge's broker says.

And Serge says, 'Of course,' because he can't explain that he's actually sitting in the disabled loo making this call, and in fact his phone will be switched off for most of the day.

After last week's scare, he's decided to bow out of Kenporter1601, and to trade from now on only as Dr Black. The surprising thing is how long it took Chicken to catch on. Using his calculator, he works out that he's in the clear. Not only has he repaid the original money he borrowed from the 1601 account to place his trades but, according to his arithmetic, he's actually overpaid by £1,343.20. But unless Chicken has done the same calculation, he won't realise this, will he? And the trouble is, Serge will never know for sure whether Chicken has decided to let it pass, or whether he's just waiting for the right moment to pounce.

The tension of not knowing makes him feel uneasy and queasy. At lunchtime he decides to bypass the FATCA cafeteria scrum and take a sandwich down to St Paul's Walk, where he can use his phone unhindered. The sky is low and almost the same colour as the river, whose futile slapping against the stones brings on melancholy thoughts about eternity, the meaning of life and the contents of his sandwich, which has turned out to be crayfish again.

He calls his broker back, and is pleasantly surprised to learn that Dr Black is worth £599,087. He decides not to repay the mortgage just yet. Instead, he calls Otto to check out how things are with him and Molly, and to make sure that his blabby tendencies are still in check.

'Yeah, you're a real mate, Soz. I'll pay you off as soon as we're in the clear.'

'No blabbing. Our secret, right?'

'Sure thing.'

'How's Molly? When's the new Free baby going to join us?'

'Six weeks to go. We've kitted out the flat with cool baby gear in non-gender-specific pastel shades. Thanks to you, Soz.'

'No worries. Have you seen Babs lately, by the way?'

'I've not talked to her, but I saw she's come out on Facebook. Heh heh.'

'No way!'

Babs a lezzie! He finds the thought vaguely sexy. Maybe he should look her up.

The thought is so distracting that he forgets to turn his phone off immediately, and a moment later it rings in his pocket. He answers without checking the caller. If he had, he might not have answered. It's Doro.

'Oh, darling! I've got hold of you at last! I've been so worried! I thought you'd disappeared from the face of the earth.'

'No need to worry, Mum. Everything's hunky-dory.'

'Because I've been reading about the terrible scandals in Cambridge. Amazing what these academics get up to.'

'Oh. Yes. Awful.'

'But your department's not involved?'

'Er . . . not a lot.'

'Apparently it was particularly bad in maths.'

'Oh, that's computational. Not my kind of maths.'

'Oh. Computational. Sounds dreadful.'

'Mm. It can be a bit fuzzy.'

'And how's the PhD?'

'Not bad. Getting there. Mum –'

'Serge, I've had an idea – why don't you come back to Doncaster for a few weeks to finish it off? You could stay in your old room, and get your head down without all the distractions of student life.'

'I'll think about it.'

'But seriously. How about next week?'

'Mm . . . but I need access to –'

'Can't you get everything online these days?'

'Not everything. But thanks, I'll definitely think about it, Mum.'

He throws the remains of his sandwich into the river, and immediately a flock of seagulls swoop and get into a fight. The biggest, most aggressive one carries off the crust, the smaller ones get a few crumbs, and there's a scrawny one with a crooked wing that doesn't get anything. He shakes a few scraps out of his bag, but the bird just flaps around in circles hopelessly. No doubt if Doro was there, she would go and buy another sandwich for it.

When he gets back to the office, people are already at their desks, but nothing much is happening. It's so quiet that he thinks at first there's been some kind of technical breakdown. Some traders drift up to the cafeteria for a caffeine fix, but the quants are mostly there on the floor. The Hamburger is trying to interest the Frenchies in his baby pictures. Lucie and Tootie are staring at Bloomberg TV on the overhead screen. The dateline says Monday 29th September 2008, and the Money Honey is interviewing some fast-talking American guy in an expensive bad-taste suit.

'What's going on?' Serge asks.

'Fuck knows,' says Lucie.

'George Bush pleading with the House of Representatives,' says Tootie.

'What d'you mean?'

'Seems they're not keen to bail out the big banks.' His acne scars dimple. 'They don't yet realise they have no choice.'

The door swings open, and in comes Maroushka: red lipstick, yellow jacket, slingback heels. A few guys turn and stare. She pauses in the doorway, then slinks along to her desk. Still they stare. What the fuck do they think they're looking at? Then he realises they aren't staring at her at all. Following their gaze, he sees a trio of men standing in the doorway who must have come in just after her: the Chief and two guys in suits – not the same class of suits as the MOTUs from Head Office were wearing last week, but average off-the-peg gear, limp polyester-mix shirts, shiny pants – sporting cheap haircuts, and looking bleary-eyed but watchful. They're the sort of guys who work in back-office compliance, or the Inland Revenue, or the Financial Services Authority – not sharp enough to earn big money, and hungry for revenge on those who do.

Serge's heart kicks up in his chest – boom! Boom! Boom! Boom!

They stand still and scan the trading floor with their bleary-but-watchful eyes. One of them leans over and whispers to Chief Ken. They're looking towards the Securitisation area. Then they start to walk.

Boom! Boom! Boom! Boom! His heart thuds as they walk past the junk bond traders, past the Frenchies, past Toby and Lucian, who look up and mutter something Serge doesn't catch. They're coming in his direction.

Boom! Boom! Boom! Boom! His heart thuds against his ribs. He cringes and bends over his keyboard, eyes shut, waiting for the hand on the shoulder. When he opens his eyes and looks up, they are already walking past the Hamburger.

Boom! Boom! Boom! Boom! He feels the faint movement of air on his neck. Then nothing. They've walked by.

At the end of the row, there's only Timo Jääskeläinen and the glass-walled office where Maroushka is fumbling in her handbag, apparently unaware of what's going on. She takes out a lipstick and a small mirror and goes to work on her mouth, puckering her lips to blot them on a tissue when she's finished. Then she looks up. One of the limp-shirt guys is staring at her through the glass wall, in that openly gobsmacked way that men do. The other is leaning over and whispering something to Timo.

Timo stands up, knocking over his chair. His cheeks are very pale. He follows Chicken towards the door, the two guys walking behind. There's that whiff of aftershave as he passes – aniseed and benzene – but the look on his face this time is unmistakeably a grimace.

CLARA: Dough

Clara's heart skips a beat. That woman's there again, waiting at the school gate. She looks a bit younger than Doro. Mint-green collarless jacket with gold buttons. Short black hair, sharply cut, fiercely dyed. Scarlet lipstick. Gold charm bracelet. The sort of woman you'd describe as Doncaster-flash.

Through her car window, Clara studies her unobserved. Why does she look familiar?

A moment later, Jason runs out and gives her a hug. They walk off together in the direction of the Hawthorns, and Clara drives over to Hardwick Avenue for a cup of tea on her way home.

Doro and Oolie are in the kitchen, up to their elbows in bread dough. Doro's dough is plumped and rounded into rolls arranged on a tray. Oolie's dough is squashed from too much kneading and greyish from her unwashed hands, peppered with small specks of unknown matter – possibly bogeys.

'Lovely, lovely,' Doro is encouraging her. 'Here, roll it into little balls and put them on here.'

Watching, Clara remembers the time before Oolie was born, when she and Doro used to make bread together. Hers were just as grey and flat.

While Doro is sliding the trays into the oven and setting the timer, Oolie asks Clara in a loud whisper, 'Did you tell her?'

'Tell her what?'

'About having my own flat. About watching filums.'

'Let's all talk about it together,' says Clara as Doro rejoins them at the table.

Then Marcus comes in with several dead teacups and deposits them in the kitchen sink.

'Hello, Clara. Lovely to see you.'

'Hi, Dad.'

She yields to the uncomplicated pleasure of his hug, the rough wool of his jumper, the smell of Pears soap and tobacco. Doro puts the kettle on and sets mugs and a jug of milk on the table. One of the mugs, with a picture of a hamster and a small chip on the rim, was a Mother's Day present from Clara, some twenty years ago.

'So how's the allotment going?' she asks.

'It's going to be a good year for apples. And plums.'

'Mm. Lovely.'

'The teachers at your school,' says Doro, changing the subject rather obviously. 'Do you get on with them?'

'Maybe.' Clara answers cautiously, wondering where this is going.

'Is there anyone . . . *special*?'

'Mother, for goodness' sake!'

Oolie is getting impatient with the conversation. 'Tell her! Tell her about the filums!'

'What films?' Marcus asks.

'Oolie wants to live in a place of her own, so she can watch films.' Clara catches her parents' exchange of glances. 'Apparently it's something the social worker suggested.'

'Did you tell her what films you want to watch, Oolie?' says Doro.

'I told her. *Girls at Play. Unin'abited.*'

'Not "uninhabited", Oolie. "Uninhibited".'

'So?' Oolie sulks, picking the shreds of dough off her fingers and rolling them into a thin sausage.

Doro turns towards Clara and mouths silently, 'P-O-R-N.'

Clara shrugs. Marcus raises his eyebrows, takes off his glasses and wipes them very slowly and thoroughly on his handkerchief.

'I think . . .' Clara begins.

Oolie pushes the sausage of dough up her nose.

'Stop that!' Doro snaps.

Oolie extracts the sausage of dough from her nostril and starts to eat it.

Doro leans across and slaps Oolie's wrist. Marcus lays a restraining hand on Doro's arm. Doro flicks it away. Oolie smirks.

★

The smell of baking bread begins to waft into the kitchen. Closing her eyes, Clara lets the smell carry her back to the kitchen at Solidarity Hall, everyone sitting around the yellow table and cheering as Doro, pink-cheeked and laughing, took a cake out of the oven. Clara was thirteen years and seven months old, and they were having a party to celebrate her menarche. Everyone was congratulating her on achieving womanhood.

It was quite confusing. She felt happy, because she was the centre of attention, and because celebrations are supposed to be happy. But what was so special about being a woman? There were millions of women out there. And this menstruation thing didn't seem so great.

Besides, she didn't want the whole world to know – and especially not her younger brother, who started to make snide remarks about bloodstains, and nudged her whenever a jar of jam appeared on the table.

'Have you heard from Serge, Mum?'

'No.'

'Me neither. He's not answering his phone.'

'I expect he's still busy with the Imperial College in London.'

'Not Imperial College, Mum, University College.' Her poor mother is obviously losing her marbles.

'He's probably working with them both, darling. No wonder he doesn't have time to answer his phone messages.'

'I bet he's got some new woman in his life. *That's* why he's lying low.'

'What happened to Babs? I rather liked her.'

'I dunno. Why do you always make excuses for him, Mother? Why don't you ever take an interest in what *I'm* doing?'

'So is there someone new in your life, Clara?'

'Oh, for goodness' sake, Mother!' Do other people's parents go on like that all the time? 'Anyway, whatever happened to *your* wedding plans? That's all gone very quiet.'

'What wedding? You never told me about no wedding!' Oolie shrieks.

Oops!

'Er . . . how would you like it, if Doro and I got married, Oolie?' asks Marcus.

Doro rolls her eyes and goes to check on the bread.

Clara drinks her tea quickly, but she doesn't hang around to listen to Marcus and Doro's heart to heart with Oolie. She finds it vaguely disturbing to be around this trio – rapidly ageing Doro and Marcus, and Oolie not ageing at all, but frozen in perpetual childhood.

What will happen to Oolie when Marcus and Doro can't look after her any more? Will Clara 'inherit' her, along with their collection of 1968 protest posters, slogan T-shirts and Marcus's unfinished manuscript? She needs to discuss this with her brother.

In the car on the way back to Sheffield, she breathes in the smell of the freshly baked rolls Doro and Oolie gave her, and wonders why Serge never answers his phone.

SERGE: *Vodka*

Serge blinks his eyes open. He's still in the trading hall, and the clock in the corner of Bloomberg is showing the same date – 29th September 2008.

That's good. The time is 18.40.

He closes his eyes carefully, then opens them again: 19.02.

'What happen?' Maroushka is standing over him with a glass of water in her hand.

Or at least, it looks like water. When she holds it to his lips, he realises it's vodka.

'Nothing. I'm fine.' He tries to demonstrate his fineness by sitting up to take a sip, but his head spins and he slumps forward on to his desk again. 'I just had a weird turn, that's all.'

'Wired? Not normal?'

'What happened to Timo?'

'Police arrested.'

'Why? What did he do?'

His heart has started up again. Boom! Boom! Boom! Boom! How long before they realise they arrested the wrong person? She places a red-tipped finger to the side of her nose and winks. For a moment, the City-woman mask slips and she looks like a mischievous twelve-year-old.

'I find out.'

Once the Fraud Squad are involved, he stands no chance. As soon as Timo starts to blab, they'll realise they got the wrong man and they'll soon track him down from that stupid Dr Black account.

What if there's some perfectly simple explanation for Chicken's 1601 account?

What if he's registered it with Compliance after all?

What if . . .?

Most people have gone from the trading floor, apart from the Indians in the Currencies corner, who are working feverishly on some late exchange deal. The rest of the quants are at Franco's, says Maroushka, celebrating Lucian's birthday.

'We go, Sergei?'

'Soon.'

He takes her hand and pulls her towards him. She doesn't resist. Her body rests lightly against his, her thigh pressing against his knee. Her perfume fills his nostrils.

'Life stands before me like an eternal spring with new and brilliant clothes.'

'You talking like crazy, Sergei.'

'Carl Friedrich Gauss. Not crazy. Sublime.'

She pours a bit more vodka into his open mouth. 'Drink.'

He coughs and splutters. 'Bloody hell. Do you always keep a bottle of that in your handbag?'

'I keep for emergentzee.'

'I love you.'

There, it's out. If he'd thought about it, he might not have said it. And she isn't recoiling in disgust, she's smiling her twelve-year-old smile again and taking a gulp of vodka.

'I still think you wired, Sergei.'

She pulls away, but lets her hand linger on his shoulder.

'Run away with me, Maroushka.'

Though he's said her name over in his head many times, it's the first time he's spoken it out loud. The consonants fuse in his mouth. She laughs. She doesn't realise he's being deadly serious.

'Why run away?'

'I have . . .'

The vodka has made him feel detached and vaguely optimistic.

> *Princess Maroushka!*
> *Hear the song of Serge!*
> *When you're facing an emerge-*
> *Entzee, you can count on me.*

If he can find the right words, if he can formulate the killer proposal, he'll make her see that despite his small size and ironic manner he's not only serious but capable, the man she's been looking for all her life without even realising it, the man who will love her and protect her and make her smile.

'I am . . .' He puts her hand to his mouth and kisses the small hard knuckles. '. . . I am Serge.'

For a moment, love swells like a heart-shaped helium balloon and rides the air, and bluebirds flutter beneath the ceiling of the trading hall. Then she laughs and pulls her hand away.

'You too much wired today, Sergei.'

'We can be wired together. We can have lots of wired babies.'

She rolls her eyes in that way he finds irresistibly sexy.

'Something abnormal happens in world market, Sergei. Timo has no importance but this has importance. Congress voted down Bush plan. Very interesting situation. Dow Jones will collapse. From this position some are winning and some are losing everything. This we must find out. We go?'

In the noisy fug of Franco's, several parties are going on at the same time. A pack of traders laid off from big-name banks in the post-Lehman bloodbath are drowning their sorrows, while others are blowing their comp, and the FATCA crowd are pouring champagne down their throats in celebration of Lucian's birthday, while listening to some suit on TV explaining that the world's tide of credit has run dry, and now, unable to borrow from each other, the big banks have stopped lending and started to collapse. Everyone seems to have forgotten about Tim the Finn, transfixed by the crisis being played out on the giant screen. Serge pushes his way through to join them as an ironic cheer goes up. The House of Representatives has just thrown out the Bush plan and voted that banks must stand on their own two feet, like everybody else. Assets they all thought were secure, assets backed by mortgages in the booming property market, assets rated triple A by the likes of Moody's and Standard & Poor's, are now as flaky as dandruff. A dam of loans, secured (apparently) on ever-rising house prices, has been breached, toxic debt is oozing into the vaults of financial institutions all around the globe. Where will it end?

'Happy birthday, dear Lucie!' somebody roars.

'Thank you, dear punters!' yells someone else, to another volley of popping corks.

Toby O'Toole shoves a glass of something into Serge's hand, and he glugs it down. Wow! What was that? Intoxicated with their own profligacy, the quants have started mixing wine and beer and spirits into the bubbly, in increasingly bizarre and disgusting cocktails, like synthetic CDOs.

'. . . Sub-prime mortgages extended home-ownership to people previously excluded . . . low-waged and unemployed . . . US interest rates shot up from 1 per cent to 5.3 per cent . . . unprecedented rate of default . . . property prices collapsed . . . blah, blah, blah . . .' the tight-jawed TV pundit drones on.

'Dear God, just give us one more year before it all folds up!' someone prays.

'Or the regulators slam us down!'

Toby raises his glass, and Serge finds himself joining in, drinking to all the no-hopers scraping to buy their dream homes, the losers and wasters who should never have been given mortgages in the first place and now find they can't keep up with their payments (surprise, surprise!), whose many-times-multiplied losses have fuelled their bonanza.

'Another year, another million!' screams one of the traders, and everybody cheers.

Serge looks around for Maroushka, wanting to share this transcendental moment with her, but she's standing on her own at the back of the crowd, not drinking, watching the TV screen with dark intense eyes.

DORO: *The sex rota*

Doro clicks off the TV at eleven o'clock and makes her way up to the bedroom, where Marcus has already been asleep for half an hour. What does he dream of, lying beneath the heaped duvet that rises and falls with his breathing, filling the small closed room with fustiness? He's been penned in his study all day, grazing in the pastures of the past. She's been out on the allotment, and her limbs ache with that pleasant well-stretched tiredness of the outdoors – and a few extra twinges in the knees and spine that remind her she isn't as young as she used to be. Missing Oolie's company, she'd found herself wondering again why Megan had run away and left her behind all those years ago.

Maybe Megan resented the newcomers, or maybe they just rubbed her up the wrong way, but she never got on with the Chrises Watt and Howe, despite (or perhaps because of) the fact that they tried really hard to re-educate her. Chris Watt, who had once trained as a nurse, helped her to control her eczema, and encouraged her to give up smoking and to breastfeed Oolie, which neither she nor Oolie found easy. Chris Howe undertook to instruct her in the basics of Marxism and free love.

Doro overheard them one day when she was washing up in the kitchen while he and Megan were finishing breakfast at the table. Crunchy Carl was under the table, tormenting a ladybird that had blown in from the garden. Chris's long grey hair was tied back in a ponytail, and he was wearing (thank heavens) pyjama bottoms and a T-shirt with the almost washed-out slogan '*Never trust anyone over thirty*', below which protruded a wedge of belly, pink and hairy. Megan was wearing Moira's blue and mauve crochet top, showing off the lacy black bra she had on underneath.

'A socialist society will liberate women from repressive monogamy, and permit them to achieve sexual fulfilment,' Chris Howe was saying, his eyes fixed on the outline of her breasts under the crochet top.

Megan said nothing.

Taking this as encouragement, he continued, 'Like, for example, under socialism, there would be nothing to stop you and me having sex together.'

'You and me?'

Megan keeled back sharply on her chair, and had to clutch on to the edge of the table to stop herself from falling over.

'Mam, what's slosherism?' Carl whined from under the table.

'Summat filthy!' Megan snapped.

As Doro sneaked out, quietly pulling the door closed behind her, she heard the sound of a slap, and Megan's voice shouting, 'Stop that, Carl!' followed by a thin whimper.

She came upon them another time, sitting at the kitchen table.

Megan was smoking, and staring out of the window. Chris, bottomless this time, had spread out a sheaf of papers on the table, and was explaining, 'You see, under capitalism the means of production are owned by rich parasites, and the working class have nothing to sell but their labour.'

'I want to be rich,' Megan said, pushing back a strand of heavy black hair that had slipped down over her face.

'You want to be a parasite?'

'Yeah, Paris, London, New York, anywhere's better than around here.'

It was a few days before anyone in the commune realised Megan had disappeared. Doro was vaguely aware that she wasn't around much but assumed she was with her mum and Crunchy Carl in Harworth and would come back, as she always had in the past.

If anyone noticed that Megan's absence seemed longer than usual, it was probably with a feeling of relief more than worry, like when a disturbing background noise goes silent – though in Megan's case it was the silence itself that was disturbing. The kids were relieved not to have Carl foisted on them in the name of brotherhood. Even Oolie seemed more relaxed without Megan constantly on at her to keep her tongue inside her mouth, and stop drooling. It wasn't until about the fifth day that they started to ask each other whether she'd said anything to anyone about going away. Doro checked her room and found that all her and Carl's clothing was missing, along with the collection of cuddly toys she kept by her bed. The clothes she'd borrowed were left neatly folded on a chair, including Moira's blue and mauve crochet top.

On the sixth day, Marcus drove the commune's ancient brown Lada up to Harworth, and cruised the streets, stopping people at random.

'Do you know someone called Megan Cromer? She's got a little boy called Carl?'

It must have been giro day, because there was a queue at the Post Office stretching right out on to the pavement, but no one knew of Megan or Carl.

''Appen she's been sold into slavery,' said an elderly woman with curlers under a headscarf. 'Like in them boowks.' The thought made her chuckle.

'Tied up and ravaged,' added her wrinkled companion.

''Appen they'll know about t' lad up at t' school,' said the woman behind the counter.

Marcus waited outside the school as the kids were coming out, but Carl was not among them. A teacher asked him what he was doing.

'I'm looking for a boy called Carl Cromer. He lives with his grandmother in Harworth, I think.'

'You'd better clear off now, before I call t' police.'

''Appen she went off wi' Silver Birch's lot,' said a man with multiple piercings standing outside the newsagent. 'Scab 'erders is always loaded. Women flock after 'em.' He snorted. 'Dutch Elm, we used to call 'im.'

A man standing at a bus stop told him, 'Never 'eard of 'em, pal, but I'll gi' you ten bob for your car.'

★

'So where d'you think she could have gone?' Doro had asked.

'Megan is Megan,' Marcus had said, which struck her at the time as an odd reply.

Weeks later, somebody found an uninformative little note that had slipped down the side of her bed.

Megan's departure spurred them to rethink the balance of power between the men and the women in the commune.

'The men always get to decide who they're going to sleep with. We think we're being liberated, but really it's just the same old crap,' said Moira, in their weekly women's meeting.

'Mm,' said Doro, who had always believed that Moira was the one who decided.

'They play us off against each other.' Moira twirled a copper strand around her finger. 'And we go along with it, because we want to be wanted.'

'Mm,' Doro agreed, thinking, it's taken Megan to bring this home to her.

'We should take matters into our own hands, and draw up a sex rota,' said Chris Watt, who had never even met Bruno. 'That way *we* could decide.'

'Mm,' said Doro, wondering how she could avoid encountering Chris Howe's pink sausage dick, should it come up for her on the rota.

After his failure with Megan's education, Chris Howe's politics had taken a move to the left, or maybe a leap into the stratosphere.

'You know where socialism will eventually come from, sister?' he asked Doro, cornering her on the bend in the stairs one day.

She shook her head, looking around for escape routes, trying not to stare at the limp manhood dangling before her.

'It'll be brought to us from outer space.'

'Oh, really?'

'Yeah. According to Posadas, any creatures intelligent enough to have devised space travel will already have created a socialist society. It stands to reason.'

★

Remembering, Doro smiles to herself in the darkness as she curls herself around Marcus's sleeping form, and feels quietly thankful that the sex rota was short-lived.

The main beneficiary was Chris Watt who, heaven knows, deserved a break.

SERGE: Lady Luck

Serge clutches his arms across his chest and hopes he won't puke in the back of the cab as it speeds and swerves through the night. It was stupid of him to get so lashed, but forgivable in the circumstances. The vodka Maroushka had given him was a necessary lifeline. A few glasses of champagne on top did no harm. The idiot thing was joining the race with the other quants to knock back those toxic combinations of champagne with whisky, brandy, beer, red wine, Pernod, Campari, fruit juice, Worcester sauce and some orange stuff that tasted like paint stripper.

At one point the barman, a small dark-skinned guy with an earring and not much hair, had tried to suggest that they ease off a bit, and Lucian, the birthday boy, had turned on him wild-eyed and screamed, 'Pour, you sad little prole! Do your fucking job!' His arms flung wide, he staggered against the table, knocking a couple of glasses on to the floor.

Another guy who worked at Cazenove, an old school friend of Lucian's, who was already well juiced, threw his arms around his pal and gave him a soggy kiss.

'Yay! If you're not getting it, you're not worth it!'

The guy was blond and tall – so tall that Serge's head would fit neatly under his chin. Serge glanced across at Maroushka to check whether she'd clocked him, but she was chatting to the Hamburger.

'All this fucking wealth in this beautiful fucking city, we made it, we earned it, and we're going to fucking drink it!' shrilled Lucian, like a mulletted prophet.

'Cos it could all dry up tomorrow!' added Toby. 'Happy birthday, ginger-boy!'

He poured the contents of his glass over Lucian's head. The

sticky liquid trickled down his face and he stuck out his tongue to catch it as it dripped down. A couple of people clapped, but most said nothing, vaguely aware even through the miasma of booze that their colleagues had gone over the top.

Serge leaned over the counter and said, 'Sorry, mate. They're not always like this.'

The barman silently lowered his head and popped another cork. It was at this point that Serge realised he had to get out. He looked around for Maroushka, but she'd disappeared.

'Thanks! Keep the change!'

Serge hands the driver a tenner, and manages to tumble out of the cab just in time to throw up acidly, yellowly, abundantly on to the pavement outside his block.

But luck is with him – he manages to keep it off his clothes.

Luck: you have to stay on the right side of this unreliable lady, you have to flatter her, study her habits, know her vicissitudes, woo her with promises and gifts. You must never, ever take her for granted. He knows Luck, and he knows her two flighty sisters, Risk and Chance. This naughty threesome hang out together on the up-and-down ladders of stock exchanges; he's met them often in examination halls; they haunt the poky corners of history, like those crones who used to knit beside the guillotine, always on the lookout for a big-head.

Before turning in to bed, out of habit, he takes a quick peep at Chicken's bank and email accounts. No action there at all today. Kenporter1601 is still empty. So far, so good. But fixed in his mind is the sickly grimace on Tim the Finn's face as he was led away from the trading floor. He must have talked to those cops by now.

What has he been telling them?

Will Chicken ask them to investigate the rogue transactions in the 1601 account?

Or does he want to keep his own trading activities in the dark?

Serge knows luck has been with him so far, but how long can it last? To keep on the right side of Lady Luck, to encourage her to see things his way, he decides to make her a small gift. He logs in and transfers £5,000 from Dr Black to Kenporter1601 – a generous interest payment for the money he has borrowed. He attaches a one-word tag to the payment: THANKS.

CLARA: Mr Gorst/Alan has a moustache

When Clara arrives at school on Tuesday morning, Mr Gorst/Alan is in the staffroom trying to organise a meeting to discuss the school's SATS results.

'We could do better.' He waves the thick printout of doom.

But she can't take her eyes off the growth of dark stubble around the lower half of his face, which could have aspirations to become a moustache or, worse, beard.

No, no! Don't go there! You're lovely as you are, Alan!

In her opinion, facial hair seldom suits anybody.

After he's gone, Mr Tyldesley whispers in her ear, 'It's like being lectured by a badly plucked chicken.'

'Or Che Gue-Bloody-Vara,' mutters Mr Kenny, loud enough for everyone to hear.

Only Heidi Postlethwaite springs to his defence.

'The Ancient Greeks regarded the beard as a symbol of virility.' (Bitch!)

Clara tries her phone once more. She still hasn't had any luck contacting the guy from Syrec, who was supposed to pick up the bags of paper and plastic for recycling. Maybe Mr Kenny was right about the regional development grant.

At lunchtime, she puts her head round the door of the boiler room, where Mr Philpott is dozing with a book open on his knee: *The Hitchhiker's Guide to the Galaxy*. He sits up with a start, and two pairs of glasses tumble off his nose on to his lap.

'Thanks for keeping the bags for me, Mr Philpott. I'll take a few more home for recycling.'

The tied black bin bags are waiting in the lobby outside the boiler room. A gust of wind through the open door catches them, and sets them flapping like a flock of outsize rooks come home to roost.

Mr Philpott helps her heave a couple more bags to her car and shove them into the boot. She slams the hatch and heads off back to her classroom. Bloody Syrec.

When she gets there, she tries the Syrec mobile number once more and, to her surprise, someone answers. It's the same teen-on-speed voice as before.

'Yeah. Yeah. Oh, shit, I completely forgot. Sorry. Yeah. Two weeks ago. Three? Where are you? Right, I'll be round. Yeah, right. Four o'clock this afternoon. Twenty quid.'

The afternoon lesson is history, Miss Postlethwaite's subject, and she's decided in her wiggly-bum wisdom that the kids of Greenhills should learn about Ancient Egypt. Maybe the old slag heaps around South Yorkshire remind her of the pyramids.

'Who can remember which river runs through Egypt?' Clara asks, keeping one eye on the clock on the wall, which is inching slowly, slowly towards 3.15.

There's a bit of shuffling and sniggering. Nobody likes to be the first to put their hand up, apart from Dana Kuciak from Poland, who doesn't mind being thought a swot.

'Please, miss, the Nail.'

'Nearly right, Dana! Well done! Now, who can get it exactly right?'

'I know, miss! T' Nob!' shouts Robbie Lewis, his hands furtively at work behind the desk. The convention is that any word beginning with 'n' can be substituted with 'nob' which is an instant cue for anarchy. There's a chorus of shrieks, groans and giggles.

Clara silently curses Miss Hippo and writes the answer up on the board.

'Who knows anything else about Ancient Egypt?'

'Pyramods!' shouts Jason.

'Yes, pyramids! Well done, Jason!'

He's actually learned something! He looks so pleased with himself she's almost ready to forgive the stolen purse.

'Will you shag me now, miss?'

'No, Jason.' But she can't help laughing. 'Who can tell me what they were for?'

'Dead bodies!' several voices clamour.

'Dead fairies,' says Dana smugly.

'And they believed that when you die your heart is weighed against a feather, and every bad deed makes your heart heavier.' Why is she peddling this anti-scientific nonsense? Maybe she should take it up with Mr Gorst/Alan. 'And only the people with the very lightest hearts are allowed into Paradise.'

A silence of thirty suspended breaths fills the room. 6F are suckers for any kind of superstitious twaddle. Then Dan Southey, whose brother works in the butcher's shop on Beckett Road, pitches in.

'Miss, our Pat fetched a pig's 'eart 'ome and it were 'eavy like a 'tater.'

'Well, people in't the same as pigs,' says Tracey Dawcey.

'Oink, oink,' says Robbie Lewis.

A pandemonium of pointing, poking and oinking erupts, and she has to quieten them down with the Look, followed up by one of Miss Hippo's tedious worksheets.

As the hand of the clock moves towards 3.30, Jason puts his head up and says,

'Why we learnin' about Ashent Egyptians, miss?'

'Well, Jason . . .' She takes a deep breath and counts silently to ten. But just as she gets to nine, the bell goes, and her problem is solved. Another day of 6F's education is completed.

She loves the silence that settles over the empty classroom at the end of each day. She loves the sound of kids ebbing away down the corridor like the sea withdrawing over pebbles. She goes around the desks, picking up the worksheets on which they've recorded their deeds, mostly the bad – 'thumped Jed', 'niked Mams fags', 'shaged Rackel Oliver'. That looks like Jason's writing.

Then she notices, through the classroom window, that a massive black four-by-four is easing into the car park. The door opens and a young guy climbs out with a mobile phone pressed to his ear, wanders around and disappears from view round the corner. By the time she finds him, he's already been directed to Mr Philpott in the boiler room, and the two of them have started loading the bin bags into his vehicle, struggling to keep them from flying all over the playground in the September wind.

'Hi, I'm Clara Free. I think we spoke . . .'

'Oh yeah, right.' He shakes her hand bouncily. He looks in his early twenties, a bit spotty, with gelled hair riffling in the breeze, low-hanging jeans and a black zip-up jacket.

'I thought you'd bring a van or a lorry or something.'

'It's okay, they'll fit in here no problem.'

He and Mr Philpott shove the last few bin bags into the four-wheel drive, which has a logo painted across the side doors: 'FIRST CLASS FINANCE: AVAILABLE, AFFORDABLE, ACHIEVABLE. WHY WAIT TO MAKE YOUR DREAMS COME TRUE?' And the same mobile number she rang earlier.

'First Class Finance. Is that you?'

'Yeah, right.'

'I thought you were a recycling company.'

'Yeah, we do that too. Multi-unlimited opportunity portfolio.'

'I see.' Though she doesn't see at all.

'Thirty quid, miss, right?'

'Actually, we agreed twenty.'

'Thirty. Take it or leave it.'

He opens the back and unloads one of the bags. Quickly she pulls the notes out of her purse. He holds them up to the light before pocketing them, gets into his four-by-four and drives off, revving so hard he leaves tyre marks on the tarmac. The wind catches the bag of left-behind newspapers and swirls them around the car park. She runs around picking them up until she is cross and out of breath.

By the time she gets back to her flat, it's six o'clock and she's ready for her only cigarette of the day, but she's stupidly run out, and the nearest shop will have just closed. Instead, she takes her shoes off, puts the kettle on, sits on the sofa and Googles First Class Finance. Nothing. Then she Googles Syrec. A website opens, with harp music and images of butterflies skimming across wheat fields, then violins soar in aspirational arpeggios while an American-accented voice-over explains how Syrec is helping us to protect our unique heritage for future generations. (Cue a pair of little blonde girls in white frocks gathering daisies in a lush meadow. Your typical Doncaster scene, in fact.) There's a Contact page with an address in Askern and the same mobile number she's been calling. That's all.

By now, she's desperate for that cigarette. She steps across the landing and rings on Ida Blessingman's door. No reply, though she's pretty sure she heard Ida come in earlier. She rings again. After a couple of minutes, Ida appears wearing her turquoise dressing gown, and smoking a cigarette.

'Oh, hello, Ida, have you got a fag . . .?'

Behind Ida, somewhere in the depths of the flat, a male voice calls, 'Who is it?'

'Nobody,' Ida shouts over her shoulder.

Through the partly open door, she sees someone streak from the kitchen to the bathroom. Although he's moving fast, she catches a fleeting glimpse of a naked male with a thin serial-killer-style moustache.

Ida snatches the cigarette from her own lips, thrusts it into Clara's open mouth, and slams the door.

Checking her Facebook page before she goes to bed, she discovers something else of interest. Her friend Tammy, from university days, has introduced a new Facebook friend called Barbara, a botany postdoc in Cambridge, with a cute pudgy face and short dark hair, who writes about her passion for the northern marsh orchid, *Dactylorhiza purpurella*, which looks like a bristly purple penis and, apparently, grows abundantly in marshland near Doncaster.

But the interesting thing is, this Barbara looks very much like Babs, Serge's girlfriend at Cambridge, whom Clara met once or twice. Although the hair's different, there's a dimply lift to the smile and an incipient double chin which seem familiar. Clara sends Barbara a friendly message confirming that she has seen *Dactylorhiza purpurella* growing at Potteric Carr, and asking whether she knows someone called Serge Free at Queens' College. Then she waters her plants, gives the leaves a polish and wishes them goodnight.

SERGE: *A cappella*

The rabbits have escaped. They're running all over the garden, and Serge is trying to chase them back into their cage. Clara is there too – bossy nine-year-old Clara – shouting at the rabbits, and at him. The last rabbit is cornered, and shooed towards the cage door, and it stops, and turns, and looks at him, and he sees that it's not a rabbit at all, it's a girl. Her nose is turned up and twitchy, like a rabbit's, but her eyes are large and brown and bright with tears. It's Babs. He tries to shove her into the cage, but she won't go – she fights back, showing her large rabbity teeth, pushing hard against his chest with both hands. He wakes up with a pounding heart; his head is splitting. He drags himself out of bed and into the shower. Sheesh, what did he drink yesterday?

When he gets into work, he finds the other quants already huddled in the glass-walled office, clutching their coffees, swapping information. Tim the Finn's problem, it turns out, wasn't a dodgy prostate at all, it was a dodgy a cappella quartet. Timo Jääskeläinen has been accused of running a scam with the other three members of his singing quartet through a series of coded texts to one or other of the songsters, who pass the information around the group and bet up to their limit, using a spread betting agency to help avoid detection, rather than going directly to the Stock Exchange where controls are tighter. Meanwhile, the wily tenor has been using the massive reserves of FATCA to manipulate the prices. This has been going on for at least two years.

One at a time, the quants and traders on Securitisation are invited up to the boardroom on the top floor to be questioned by Detective Inspectors Birkett and Jackson, who have been called in by the FSA, which was alerted when controllers in the back office at FATCA picked up irregular movements of equities linked with Timo Jääskeläinen. They couldn't prove the connection since he wasn't actually doing the spread betting himself. The mobile phone company provided the police with details of his contacts, but it appeared he was only texting guys in his a cappella group about songs in their repertoire. What is still unclear is the amount of cash they've managed to stash away, and where it is.

'I'd do it, if I could get away with it,' Toby O'Toole shrugs with a mixture of disapproval and admiration. 'It's a victimless crime, isn't it?'

'*Le banking, c'est toujours un casino,*' one of the Frenchies adds.

'Personal fraud is not good for bank reputation,' Maroushka says. 'Average people must retain belief in banking system. He should be more careful. What you think, Sergei?'

'I think you're right. As always, Maroushka. How's Chicken taking it?'

'He remains calm.'

Toby smirks, fixing Serge with his pale eyes. 'You should have met him before he was sent on the anger management course, Freebie.'

'Anger? I find him quite . . .' It's hard to define Chicken's appeal – a mixture of charm, energy and good clothes.

'Charismatic is the word you're looking for. They teach them that too. Send them off into the woods with paint-ball guns to learn leadership. You didn't know?'

Serge keeps quiet. Tootie's combination of private cynicism and public arse-licking can be hard to take.

'You're so like young Lucie. Another innocent soul who worships at Chicken's altar. By the way, he sends his apologies for last night. Called in ill today. Sick as a ginger dog.' He grins unpleasantly. 'Doesn't know when to stop.'

Serge, when it's his turn to be interviewed in the boardroom, says and asks as little as possible, hiding his nerves behind a mask of nonchalance. DIs Birkett and Jackson are hiding behind a mask of tight-lipped professionalism.

He tries to work out from their expressions whether they suspect anyone else, but all he can deduce is that they're investigating Timo's contacts, and he's not on their suspect list yet.

'Did you notice he spent a lot of time in the toilet?' asks DI Birkett.

He shrugs. 'Not really.'

As soon as he gets home that evening, he turns on his laptop and checks the hacked accounts. Kenporter1601 is empty again. The £5,000 he transferred into it has disappeared, and it hasn't reappeared in Dr Black. It means his payment's been accepted. That's positive.

From the fridge he grabs a bottle of cold lager, and strolls out on to the balcony of the penthouse, breathing deeply, noticing the autumnal glimmer in the air and the golden evening light enamelling the rooftops of the city. The knot in his stomach loosens, his shoulders relax, the cold beer slides down like silk. Here under the wide sky his soul opens out and philosophical insights gush in. He thinks of Tim the Finn sweating in a cell somewhere, confused from terror, trying to remember what he has and hasn't said, his Porsche still crouched in the underground car park, waiting for an owner who may never return. It could have been him.

No, he won't get too greedy. His £5,000 payment of thanks has been accepted. Now is the time to concentrate on boosting his legitimate bonus by putting all his efforts into his day job. So long as he stays at FATCA, he'll always have the possibility of an investigation hanging over him. He'll never know when he's in the clear, nor ever be free from the fear of being caught. He must be careful. But he's not quite ready to leave yet.

'Run away with me,' he'd said, and she'd laughed, not cruelly, but unconvinced. He needs time to win her round. Because love is the ultimate pay-off.

Because love is the thing that money can't buy (but it helps).

Because when he leaves, he wants to be sure she'll come with him.

DORO: *Stringy*

Doro knows she loves Marcus, with that deep companionable love that's stood the test of forty years, so she's surprised to find herself feeling a bit flustered as she prepares to accompany Councillor Loxley on a fact-finding tour of the allotments on Wednesday. After showering, washing and blow-drying her hair, she dabs on a bit of eye make-up and lip gloss, squirts some Chanel No. 5, relic of a long-ago airport splurge, behind her ears, and stands in front of the mirror studying herself with a nagging feeling of dissatisfaction. Where did those eye-bags come from? How long have there been two vertical lines between her eyebrows? And those saggy pouches on each side of her chin – when did they appear? She can make them disappear if she smiles. That's better. Trouble is, she'll have to go around smiling all day. Maybe that's why old women always look so bloody happy.

Next she looks through her drawer for a suitable T-shirt. '*Let a hundred flowers bloom.*' She pulls it over her head, looks in the mirror, and the feeling of dissatisfaction returns. The T-shirt – like all her slogan T-shirts – looks faded and outdated. Instead, she opts for a white tailored blouse she bought for some formal college event and a pair of blue linen trousers which still fit snugly around her hips, though the zip strains a bit. She brushes her hair so that it parts on one side. Then on the other side. Then she brushes it backwards and lets it fall naturally. The broad silver wings above her ears are quite attractive, she thinks. At the last moment, she puts on a necklace.

By the time she gets to the allotment entrance, slightly out of breath, a few minutes after four thirty, he is already waiting there. His black BMW is parked by the fence and he is leaning on the bonnet talking into his mobile phone, looking suntanned and relaxed in an open-necked check shirt and grey slacks. A slightly frayed Paul Newman comes to mind.

'Ah, Mrs Marchmont!'

'Hello, Councillor Loxley. It's very good of you to spare us some of your busy time,' she coos. (Why is she talking like this? Shouldn't she be more assertive?)

'My pleasure. I've had a chance to look through the paperwork.'

'And?'

They've started walking as they talk, following the lattice of grassy paths around the allotment beds.

'You have to realise the Council stands to make a sizeable sum on this sale . . .'

'But you can't! People have been gardening here for years; growing food for their families!'

'. . . to plough into essential frontline services. The Council can't afford to let a valuable resource like this remain undercapitalised.'

'This isn't a resource, it's a paradise!'

This isn't going at all right. She's supposed to be winkling out information and subtly persuading, not haranguing him.

'I'm open to persuasion,' he says, and his hand accidentally brushes against hers as they walk.

She leads him past Ada and Danny's fruit bushes and Reggie's spectacular leeks, around the upper border of the allotment where Ian West's runaway champagne vines are leaping through the hawthorn hedge. The sun is low but still warm, the air so humid that you can almost breathe the dew before it falls and catch the glimmer of midges' wings in the shade, waiting for dusk, when they will come out and pounce. The plants in the vegetable beds breathe in the moisture too. Their leaves are erect, their fruits and seedpods swell with juice. Fat songbirds, gorged on fruit and flies, warble in the highest branches, piercing the stillness framed by the faraway murmur of traffic, the quiet chit-chat of human voices, the tap-tap of a hammer as someone repairs the roof of a distant hut.

The councillor pauses by a bed of runner beans to watch a wiry suntanned old gent tightening up the wires that hold the supporting canes together.

'Malcolm Loxley, from the Council.' He proffers his hand. 'On a fact-finding tour.'

The old man wipes his palms on the sides of his trousers.

'Harry Stringfellow. I 'ear t' Council's gooin' to shut us down.'

'Don't you believe everything you hear. Nothin' decided yet. We're still carrying out the impact assessment.'

'But don't you have to go out to tender? Don't you have to consult?' asks Doro.

'I'm consulting now.' He turns to the old man. 'Great beans you've got there.' His voice has altered slightly, become rougher, more regional. 'My granddad were a great gardener. He grew some smashin' runners.'

A sleek blackbird, heedless of their closeness, starts tugging a worm out of a heaped bed. They all watch, entranced by this clash of forces, pink versus black, resistance versus determination, until the gardener claps his hands to chase the bird away and the worm recoils pinkly into the dark soil.

'Greedy buggers. Always on the scrounge,' says the councillor.

Doro, who had sided with the blackbird, attracted by his glossy beauty and urgent hunger, says nothing.

''Ere,' says the old man, picking a few fat sticks of beans, 'try these, pal.'

'Thanks. I'll have them for my tea tonight.'

He takes the beans, shakes hands and moves on.

'Come and see my patch.'

She leads him down a narrow track through the heart of the allotments towards the lower plots, where the sun has already dipped away and the cooling air has started to release beads of moisture on to the grass.

'You know, most people who come here haven't got much money, and it's an escape for them. Another world. No stress. Companionship. Fresh food. Gentle exercise. Healthy lifestyle.' She laughs. 'What else can I say to convince you?'

He laughs too, wrinkling his eyes. 'You're a great persuader. You should go into politics, Mrs Marchmont. Then you'd see how hard it is to make these decisions.'

She cuts off three fat rosy rhubarb sticks and hands them to him.

'Here, something for your supper.'

'When I were a kid, we always had rhubarb pie on a Sunday.'

She wonders who will cook the rhubarb for him tonight. 'I didn't like rhubarb when I was a kid. Too sharp. Now I cook it with honey and ginger. It's delicious. Oolie – my daughter – loves it. You met her, d'you remember?'

'At the school. How's she doing?'

'Fine. She's working at Edenthorpe's.'

'Everybody has a contribution to make.'

There's something in the Yorkshire flatness of his voice that sounds authentic, unpretentious and kind, not the type to be in league with developers and crooks. She finds herself confiding, 'It means a lot to me – to us – having this place to come to together. We've had so much happiness here on this allotment.'

'You've still not persuaded me,' he says in a voice that sends a shiver through her.

They stand like that for a moment, listening to the birdsong, feeling the coolness of late afternoon settle on their skin. She completely forgets to ask about the timescale or the tendering arrangements for the proposed development.

SERGE: Why apologise?

Asian stock markets have plunged on the news of Monday's bailout failure. Bank shares are in meltdown. People with cash have started buying gold. But the quants huddled in the glass-walled office on Wednesday are mulling over events closer to home. Without Tim the Finn to keep them in line, they spend more time in here, gossiping, exchanging information. The Hamburger has brought in a box of Mozartkugeln to cheer them up. Maroushka has gone up to the cafeteria for some coffees. It's getting quite pally.

'I've completely forgotten. What did I say?' asks Lucian Barton nervously.

'You called him a sad little prole,' says Toby O'Toole.

'Crikey!' A look of agony flits over his freckled features.

'Maybe you can apologise to the barman,' says the Hamburger, passing around the chocolates.

'Apologise?'

'Yeah,' says Toby solemnly. 'We'll all go with you and hear you apologise. It would be the decent thing to do, Lucie.'

Apologise? Decent? What's going on? Serge wonders. Nobody here thinks that way.

'Crikey!' Lucian looks around the circle of deadpan faces, as if he's hoping they'll suddenly break into a grin.

'What d'you think, Maroushka? Should he apologise?' Toby turns to her as she comes in with a tray of coffees.

'What for apologise?'

She sets the tray down and hands around sugar sachets and spoons.

'For calling the barman a prole.'

'But is true, no? He is proletarian.'

'I know, but it's rude to say it.'

'Why is rude to be proletarian?' Maroushka has that mildly exasperated look which Serge finds so irresistibly sexy. 'If someone is proletarian he must work hard to improve his situation.'

Toby sniggers openly. 'Like Lucie said, all this fucking wealth, we made it, we earned it!'

'Crikey!'

'Why apologise for truth? Is normal that clever persons get more money than average persons. I am studying five year in prestigious Zhytomyr State Technological University, I have been first in my class. I am earn billions of hrivny for these bloodsucking oligarchs. I too should be rich!' Maroushka swivels round on the swivel chair which used to belong to Timo. 'What you think, Sergei?'

'I think . . . er . . .' he hesitates, noting Maroushka's fiery eyes and crimson cheeks. 'I think he should apologise. Because however clever you are, it doesn't give you the right to abuse other people.' And seeing her lips pucker poutily, he adds, 'As you so rightly said, Maroushka.'

The barman, who it turns out is called Jonas, has to be summoned from the back kitchen. He comes in sheepishly wiping his hands on his apron. Despite his exotic appearance he has a quiet South London accent.

'What am I supposed to apologise for?'

Serge catches the barman's eye as he stares at them. He clearly doesn't remember them at all.

'No, *he's* come to apologise to *you*.' Toby gives Lucian a little shove between the shoulder blades.

He stumbles forward. 'Yeah, sorry, man. I was well out of order.'

'No problem. Water under the bridge. I'd forgotten.' Jonas backs away in the direction of the kitchen, but Toby won't let it rest.

'He called you a sad little prole. Remember? He ordered you to pour the drinks?'

Serge is beginning to feel uncomfortable. There must be some age-old rivalry playing out here. The Hamburger and Frenchies are keeping their heads down, studying the wine list.

'Oh yeah.' Jonas blinks. 'It's all right. It's cool. We all get pissed sometimes.'

'It was my birthday. I was away with the fairies,' burbles Lucian, relieved that the barman isn't pushing for a confrontation. 'I mean, we do get decent compensation, but . . .' He smiles wetly.

'Tell him, Lucie,' Toby interrupts. Some weird mood has come over him. 'Tell him what you earn. Tell him about your bonus.'

Jonas's eyes flick from Lucian to Toby, trying to work out what's going on between them.

'It's all right, man. No stress.' Jonas looks over his shoulder towards the kitchen.

'Some people think we're overpaid,' Toby persists. 'I bet *you* do. Know what? You could be right. But no one'll stop it, because they're all fucking scared we'll fly away to Singapore. And all these bars, shops, the City – the whole bloody country – it'll all close down.'

His arms sweep outwards to embrace the long mirrored bar with its ranks of bottles and glasses. Jonas, who seems an okay kind of guy, shuffles backwards.

'Yeah, I get that. It's just . . . I mean, what do you guys do, to earn all that money?'

'We design algorithms for trading derivatives?' Lucie's voice takes on that ingratiating upwards lilt.

'Derivatives?'

'Things that derive their value indirectly, from underlying assets? Like mortgages, securities, futures?' he gabbles. 'For example, futures options on bananas – they give you the chance to buy tomorrow's bananas at today's prices? Or wheat? Or coffee? You gamble the price'll go up?'

'Or you can force it up,' adds Tootie. 'And you can trade options, just like bananas. But with no weather problems, no storage or transport costs, no strikes.'

'So it's . . . kind of gambling?'

'Not gambling! Because new mathematic eliminates risk.' Maroushka's cheeks are flushed. 'Very soon all trading algorithmic high-frequency computerise non-stop profit.'

Jonas stares, like he's astonished a creature of such loveliness can speak. Serge catches his eye and shakes his head, but the poor sap is still grinning hopefully. He really thinks he stands a chance.

'Banks perform vital functions in the economy, arousing capital for businesses and housebuyers,' the Hamburger interjects in a mild tone. 'But I think the society with excessive unequality is sometimes breaking apart.'

The Frenchies, who haven't taken much notice up till now, look up sneerily.

'Breaking down,' one of them corrects.

'Breaking up,' says the other.

Maroushka's exasperation has stepped up a notch.

'No, no! This is all Communist propaganda! Free market is superior form of economic organisation. I have experienced life in planned economy. Bad food. Bad clothe. Bad house. Everything stink of cabbages!' She wrinkles her nose. 'Lazy and stupid persons rewarded for sitting on bottom all day. What you thinking about, Sergei?'

'Nothing,' he sighs, thinking about the smell of boiled cabbage, stale joss sticks, the damp mousey whiff of Solidarity Hall; baggy dungarees, saggy cheesecloth skirts; the clack-clack of knitting needles; Doro and Marcus laughing as they argue over some principle around the painted yellow table cluttered with overflowing ashtrays, and bottles and glasses that glisten in the candlelight, because the electricity has been cut off again. And Doro suddenly hugging him tight and whispering, 'We're going to create a better world for you, Serge.'

DORO: *Saggy grey*

Doro spoons herself around the curve of Marcus's sleeping back, nuzzling the grey curls which smell faintly of cigarette smoke, herbal shampoo and dreams. He stirs, pulling her towards him, murmuring a cadence of words and snuffles which could be a declaration of love or an analysis of Volume II of *Das Kapital* or some dreamtime combination of the two. She presses her face into his warm nape and covers his shoulder with small kisses, which already taste of betrayal. In the back of her mind she's wondering how to respond to the email which came this afternoon, a week after her walk around the allotment with the councillor.

Can we meet at the allotment next week? Malcolm Loxley

In fact, she's decided how to respond; what she's wondering is what to wear. She hasn't replied yet – she'll leave it until tomorrow, for decency's sake – but she's inspected her underwear drawer, sighed over the assortment of washed-out baggy knickers and grey overstretched bras, and concluded that she must go shopping. If many-splendoured love should strike, or even just lust, she doesn't want to be caught out in saggy grey.

The last time she was unfaithful to Marcus was more than twenty years ago, during the miners' strike, and she wonders, when was he last unfaithful to her? In those days of course unfaithfulness had no meaning, because jealousy and possessiveness were relegated to the dustbin of history, along with private property and the nuclear family. If the green-eyed monster ever showed his claws, you smiled bravely and carried on, because admitting you were jealous meant you were mired in atavistic bourgeois ideology, which was even worse than being two-timed. Because she truly loved Marcus, even though she wasn't always faithful to him, she spared him that indignity by keeping her infidelities to herself, and doubtless he did the same for her. (Unlike Moira, who always wanted everyone to know what a great time she was having, and with whom.)

Anyway, the main thing about communal living wasn't sex – though that's mainly what people remember – but creating a new type of human being: liberated, unselfish, unmaterialistic, committed to the common good. Okay, so it wasn't as easy as they'd thought. It didn't stop lovers feeling jealous, nor comrades hoarding chocolate, nor parents favouring their own kids. But their motives were honourable. And their wonderful children – Clara, Serge, Otto and Star, Toussaint and Kollontai (though they were only part of the commune for a short time) and especially Oolie – are a credit to them.

'I love you,' she whispers into Marcus's sleeping ear, and snuggles closer, stroking his loose belly, the flaccid skin of his shoulders and arms. Their bodies have grown old together, baggy and comfortable like their underwear, and if they no longer achieve the passionate heights of their experimental years, and their lovemaking is now less frequent than it was, it is still tender and affectionate.

So why this unexpected itch of desire, this snag in the cosy fabric of their lives?

Malcolm Loxley isn't even her type – no, it's not him, it's her. It's her sixty-year-old body trying to kid her she's thirty again. Just one more time.

CLARA: Sweeteners

When Clara drops by at Hardwick Avenue on her way home from school on Thursday, the first thing she notices is a musty odour of stale cooking, wax polish and unventilated corridors. It reminds her of . . . what? She sifts through her smell-memory. Yes, her grandparents' house in Norwich used to smell like that when she visited as a child. It's the smell of old people, faint but unmistakeable. In the sink is a heap of unwashed dishes, and a bundle of dirty washing has been left beside the washing machine, in which another load is waiting to be taken out and hung. Things are definitely going downhill around here. She puts the kettle on and hunts unsuccessfully for a packet of biscuits.

Doro is out at an allotment meeting, and Marcus is upstairs on his computer, so she and Oolie end up having a cup of tea together in the kitchen. Oolie heaps two spoonfuls of sugar into her tea, then stirs in half a dozen sweetener tablets.

'Are you sure you need all those sweeteners, Oolie?'

'Mum says I gotter 'ave 'em to keep me weight down.'

'It's cutting out the sugar that keeps your weight down, not adding sweeteners.'

'Mum says I'm turning tubby.'

'But you're supposed to have them instead of sugar, not as well as, Oolie. Isn't it too sweet?'

Oolie stirs determinedly. 'Mum says I've gotter 'ave sweeteners.' She slurps and sucks in air to cool a scalded tongue. 'Ooh, that's 'ot!'

Clara shrugs.

'That's me, innit, when I wor a babbie?' Oolie points at the framed photograph on the wall below the clock, of the Solidarity Hall commune, taken sometime in the 1980s. 'I wor right tubby then, worrent I? Mum says I'm getting tubby again.'

Clara looks at the picture, which she must have looked at dozens of times, without really noticing. There's Oolie, a cute tubby toddler, holding Megan's hand. Megan is frowning, staring at the camera. Despite the different hair and younger features, Clara recognises at once the woman at the school gate. The shock of recognition is so intense that it takes her a moment to register that Oolie is still pointing at the picture and saying something.

'Mum thinks it were me what started it but it worrent.'

'Started what?'

'You know. *It.*'

'I don't know who you mean.'

Oolie wanders through into the sitting room, picks up the remote control of the television and starts to play with the buttons.

Too late, Clara realises what Oolie's talking about. 'Who was it? Who started it?'

But Oolie has started flicking through the channels.

'It worrent me, it were them lads.'

'Which lads? Tell me, Oolie. Tell me.'

Oolie flicks faster, muttering something to herself.

'You can talk to me, you know. I'm your best sister. I won't tell Doro and Marcus, if you don't want me to. Oolie?'

Oolie shakes her head in that infuriatingly stubborn way.

'I wanna see if Russell Brand's on TV.'

The A6182 is scattered with spinning leaves and fallen branches from the autumn gales as Clara drives home. She drives carefully, replaying her conversation with Oolie in her mind. As soon as she gets back to Sheffield, she tries Serge again.

No reply.

Furious and curious, she sends him a text and an email. Then she invites Ida over for a reheated risotto and a glass of wine, which they eat in front of the TV.

Before bed, she checks online for new messages. Her heart thumps a spare beat. There's nothing at all from Serge, but there's one from Barbara on Facebook.

You can tell that fart-faced brother of yours that next time I come to London I'll break into the bank where he works and I'll wrench his balls off with my bare hands and fry them in olive oil with garlic and thinly sliced Dactylorhiza purpurella.

DORO: Undies

Doro isn't sure from his email whether Malcolm Loxley's invitation to meet at the allotment had a sexual overtone. It could just be that he wants to top up on his greens and beans. But just in case, she heads into town on Saturday afternoon, pausing for a moment to wonder what's going on as she pushes past the queue outside the branch of a building society, before making for Marks & Spencer.

It's quiet in here – everybody's out in the street, enjoying the breezy autumn sunshine and buzzing with the crowd. Inside the cool fluorescent-lit shop, she riffles through the undies, letting the satin and lace slide through her hands, wondering what's got into her. Her body feels strangely alive and buoyant, as though all the saggy and lumpy bits can be held in place by optimism alone. Yes, it's optimism that makes her pick out the creamy satin underwired push-up bra with matching lace-panel camiknickers, and try it on in front of the mirror – 36B, that's still her size. The wanton luxury of the satin makes her skin tingle like a caress. She puts two in her basket – one cream and one black. Should she be doing this?

Yes. Because she knows that soon enough there will be Velcro fastenings and incontinence pads and hearing aids; there will be crumbling teeth, and aching joints, and hair that falls out in clumps, and pain and disease, and huge chasms in her memory which swallow up months and years of her life. But just now it's summer, and her body is still more or less functioning – in fact, in some areas it seems to be going into overdrive – and there's a man with gimlet eyes waiting for her, and nothing else really matters.

She slips her credit card into the reader and punches in the code: Serge's birthday. One day, she will forget even that.

The girl smiles and hands her the bag with her purchases. 'Have a nice day.'

'I intend to,' says Doro.

SERGE: Angels

Autumn arrives in the City with a rattle of wind, knocking branches off trees, flicking slates off roofs, and bringing another set of shocks to the markets. The Irish economy is blown away. Icelandic banks, riddled with toxic debt, fall like so much rotten wood. Even with the ban on shorting, stocks worldwide continue to twirl downwards like lost leaves across the sky. Already some of the big-name banks have started shedding staff: 5,000 at Lehman Brothers, and about the same at Merrill Lynch. Credit Suisse, UBS, Barclays and Nomura are laying off hundreds, and mighty Citigroup has warned of 1,500 cuts. Even mega-mighty Goldman Sachs are threatening to sack one in ten of their London workforce. Fear infects the trading floors of the City, and the quants are not immune – though at FATCA all is calm, no one quite knows why. Serge keeps his head down and concentrates on riding the currents; he has enough other things going on to keep his anxiety levels high.

His searches for property in Brazil have become more purposeful. He has identified a location, a stretch of coast, a minimum number of bedrooms (two) and a maximum price ($500,000). He adds in air conditioning and a pool as requirements. But will that be enough to tempt her? One night, out of curiosity, he tries Googling that town she says she comes from. He has to experiment a bit to get the right spelling – Zhytomyr. It definitely looks like a place to avoid. No wonder she wants to hop over to the West. No busy brightly lit streets with bars and boutiques, but big shabby concrete buildings, grim squares with sad people in shapeless clothes, and dreary statues of guys no one has heard of – some geek who claims to have invented space travel (ha ha) and some bloke with a bad suit and a goatee beard, who looks vaguely familiar. He enlarges the view, and an image straight out of his childhood hits him in the eye. Hey! It's Lennie the Leader! What's he doing there?

*

Meanwhile, the heat in the quants' glass-walled office is intense, not from the sun, which seems to have said goodbye for the year, but because of the competition to become the next incumbent of the swivel chair. Chief Ken is taking his time naming the successor to Tim the Finn, almost as if he's playing with them, like so many juggling balls tossed up in the air.

Maroushka tries to stake her claim by twirling in the Finn's swivel chair, showing off her legs. If it were a matter of legs, or even of maths, she might possibly stand a chance. But she's relatively new, her visa situation is still irregular. And besides, look, she's a girl. And it's not just that – there's a general feeling, not vocalised but expressed in smirks and sighs, that to be managed by Maroushka would resemble being indentured simultaneously to Kristin Davis and Attila the Hun.

Toby O'Toole clearly wants the job because he's been sucking up blatantly during Chicken's more frequent visits to their area, asking advice about new investments which are beyond Ken's ken, chatting about golf and generally brown-nosing. Toby is efficient and clever, but there's that ugly angry streak in his personality which scares people off.

From what Serge can make out, most people favour the Hamburger to succeed Timo Jääskeläinen (except Maroushka, who favours herself), because he's the longest-serving member of the desk, a sound mathematician and a calm, good-natured guy. However, after the a cappella debacle there's a mood emanating from New York Head Office that continentals are not to be trusted. This affects the Frenchies, too, especially since they usually head off home to Paris on the late Eurostar on Fridays, rather than joining the others at Franco's.

Lucian is too wet behind the ears, so that leaves him. He's as good a mathematician as Maroushka, but he's not been there long enough, and he hasn't been capitalising on his advantage, because he doesn't want to attract the extra scrutiny. He needs to hedge his position, to have some insurance in place should his personal situation start to unravel, and to quietly plan his escape. In fact, he needs a little protection portfolio, like the portfolios he assembles for the markets, to offset the risk and save his skin in the worst eventuality. A portfolio of emails, for example.

> I want to taste your kum.
> I will walk all over your naughty willy, it will hurt.

What if . . .?

Up to now, he's been covering his traces by marking the emails he reads as unread. But what if Chicken opened his inbox and found new messages that had already been opened by someone else? Not to actually blackmail him of course – that would be low, as well as risky – but just to nudge him to an awareness that whoever was accessing the Kenporter1601 account was accessing his emails too. Take today's early morning classic from Juliette.

> I waiting for you, you naughty boy, come Friday 6 p.m. and you will have
> to do every dirty thing I say else I will punish you.

Serge reads it and, for the first time, he closes it without restoring it to 'unread'.

Later, sitting on the tube, avoiding the dawn-red eyes of his fellow travellers, he ponders the implications of what he's done, and breaks into a cold sweat.

In Timo's absence, Chicken has taken to attending their morning meetings in the glass-walled office once or twice a week. He doesn't contribute to the discussion of algorithms, much of which is above his head, but he likes to share the benefit of his wisdom with the young ones.

'You know what the real threat is to this country?' Serge hears him asking Lucie, who says nothing, but raises his eyes, waiting for enlightenment.

Chicken snaps his teeth. 'Too many women in burkas. Think about it.'

Lucie bows his head like an acolyte at communion.

'You've got a point, Chief Ken,' smarms Toby.

Burkas? thinks Serge. Could Chicken be very slightly mad?

'You know what's wrong with this country, Freebie?'

Chicken pulls up a chair beside him, and Serge feels the rabbit-kick of panic in his guts. Has he checked his email yet?

'Er . . . the weather . . .? Crime . . .? Drugs . . .? The Government . . .? Poor performance in sporting events . . .? Burkas . . .? I dunno.' He puts on his disarming smile.

A range of expressions flickers over Chicken's face like a pinball machine as the ball of thought bounces around.

'The public sector. There's too bloody much of it, Freebie.'

'Oh yeah?'

'Civil servants. Bureaucrats. Planners. Social workers. Town hall busybodies. Pen-pushers. Clip-counters. Thumb-twiddlers . . .' His face glows and quivers as the score mounts.

'What about schoolteachers, dinner ladies, professors . . .?'

'They're not productive. They don't produce wealth, like you and me.'

'Me?'

'Exactly. We pay for it all. And their bloody pensions.'

'I learned maths –'

'Exactly. Why should I pay for somebody else's kids to go to university? Let them pay for it themselves.'

'Doctors and nurses . . .?'

'Don't knock nurses, Freebie. I won't have anything said against nurses. Angels.' His voice thickens. His eyes have gone misty. 'When our son Willy was in hospital . . .'

'Angels. Well said, Chief Ken!' Toby's voice quivers with phoney empathy. Shameless.

'I think biggest problem in this country is too much taxes,' says Maroushka, twirling round in her chair. 'In my country nobody pay tax. Is voluntary. Only pay pensioners and persons too unintelligent to avoid.'

She looks so lovely in a tight tailored sea-grey dress, Serge wonders whether it's worth trying to convert her to a more enlightened view, in anticipation of a possible meeting with his parents, but she has that don't-argue-with-me look about her. Anyway, who in their right mind argues for higher taxes?

Chicken turns, eating her up with his eyes.

'Too right, Mary. Disincentive. If it goes up any more, I'll just give up working altogether. Be a layabout. Sign on the dole.' He chuckles. 'Trouble is, there's a lot of ignorant bureaucrats who don't understand City bonuses, think they can be regulated. Like that prick Adair Turner from the FSA saying most of what we do is socially useless. I'd like to give his bollocks a nip! Grrr!' He twists his head sideways and snaps his white pointy teeth. 'We're the main growth industry in this country. We create wealth. We give employment to thousands. Our employees pay taxes. What's not socially useful?'

Serge keeps quiet, for something similar has occasionally crossed his mind. Wasn't Doro recently ranting in the same vein? Something to do with dog shit. Though, when you think about it, lots of quite nice things are socially useless – banoffee pie, perfume, shoulder pads, mooching, to name but a few.

'Talking about contributing to society,' Chicken glances at his Rolex and rises to his feet, 'I've got another meeting to attend. At Number Eleven.'

At lunchtime Maroushka grabs her matching sea-grey jacket and vanishes before he can follow her. He can't face the cafeteria, so he walks down to Franco's, half hoping Jonas will be there, but only the sulky bar girl is on duty. The food at Franco's is Italian, classy, served in small pretentious arrangements on outsize square plates. Running his eye down the menu he feels a massive hankering for a Barnsley chop served with chips and Daddies sauce. But he settles for agnolotti alla zucca, seats himself in a corner, takes his phone out of his pocket and calls his broker.

He still has open positions on several holdings, and the market's dipped below 4,000. It dropped 315 points yesterday, its biggest tumble in five years. He buys back half of his Endon holding, which he reckons has probably fallen about as far as it's going to, but extends

Edenthorpe Engineering, in anticipation of further falls. Then he orders a double espresso.

While he's waiting, his phone rings in his hand. It's Clara. He jabs the red Off button, but it rings again, and he surrenders to the inevitable.

'Hi, Claz. Good to hear from you. How's things?'

'At last. Listen, you little ferret-fucker, I've been talking to Babs. She says you're not in Cambridge at all.'

'I . . . I've been working with a team at Imperial College –'

'Don't dig yourself in deeper, Soz. Just listen. Out of the goodness of my heart, I'm going to give you till the end of next week to tell Doro and Marcus yourself. You've been conning them all along, haven't you?'

The worst thing is the undisguised glee in her voice.

'It's not how it seems, Claz. Sheesh!'

'Don't you sheesh me, hamster-killer. What are you?'

'Okay! Okay. I'll tell them myself.'

He fumbles for the Off button, but before he can switch off it rings again. It's Doro.

'Hi, Mum. Good to hear from you. How's the frozen North?' He plays for time.

'Everything's fine up here. It's nice to talk to you at last, darling. You've been so elusive. How are things?'

'Good. I'm good. Mum –'

'Have you heard from Clara?'

'Yes, she just rang. The thing is, Mum –'

'I'm so glad. She was worried that she couldn't get in touch with you.'

'Mm. We had a good chat.'

'Lovely. And how's the PhD going?'

'Fine. Good. The thing is, I've got something –'

'I'm so proud of you, darling. Doing all that cutting-edge research. For the advancement of human knowledge. It's sad that so many young people nowadays only think about making money. You know, when we were young in the sixties, we thought that if you had ability and education you should see it as an opportunity to help others less able than yourself. Believe it or not, people wanted to use their skills for the betterment of humanity. I suppose it seems old-fashioned to your generation. Nowadays, people who have brains just see it as a licence to fleece others. Look at Marcus, he's so brainy, but he never for one moment . . .'

She prattles on like that. At the end of ten minutes, Serge feels emotionally drained.

'Are you still working down in London on that project?' she asks abruptly.

'Er . . . yes . . . no . . . not exactly.'

'So you're back in Cambridge?'

'Yes. I mean . . . not completely. The thing is, Mum –'

'That's wonderful, because Oolie and I are planning a little outing. We thought we'd come and spend a day with you in Cambridge. What about next weekend?'

DORO: The spider

Oolie is excited about their trip to Cambridge at the weekend, but Doro is more excited about her trip to the allotment this afternoon.

It's been raining all morning, but now the sun is out, beaming gold between clumpy cloud towers massed overhead. The rain has chased the other gardeners away, and it looks like they have the place to themselves. The insects have gone too, but the birds are back, tapping and pecking impatiently at the fruit, knocking it to the ground, rustling droplets off leaves, beaking at the moist earth, gorging on worms that have wriggled to the surface, poking and pulling, scarcely bothering to flap away as Doro and Malcolm Loxley thread their way once more between the vegetable beds and fruit trees that are already bowed with ripening apples, plums and pears.

He's wearing a white shirt and grey trousers, and carrying a briefcase. She's wearing a flared skirt and a silky top, cut low to reveal the deep V between her breasts created by the wired and padded up-push of the black lacy bra she bought at Marks & Spencer. She looks down and sees the tops of her breasts wobbling as she walks. Has he noticed too? He shows no sign.

At the seats by the communal water tap, he sits down and opens his briefcase. 'I thought you might be interested to see these.'

He passes Doro a bunch of papers which she studies attentively to conceal her embarrassment at having misread his intentions. They are the minutes of a council sub-committee meeting about the allotments, in which Councillor Loxley is on record as urging a moratorium on the development and a full review. Looks like he really did want to discuss the development, after all.

'So you're supporting us? Was it the beans that did the trick, or the rhubarb?'

He smiles. 'I'm open to all possibilities.'

'What possibilities?'

'We could reach an agreement with the developers to use part of the site for a retail park –'

'What do we need a retail park for? Half the shops in the city centre are empty as it is.'

'It'd give the city a boost. Create jobs. And there're grants available for environmentally sensitive development –'

'You think pouring cement over this would be environmentally sensitive?' She knows she should stop interrupting him, but the words just keep tumbling out.

'Depends how it's done. Part of the site could be dedicated to a socially valuable utility such as a nursery school, a doctors' surgery or – and this would be my favoured option, Mrs Marchmont –' he smirks at her like a card player who's just about to pull a trump '– a sheltered housing facility for the learning disabled.'

She winces, and covers it with a smile. If only some of the other GAGAs were around to back her up. Ah, here comes someone! It's Winston Robinson walking up the path with two bulging carrier bags in his hands.

'Hi, Winston. Come and join us! We're just discussing the development plans for the allotment.'

But Winston shakes his head. 'Gotta get home to the wife, else I be in trouble. Just come to pick me some plums before the rain knocks them down.' He digs into the bags and pulls out a large handful of ripe Victorias. 'Here. Plenty more where these come from. Tree gone berserk! Help yourself.' He hurries off.

She drops a few plums in her bag, and one into her mouth. The juice dribbles down her chin. The councillor takes a bite out of a ripe plum, and stows a couple more in his briefcase.

'They get everywhere, don't they?'

'Plums?'

'Our coloured brethren.'

The shock of his words hits her like a splash of cold water.

'He's very nice,' she retorts, aware of the lameness of her answer.

Most of the GAGAs have long ceased to notice that Winston is their only black member. What shocked her most was the unguardedness of his speech, his casual assumption that she'd agree. She sees him flush as he realises his mistake.

'Oh yes, indeed. Many of them are. Don't get me wrong.'

'He's not one of them, he's one of us.'

For the first time, his eyes rest on the deep V between the wobbling bulges of her breasts. She feels herself blush, wishing they were more hidden and less wobbly. She can't understand what came over her that night as she lay beside her sleeping husband, what niggling little demon had urged her to go out dressed up like this.

Suddenly a large drop of water splats on her bare forearm. A thunderclap follows, and a gust of wind snatches the papers from her hand. As she grabs for the flying documents the heavens open, and huge soft raindrops drench them like a tepid shower. She races down the slippery paths towards her own allotment hut, fumbling in her bag for her bunch of keys. He follows, skids on a patch of mud, slips over and, as he hits the ground, his briefcase bursts open. He rights himself and flails around, catching at the contents which have spilled out over the claggy soil. She dashes to help him, scrabbling among wet gooseberry bushes to pick up the damp papers, pens, rulers, tissues, fruit pastilles, rubber bands, Winston's plums, and a small foil-wrapped item which she realises as she hands it over is a condom.

'Here.' She can feel the heat spreading through her cheeks.

'Thanks.' Avoiding her eyes, he slips it into his pocket.

'You'd better come in!' She pushes the hut door open, flicking wet hair out of her eyes. Rivulets of water run into the V between her breasts. He follows, shaking himself like a dog, brushing against her in the narrow space, an intruder invading her little domain.

The allotment hut is small and fusty, but dry. The shelves are piled with packets of seed, balls of string, gardening gloves, secateurs, trowels and hand forks, sticks, plant labels, catalogues, plastic ties, tubs, jam jars and tins of fertiliser, slug pellets, rooting powder, liquid manure, weed killer and other substances no longer in their original containers. She's forgotten what they are, but if she could remember she's sure they'd come in handy. Stashed in the corner are the larger tools: fork, shears, loppers, spades, a rake. On the other side is a small cobwebby window and in front of it two canvas chairs and a folding table, where she and Oolie chat over cups of tea. She wishes she was here with Oolie, and not with him.

There is a carpet off-cut on the floor, but it is slightly damp. There is a primus stove, but it is out of gas. There is a tin of powdered milk, but the lid is lost and the powder has set like concrete. There are mugs, but slugs have crawled all over them. There was a packet of biscuits, but mice have eaten even the crumbs. There are, however, two tea bags.

'We're not very well equipped, as you can see.' She laughs to cover her embarrassment.

He says nothing, studying her.

She wishes she'd worn a different top – a T-shirt with a slogan that would spark conversation and conceal her breasts, which are heaving, bodice-ripper-style, beneath the clinging silky fabric, from panic, exertion, excitement or a terrifying mixture of all three. She thinks about the anticipation with which she tried on the bra in the shop, and realises she's made a terrible mistake. How the hell is she going to extricate herself?

'Have a seat.'

She indicates a canvas chair, and lowers herself on to the other one, but he remains standing, blocking out the light from the window with his bulk. The rain is still hammering on the roof and peals of thunder seem to be getting closer. They could be here for quite some time.

'So about this development. You think it might . . .?' she witters, her voice scratching the silence.

'Include a sheltered housing project? Yes.' His eyes are fixed on her.

She shivers. 'But you were talking about a horrible retail park. Here in this lovely place . . .' She gestures vaguely towards the window, where a fat spider is legging along a silken thread towards its dinner, a trapped fly buzzing helplessly in a corner of the web.

The spider pounces. Ah! She jumps. Her sharp intake of breath echoes a ripping sound; the canvas beneath her starts to split and leaping to her feet she barges into him, because he is standing too close beside her in the confined space. He grabs her in his arms and pushes his face towards her; she feels his mouth on hers; she smells his musky aftershave and the feral under-scent of his warm skin. She takes a step back and her foot catches the spikes of the rake; the wooden handle whacks up against her head. Next minute, they're rolling around on the slightly damp carpet piece.

The worst thing is, she realises she has only herself to blame.

She starts to struggle, knocking into the tumbled tubular furniture. 'Don't . . .'

He covers her mouth with his; his weight is crushing.

'C'mon, Dorothy. You know it's what you really want!'

'No! I just wanted to talk about . . .'

His hand is inside her skirt and fumbling upwards. Should she scream? But no one's there to hear. Try to keep him talking.

'. . . the plans . . .'

She must keep her cool and get his mind back on to the development.

'That disabled housing scheme?' She turns her head to free her mouth from his, 'I'd like to discuss –'

'Let's talk about that later.'

He takes her face between his hands and starts to kiss her again. Her head is jammed up against the wooden wall of the shed, and from the corner of her eye she can see the spider who, having finished his lunch, has slithered back up his web and seems to be watching them with interest.

'. . . the retail park . . .'

'This is just between you and me.'

'No! Please! Tell me about the retail park!'

'You know you've been waiting for this.' One hand is up inside her silky top.

'Will there be a Marks & Spencer . . .?'

'C'mon, Dorothy.'

'Or British Home Stores . . .?'

She tries to wrestle, but her movement seems to spur him on.

'Did anyone tell you . . .?'

The other hand is in her knickers.

'Or Sainsbury's!' she screams. 'No! Stop!'

'. . . what a great body you've got . . .?'

Now he's fumbling with his zip.

'. . . for someone of your age?'

'Someone of my . . .?! Yaaagh!'

She kicks out and catches the blade of a spade wedged between the prongs of the fork, which is hitched through the pruning loppers. The stack of tools topples down on him. The blade of the pruner catches him on the cheek. Blood spouts and trickles down his jaw to the corner of his mouth, giving him a vampire grin. If only she could plunge a stake through his heart. Where did she put the secateurs?

A quick movement by the window catches her eye – the spider scuttling down his webby trap. And beyond the web, beyond the window, a face, familiar, fleetingly glimpsed – whose face? She freezes.

'Oolie!'

'What's the matter?' He sits up abruptly. 'I thought you wanted . . .' The blood dribbles down his chin on to his shirt.

She passes him a tissue from her bag. 'I think you'd better go.'

He scrambles to his feet and straightens his clothes. Doro hitches up her top, hitches down her skirt, and opens the door of the hut. It's still raining, but not so heavily now. There's no sign of anyone at all outside.

'Goodbye, Mrs Marchmont,' he says.

His eyes are flinty. His voice is steely. A dribble of blood is still running down his face. He picks up his briefcase.

'I'll remember your enthusiasm for Marks & Spencer.'

He slithers away over the slimy ground.

Doro waits until he's out of sight, then she slumps down on the remaining canvas chair and wishes there was some gas in the primus. She could murder a cup of tea. Surely, even if her intentions were a bit out of order this morning, surely she has the right to change her mind, once she realises he's a man besotted with retail parks; a man bothered by the colour of people's skin; a man who says she's attractive *for someone of her age*?!

The fleeting image of Oolie's sweet face at the window must have been a vision, sent to save her. The spider has vanished from his web, gone creepabout, but looking out through the dusty glass she sees someone else striding across the allotment, head bowed against the rain. Someone with round glasses and brown overalls and – oh bliss! – he's carrying two cups of tea in his hands.

'Oh, thank you, Mr Philpott! How did you know . . .?'

'I saw you with that councillor. Everything all right?'

'Yes. Fine. I mean –' how much has he witnessed? she wonders '– not really because they want to use half the allotment for a retail park, and half for some social housing project.'

He sighs. 'There's something rotten in the state of Donny!'

'Yes. Quite. I tried to stop him but . . .'

She hopes this will explain her dishevelled appearance, and any rolling on the floor he may have noticed. It just goes to show, you're never as alone as you think on an allotment.

CLARA: *Umpy fashional*

'Oolie, you really mustn't make a habit of this.'

Oolie-Anna sidles into Clara's classroom and sits down opposite her at the teacher's desk, fingering a box of coloured crayons.

'I wanna talk to you.'

'About films again?' Clara sighs.

It's just turned four o'clock, the kids have all gone, and in this quiet breathing space at the end of the day, she's replaying her lessons in her mind, reflecting on what went well and what she could have done better.

'Not filums.' Oolie points towards the window. 'Did it come back?'

It takes Clara a moment to realise that she's talking about the hamster. It's odd, but sometimes she thinks she does see signs of his presence – little black crumbs which could be hamster pooh in the book corner, shreds of paper, crumbs of crisps and sandwiches mysteriously cleaned up. She wonders whether Oolie has a confession to make.

'Did you come to talk about the hamster?'

'Not t'ampster.' Oolie shakes her head again. 'It's about Mum.'

'So what's she done now?'

Clara feels a stab of impatience. Really, Doro and Oolie are both impossible in their own ways. Her dad must be a saint to put up with them.

'She's been shaggin' that man.'

Clara catches her breath and tries to keep her voice calm. 'What man?'

'You know. *'Im*.'

'I don't know. Anyway, how do you know who she's been shagging?'

Oolie's vocabulary has got racier since she's been working at Edenthorpe's, but it's not clear how much she actually understands.

'I seed 'em. Up at t'allotment. Dad said I 'ad to get Mum, and she worrent in't garden, so I went up to t'allotment.'

'Oolie, you're making this up.'

'No, I told you, I *seed* 'em.'

'What did you see?'

'I seed 'em shaggin'. On t' flooer.'

'When?'

'*I* dunno.' She pouts mardily, annoyed at being disbelieved. 'It was rainin' and they was at it. In t' 'ut.'

'Who was the man?'

'You know – 'im wi' grey hair.'

Clara does a mental check of all the grey-haired men she knows. There's probably some perfectly simple explanation.

'Are you sure it wasn't Dad?'

'Course I'm sure. I'm not daft, y'know.'

'I know you're not, Oolie.' She recognises her sister's sensitivities. 'Was it Mr Philpott? You know, the man who helped us try and catch the hamster last time you were here?'

She knows Mr Philpott also has an allotment up there. But shagging her mum? Mind you, she wouldn't put anything past Doro these days.

'No, it worrent 'im. It wor t' tall one.'

'What tall one? Have you seen him before?'

'I seed 'im at your school.'

Clara's mind flashes back to the previous occasions when Oolie came to her school.

'The head teacher – the one with the hamster?'

'No, but I wun't mind shaggin' 'im. No. You know. *That day.* Wi' all't potty plants.'

She must mean Community Day in September. Oh, the chaos!

'You mean the councillor?'

'I dunno if he's consular or what.' She shrugs.

'Oolie, try to remember.'

'I *do* remember. I just don't know 'is name.'

Clara finds her heart is beating too fast. She doesn't quite believe her sister, but she doesn't altogether disbelieve her, either.

'What were they doing?'

'I told you, they was shaggin'. On t' flooer. He were on top of 'er.' Oolie slumps back in the chair grumpily, exhausted with the effort of so much verbalisation.

'Okay, Oolie.' Clara kneels beside the child-sized chair and puts her arm around her. 'Thanks for telling me. You've done really well to remember all that.'

Oolie beams. 'I runned all the way back. I got reyt wet.'

'Come on. I'll take you home.'

Just as Clara pulls into the drive at Hardwick Avenue, the front door opens, and a young man with fair hair bursts out into the porch. Behind him the door shuts with a slam. He stands there looking nonplussed, grasping a sheaf of papers and fumbling to open his briefcase, at the same time as he tries to wrestle himself into his jacket.

Oolie runs up and gives him a hug.

The papers slither out of his hands on to the ground, where a gust of wind catches them and scatters them over the garden. Clara gathers them up and hands them over, thinking, why does he have that pathetic little beard?

'Hi, I'm Clara. I'm Oolie's sister. Do you two know each other?'

'It's Mr Clemmins. Him what said I gotter 'ave me own flat and watch filums.'

'Mike Clements.' He stretches out his hand for Clara to shake. It's firm, hot and sweaty. When she doesn't say anything, he adds, 'I think I might have got on the wrong side of your mother.'

Clara and Oolie exchange glances.

Clara says, 'That can happen.'

Then the door opens again and Doro sticks her head out.

'What's going on? Oolie? Clara? What are you doing?' She turns on the young man. 'You still here? Why don't you clear off? And take your bloody tick-boxes with you!'

Oolie whispers to Clara, in a voice loud enough for everybody to hear, 'Mum don't like him. She says he's umpy fashional.'

'That's enough, Oolie,' says Doro.

'Let's just say I've been tested to my limits,' says Mr Clements, stuffing the flyaway papers into his briefcase and legging it down the drive.

Shame about the beard, thinks Clara.

SERGE: The bridges over the River Cam

On the last Saturday in October, Serge strolls around the cloister of his old college, trying to summon up waves of nostalgia, but all he feels is an intense anxiety kettling him in. He's holding a carrier bag of letters he picked up from the Porters' Lodge a minute ago. They're mostly from his bank. They're mostly addressed to Dr Black, Queens' College Cluedo Society. The only one he's opened so far asks him to contact his branch immediately. He doesn't bother to open the others, and tries to push the thought of their contents to the back of his mind for the moment.

Just before one o'clock, he positions himself in front of the Queens' College gatehouse and looks out down Silver Street. Here they come, ambling along hand in hand, Doro smiling and giving a running commentary on the buildings and people they pass, Oolie doing a little skip on every third step. What the fuck is Doro wearing? He can't believe it. Dayglo pink circa 1990. With pointed lapels. Jeezus. Oolie's not much better, in a white Puffa jacket that makes her look like a Michelin lady, but at least she probably has the excuse that Doro chose it.

As soon as she spots him, she lets go of Doro's hand, and runs up to hug him.

'Hiya, Sausage.'

'Hi, Oolie. Hi, Mum.'

Hugs all round. Simple happy hugs. Tears prick his eyes. If only he could dump his burdensome secret. If only he didn't have the letters in the carrier bag, which he's doomed to lug around like a ball and chain on his heart. If only he could be a part of their simple happy world.

'Shall we go and get a punt?'

'Aren't you going to take us up to your room, Serge? Oolie's longing to see your room.'

'No, not at the moment. It's not very convenient. You see –' he lowers his voice to a whisper, he's prepared this '– a friend of mine, she's in an all-women's college, and she's met the love of her life, at least, she thinks he's the love of her life, but she can't take him back to her room because men aren't allowed. So I said she could use my room. Seeing as I'll be out all afternoon. You know,' he smiles disarmingly, 'the course of true love . . .'

Doro smiles sympathetically. 'You'd have thought they'd have got rid of those archaic paternalistic rules by now.'

'Are they shagging?' asks Oolie.

Scudamore's punt hire is just around the corner. He gets into the punt first, stows his carrier bag under the seat, and helps Oolie in. She jumps heavily, making the boat rock.

Doro shrieks.

The young man from Scudamore's says, 'Don't worry. They're very stable. Seldom capsize.'

Serge stands at one end wielding the pole. It's ages since he did this, but once you get into the rhythm it's not that difficult. It helps to be tall and to have a torso that ripples under a tight T-shirt but, despite having neither of these, the two women in his punt are looking at him adoringly. He pushes off – swoosh!

It's one of those perfect October days, sunny and clear, with golden leaves floating along the black water and late tourists clustering on the bridges like birds preparing for their winter migration. The air is crisp and cold, but he's already worked up a sweat as he manoeuvres their way under the Mathematical Bridge. His spirits lift as he gives the usual spiel about tangents and radial trusses.

'Actually, it's the main reason I came to Queens' College.'

'I can't see any tangerines,' says Oolie.

'You're so clever, darling,' says Doro.

So far, everything is going swimmingly.

There are still plenty of punts on the river. Between King's College Bridge and Clare Bridge they glide along The Backs, serene lawns stretching down to the river, willows drooping weepily. At last, that tingle of nostalgia.

Oolie trails her hand in the water, which she flicks at Doro from time to time.

'Stop that, Oolie,' says Doro. 'Sit properly, else you'll make the boat tip over. Such a pretty place. What a pity it's the preserve of the privileged few. I wish my students from Doncaster Tech had something like this. I've always believed beauty is good for the soul. No, put it back in the river, Oolie. It's dead.'

Serge is only half listening. He's concentrating on following the route of the underwater towpath, and keeping his eyes out for rogue punts.

They pass Trinity and approach the Bridge of Sighs, where there's the usual logjam of punts waiting to go through one at a time. Some of these punters are really useless, especially the women, spinning and bumping into each other with little girly shrieks. He stows his pole, and lets the punt drift slowly towards them. Then he spots her, sitting with her back to them, up ahead in the logjam of punts. Bright-yellow jacket and long dark hair. Maroushka! What the fuck's she doing here? And how can he avoid having to introduce her to Doro and Oolie, who would without a shadow of a doubt ruin his chances for ever?

She hasn't seen him yet. He's still got time to turn.

He raises the pole and jabs it hard into the water. The punt stops, jerks and spins sharply to the left, clunking another punt that is just pulling in alongside them. A wave of water pours in, drenching his coat, which he tucked under the seat with the carrier bag. Doro and Oolie are shrieking, clutching on to the sides of the punt, which is still rocking, letting in big splashes on each side that slosh around their feet. He tries to push off, keeping his head down, but all the other occupants of the punts are looking now, laughing. These kinds of collisions are part of the fun of the river. He misjudges, pushes too hard, and they rebound with a judder against the opposite bank, almost tipping into the water. A low-hanging willow sweeps over the prow. There's a sudden splash.

A scream. Another scream.

'Serge! Oolie! She can't swim!'

Doro is pulling off her dayglo pink jacket. In the moment it takes him to work out what's happened, there's another splash at the side of their punt, a dark head pops up, looks around and disappears under the water again. Serge dives in too and swims over to where Oolie is flailing, trying to grab at the willow tree, burbling as she spits out a mouthful of leaves. By the time he reaches her, the other man already has his arm under her, lifting her head out of the water. Oolie's hands are around his neck, pushing him back under as she thrashes about.

'Stop fighting, miss! We've got you!'

Oolie gazes into the deep African eyes of her saviour and goes limp. Between them, with Doro pulling at her legs, they heave her back into the punt. The young man swims back and retrieves their pole.

'D'you want to come in our boat?' asks Oolie, squinting flirtily with her eyes.

He shakes his head, laughing, flicking silver droplets off his tight wet curls, and clambers back into his own punt.

'Is everybody all right?' asks the young Asian woman in the yellow jacket.

Fifteen minutes later, they are disembarking at Scudamore's pontoon, Oolie squeezing the water out of her Puffa, Serge dripping and shivering, Doro trying to wrap her dayglo pink jacket around him.

'Let's go back to your room and have a nice cup of tea and warm up.'

'The thing is, Mum –'

'Don't tell me they're still at it! We've been gone nearly two hours.'

'I know, but you see –'

''E were reyt gorgeous, that nigger. I wouldn't mind shaggin' 'im,' says Oolie.

'Oolie, will you please stop using that word!'

'I thought we could drop in on Otto,' says Serge, improvising desperately. 'He's got a flat near here. I told him you were coming to Cambridge. He'll be thrilled.'

He tries to remember where Otto said their flat was. Mill Road somewhere. It must be one of those flats above the shops.

'Are you sure, darling? We'll ruin his carpet.'

'Put it this way, Mum, he'd be really upset if he knew you were in Cambridge and didn't go and see him.'

'Really?'

'Otto! Otto! I want to see Otto!' Oolie chants, clapping her hands.

'His girlfriend's pregnant. They'll be having a baby soon.'

'Babbie! I want to see t' babbie!'

'It's not been born yet. At least, I don't think so.'

When did Otto say it was due?

As they talk, he's already leading them away from Queens', up Silver Street, past Emmanuel, through Parker's Piece, slimy with trodden leaves, and on to busy Mill Road. Did Otto say their flat was above a café or a travel agent? Mill Road is much longer than he remembers it. It's almost five o'clock by now; the sky is clear and cold, the pavements are bustling and the street beginning to snarl up with traffic puffing out exhaust fumes that vaporise in the chilled air. There's something missing, though. He had a carrier bag before. Shit, he must have left it under the seat of the punt. Hopefully it'll still be there later.

What time do Scudamore's close? Or should he turn back now?

'Are we nearly there?' Oolie's teeth are chattering.

'Nearly.'

They stop in front of the parade of shops near the turning to the cemetery. There's no travel agent, but several cafés. Serge pulls his mobile phone out of his jeans pocket, but it's wet through and won't even switch on.

At that moment, a minicab draws up a little way ahead, and toots its horn.

Serge goes over to the driver and taps on the window. 'Excuse me, mate . . .'

The cab driver ignores him, and gets out on the other side, to open the door for a couple who have just appeared on the pavement. The woman is heavily pregnant, clutching her belly. The man is Otto.

'Hi, Otto!' In an instant Doro has her arms around him. 'How lovely to see you after all these years. You're looking so well. So tall! What are you up to these days?'

'Er . . .' Otto's eyes swivel.

Oolie has her arms around Molly, whom she's never met before. 'Can I see your babbie?'

Serge catches Otto's eye. 'I can explain. If we could just come up to your flat for a minute . . .?'

Otto looks like he's on the edge of a serious panic.

'Yeah, man, like we have to go to hospital right now?'

'I thought you said six weeks . . .'

'Yeah, but Molly's waters have broken?'

'I were in't water!' Oolie cries. 'It were brilliant. I were saved by this 'unk!'

'You'd better get going! How exciting for you!' cries Doro as Otto and Molly extricate themselves and clamber into the taxi. 'Good luck! Good luck!' She blows kisses with two hands as the taxi pulls away and joins the crawl of rush-hour traffic.

'We'll come back very soon to see the baby!'

CLARA: *Scarper*

On Sunday night, Clara phones Doro and tries to wheedle out the truth behind Oolie's tale of sex on the allotment. But Doro at once hijacks the conversation with a rambling account of a visit to Cambridge, and it's only after ten minutes that Clara realises something weird is going on: how could Doro visit Serge in Cambridge if, as Babs said, he was living in London?

'Cambridge? You were in Cambridge?'

'That's what I said. Haven't you been listening, Clara?'

'So you visited Serge's room?'

'Not exactly. He said someone was using it, a girl. We called on Otto, but . . .'

'Mhm,' says Clara, thinking she must drop Babs another line, and see whether she has an address or phone number for Otto. 'So did he say anything about getting a new job?'

'For goodness' sake, Clara. What is this? The Inquisition? He's still trying to finish his PhD, darling. I know it's been going on for ages, but I think he's almost there.'

'Mhm.'

Why has her mother been so grumpy recently? Surely she must be well past the menopause by now.

She could so easily, now, let slip casually into the conversation what Babs told her about Serge. But she holds back. It would be mean and snitchy, and against the spirit of Solidarity Hall. She doesn't want to be that kind of person. And although Serge's refusal to accept responsibility is annoying, he's still her little brother, and she realises that in some weird way she still feels protective towards him.

A flash of memory brings back an image from long ago: they're all standing in the garden, Serge in his pyjama bottoms, Otto wrapped in his crocheted blanket and baby Star in her saggy nappy, all whimpering and sobbing as they survey the bloodied and mangled corpses of their twenty-six rabbits.

'It's only a fox,' she says, trying to sound calm and grown-up, trying to keep down the scream that is building up in her own throat. 'C'mon. We mustn't be late for school.'

Recalling the night of the rabbit massacre makes her shudder even after all these years – the dreadful feeling of responsibility compounded with helplessness still haunts her in moments of stress. She didn't hear the commotion that night – she was sleeping in the front attic – but she came down first in the morning and saw the remains of the carnage all over the garden.

And buried in the back of her mind is another of the unresolved mysteries of her childhood, something Serge told her that day that stuck in her mind.

He said Megan was down there in the darkness of the garden, yelling at the fox, 'Get away wi' you!'

And someone else, a man, had shouted, 'Scarper!'

That word – a familiar word, from her childhood.

An old-fashioned word, very English, not a word an Italian would know.

So *who* was it?

Because after Mrs Wiseman taught them the Facts of Life at school, she'd counted the weeks, and she worked out it was exactly nine months after the night of the rabbit massacre that Oolie-Anna was born.

SERGE: *Vilification*

Serge opens his eyes and tries to blank out the ghost rabbit, but it's still there at the foot of his bed. He's been dreaming that dream again. The ghost rabbit digs silently, tunnelling with its horrible sharp claws. What's it looking for? Something lost. Then he remembers – the carrier bag of correspondence from his bank, which he left in the Scudamore's punt on Saturday. He phoned, of course, but the dozy guy on the other end of the line knew nothing, and obviously wasn't prepared to go and look.

'Maybe it fell in the river.'

Maybe it did, but there's no harm in checking, is there, wasteboy?

He frets as he pulls on his clothes, wondering what he should do now. Certainly, visiting his local bank branch, as advised in the one letter he opened, is not an option.

There are losses and losses. On the early radio news, someone from the Bank of England is announcing that the world's financial institutions have lost $2.8 trillion since the summer of 2008. It leaves him cold.

As often, after that dream, he's left feeling disoriented, as if the world is slightly off-kilter, but nobody's noticed, or else they're all pretending everything's normal. Look at the politicians. Alistair Darling and Gordon Brown have been ratcheting up the anti-banker rhetoric, it's the sort of thing that really gets Marcus and Doro going, but it's completely meaningless. They talk as if they still have some power in relation to the City, when everybody in the City knows they've lost it. There was a point last year when they could have acted, put some regulations in place, enforced transparency, but they bottled out, and now the banks have got the bailout money, why should they behave any different? It's the ultimate risk-free gamble. If they win, they keep the takings – and if they lose, Mr Taxpayer will pick up the tab. There's no point moaning about it. It's not their fault. It's just what they do, like rabbits breeding.

*

Chicken has a good line on this.

'You know what's wrong with this country? The whole country depends on banking, but they don't like bankers. Ha! It's the politics of envy gone mad.' Serge overhears him chuntering to Toby and Lucian at the next desk. 'They think there's a better way of banking. More ethical. Lower bonuses. What would happen if they tried to make us cut our bonuses? See, we're just as trapped by the system as they are.'

'Interesting point, Chief Ken,' smarms Toby, 'but will they actually *do* anything?'

'No chance.' Chicken flashes his predator teeth. 'Because if they try, we'll all up sticks and move to Singapore, won't we?'

'Course we will,' Toby nods. 'Or Liechtenstein.'

'See, the boys at Barclays've got the right idea. Don't accept the bloody bailout money. That way, the Government can't stop their executive bonuses. They've raised the money they need in the Middle East at 14 per cent, no strings attached.'

'Isn't the Treasury deal only 10 per cent?' asks Lucie naively.

'It's all tax deductible. Let the taxpayers take the hit. Let the pension funds take the hit. That'll teach them to bloody interfere.'

'Isn't that a bit . . . sort of . . . unethical?'

Chicken throws back his head, clucking with delight.

'Banks don't have ethics, Lucie, they have cost centres. What do you think, Maroushka?'

Maroushka has just come in with a coffee from the cafeteria and is heading towards her desk. She's wearing red today, not shouty London bus red, but a deep, subtle, rosy red that swirls around her knees as she walks.

'What I think about what?'

'The vilification of bankers in the media. Has it gone too far?'

'What is mean vilifiction?'

'You know, the way they run them down.'

'Run down with car?' A tremor of emotion crosses her face.

Chicken chortles. 'No, just with words.'

'Words!' She shrugs. 'In my country exist nothing only words! Car is better.'

★

As she logs into her computer, Chicken's shiny predator eyes are fixed on her hungrily. Serge feels a lurch of despondency. So that's it – Tootie the Terrible will be elevated to the swivel chair, and Maroushka will be elevated to the soft off-white aptly named shag-pile rug on Chicken's office floor. They say Chicken has shagged most of the female staff at FATCA, so there's a certain inevitability to it.

And what will happen to him? Yes, the visit to Cambridge did set him dreaming. All that silence and old stone. Golden light. His splashy afternoon with Doro and Oolie on the river. And Otto and Molly, with their new baby. Coochie-coochie-dribble-dribble-bluh-bluh-bluh. Maybe it's time for him to settle down too. He must remember to give them a call. Buy them a nice present. Something expensive and useless that they'd never get for themselves.

He keeps his head down and musters some equations, waiting for Chicken to go away so he can sneak into the disabled loo with his phone, but next time he looks up, Maroushka and Chicken are in the glass-walled office poring over some printouts. He can't hear what they're saying, but he can see her giggle, and Chicken's leery smile. Doesn't she realise this guy is just after her body?

Hear the song of Serge!
This Chicken is a scourge . . .

He isn't going to give her babies and lasting love. Or maybe she realises, but doesn't know how to tactfully put him off. Girls are sometimes scared to assert themselves. Chivalrous thoughts spring into his head. For the first time, he feels a stab of something resembling hatred for Chicken, his inane opinions, his lack of irony, his sheer animal physicality.

Over in the Currencies corner there's a sudden roar of voices. Something big has obviously happened on the markets. He glances up at the Bloomberg screen. The Icelandic government has just hiked interest rates to an incredible 18 per cent. Waves of frenzy roar around the hall as the traders race to cash in. The whole world's gone mad. Even Chicken has come out on to the centre of the trading floor, and is standing there with his arms spread wide, his face lit up with inner joy, like a saint waiting to be whisked up into heaven.

On his way towards the exit, he stops for a moment by Serge's desk.

'Can you pop up to my office at four o'clock, Freebie? Something we need to discuss.'

DORO: Woolies

On Tuesday afternoon, while Oolie is at college, Doro catches the bus into the city centre, and makes her way to Marks & Spencer. Despite the rain outside, the store is almost empty, and even the few people wandering around seem to be more browsing than buying. She hurries past the underwear display without so much as turning her head. In her bag is the new underwired cream bra, the one she hasn't worn yet, and the receipt.

'It isn't very comfortable.' She hands the bra to the shop assistant. 'I'd like a refund.'

What she doesn't say, because it would be too humiliating, is that she was wearing the black satin bra last night when she was undressing, and Marcus had stared at her long and thoughtfully and said, 'Keynes believed that this latest stage of capitalism, characterised by financialisation of the economy, represents the domination of speculation over enterprise.'

In other words, he didn't even bloody notice.

Afterwards, she makes her way to Woolworths to buy a new mop. She's learned her lesson: housework is more appropriate for a woman of her age than flashy underwear.

'Cash or card?'

The shop assistant is a middle-aged woman with stiff yellow hair standing up from her head like sprayed-on insulation foam. She takes the card and inserts it into the machine while Doro watches. Something about her is very familiar. She looks up and meets Doro's eyes, stares, and breaks into a hesitant smile.

'Aren't you her that used to live in t' old Coal Board offices?'

Doro nods, puzzled. 'I know I know you, but . . .'

'Janey Darkins. Askern soup kitchen. Remember?'

'I remember!' laughs Doro. 'Such a long time ago. You must have thought we were all bonkers.'

'Just a bit.' Janey smiles. Her teeth are perfect, and far too white.

'We thought there was going to be a revolution.'

'Aye, so we gathered.'

'And you embodied the revolutionary aspirations of the working class.'

'By 'eck! We only wanted to keep the pits open, and save the lads' jobs.'

She pauses, and her face shows its age beneath the yellow styrofoam hair.

'But you were there when we needed you, duck. Remember when Maggie called us t' enemy within?'

'I remember that.'

'It were only nutters like you that stuck up for us. There's never no shortage of folks to shout for them wi't money on their side.'

'What happened to you after they shut the pit?' asks Doro.

'Jimmy and me split up. But it weren't all bad. I went to college and got me O levels. It were because of that Italian bloke – Bruno. He lived at your place, didn't he? He taught us a thing or two. Not just about spaghetti, neither.'

'I didn't know you and Bruno had a thing going.'

'I still get a letter from him now and again. He's married now.'

She fumbles beneath the counter and pulls out a photograph of a family: two girls, not yet in their teens, a pretty dark-haired woman in a pink dress, and Bruno, older, greyer, hairier, somehow sadder, but still heartbreakingly gorgeous. Seeing the photo she feels a stab of envy, not just towards the woman in the pink dress, but towards Janey, who at least got a photo from him. Against all reason and all experience, she had felt in her heart that he really belonged to her.

'Did you know Megan? Megan Cromer?'

'You mean Megan Risborough?'

'She said she was called Megan Cromer.'

'She were always a fibber. Her and her scab husband.'

'Bruno said her husband used to beat her up.'

'I'd have beat her up mysen if I could've got me hands on her.'

Doro laughs, wishing she could be as free of guilt and political correctness.

'But there was always something a bit sad about her. The way she had all those cuddly toys on her bed. The way she left her son to be looked after by her mum. As if she'd never quite grown up. Even the way she lied about her name. Like she wanted to be someone else.'

'She fibbed about a lot of things. She put it about that Bruno were the dad of that kid she had – the little mongol girl.'

'You mean . . .?'

'Couldn't have been, duck. I know, because he were with *me*. Look at the dates. Any road, you can ask her yoursen. She's back in town. Living up Elmfield. Spends all her time looking after her grandson. She's been in here once or twice.'

'I remember the day Bruno brought her back to the house.'

Janey chuckles. 'He spread himself about a bit, din't he? Mind, he weren't the only one.'

An urgent thought pushes into Doro's mind. 'Did you know about the fire?'

'There was talk about it at the time. Wasn't it some lads from the Prospects?'

'Is there gooin' to be any service around 'ere today, or are you two lasses set for gabbin' till closin' time?'

An elderly gent in a peaked cap, with thick glasses and a conspicuous hearing aid, is holding out a pair of green satin boxer shorts. Behind him, two impatient shoppers have formed a queue.

'Sorry – we haven't seen each other for ages. We're catching up on twenty years' worth of gossip.'

'Aye, we could all hear,' says a brisk woman in a too-tight skirt, next in line. 'My advice is, take up lesbianism, duck. Or be a nun.'

'Or both,' the old gent adds.

'Give them here, love.' Janey takes the satin boxer shorts. 'Are you buying them or returning them?'

'What d'you reckon?' he chortles.

'Get on with it,' snaps the too-tight woman. 'Some of us've got jobs to do.'

'I'll catch you another time,' says Doro to Janey. 'We'll go for a coffee.'

'Can I come too?' asks the old gent.

'Grow up, granddad,' says the woman.

'What happened to June, by the way?' says Doro, pausing to gather her shopping.

'She died,' says Janey. 'And Carl, Megan's boy. Din't you read it in the papers?'

SERGE: Green shoots

'Can I get you a coffee? He'll be over in a minute.'

Noelline, efficiently slinky in pencil skirt and pussycat-bow blouse, ushers Serge into Chicken's office, which occupies a corner of the top floor with huge curved windows facing south and west. He gazes at the wide loop of the river, a red bus crawling over London Bridge, St Paul's dome, and beyond that the endlessly unfolding drama of the sky, where clouds scud around the tops of money towers even taller than FATCA.

Inside, the furniture is all hunky mahogany and manly black leather in the style of an Edwardian gentleman's club. There are hunting prints on the walls, and a rather tacky oil portrait in a gilt frame – it must be Caroline, bleached, tweaked and weighed down by jewellery. He recognises her from the photos he downloaded from the memory stick and . . . where *has* he seen her before? The two non-window walls are lined with bookshelves, packed with rows of identical leather-bound volumes: the complete works of Charles Dickens; the complete works of Sir Walter Scott; the complete works of Anthony Trollope; the complete works of Jeffrey Archer. Obviously Chicken is a bit of an intellectual. On the shelves behind the desk are gilt golfing trophies and framed photographs. Here's one of Chicken with the Gant golfing Apollo. Here are Chicken's kids, William and Arabella, neat and shiny in their school uniforms – Arabella with her dimples, William with his button nose and almond eyes.

'That's Willy Wonka. He's quite a little character.' Chicken has entered the room behind Noelline, who is carrying a tray with a cafetière and two cups. 'Have a seat, Freebie.'

Chicken relaxes into his chair with his back to the window, his legs stretched forward under the desk, watching him with hunting-dog eyes. Serge feels exposed in front of the vast light, as if Chicken can see right into his flaky Zegna-clad impostor soul. His palms are sweating, but fortunately Chicken does not shake his hand. Serge can smell his aftershave – musky, pungent, sinister – it reminds him of . . . He closes his eyes and remembers the scene in the garden on the morning of the rabbit massacre – the smell of the fox. His mind races through vivid worst-case scenarios: they sack him; they call the Fraud Squad; he's publicly humiliated in front of the team, in front of Maroushka.

'My adopted sister –' he can hear his own voice stumbling over the words pathetically, ingratiatingly '– she's like Willy . . .'

In Doro-speak, he's reaching out for their 'common humanity'. But is Chicken human?

'Down's syndrome?' Chicken clucks, suddenly morphing from a Dobermann into a big soft Mother Hen. 'Most people don't know the love – the sheer sunshine they bring into your life. Would you believe it, Freebie, the Nazis tried to gas them? To stop them breeding? Built gas chambers for them, before they started on the Jews. Monstrous!' There's even a glint of a tear in his eye as he says, 'Yes, little Willy's shown us what really matters in life.'

Serge can feel a sniffle coming on too. Shit, they're both sniffling. This is surreal.

'You must be wondering why I've called you up here, Freebie.'

'Yes. Love. The perfect algorithm.' He mumbles disconnected words. His heart is rolling all over the place.

'We're developing another CDO investment. The premise is simple. Housing market recovery.'

'Housing? Recovery?' So – after all that – nothing to do with the 1601 account. Serge's shoulders loosen. He smiles. Phew!

Chicken notices the smile.

'I know what you're thinking, Freebie. But look at it this way. There's a lot of evidence now that the crash of 2007 has gone too far. We're due for a correction. The latest housing data is positive. Everybody's waiting . . . we'll be the first to take it to market. Scoop up all that cash that's out there looking for a better rate of return. We're going to call it the Green Shoots Fund.'

In two minutes, Mother Hen has morphed back into Dobermann.

'Green Shoots. Like an eternal spring with new and brilliant clothes,' Serge says.

Chicken looks at him oddly.

'Maroushka's heading it up, and she's done a great job, no doubt about it. Brilliant girl. We're almost at the rating stage. You know, the usual bundle of debt. Structured in tranches according to risk level. Now, for this to be launched successfully, we need to secure triple A rating for the maximum proportion of tranches. You're with me?'

Serge nods.

'But there's a small problem, Freebie. We have to sell it to the rating agencies in this unhelpful climate.' He leans forward over the desk, studying Serge's face. 'We have to sell it to the rating agencies and . . . in my opinion, Maroushka's not the girl to do it.'

'Why?' A cold dribble of sweat runs down the inside of Serge's shirt. 'Why not?'

'This is strictly in confidence, Freebie, just between you and me, yes?'

Serge feels his heart thump. 'Sure.'

'She's a girl. She's young. She's Ukrainian. She's only here on a student visa. And the way she looks – to a lot of people in the City, someone like that lacks credibility. Gravitas. Don't get me wrong – I have the greatest respect for . . . But you know, achieving a triple A rating is all about confidence. The markets need constant reassurance. Otherwise, panic. What I'm saying is, bright though she is, Maroushka doesn't look like someone who inspires . . .' He pauses in mid-sentence. His birdy eyes swivel. 'You went to Cambridge, didn't you, Freebie? And it's along the same lines as your ABS but with less exposure to buy-to-let. Bigger proportion of straight residential and commercial. New developments. Green shoots. You get my drift?'

Outside the window, a great bank of cumulus is drifting across the sun, and it has the cloudy shifty shape of a crouching rabbit. As he watches, it gets fluffy at the edges, insubstantial – but look, the sun has been swallowed up, and now the cloud itself is changing, bulking up, the rabbit has grown wings, a beak, and great streamers of light are flowing between its claws.

'You mean you want me to . . .?'

'Exactly. We're meeting them on Tuesday week at Canary Wharf, so you've got a fortnight.'

'I'm not sure I . . .'

'Fortune favours the bold, Freebie! Green shoots. Go for it!'

Chicken stands up. Serge stands up too, wondering what exactly he's agreed to.

SERGE: *The correlation skew*

She's clever, this girl. This algorithm she's made – it's beautiful. Clean, simple, economical. She knows what she's doing. She sits beside him, tracing the lines with her scarlet fingertip, explaining, 'I have made improvement to random factor loading model to capture risk specific to super senior tranches.'

He can't fault it.

He told her Chicken wanted her to run it past him, to see whether it needed tweaking. He didn't tell her Chicken wanted him to . . . what exactly does Chicken want him to do? Steal her algorithm and pass it off as his own? Explain to her that she lacks gravitas? If he could suggest improvements, there'd be a case for a working partnership, but apart from tidying up her grammar she doesn't need his help.

It's past ten o'clock, and nearly everyone has gone. There are a few nightbirds squawking over on Commodities. A vacuum cleaner is whining away somewhere. But in the glass-walled office it's quiet. He can almost hear her heart beating.

'It's perfect, Maroushka. A perfect example of modelling single-tranche CDOs in the presence of a skewed correlation curve.'

What he means is – *you're* perfect. The curve of your cheek. The wisp of dark hair straying across your creamy forehead, which is now puckered in a frown of concentration. He holds his breath and slips an arm around her, feeling the warmth of her back, the smallness of her shoulders under the red fabric.

'And I can see you've already developed an appropriate pricing methodology across the different classes of multi-name claims.'

'Also exotic CDOs and CDO2s. Advanced algorithm can price and calibrate multi-name factor models between bespoke and standard indexes portfolios.' She says it with a hesitant giggle, as though afraid of boring him. 'Is good. Yes, Sergei?'

He can smell her perfume. He touches the miracle of her skin.

'Yes. Is good.'

Next moment, their arms are around each other and their mouths are locked together, their tongues like hungry molluscs devouring each other . . . Okay, not molluscs. Her lipstick is smudged like a little kid who's overdosed on red jelly.

'Run away with me, Maroushka.'

She laughs. 'Why you always running away, Sergei? We stay here, make good money.'

'Because you're too good for this world, Princess. Because it's all going to come crashing down.'

'When it crash down we will be rich.'

'We could be happy together.' He pulls her to him, holding her tight in his arms, and kisses her again and again. 'Being rich isn't everything.'

She struggles free from his embrace.

'In my country, Sergei, rich is everything.' Her eyes are blazing. 'In Soviet time, all persons were average. Now we have rich elite. These persons are more intelligent. I also am intelligent. So why not me?'

His spirits sink and melancholy settles over him like a grey fog, damping out any possibility or hope of future joy; for he realises, in this moment of truth, that he will never, ever in a million years be able to take her home to meet Marcus and Doro.

DORO: *Greens not greed!*

Outside the Doncaster Mansion House, on a Monday in November, Marcus and Doro are participating in a colourful pageant of democracy in action. The council meeting is due to start in thirty minutes, and the railings are festooned with banners made of painted sheets – 'KEEP GREENHILLS GREEN!', 'VEGGIEPOWER!', 'REMEMBER DONNYGATE!' – which flap damply in the fitful wind. Sheltering on the top step, in the cover of the doorway, Doro surveys the crowd – almost a hundred, she reckons – and brandishes a placard proclaiming 'GAGA!' above a picture of a cabbage. Down in the street, amidst a forest of home-made placards, the Rossington colliery band, invited by Reggie Hicks, plays 'The Red Flag'. Milling around, trying to sell their newspapers, are the usual suspects – the British League of Trotskyists, Barnsley Anarchist Alliance, Legalise Trepanation, and Pontefract United Liberation Party – who swell their numbers while pursuing their own obscure agendas. A fine drizzle is falling, but their spirits are high.

Reggie has been delegated to address the Council in the chamber, and Ada Fellowes will present their petition with more than 200 signatures (some faked), too late to affect the planning decision. Doro, who suspects it's all a game which they lost long ago, resigns herself to standing on the steps and shouting. It takes her back to the old days of demos and marches, and she's glad she persuaded Marcus to come along – he was reluctant at first, but here he is, standing on the step below, waving his placard and yelling, 'Greens not greed!'

As members of the Council arrive in ones and twos, the crowd jostles forward crying 'GAGA!', 'Legalise now!', 'Out! Out! Out!' She's keeping an eye out for Malcolm Loxley, trying to decide whether to face him boldly or look away and pretend she hasn't seen him.

Suddenly, at the far end of the High Street, a small but very noisy band of demonstrators appears, waving clenched fists and chanting, 'All Power to the Allotments!'

'Who the hell are they?' says Marcus.

She can just see PISSF in large black letters on the red banner, but as they approach she reads Posadist International Socialist Solidarity Front. In one corner is a hammer and sickle. In the other, a flying saucer.

'Er . . . do you recognise the fat guy with a ponytail, holding the banner?'

'Isn't it Chris . . .?'

'. . . Howe!'

He looks sleeker, neater, almost jaunty, despite his paunch.

'Comrades!'

He recognises them in the same instant and, dropping his end of the banner, pushes through the crowd.

'Marcus! Doro! Great to see you. Didn't realise you were still around here!'

Marcus grips him in a bear hug. 'Good to see you, Chris! Have you come to support us?'

'Allotments are the new vanguard of class struggle in deindustrialised Britain, comrade! You know what Posadas said? When extraterrestrial intelligence brings us socialism, it will be embraced first by neo-Narodniks and dolphins. Hi, Doro! Glad to see you're still keeping the faith!' He reaches out and grabs her hand.

Doro responds coolly. She still hasn't altogether forgiven Chris for his part in what happened in 1994. Okay, so he wasn't to know, when he went down to answer the doorbell wearing only a T-shirt, that it would be the police at the door. But surely he should have had the gumption not to shout over his shoulder, 'It's the pigs!'

And when the police pushed past him into the hallway, any sensible person would have gone and put some more clothes on, instead of which he stripped off his T-shirt too, and cried, 'Take me away into the night, fascists!'

Which of course they did.

'Yes, I'm actually one of the allotment gardeners, Chris.' She smiles thinly.

It seems funny in retrospect. In fact, it might have seemed funny at the time, if it hadn't been taken to heart by Oolie's then social worker, who became convinced that Solidarity Hall was a den of paedophilia and satanic ritual abuse, and unleashed a tsunami of investigations that eventually drove the Chrises away.

'Toussie, Kollie . . . do you remember, Doro?'

Two shy tall young people with stringy dyed-black hair, Goth clothes and pierced eyebrows push their way forward and she gives them warm hugs.

'Look how you've grown! What about Chris? Is she with you?'

'Er, Chrissie and I split up,' says Chris. 'This is my new partner, Mara.'

A shy, dark-skinned, stunningly pretty girl, about the same age as Toussaint and Kollontai, glances up at Doro.

'Hi.'

Then she fixes her eyes back on Chris in an adoring gaze.

Looking around the group, Doro realises they're all about that age, and most of them are girls, and most of them are looking at Chris Howe in that moony-eyed way. Oh God! So he finally became a guru.

The guru whips a megaphone from his shoulder bag: 'Comrades! Citizens of Doncaster! Allotment holders of the world!'

Before he has even come to the end of his sentence, the moony-eyed girls start to clap, then the whole gaggle of youngsters bursts into cheers. Doro flinches, takes a step back, and steps on the foot of someone trying to shove through the crowd behind her into the building. She turns – it's Councillor Malcolm Loxley. Their eyes meet.

'I bring you greetings from the radio galaxy of Cygnus!' bellows Chris Howe into his megaphone.

The councillor glances at her placard. His lip curls, ever so slightly. Then he looks right over her head and pushes past her towards the council chamber.

Red with fury, she tries to follow, but an usher bars her way.

Despite the oratory of Reggie Hicks, despite the 200 signatures on the petition, despite the music and the shouting, despite the fight that broke out between the PULP and the BLOT, and the theft of the Posadist megaphone by extremists from the Barnsley Anarchist Alliance, who taunted them – BAA! BAA! – the motion to sell off the allotment site for redevelopment was carried by forty-four votes to eight, plus five abstentions, with the stipulation that part of the site must be used as a sheltered housing facility for 'the learning disabled'.

It's after one o'clock by the time Marcus and Doro get home, feeling tired, and a little hoarse. Doro flings herself on the sofa, wishing she had worn a more comfortable pair of shoes.

'What's for lunch?' says Marcus.

'There's cheese and lettuce. And half a bottle of wine in the fridge.'

'Shall I make a sandwich?' he asks in that hesitant tone that implies he is too incompetent for this important task.

'Take a risk,' she says.

They munch their sandwiches sitting side by side on the sofa, watching the news on TV. The Obama election victory still hogs the headlines. Thirty-seven people have died in Afghanistan, another twenty-five in Iraq. Miriam Makeba has died.

There's nothing at all about their demo, not even on the local news.

'Shame. It was a good turnout,' says Doro, sighing as the food and wine strike their comfort target.

'Made me feel quite nostalgic,' Marcus says. 'It's years since I had such a good shout! I'm glad you persuaded me to come along.'

'I just wish there weren't so many loonies – it gave the wrong impression.'

'We were loonies once.'

'But never as loony as that,' she says.

'Loonies perform a vital function. They challenge the orthodoxies of the day.'

'Oh yeah?'

'Just think. Without loonies, there'd still be slavery and child chimney-sweeps.'

She pours the last drops of wine into his glass and puts her arms around him.

'I love you, loony,' she whispers, ruffling his hair, still damp from the rain.

'I love you, Gaga,' he whispers back. 'Partner in struggle. Life companion.'

He pulls her towards him on the sofa, his hands warm and familiar, and covers her face with kisses. She leans against him, feeling inside his shirt with her fingers to the softer private skin with its fine fuzz of curled greying hair. He unbuttons her blouse, and takes her black-satin-clad breasts between his hands.

'You know, you're a very attractive woman . . .'

She shuts her eyes, crosses her fingers behind his back, and wills him – *please, please, please* – don't say 'for someone of your age'.

And he doesn't.

PART FOUR

Fairyland

SERGE: AAA

It's Tuesday 11th November, about four o'clock. Serge, Maroushka and Chicken are in a taxi crawling over the Limehouse Link towards Canary Wharf. Chicken and Maroushka are sitting side by side, unnecessarily close, on the forward-facing seats. Serge is sitting with his back to the driver on one of the fold-down seats, with a document case on his knees, which are almost touching Maroushka's – he wants to touch them, but has to stop himself, because of Chicken. Maroushka is wearing a black cashmere coat, casually unbuttoned, over the same deep-rose dress and sheer black tights that accentuate the curve of her knees. Her lipstick matches the red of the dress, sultry yet understated. Chicken is also wearing a black cashmere coat over a black bespoke suit, with a creamy Brioni shirt. Serge is still wearing his cut-price Ermenegildo Zegna, but he's treated himself to a new Brioni shirt, which caresses his body as it sways and jerks with the movement of the taxi. He would rather be caressed by Maroushka, but that's not an option at the moment.

Maroushka squeals with delight as the fairy-lit towers of Canary Wharf rise out of the dusky sky, as if she's never seen them before. Chicken recites the names of the buildings, like a father pointing out the constellations of heaven to an excited child.

'HSBC. Citigroup. Barclays. Clifford Chance. Credit Suisse. Bank of America. Merrill Lynch.'

She cranes and twists in her seat, bringing her thigh into contact with Chicken's. Serge is particularly annoyed, not only because he has his back to the view, but because he wanted to come on the Docklands Light Railway, which would have been infinitely quicker and more comfortable, but Maroushka had flatly refused on the grounds that trains are too popular and she only travels by taxi. And because nothing has progressed between them since he kissed her last week. And also because, if he hadn't stuck his neck out with Chicken, she wouldn't be here at all.

The taxi drops them at the foot of another glass-and-steel tower where the rating agency has its offices. They take the lift to the top floor, and are ushered into an anonymous corporate meeting room.

'This is Serge Free. I spoke to you about him on the phone.' Chicken makes introductions. 'And this is Mary Malko, one of our brightest quants.'

'How do you do.'

The two guys from the rating agency shake his hand briskly, and linger over Maroushka's. It soon becomes clear that the shorter, older one is the subordinate. The young tall one with the blunt nose and big ears looks vaguely familiar, but Serge can't place him. He invites them to sit. Coffee is brought.

'Go ahead, Serge,' says Chicken.

Serge opens his document case and clears his throat.

'This investment represents a new model of portfolio design for the post-2007 trading environment that significantly extends the standard Gaussian copula model of default loss. We have randomised recovery rates, drawing on the established effect of inverse correlation between recovery rate and default frequency.'

The older, smaller man is taking notes and glancing up at Serge, who is keeping an eye on Chicken, who is watching the tall blunt-nosed man, who is staring at Maroushka. Maroushka is looking out of the window.

How can she stand it, hearing him speak her words, without wanting to interrupt or clarify? If he were her, he would be furious at the way Chicken has hijacked her work and handed it over to Serge to present. Originally, he had planned to exclude her from the meeting altogether, but Serge had put his foot down and insisted she should be invited to attend. The strange thing is, she doesn't seem to mind. Maybe it's because she's a girl.

The room they are in looks over a wide vista of skyscrapers and connecting plazas that all seem brand new, contained by the loop of the river, which from most places in London looks filthy brown, but here looks like heritage Father Thames. At ground level is a genuine quay where actual boats are moored and live seagulls squawk. As dusk draws in, lights sparkle from the surrounding towers and the streets and quays down below, and the whole place looks a bit like a scene in a computer game – cleverly designed but unreal, all constructed out of unlimited upside. People have already started to swarm out of the offices into the plazas of shops and bars as he reaches the end of the presentation, and they break for coffee and questions.

'All right, Maroushka?' he asks in a whisper. 'What d'you think?'

'We pay good fee they make good rating,' she says, without looking at him.

On his left, he can hear Chicken talking to the blunt-nosed man.

'I've brought my handicap down to eleven.'

The man – his name is Smythe – puts a hand on Chicken's shoulder. 'We'll have to get away for a game before Christmas, Ken.'

That's it – the golfing photos. He's the golfing Apollo with the golden curls, except now he has an anonymous bankers' haircut, which makes his ears and nose look big. In the photos he was wearing a polo shirt, but the suit he's wearing today is a real beast, wool-silk-weave fabric, probably bespoke, with an Italian cut. They stand, two confident good-looking guys, showing toothpaste-white teeth to each other, as if they're posing for some men's magazine photo shoot.

'We've made copies of the paperwork. Let me know if you foresee any problems, Tony,' says Chicken.

Seems like he and Chicken are old pals. That's convenient.

SERGE: *Hoover*

Otto and Molly have a baby girl. She's called Flossie, in honour of Free Open-Source Software, Otto told him, blabbing with pride. They sent him a photo-text of a little blob in a white knitted hat. He sent them a voice-activated digital picture frame, which he found online, with 4GB of memory and MP3 and video playback, which will allow them to store and flick through all their pictures at a simple command, as well as baby noises and first steps and all that. The demo looks really cool – he might even get one for himself.

Otto has been down to Scudamore's punt hire and asked about a carrier bag full of letters, but drawn a blank. He has also walked with Molly and baby Flossie along the river past Magdalene Bridge as far as the lock at Jesus Weir. From among the flotsam of dead branches, plastic bottles and lost shoes, they managed to pull out an envelope addressed to Serge at Queens' College, but all it had in it was a flyer for the Cambridge Playhouse, six months out of date.

He doesn't feel too worried, though, because Chicken came down to the trading floor today with a bottle of Veuve Clicquot to celebrate the success of Green Shoots, which has been awarded a triple A, and is now in the hands of the marketing team. Maroushka got a bit tipsy, and snogged him afterwards in the lift, and he even got to feel her tits. She's got a new outfit – dark brown with sparkly buttons.

The stock market has been drifting down since the start of November. Later in the afternoon, while no one is in the glass-walled office, he prints out the graph of surges and retracements over the last six months and analyses it; as well as the daily up and down movements, there's the larger pattern, which fits the Fibonacci model almost uncannily. It's approaching Phi – the turning point. Soon the market will bottom out and, when the upswing starts, it will accelerate fast as everybody rushes to cash in. He phones his broker and by five o'clock he's doubled his holdings of SYC, and sold his entire holding of Wymad, Endon and Edenthorpe Engineering. He'll lose the extra bit he could have made by holding on until the last minute, but why risk it when he's already quids in?

Afterwards, he's careful about switching his phone off because Clara has been texting him. She says she wants to talk to him about Oolie. No doubt there'll be a ticking-off about lack of attention to safety on the river or some such crap. Oolie had a great time. In fact, he'll have to warn Otto – Doro says she can't wait to go down to Cambridge again.

By nine o'clock, he, Maroushka and the Hamburger are the last three of their team left in the office. Even most of the traders have gone. Maroushka is working away mysteriously, frowning over her keyboard, and Serge pretends to be working too, waiting for the moment when the Hamburger leaves and they're on their own. Will he be able to undo those sparkly buttons? And what will she have on underneath? That skirt – it's short, but tight. And he's always found women's bras a challenge. Thinking about this, planning his strategy, is making him feel incredibly horny.

> *Princess of maths!*
> *Put your numbers aside,*
> *And open your . . .*

'*Gute nacht*, Serge, Maroushka!'

The Hamburger heads for the exit. At last!

For form's sake, Serge waits three long minutes before making his move. He sidles over to the door of the glass-walled office.

'Hi.'

Not one of the great chat-up lines, but it has the benefit of simplicity.

'Hi.'

She's still got her eyes glued to her screen, so he goes up and rests a hand on her shoulder. She doesn't move. He skims her dark hair with his lips.

'What are you working on, Princess?'

'End of housing recession. Green Shoots is having good success in marketing.'

Personally, he wouldn't have given the investment a triple A, despite Maroushka's bravura maths, but maybe that's why he's a lowly office-bound quant, while Tony Smythe and Chicken stroll the golf courses of the world clad in Gant.

'Green shoots – like Gauss's eternal spring with new and brilliant clothes.'

She looks up at him, laughing.

'I like you, Sergei. You always thinking about some interesting philosophy.'

'Love's my philosophy, babe.'

He bends and takes her face between his hands and kisses her, softly at first, then with a growing crescendo of passion, seeking her tongue with . . . oh no, not the hungry molluscs again. She's pushing him away, not like she means it, but playfully, giggling, and he reaches his hand inside her dark-brown jacket, feels the warmth of her breast through the flimsy fabric of her top while she wriggles, then she sighs, then goes still, eyes closed, cradled in his arm, murmuring, 'Sergei!'

Yes!!!

He fumbles with the diamanté buttons. Not so much the buttons as the buttonholes. Bloody hell, they're tight. He fumbles, he tugs, tugs a bit harder, then . . . ping! A button arcs through the air, bounces one-two-three times, and rolls away under the desk. She sits up, opens her eyes.

'No, Sergei, those buttons is for decoration only. Not unbutton.'

'Oh, I see. I'm sorry. I'll find it for you.'

He gets down on the ground and starts to search. His face is at the level of her gorgeous knees, slightly parted, with her skirt riding up over sheer black tights. Tights can be a problem, but he'll deal with them once he's found that bloody button. Is that it, lurking in the corner by the bin? He crawls under the desk. No, a five-pence coin. He pockets it. His stiffy is wavering, but he can't give up now.

VRURURURURURURUH!

There's a sudden roar by his ear like a jet taking off. He jumps up, bangs his head on the desk – ouch! – then everything goes black for a moment. Next thing he hears is Jojo the cleaner's voice: 'Do you mind if I just hoover up in here, love? I want to get off early.'

The whine of the vacuum cleaner fills the small office, the rasp of suction, and a rattle as something large and hard is sucked up through the plastic tube.

'Stop! Stop!' shrieks Maroushka.

'Stop!' He yells desperately from under the desk. But Jojo can't hear above the noise of the machine, so he lunges forward and pulls the plug out of the socket by the door.

'What's up?' says Jojo.

Maroushka shows her top, with its missing button.

'I think it's in there.' Serge points to the cylinder. 'D'you mind opening it up?'

'I'll tip it out,' says Jojo, and straight away unclips the cover of the cylinder and flips the contents on to the office floor.

Inside is a clotted mess of grey-brown dust, matted hairs and shrouded lumps of indeterminate debris. He holds his breath and starts to poke it with his fingers, sending a grey coil of powdery dust snaking upwards.

'No!' says Maroushka, coughing. 'Is okay! Never mind!'

He fingers the button-sized lumps. Where the fuck . . .?

All that matted crumbly filth reminds him of the understairs cupboard at Solidarity Hall where bags and wellies were kept, and where lost things disintegrated into the grot of ages.

'I'll find it! Don't worry, pet!' Jojo digs in with gusto, her plump rubber-covered fingers squeezing and sifting. 'It's gotta be some-where in here!'

This is ridiculous. He definitely heard the sound of something large and button-like being hoovered up. And he knows with a deep gut certainty that if he's ever to make any progress with Maroushka, he's got to find this button – their future happiness depends on it.

'Please, never mind. You making more dirty than you cleaning.'

Maroushka coughs, pushing back a stray strand of hair, and

leaving a smudge of brown dust on her cheek. He kisses it tenderly, but his stiffy has well and truly shrivelled away.

Then all three of them start poking through the filth, coughing in the opaque air. They fish out, between them, a pound coin, two euros, a twenty-pence coin, a small lump of brown stuff wrapped in silver foil, a dead cockroach, several paperclips, two pen tops, a small brown memory stick that looks like a dead cockroach (hey?), a false fingernail, a contact lens and something which looks like a green shoot, but turns out to be a shard of lettuce from someone's sandwich. No button.

He stares at the memory stick poking out of the clumpy dust. Should he pretend it's his? Just as he's about to pick it up, Maroushka bends with a little giggle and slips it in her pocket.

It's half past ten by the time Jojo has vacuumed up the mess on the floor, and they've thoroughly washed their hands, turned off their monitors, and are riding downwards together in the lift.

'I am sorry for this cleaner,' says Maroushka. 'She has no ability to improve her situation. She has proletarian mentality.'

He leans towards her and says, 'Can I take you out for a meal or something, Venus? To compensate for the loss of your button?'

She shakes her head.

And, to be honest, his pang of regret is tempered by a touch of relief.

You can't hurry love. This girl – she's worth waiting for. She's not just a quick office-floor shag. Despite the button incident, he feels buoyant with optimism as he takes the stairs two at a time up to his penthouse, her kisses still fresh on his lips. It can only be a matter of time before he brings her up here, to marvel at the rooftop view, and pop a bottle of bubbly, and then . . .

On the bookshelf Maroushka's shoes are standing stiffly to attention, waiting for her to come and claim them.

Not long now.

Maybe in future years they'll look back on this evening spent sifting through the contents of the office vacuum cleaner, and smile.

★

Sitting up in bed with his laptop that night, as is his habit, he logs into Kenporter1601's online broker account before going to sleep – not to trade of course, but just to see.

What he sees is that Chicken sold £525,000 worth of Edenthorpe Engineering shares this afternoon, about half an hour after Serge did. Jeez! A coincidence? A pattern? No, it can't be a coincidence. Chicken must have known about his trade. But how? The price has dipped right down to 102p. If he'd sold at that price he'd have made an extra few thousand. Has Chicken been snooping on him, when all the while he thought he was the one doing the snooping? He feels the rabbit-squeeze in his chest.

He checks the email account for new information. Here's a message from Juliette reminding him about an appointment on Friday – 'you naughty boy, you'. How great to be a fly on the wall at one of those sessions! But what's this pesky little message there at the bottom of the list?

Tomorrow. Mx

Barely two words, but enough to set his heart plummeting like a market in free fall. The email address reveals nothing – a-string-of-numbers@yahoo.com. He notes it down, but daren't risk a reply. He rereads the message, reads between and behind the lines – 'M'. It has to be her – who else? And 'x' – a kiss.

DORO: The letter

Doro trundles the Hoover around upstairs, cursing the rain that has kept her in all day. Since she retired from her part-time lecturing job at the end of last year, and Oolie started working at Edenthorpe's, she has free hours at her disposal, hundreds of them. If she strung them all together, she could write a book, like Marcus, or learn a language or take up golf. Instead, she fills them with housework, which she loathes because it's endless, and cups of tea, which she often leaves undrunk. Cleaning must be some primeval female instinct, for Marcus took retirement three years ago without feeling any increased urge to hoover. So much for 'new man'.

She can't understand why he's suddenly so keen to get married, but Oolie-Anna seems to have taken the idea in her stride. In fact, Oolie's far more excited about being a bridesmaid than about being adopted, since the latter doesn't involve dressing up, and neither Marcus nor she could suggest any other advantages. When they've fixed a date, she'll have to start making preparations, which no doubt will be left up to her.

In the study, Serge's former bedroom, the Hoover bumps against a box of papers sealed with sticky tape that hasn't been opened since they moved from Solidarity Hall in 1995. Maybe it's time to dump some of this old irrelevant junk? She opens it for inspection and a piece of paper flutters to the ground.

Dear Everybody,

By the time you get this, I will be far away.
I had a chance of happiness, and I had to take it.
Look after little Julie-Anna.

She was always more your than mine, and now she is all yours.
If we ever meet again, I hope you will understand.

Yours sincearly,
Megan Cromer

The writing is small and round, like a child's, with circles for dots above the 'i's, and that single spelling mistake near the end. She reads it through twice, and is so bowled over by the rush of emotion it brings, she stuffs it back quickly into the box. But the questions persist in her mind as she trails around the house with the Hoover.

Where is 'far away'?

What 'chance of happiness'?

The first time she read it, twenty years ago, she'd dismissed it without a thought. Now it seems ludicrous and melodramatic. 'If we ever meet again, I hope you will understand.' Straight out of Mills & Boon. She's suddenly filled with fury at Megan, which political correctness wouldn't let her feel at the time. As if *her* happiness was what mattered. What about Oolie's happiness?

Even the names are a question.

Why Megan Cromer? What was she hiding? Or did she already know that she would run away one day?

Why Julie-Anna? Was it a simple mistake, or a refusal to accept the name they'd given her?

She recalls the scene in the sitting room at Solidarity Hall, Chris Watt trying to get her to breastfeed the baby, Megan's sullen exhaustion, and Chris Howe and Fred bounding in, so pleased with the name they'd come up with. Megan had nodded blankly, staring at the fretful, unresponsive baby. Doro feels a stab of guilt. 'She was always more your than mine.' Maybe there was some truth in that. But the commune had been able to give Oolie so much more than Megan could have done on her own – why should she feel guilty? 'Now she is all yours,' Megan wrote, and Doro's life was set on a different course, like a planet that shifts its axis of orbit.

The older kids also adapted to Oolie's arrival in their family. Clara became more responsible. Serge and Otto withdrew into their own geekish world. It would be nice to talk to them about those days, to explain what it was all about. But why burden them with that old forgotten stuff? Clara's doing a great job with those difficult kids, not just thinking of me-me-me all the time, as many of the young do today. And Serge hasn't gone down the easy money road, as he could have, with his brains, but is toiling at the frontiers of knowledge. And little Oolie is so resolutely cheerful, despite all the setbacks she faces. Her kids have done her proud.

She switches off the Hoover, and heaves the old box of papers on to the landing – tomorrow, she'll get Marcus to help her take it to the recycling dump. On the way back, she'll stop off at the Oxfam shop, and sign on as a volunteer.

'Shall I make something for supper?' he calls up from the kitchen.

Yes, the winds of change are really blowing through her life.

SERGE: *You naughty boy, you*

In other words, today: 07.45, 14th November 2008, according to the Bloomberg TV channel suspended from the high ceiling of the trading hall.

She's not in yet. Serge hangs his jacket on the back of his chair and switches on his monitor. He didn't sleep much last night. An exhausted tic pecks away at the lid of his right eye.

But Green Shoots is doing well, and there are other signs of recovery in the housing market. In a show of confidence, Persimmon, the house builder, has reversed provisions it had taken against falls in house prices. The Icelandic banks have stabilised too, thanks to a $2 billion IMF loan.

At Edenthorpe Engineering, however, things are not so rosy. A newsflash reveals that the shares have collapsed to 85p and there are rumours of receivership. Surely it can't be just his own short selling that brought this about? Serge does a quick search on BBC Business. Seven hundred jobs at risk. Shit! He shuts his eyes and tries to block out the hum of his conscience. But even as he's grappling with his scruples, another voice is whispering: 'If you'd held on and bought back at 85p, you'd have made shedloads more.'

While he's reading the screen, he doesn't notice that the room has fallen quiet around him. He looks up to see all eyes are turned towards the door. Chicken is standing there, with one of the American suits beside him – Craig Hampton or Max Vearling, he can't remember which. They whisper together, surveying the scene.

What are they looking at? Who are they looking for?

Chicken's Dobermann gaze rests on him. His guts lurch.

That email: 'Tomorrow. Mx.' A carelessly omitted vowel. Yes, it's Max Vearling. There he is, staring straight at Serge, with a sly half-smile. So this is it, the word in the ear, the quiet hustling away to a private room where Inspectors Birkett and Jackson or some goons from the FSA are lying in wait. What a fool he'd been to break the rules. What an utter fool to think he could get away with it.

He tries to keep calm as he looks around for an escape route, though his pulses are hammering so hard he can barely think. There's no exit from the trading floor – or at least, there is, but Chicken and Max Vearling are blocking it. Then they start to walk slowly forward between the desks. They are heading towards the Securitisation area – straight towards him.

'Good news from Persimmon, hey?' Toby O'Toole leans back in his chair as they pass.

Bless you, keep them talking, brown-nose boy!

Max Vearling pauses for a moment to exchange pleasantries, but Chicken is still advancing. He stops by Serge's desk, and says in a low voice, 'Interesting developments at Edenthorpe Engineering, hey, Freebie?'

A flash of blinding panic strikes Serge's visual cortex. For a second, the room goes black. Then light floods in, strobing as in a nightmare. He jumps to his feet and, dodging past Chicken, sprints in the opposite direction down to the end of his aisle without looking round, almost knocking the Hamburger out of his seat, takes a left, and then legs it up between the desks of the next aisle. People stare, but nobody tries to stop him. As he runs, the world around him seems to slow down, to collapse into slow motion. On the side, his colleagues are waving their arms like lazy swimmers, as though the huge hall is filled with water instead of air. Big glassy bubbles are rising to the surface, and he is drowning, drowning.

When he reaches the door, he stops and glances over his shoulder. Everybody is staring at him, their faces distorted through the deep sea swell, their mewing voices unintelligible like seagulls. He shoves at the door and stumbles out into the lobby, gasping for breath. A stroke of luck – the lift is waiting there. He pushes the button and lets himself down, down through the rattling oesophagus of FATCA into the sunlit atrium of the reception – AUDACES FORTUNA IUVAT – past the chirpy girls at the desk, and out on to the pavement. Sunlight slants in broad beams between the lofty buildings. No one is around. He starts to run.

At the end of the street, he bears right into a narrow alley which after a couple of blocks ejects him into Paternoster Square and he races across the bricky expanse – where did those bloody sheep come from? – towards St Paul's. His breath comes in hoarse pants through his open mouth. His chest is bursting. His eyes are inexplicably wet and misted. He keeps on running, running.

Then suddenly – pfwhat! The pavement leaps up and thumps him in the face. His arms flail but his legs are caught, entangled in a snare which on closer inspection turns out to be not a snare but a leather lead. At one end of the lead is a large disgruntled poodle, now yelping with annoyance. From his pavement-level view, all he sees at the other end is a pair of pink leggings tucked into shiny black high-heeled boots. A few inches away in front of his eyes is a steaming mound of freshly laid dog pooh. A trickle of blood, presumably from his nose, is leeching towards it. Even in this addled state, a lucid thought flashes into his mind: 'Sheesh! This could have been so much worse!'

The pink-leggings lady tugs at the lead, jerking it tight around his ankles, which makes the dog yelp again. Looking down with an inscrutable smile, she murmurs,

'You naughty boy, you!'

You naughty boy, you. In the depths of his brain, the phrase rings a bell.

Could it be . . . Juliette?

He closes his eyes and lets blackness descend.

SERGE: Thwack!

How much time has passed? Serge isn't sure. He reaches up to touch his nose. Amazingly, it's still there, but it's sticky and much too big, and it's sending out pulse-waves of pain into his forehead. His eyes are also not working properly. He blinks slowly, and when he opens them again the room swings back into focus – the bulky cream faux-leather sofa where he is lying propped up on an Indian mirror-work cushion, the TV blaring away in a corner. A blood-soaked hankie is swimming in a bowl of pink water on the floor beside him; a fat brown poodle is snuggled up against his thigh. Above the noise of the TV he hears the intermittent crack of a leather whip and the ecstatic groans of Juliette's client in the next room. Crumbs, that woman must pack some strength.

He tries to get back to sleep, but the noise is disturbing. On the television, there's something about the G20 summit, world leaders congregating in Washington to sort out the global economic crisis. About time. If he wasn't feeling so bad, he could probably come up with a few ideas himself. He knows times are hard, but you'd have thought the PM could have forked out for a better suit. A couple of studio guests are discussing the need for bank regulation – an earnest young woman in a chain-store jacket who keeps going on about a society based on shared prosperity (what shared prosperity? She's living in Doro-Doro-land – nice legs, though) and a City guy who blames the Government ('Ill-judged interest rate hike . . . property prices collapsed . . . only now starting to see green shoots of recovery . . .'). The camera pans in for a close-up. Crumbs! There's Chicken in all his tailored glory, his sharp predator teeth snapping on the words as he talks.

At five o'clock, he hears murmured goodbyes in the hallway, the click of a door, and a few minutes later Juliette enters carrying two cups of tea. Serge takes a gulp and feels better at once.

She gives the poodle a slap on the rump. 'Budge over, Beastie.'

It sighs and snuffles as she squeezes on to the sofa beside it.

She's changed into a plain pale-blue dress, shaped around the bust and pulled in at the waist, which looks quite kinky, a bit like a nurse's outfit. Some men get off on that sort of thing. She must be in her forties, too old for him. Tired lines around her eyes, but her face is nice.

'How are you feeling, pet?' She cups a hand under his chin, twists his head towards the light, and presses along the bridge of his nose with her thumb. Her hands are small and smell of soap.

'Ouch!'

'Trust me – I'm a nurse.'

'No kidding?'

'Though now I'm a full-time See Eye practitioner. Some people find it embarrassing, but I think of it as a public service.'

See Eye? Is this a euphemism for kinky whiplash activities?

'I know what you're thinking. But have you ever tried it, pet?'

'No. I imagine it must be a bit painful.'

'Not if it's done properly.'

He glances surreptitiously at her feet. They look quite small. Size eight, she said in the email.

A question pushes itself up to the bruised surface of his brain. 'Er . . . how did I get here?'

'In a taxi. I was going to phone an ambulance but you begged me to give you another chance. I couldn't just leave you bleeding on the pavement, could I?'

'Wow. A Good Samaritan.' His voice chokes with tears. 'But . . . weren't you scared? A strange man . . .?'

'Beastie looks after me if any of my clients get frisky. He can be quite fierce, eh, you naughty boy?'

Beastie woofs and thwacks Serge's leg with his tail.

The room is close and hot. His head is throbbing terribly, and flashes of light pop at the perimeter of his vision. There's a faint smell of something disgusting, which he realises after a moment is the dog.

'You been a naughty boy?' she cajoles.

'No. Honestly. Thanks, Juliette. It's not my thing.'

She rubs the dog's belly and he grunts with pleasure and rolls on to his back, pawing the air with his huge hairy mitts.

'You work in the City, do you?' she says.

'Yes. Well, I . . . I'm not sure any more.'

'I have a lot of City gentlemen among my clients. I get rid of all the . . . congestion.' She folds her hands together. 'Think about it, pet. I'll do it for free. Nothing to be frightened of. You're in the hands of a professional. Bathroom's through there if you want to clean up before we start.' Her voice is flatly matter-of-fact, with a slight regional accent he can't place.

He staggers to his feet, wondering whether he should just make a run for it.

'Hello, spud,' he greets the wan battered face in the bathroom mirror. His nose is a crust of dried blood, still oozing slightly, and a purple bruise is spreading upwards, puffing out the skin around his eyes, making everything look blurred. He cleans his face up with tissues from a lacy tissue dispenser. For someone with such a strapping occupation, Juliette's tastes seem surprisingly girly. The bathroom is cluttered with bottles and potions, brushes, scissors, tweezers, vitamins, lipsticks. Her perfume is Miss Dior Chérie – the same as Babs's. He squirts a bit on to his wrist and sniffs for old times' sake. Memories flood back. Dear Babs. She was a good woman. One of the best. He hopes she's found happiness in her new life. Her new squishy lesbian life. His cock stirs. For some reason, his eyes are full of tears.

Outside the bathroom door, Beastie growls.

'Are you all right, pet?' Juliette asks as he stumbles back into the sitting room and flops down on the sofa.

'Fine, yes. Just a bit . . . weird.'

He shivers, although the flat is sultry. His head is throbbing again and new arrows of pain are shooting outwards to his temples.

'We don't have to do it right away, George. Maybe later. After I've done with my clients.'

George?

'Right. Yeah. Or . . . maybe another time?'

He tries to stand, but his legs give way. As he surrenders to gravity, another connection clicks in his brain: 'Six o'clock Friday, you naughty boy, you.' If he's still here, he could witness the flagellation of Chicken, maybe even get some pics with his mobile phone camera – useful if Chicken needs encouragement to overlook the irregular transactions in the 1601 bank account.

'Actually, I do feel a bit rough. Could I just stay . . .?'

Juliette looks concerned. 'No rush. Stay as long as you like, pet. I've got a client coming at six.'

She fetches a glass of water and hands him two small capsules. 'Here, take these. They'll help you sleep. You can stretch out on the sofa. Shift over, Beastie!'

She gives the dog another slap. It lurches on to the ground, shakes itself morosely and yawns. Its breath smells of . . . actually, he prefers not to remember. Then the doorbell rings.

'Excuse me, pet. Try to get some sleep.'

Beastie follows her out.

He hears a man's voice in the hall. Is it . . .? He strains to hear but the voices are too low to make out above the burble of the television, where *Xena: Warrior Princess* has taken over from the news. The pills he took haven't lessened the pain, but have made him feel woozy. A few moments later, he hears the crack of the whip and the terrible shuddering groans.

A huge blanketing drowsiness descends on him.

Strangely alert now, he jumps to his feet. How very peculiar: his legs seem to be working again – in fact, they're working 110 per cent, making his steps long and bouncy, like he's walking on the moon. Miraculously, his iPhone is still there in his jacket pocket. He's not going to miss this chance. Switching on the camera function, he creeps out into the corridor.

One door is slightly ajar. He puts his eye to the gap. As his vision adjusts to the darkness he sees two figures in the room: Juliette, in pink leggings and black stiletto boots, standing astride a man crouched on all fours – a chunky muscle-packed man, naked but for a leopard-skin posing pouch. She's wearing a studded leather bra which squeezes her breasts into awesome pointy cones like a warrior princess. The crack of her whip splits the darkness, and the man lets out a long shuddering groan.

'Tell me, you naughty boy!' Juliette hisses. 'Tell me the bad things you done!' She jabs the man with her heel.

'I did nothing unlawful, mistress.'

'You must have done something bad, else you wouldn't be here, would you?'

Thwack!

'I don't know. I can't remember.'

'I can't remember, *mistress*.'

Thwack!

'All right. I opened an unregistered account. A victimless crime, mistress!'

'It's still a crime, innit?'

Thwack! The whip flickers in the half-darkness. Serge holds the camera up and clicks again and again through the gap of the door.

'Okay, we created a financial instrument,' the kneeling man moans. 'Look, if there's a way of making loadsamoney, somebody's going to find it, aren't they? You can't stop it. It's human nature.'

Thwack!

'They should've passed a law against it. Useless politicians. Clueless. All on the take.'

Thwack!

'So this instrument? It done a naughty thing?'

'It wasn't me, it was it. The regulator should've stopped us. You can't blame me!' He talks fast, stumbling over the words. Flecks of foam dribble from his mouth. 'It stands to reason, if there's no law against it people are gonna do it, aren't they?'

'Do what, you moral maggot?'

Thwack!

'Create a dodgy fund. Flog it to the investors. Knowing it'll fail! Aagh!'

'That's better. And?'

In the doorway, Beastie is snuffling with excitement. The man is breathing hard, his arched shoulders shuddering. Serge finds himself shuddering too.

'I wiped out an engineering works! Aagh! I killed my sister's hamster!'

'Now we're getting there!' screams Juliette. 'And?'

'I lied to my mum!'

He falls forward, sobbing uncontrollably.

When he wakes, his eyes are still full of tears and his nose hurts.

DORO: *Flossie*

On Saturday morning, Doro and Oolie set out for Cambridge. Doro hasn't managed to contact Serge yet, but she's taken her mobile, and keeps trying. She's also obtained Molly and Otto's number from Directory Enquiries, so she can drop round afterwards with a pretty green, mauve and white bonnet (the suffragette colours) that she's crocheted herself.

Oolie gazes out of the window of the train and burbles her latest thoughts about her bridesmaid's dress, while fields, trees and anonymous towns flit by, all dampened by November drizzle. Doro stretches her legs and unfolds the *Guardian* she picked up at the station. The pound is plummeting. G20 world leaders sound off about the recession, as though they'd predicted it all along. Gaza is under siege. Wildfires rip through California. But her mind keeps wandering back to a recent telephone conversation with Clara.

When she was Clara's age, people still used to talk about 'making love' for having sex, which sounded romantic, or 'sleeping with' someone, which sounded nice and cuddly. And then, okay, when they got into sexual liberation people started saying 'fuck', like it was a political statement, decolonisation of language, rejection of prudery, etc. But 'shagging'! She shudders. How could her own daughter accuse her of that?

She buys herself a double-sized cup of tea from the trolley, and a chocolate muffin for comfort, which she shares with Oolie.

By the time they get to Queens' College Serge still hasn't answered her calls, so she asks in the Porters' Lodge for his room number.

The man behind the desk gives her a funny look. 'He's been gone over a year.'

'Oh. Really? The name's Serge Free. F-r-e-e.'

'Yes, I know how to spell it. He left last summer.'

'Are they still shagging up there?' chirps Oolie.

'No. I don't think so.' Doro's brain is still trying to process this indigestible information.

'Can we go to the river and see if that 'unk's there?'

'No. Let's visit Molly and her baby, instead.'

'Yeah! I wanna see t' babbie.'

Molly and Otto's flat above a hairdresser's on Mill Road is tiny, warm and filled with that sweet stinky baby smell that brings on a rush of emotion to Doro. Molly greets them at the door, tousled, barefoot and wearing a milk-stained dressing gown. The baby is tucked into the dressing gown, guzzling away.

'Oh, she's lovely!'

'What's she doing?' says Oolie.

'She's feeding, love. That's how babies get their milk.'

'Yeuch!'

They sit on a small sofa in the sitting room, which is also the dining room, kitchen and Otto's office, while Molly finishes feeding the baby. A long curl of reddish-brown hair trails across her cheek and down on to her breast, reminding Doro of Moira.

'It's nice to have visitors,' says Molly. 'Otto's often away at weekends. Jen comes over sometimes. You know, Otto's mum?'

'Oh yes, I remember Jen.'

'They live quite nearby, in Peterborough, Jen and Nick. He's still teaching. She's working as a solicitor.'

'Jen and Nick are still together?'

'Yes, she has some funny tales to tell about the commune. She says you were all bonkers!'

'Mm. Some more than others.' Doro has a vivid memory of Jen, wearing only a pair of knickers, practising primal screaming in the garden. Now a solicitor, eh?

'And what's Otto doing with himself?'

'Otto's at a conference about Free Open-Source Software. It's his big passion. That's why we called the baby Flossie – F-O-S-S. The French geeks stuck an 'L' in for femininity.'

'Ha!' So all that anti-patriarchal upbringing didn't change anything much. 'Can I hold her a minute?'

Molly passes her to Doro to hold, while she goes to make the coffee. Doro gazes into the dark glassy eyes and remembers Clara, Serge, Otto, Star, Oolie – so many babies she held – the warm sleepy bulk of new life. If only Clara and Serge would get a move on!

'Hello, Floss-Floss-Flossie!' She moves her face into the baby's field of focus, smiling full on and jiggling her head.

'Hup!' says Flossie, and lets out a dribble of curdy milk.

'I wanna hold her!' Oolie makes a grab.

'Sit down. Don't grab!' Doro has a sudden flashback to an unfortunate hamster incident years ago. 'Hold your arms out carefully!'

'Shall I get my tits out?'

'No, it's all right.'

'Hup!' says Flossie.

'In't she cuddly? I'd sooner 'ave a babbie nor a 'amster.' Oolie gazes down into the little baby face, which now seems to have dropped off to sleep.

Maybe it wasn't such a good idea to come here with Oolie. Doro feels a sinking in her guts, in anticipation of the question that will inevitably come next.

'Can I 'ave a babbie?'

'I don't think –'

'They're quite hard work!' Molly laughs, carrying the tray with a dancer's grace, her loose curls falling forward as she places the cafetière and cups on the low table. How pretty she is, thinks Doro. And how nice it is to be old enough to enjoy another woman's beauty without feeling that little prick of rivalry.

'I'm good at 'ard work,' says Oolie.

'Schrrrup . . .' Flossie murmurs from the depths of sleep.

'I can't tell you how grateful we are to Serge.' Molly pushes her hair back from her face to pour the coffee. 'Without him, we'd be out on the streets.'

'How d'you mean?'

'Lending us the money, when they were going to foreclose on us. Otto says he's more like a brother than a friend.'

'He lent you money?'

'Yes. Don't sound so surprised!' Molly smiles, stirring four spoons of sugar into her coffee. (How can she take so much sugar and not get fat?) 'He's a really nice guy.'

'I know he's nice. I just didn't know he had any money.'

'Well, I think they get paid quite well in the banking world.'

'The banking world?' She tries to keep her astonishment out of her face. 'Oh yes. Of course.'

'Anyway, it was nice of him to help us out.'

'Mm. Which bank is it he works for? It's completely slipped my mind.' Doro gives a little dotty giggle.

'Eff – something. I've forgotten too,' Molly laughs.

'I don't like coffee. Ent you got no tea?' Oolie interrupts sulkily.

'You sit!' says Doro to Molly, jumping up. 'I'll get it!'

She's glad to turn her back on Oolie and Molly for a moment, and gather her thoughts. She can hear Oolie saying, 'Mum says I can 'ave a babbie, if I'm good.'

She wishes that bloody smug Mr Clements with his checklists of 'blossoming individuality' could hear this.

'Where d'you keep the tea bags?' she asks.

'Are you gonner get your tit out again?' asks Oolie.

'Not now. Cupboard above the sink. I think it's called FATCA? Does that ring a bell?' says Molly.

'Ent you got no sweeteners?' asks Oolie, stirring four spoons of sugar into her tea in imitation of Molly. 'Mum says I gotter 'ave sweeteners.'

'Yes, that's it!' says Doro.

It isn't until they're on the train back to Doncaster that she realises she still has the crocheted bonnet in her bag. Oolie is asleep, snoring with her mouth slightly open. Serge's phone is still switched off. Doro watches the landscape fading from daylight to dusk as it flies past, imprinted with the emotions of all the other times she's travelled up here. It seemed crazy, exhilarating, their first journey north in 1969.

Looking back, as she increasingly does these days, she finds herself wondering what it was all about. They'd been so certain in those days; so convinced of the rightness of their mission. Her whole life since then has been a journey backwards into uncertainty – from knowledge to doubt; from black and white to shades of grey; from taut to baggy, like underwear; from rigid to squashy.

SERGE: Bye-bye, Beastie

'Wake up, sleepyhead.'

A woman is standing over Serge with a cup of tea – she's wearing a fluffy dressing gown and pink slippers. In his bleary state, it takes him a moment to recognise Juliette.

'Oh, thanks. How long have I been asleep?'

'It's Saturday afternoon. Are you feeling better?'

'Saturday? Oh, shit!'

'How's the nose, pet?' She cups her hand under his chin and jerks his face round. 'Does it still hurt?'

'A bit.'

'There's some swelling. Maybe a hairline fracture.'

'I should get going.'

'Wait till you feel better. We don't want you passing out on the underground.'

'No. I guess not.'

Feeling wobbly and strangely weepy, he sinks back on to the sofa in front of the TV, where they're still on about the G20 summit. The crisis has sprouted a field of overnight experts tut-tutting about the runaway sub-prime mortgage market; too much risky lending has resulted in no lending at all, because no one knows what any bank's assets consist of. Billions of pounds' worth of derivatives that may not be worth the paper they're written on have been sold and resold. Cases have come to light of mortgages secured on non-existent properties, mortgages written up to people who never existed, mortgages secured in the names of people who are already dead. It seems everyone was in too much of a hurry making money to check. He listens with detached interest. It all seems rather seedy and meaningless.

Images from last night nudge his brain. What happened in that room? He struggles to remember. Something to do with a dog.

'What d'you want for breakfast, pet? Bix or flakes?'

Sounds like dog food.

'I'm not that hungry, thanks, Juliette.'

The television news has moved on from the G20 summit. Twelve miners killed in Romania. Israel blockades Gaza. Britney Spears charged with dangerous driving. What a terrible mess the world is in.

She leans forward and snaps the television off. 'It's a wonder you didn't have nightmares, sleeping with that on all night.'

'Maybe . . . Juliette, do you ever –?'

'That's another thing I don't get – why d'you keep calling me Juliette?'

'I thought . . .'

'My name's Margaret, pet. I told you. Don't you remember?'

So Juliette must be her 'professional' name.

'And you said yours is George. Such a nice name. Like the saint.'

Serge nods silently. He feels some affection for St George, who is the patron saint of Doncaster, but he can't remember ever having adopted his name. In fact, he has no recollection of this conversation at all.

She heaves a large black bag with a padded shoulder strap on to her shoulder.

'I need to pop out to see a client, George. Will you be all right on your own for a bit?'

'Sure.'

'I'll leave Beastie here. He gets snarky sometimes when I'm working. Possessive. You naughty boy.'

Beastie woofs and thwacks his tail.

'If you feel like going out, there's a nice W-A-L-K through Smithfield Market and down towards St Paul's. Don't forget to take a pooper bag. Some people are so intolerant. You'd be amazed the fuss they make. I mean, it's just nature, isn't it?'

'Mm.'

'Help yourself to anything you fancy from the fridge.' She waves in the direction of the kitchen and disappears. 'Bye, George! Bye-bye, Beastie! Bye-eee!'

*

After she's gone, he goes into the kitchen and puts the kettle on. He's feeling hungry now, though his face is still throbbing. He opens the fridge, but all it contains are the rancid remnants of a curry take-away, two dried-out crumpets and a monster sausage in a plastic skin. He takes it out cautiously. It looks like no sausage he has eaten before – in fact, it looks like a giant penis sheathed in a giant con-dom. He cuts a slice. The taste is bland, faintly meaty, faintly chemical. The texture is rubbery. He has to force himself to swallow. Beastie has followed him into the kitchen and is sniffing eagerly at the open fridge, nose quivering, thwacking Serge's leg with his tail.

'Go away, Beastie.'

The tail stops thwacking and Beastie growls. Serge holds the monster sausage up to his nostrils. The smell is not nice. Then he sees, in faint print, on the plastic skin: 'Top Dog Doggie Dinner'. Ah. He remembers their first encounter, with Doro, outside St Paul's – Doro's incandescent rage, Beastie's determined crap, Juli-ette's humiliated retreat. This explains the poor mutt's toilet habits. As he's about to return the sausage to the fridge the poodle, with a sudden leap he wouldn't have thought it capable of, snatches it from his hand and carries it off to the front room. By the time he's tracked it down behind the sofa, there's nothing left but shreds of chewed-up plastic skin. Too bad.

He dampens the shrivelled crumpets under the tap then toasts them (an old Solidarity Hall trick) and eats slowly, gazing out of the window. All before him is a vista of drab apartment blocks and mangy grass dotted with leafless trees. The room is small, stuffy and cluttered with knick-knacks, chipped souvenirs from dismal seaside towns, faded Monet prints, china animals. Everything seems so banal, could it really be the setting for the brutal drama he wit-nessed last night? Or was that all a dream? Hang on – didn't he take some photos? He fishes his iPhone out of his jacket pocket, but there's only an out-of-focus picture of St Paul's dome.

The room where Juliette (he can't think of her as Margaret) sees her clients, the room sandwiched between the bedroom and the sit-ting room, is locked, so he tries the door to her bedroom. Beastie has reappeared, snarling and snapping, his tongue hanging out, his breath warm and foul. He shoves the dog out with his foot, shuts the door and sets about examining the room. There's the usual girly paraphernalia – undies, tights, tampons, tissues – nothing to suggest whiplash activities.

Surely she must keep an appointments book, or some record of her clients. On her bedside table is a paperback novel called *Under the Duvet* and beneath it a booklet that turns out to be a manual for some equipment which looks like a mini-washing machine attached to a bed. Aqua-Clinic Colonic Hydrotherapy. Weird. On the wall there's a photo of Juliette, much younger, in a nurse's uniform a bit like the one she was wearing today. Maybe she really is a nurse. All the while he's investigating the room, the dog yaps and scratches outside.

He opens the door carefully, but Beastie is waiting and hurls himself through the opening, teeth bared, snarling. He tries to slam the door, but unfortunately slams it on Beastie. The dog lets out an agonised yelp and falls on the floor, thrashing its body from side to side. A dribble of blood spurts on to the carpet.

He's standing there, wondering what to do, when he hears the noise. The whiplash crack. The long-drawn shuddering groan. He freezes, all his senses jangling. Now, in the daylight, the sound seems less human and more mechanical. The strange thing is, it seems to be coming not from the locked room next door but from the far end of the corridor. In fact, it's coming from outside the flat. He looks down at Beastie, expecting some reaction, but the dog seems to have passed out. Or maybe he's dead. Remorse seizes him. What a scumbag he is. This is how he repays Juliette's kindness – by killing her pet! Then he hears another disturbing sound: ping-ping!

Quickly, he heaves the dog's limp body into the bedroom and closes the door. There's only a small smear of blood on the carpet – he'll deal with that later. He puts his eye to the spyhole in the door, but the face in the lens is too small and distorted to recognise. He hesitates. Common sense tells him to pretend there's no one at home but, half hoping to see Chicken standing there, he opens the door.

'Hi.'

'Hi.'

A blush rises to Serge's cheeks.

'You are also waiting . . .?'

'She's gone out,' Serge says.

'I have an appointment. I am rather early.'

'D'you want to come in and wait?'

'Thank you.'

The Hamburger follows him through into the sitting room and sits down stiffly, knees together, at one end of the spongy sofa. Serge sits down at the other end. Between them is a metre of embarrassed silence.

After a moment, the Hamburger asks politely, 'You are often coming here?'

'No. It's my first time. I'm a bit unsure . . .'

He wishes he hadn't opened the door. He wishes he could call a vet to check on Beastie. He can hear a faint whimpering sound from the bedroom. The Hamburger hears it too, but mistakes its source.

'There is nothing to fear, Serge. Some initial discomfort. You get quickly accustomed.'

'You do?'

'You will feel better after.'

'That's what I'm hoping,' he mumbles.

'The nature of our work is not healthful. Too much sitting on the underbottom. It is sensible to seek relief.' The Hamburger shuffles about on the sofa.

'Mm. Yeah.'

'I thought you may be unwell when I saw you were running away the other day.'

'Yeah. I felt . . . like crap.'

'A sudden urgency?'

'Yeah. Exactly.'

'I think Margaret can help you.' The Hamburger nods slowly. 'So you have not heard about Maroushka?'

'Maroushka?' Serge's heart thumps in his chest.

'The *Nutte* has been promoted.'

'Promoted?'

'Yes. Max Vearling announced yesterday, after you run away. But I have always considered her approach unsustainable. Not skill. Corruption.' The Hamburger sniffs the air as he speaks.

Serge sniffs too. Their eyes meet, and each looks away quickly. There are some thoughts which cannot be spoken. The stench of corruption is palpable. In fact, it seems to be coming from behind the sofa.

After a moment's silence, the Hamburger grins awkwardly. 'So it is your introduction to the See Eye.'

'Er – what exactly is the See Eye?'

'You are not coming for the colonic irrigation?'

'Oh. I see. C.I.' He forces a grin on to his face, but his heart is jumping about wildly. That diagram of a washing machine attached to a bed. The hosepipes! The horror! He leaps to his feet.

'I have to go. A sudden . . . urgency! Will you give Juliette my apologies.'

'Juliette?'

'Sorry – Margaret. I thought she was someone else. You know how once you get an idea in your head . . .'

'Really, Serge, my friend, there is nothing to fear . . .'

The Hamburger's voice trails him down the corridor and out through the door.

He presses the button, and a few minutes later the lift arrives. It comes to rest with a loud whiplash crack. He gets in. With a long shuddering groan it carries him down to ground level.

CLARA: The moggidge

The news was on the local radio. Edenthorpe Engineering is to close with the loss of up to 700 jobs. By the time Clara gets to school, everyone in the staffroom is talking about it. Mr Tyldesley compares it to the demise of coal mining. Miss Postlethwaite likens it to the fate of the handloom weavers in the eighteenth century. Mrs Salmon worries about dicky dodgers claiming free school meals. Over by the photocopier the other teachers are chuntering darkly. Mr Kenny sees it as an excuse to break the smoking ban. When Mr Gorst/Alan arrives to announce the news, the whole staffroom is already wreathed in smoke and gloom.

Clara counts the children in her class whose parents work at Edenthorpe. Dana Kuciak, Tracey Dawcey, Jason Taylor – and doubtless some others. Families thrown into insecurity. Parents arguing in the night about money. Kids nervy, anxious, playing up in class, getting behind with lessons. There'll be teasing and bullying too.

Ner-ner, you've got manky pants! Ner-ner, your mam got them trainers in Netto's!

And what about the shops and local businesses? Will people still afford to buy meat from the butcher's shop in Beckett Road? And when the kids are old enough to go to work, where will they go?

'What I don't understand,' she says, 'is why? I mean, why do sub-prime mortgages in America close down a perfectly good engineering works in Yorkshire?'

'It's globalisation,' says Mr Tyldesley.

'It's the bloody bankers,' says Mr Kenny.

'It's just like the great tulip bubble, isn't it, Alan?' simpers Miss Hippo. (Bitch!)

At lunchtime, just as she's about to slope off to the staffroom to continue the discussion, Jason Taylor stops her in the corridor.

'Please, miss, will you sponsor me?' He waves a sheet of crumpled paper at her, covered with wobbly hand-drawn lines.

'You know I can't, Jason.'

'Please, it's for me mam, miss,' he wheedles. 'To get a new cooker.'

His face has greyish streaks and smudges around the eyes, as though he's been crying.

'I'm sorry, Jason. What happened?'

'Cooker blew up, and now Edenthorpe's closed down, she in't got nowt comin' in, and she's gotter choose between a new cooker and payin' t' moggidge.'

Could this be true? With Jason, you never know what to believe. He may be near the bottom of the class when it comes to reading, but he's quick to sniff out a business opportunity.

'But that only happened today, Jason. How can she be behind already?'

His reply is pat, as if he anticipated the question. 'She can't get a new cooker on't catalogue because of 'er mobile contract.'

'But why –?'

'Because we went to Cromer for us 'olidays, miss. With me nana.'

'Cromer?'

'Last August. Nana's got a caravan there. It were reyt good. I got off with this girl. But Mam missed a month on 'er mobile contract. Then t' cooker blew up. Then she gorra letter saying if she don't pay t' moggidge they gonner reposition us.'

'Reposition?'

'Take the 'ouse off of us, miss.'

He stares at the floor in front of her feet.

She wants to put her arms around him and hug him, but teachers can't do that any more. In the back of her mind she's wondering how much of this convoluted report of the Taylor family's finances is true, and how much is Jason's invention. Did the cooker really blow up? Was anyone hurt? Why does Mrs Taylor have a mortgage when everybody else around here is a council tenant? And why does the word 'Cromer' tinkle like a distant bell in her memory?

'Can't your dad help, Jason?'

'Me dad's dead, miss. 'E were a war 'ero. That's why they give 'er a moggidge.'

'Really?'

Is he acting, or does she detect a touch of pride in his voice?

'They said it made no difference 'e were dead cos she could count 'is earnings like if 'e were still alive.'

'Who said that?'

''Im what fixed t' moggidge. First Class Finance.'

Clara sighs, knowing she's beaten on this one.

'Your mum needs some proper advice, Jason. There's the Citizens Advice Bureau.'

'She's been there, miss. They can't do nowt.'

'Why doesn't she ask that councillor she met on Community Day? Malcolm Loxley? Maybe he could help.'

Jason picks up his sheets of paper with a shrug. 'I'm gonner see t' caretaker. I bet 'e'll sponsor me for a cooker.'

A moment later, she sees him passing in front of the classroom window, heading in the direction of the boiler room.

At four o'clock, Clara is waiting in her empty classroom for Oolie to be dropped off by Edna, the manageress, on her way home from Edenthorpe's, because Marcus and Doro have gone to a meeting about the allotments. She tidies away the debris of the day and sorts the reading books by level, keeping an eye on the clock. Soon Oolie's job will be coming to an end too, she thinks. Just as she was beginning to break free and get a life of her own. Even the bit of financial independence – the holiday money saved in the tin, the freedom to buy sweets when Doro's back is turned – has boosted her confidence. Other families will of course be hit much harder. Jason is still outside, she notices, shifting from one foot to the other by the gate as he waits in the rain. Why doesn't he come inside and wait in the hall? His cotton hoody is pulled up over his head, but it's completely soaked. Everything about him looks grey, soggy and shrunken.

At last, Edna's silver Corsa pulls into the car park, and Oolie clambers out of the passenger seat holding a plastic bag over her head. Clara waves from the window, pulls on her raincoat and goes out to greet her. They wave as Edna drives off.

Then Jason sidles up. 'Ey up, miss. Is that your spazzie sister?'

He and Oolie exchange grins of mutual recognition.

At that moment, a woman in a black raincoat with a red umbrella hurries up, stepping carefully around the puddles in her red high heels – yes, it's Megan. Clara's sure of it. Her face is older and her hair, which used to be long, is short and sleek. But her eyes are the same – wide, grey-green, watchful.

'Sorry I'm late, pet,' she says, as Jason runs up to her.

'Megan?'

Clara steps forward, smiling hesitantly, not sure how much warmth is in order, and Megan smiles back. Then Megan's eyes fall upon Oolie and her smile vanishes. She stares. Oolie stares back.

'Julie? Julie-Anna?' she says in a low voice.

'Oolie-Anna, silly,' says Oolie.

Megan bursts into a long quavering sob.

'What's up with 'er?' Oolie whispers loudly.

Megan drops her umbrella and grabs Oolie in her arms.

'Gerroff!' Oolie pulls back, splashing into a puddle, taking Megan with her.

'Hey, Nan! Watch out for t' Mighty Duck!' Jason takes a running jump into the puddle beside them.

Muddy water splashes everywhere.

'Give over, Jason!' cries Megan, still hanging on to Oolie.

'Duck! Duck!' Oolie wriggles herself free of Megan's embrace, and stamps in the puddle.

'Stop it, Oolie! Stop it, Jason!' yells Clara.

But they've worked themselves into a state of giggling hysteria with their stamping and splashing. Megan has pulled out a tissue from her pocket and is dabbing her eyes, which have two large black panda-circles of running mascara spreading on to her cheeks. The rain has intensified. All of them are soaked.

'Megan? I'm Clara,' says Clara to Megan. 'Don't you remember me?'

'Course I do, love!' She whips out another tissue and drops the packet into the puddle – her hands are shaking so much. 'Where are you living these days?'

'I'm in Sheffield now. But Mum and Dad are still in Doncaster. Hardwick Avenue. D'you remember Marcus and Doro?'

'Course I do, course I do, love! How are they?'

'Fine. Why don't you come back and say hello?'

Megan hesitates.

Jason says, 'Yeah, Nan, let's go!'

'Come! Come!' cries Oolie.

A gust of wind catches the red umbrella, and twirls it up into the sky.

DORO: Only a broken bowl

The allotment gardeners' meeting turned out to be more a wake than a plan for action, and Doro, thinking about her little hardy cabbage seedlings that would now never grow into cabbages, suddenly burst into tears and had to be driven home and consoled by Marcus.

Which is how they happen to be in bed together when the doorbell rings, at four thirty, and she suddenly remembers that Clara will be bringing Oolie home today. She jumps out of bed and scrambles into her clothes. To face Edna and Oolie in a state of half-undress is one thing – to face her older daughter's sly and slightly patronising smirk is quite another.

'Hold on, I'm just coming,' she yells, though Clara has her own key, and has already opened the door by the time she's racing downstairs, still buttoning up her cardie. 'I was just having a little snooze,' she says, catching Clara's eye. 'You know? A woman's right to snooze?'

'I've brought some visitors,' says Clara.

Behind Clara, in the hall, Oolie is shuffling out of her wet coat, and a woman and a boy are wiping their feet.

'Hi, come in,' says Doro, studying them curiously. Who are they? The boy looks vaguely familiar: pale skin, large grey eyes, the way he shuffles in his shoes. The woman looks familiar too. She's smiling at Doro, enjoying her stupefaction.

'Hi, Dad,' says Clara, grinning at Marcus, who is shambling down the stairs in his socks, still zipping up his jeans. 'Were you having a snooze too?'

'Mm.' He rubs his eyes. Then rubs them again. 'Megan?'

Yes, it's Megan. Doro's head spins with a rush of mixed feelings.

'How lovely to see you,' she says, hoping the words sound more sincere than she feels. Sometimes, the past should stay in the past: it's been invading the present too much recently.

'I bumped into Megan outside the school,' says Clara. 'She's Jason's grandmother.'

'I see,' says Doro. (Isn't Jason the same boy who caused havoc with Oolie on Community Day?)

'And Jason is Carl's son,' Megan says, shaking out a red umbrella. 'Remember Carl?'

Doro remembers the sullen little boy despatching insects under the kitchen table; and she remembers what Janey said.

'He died . . .?'

'Roadside bomb. In Helmand. It was in all the papers.' There's sadness and a touch of pride in Megan's voice. 'He wasn't even that keen on the army. He wanted to go to university, like you lot. He loved to listen to your talk. Remember, he used to sit under the table and listen? But his school didn't do A levels, and the college was useless. So he joined the army. Said he wanted to travel.' Her head droops and, despite her jaunty lipstick and high heels, she suddenly looks poor and old.

''E were a war 'ero,' says Jason.

What a terrible shame. What a terrible waste, thinks Doro.

'Come in and have some tea,' she says.

They follow her through into the kitchen. The remains of lunch are still on the table.

'Have a seat. Sorry about the mess.'

'Remember t' muck in t' old Coal Board offices?' Megan grins, then catches Doro's eye. 'Sorry, I didn't mean no offence.'

Doro bites her tongue. Megan was never at the forefront of the domestic brigade. Bustling with resentment, she clears the table, puts the kettle on and searches for some biscuits, but they've all disappeared – Oolie must have discovered her secret hiding place. All she can find are some ancient cream crackers, soft with age, which she puts in the bin.

Jason and Oolie are sitting on the sofa, squabbling over the remote control. She can see them through the open door.

'D'you like Russell Brand?' asks Oolie.

'He looks like a poof,' says Jason, 'wi' long manky 'air.'

'I want to shag 'im.'

'Only spazzies fancy Russell Brand.'

'Shut it, Jason,' growls Megan.

'Talking about long hair, we bumped into Chris Howe the other day,' says Marcus. 'Remember him?'

'Him what was always showing off 'is little chipolata?' Megan laughs, then falls silent, looking from Marcus to Doro to Clara.

What's going on? Doro feels a twinge of unease.

'I saw Janey Darkins in Woolworths. She said you're living in Elmfield.'

'That slapper. Less I seen of her the better.'

Doro is startled by her vehemence. Then she remembers. Bruno.

'Do you still hear from Bruno?'

She shrugs. 'He went back to Italy, din't he?'

Doro pours the boiling water into the old brown teapot and, without looking up, remarks, 'Janey said he's not Oolie-Anna's father.' She tries to drop it casually into the conversation, but it falls like a brick into a well of silence.

Clara looks around with a funny smirk on her face. Megan opens her handbag, and starts to sift through its contents. Eventually, she pulls out a packet of Marlboro and a plastic lighter.

'Mind if I smoke?'

'No. But . . .'

'It's none of her business, is it?' She draws deeply and puffs out a sigh of smoke.

Marcus finds an ashtray and puts it in front of her on the table. Doro thinks she catches a quick exchange of glances between him and Megan.

'Haven't you got any biscuits?' asks Clara, setting out the teacups and milk jug.

'No,' says Doro.

She pours the tea in silence, as though to speak might disturb the herd of elephants that have gathered in the room. Megan is watching Oolie and Jason through the open door. Doro cannot read her expression.

Clara calls through the open door. 'Oolie, Jason, d'you want some tea?'

They come bouncing in, nudging each other.

'In't there no biscuits?' asks Oolie.

'Somebody ate them all,' says Doro. 'I wonder who that could be?'

'It were t'amster,' says Oolie. 'I seed 'im. Little bugger.'

Doro laughs. Winding people up is something else Oolie has learned at Edenthorpe's. 'Oolie, what a terrible fib!'

'When I 'ave me own flat, I'm going to 'ave a 'amster.'

'Is she going to have her own flat?' asks Megan.

'Yes, cos Mr Clemmins says.'

'Who's Mr Clemmins?'

'Mr Clements, the social worker,' says Doro. 'It's still under discussion. I suppose, now you're back –' She stops. Her heart is beating wildly. Now Megan is back, will she snatch Oolie away? Will she take over Oolie's life?

'I'll help,' says Megan. 'I mean, I'll help keep an eye on her. In her new flat. If you don't mind.'

'Why should I mind?' says Doro, wondering why she does mind so much.

'Miss killed our school 'amster, din't you, miss?' says Jason.

'Jason, what a porker!' says Clara.

'D'you want to see my bedroom?'

Oolie grabs Jason's arm, and pulls him towards the door. He grins, showing teeth like crooked grey pegs.

'I think I've made a 'it, miss.' He winks at Clara.

What a horrible little boy, Doro thinks; no wonder Clara gets shrewish, having to put up with a class full of kids like that all day, every day.

'I'll come too,' says Clara, and they all troop upstairs, stamping on the treads like a wooden-legged army.

Megan watches them go, with that catlike expression in her grey-green eyes.

'She's a reyt little biddybob, in't she?'

She pulls cigarette smoke deep into her lungs, and expels it with a cough. Doro notices that her hands are trembling.

'Thank you for letting us have her,' says Marcus.

His eyes meet Megan's once more, and Doro thinks, yes, that was the right thing to say, but there's something still unsaid, something waiting to be said.

'What I don't understand,' she says, letting her resentment bubble out through her facade of politeness, 'is how you could just go off and leave her.'

Megan starts coughing again, leaning over and covering her face with her hands.

Upstairs, the wooden-legged army seems to have gone into battle. There's a clatter on the floorboards, and a crash, followed by a scream. Marcus jumps up and races up the stairs.

Doro rolls her eyes and sighs. 'Kids!'

Then she notices Megan has started to cry.

'I'm sorry. I don't want to upset you. But I just want to know why you left her behind.'

Megan hunts through her bag for a tissue, saying nothing.

'Didn't you love her? Didn't you miss her?'

Megan starts to sob, keening like a child.

'He wouldn't have her. He said he'd have Carl, but not Julie.'

'Who was he?'

'Just another bloke. A businessman. From Leeds. It didn't even last that long. He said I had to choose between her and him.'

Doro moves her chair close and puts an arm around her. 'And you chose him?'

Megan moans. Her eyes and nose are streaming. 'I thought she'd be happy wi' you lot. I thought you'd look after her better'n I could.'

She dabs hopelessly with her sleeve. Doro fetches a roll of kitchen paper and puts it on the table.

'You thought she'd be better off here, because Marcus was . . .'

'Yes. You're blaming me like I'm some kind of monster, but I thought he'd have told you by now.' She gets out another cigarette, but her hands are shaking so much she can hardly keep the flame to the tip of it. 'And because of you, Doro. The way you loved her. Thank you for looking after her. I never said thank you, did I? She's turned out lovely.'

'It was . . .' Doro pauses, trying to catch the thoughts whirling through her head.

My duty? Just one of those things? Somebody had to? Worth-while? A pleasure?

'It was nothing!' Marcus yells down the stairs. 'Just a broken bowl.'

The darkness is absolute. Then after some time, a faint grey oblong appears behind the curtains, with a stripe of pale silver down the middle, where the curtains don't quite meet. As she lies watching, the grey lightens, and now she can hear birdsong. A thrush. A black-bird. And some sounds she doesn't recognise. She listens. It must be dawn. How long has she been lying here, trying to get back to sleep? In the darkness of the room she can hear his breathing – short, shallow breaths. No snuffling.

'Marcus? Are you awake?'

'Yes. Are you?'

'Yes.'

'You're not angry with me, are you, Doro?' He folds her in his arms, pulling her close into his sleepy warmth.

She wriggles a bit, then relaxes. 'No, not very.'

'Not very?'

'But why didn't you tell me?' She's glad it's dark, and he can't see the tightness around her mouth.

'I wasn't sure at first. Then the longer I left it, the harder it was to tell you.'

'I wish you'd told me.'

'I wish I had too. But it wouldn't have made any difference, would it?'

She thinks of the ways her life might have been different without Oolie. She might have moved back to London. She might have risen in her career and become the principal of her college. She might have gone to Italy and married Bruno. She might have written a bestselling novel. She might have become a guru. She might . . .

'No, probably not,' she says.

CLARA: The SPA

Clara settles her class down with the age-old trick of asking them to write about their family, and wishes she could sneak off to the staff-room for a fag, à la Mrs Wiseman, but instead she gazes out of the window, and finds herself wondering whether that broken bowl yesterday, still half full of Oolie's breakfast porridge, was an accident, or whether Jason pushed Oolie on purpose. The way he grinned when Clara reprimanded him was a giveaway. It's odd that he isn't in school today, but his attendance is patchy at the best of times.

She notices that someone has left a scattering of little black chippings under her chair again. She must mention it to the cleaners before she goes home.

But at home time, Robbie Lewis sidles up to her.

'I just got a text off Jason, miss. The bailiffs is coming to their 'ouse. 'E says can you go round? It'll be a reyt laugh.'

If Jackie and Jason are really being evicted there's probably nothing she can do, but she decides to call in anyway.

It's after four, and the traffic is building up as she weaves her way through the estate. Jason's house is in Hawthorn Avenue, known locally as The SPA. As she turns into the small road of scruffy red-brick semis, she sees a sleek black shiny four-by-four with 'FIRST CLASS FINANCE' written on the side, parked on the verge. She rings the doorbell and Jason appears, almost swallowed up in a man-sized sweatshirt, a shifty smile on his face.

'Mam, me girlfriend's here!' he calls indoors.

The house is incredibly warm and smells of fried food, cat pee and air fresheners. A television is blaring somewhere, booming voices pierced with blasts of laughter like gunfire. The floor is covered with debris – scattered clothing, shoes, packaging, random bits of broken plastic – as though people have fled from a battlefield.

Bulging cardboard boxes are lined up along one wall. As she stands in the hall wondering whether she remembered to lock her car, Mrs Taylor appears, looking fragile and girlish in skinny jeans and a white blouse.

'I got a message . . .'

'Come in, miss. Put the kettle on, Jason.'

'I saw Mr First Class Finance's car outside . . .'

'Trev Fertle. Tricky Trev, we call him. He does a lot of business on t' SPA.'

'Why's it called The SPA?'

'Single Parents Avenue. We've all got mortgages. Now he wants me to consolidate.'

'What does that mean?'

'I think it means taking out another loan. But see, I lost my job . . .' She sighs.

'I'm sorry. Jason said the bailiffs are coming. And you need a new cooker.'

'What bailiffs? What cooker? That kid! Jason? What you been telling everybody?'

Before he can answer, the doorbell pings.

Mrs Taylor opens it a crack. 'You can't come in, Trev. I've got company.'

But the visitor has his foot wedged in the door; he forces it open, and shoves past her into the hall. Clara hovers in the living room, wondering whether to intervene.

'You've really let me down, Jackie!' Mr First Class Finance is more gelled-up and speeded-up than ever. 'See that out there, Jackie? You know how much that cost? Fifty grand. How'm I gonner pay it off?'

He jiggles from foot to foot. His jeans look ready to dislodge and slip over his hips any minute.

'I told you, I lost my job. I'm owing on my mobile contract.'

'I've got a business to run, Jackie. I've got expenses.' He kicks one of the boxes, denting the cardboard. 'Planning to do a flit? Leave me in the shit?'

'Give us a break, Trev. Just a couple of weeks.'

'You've been a bad girl, Jackie.'

313

Clara can't see the look in his eyes, but she can hear the menace in his voice.

'I like bad girls. You know I've always fancied you, Jackie.'

He reaches out a quick hand. Jackie pulls away.

'Don't be a tosser, Trev.'

Clara steps into the hall, ready to back her up.

Trev's eyes glimmer with recognition. 'Weh-hey! The sexy school teacher too!'

'For heaven's sake!'

'Lay off me mam! And me girlfriend. Or I'll do yer!' Jason puffs out his shoulders in his baggy T-shirt.

'You, you little minger? Don't make me laugh. See this?' He unzips his black jacket and grips Jason by the ear, pulling his head down towards the label. 'Ver-soddin-sachy. Now fuck off while I see to these ladies.'

'Ow! Gerroff!'

'Stop that this minute!' Clara snaps in the voice she usually employs with playground bullies. 'You're assaulting a minor!'

She grabs his sleeve. He pulls back. With a tsic-tsic-tsic-tsic of rending cloth, it comes away in her hand.

'Now look what you've done! You know how much this cost?' His face is like a purple storm in which the pimples glow like pinpricks of fire.

'Looks like Ver-soddin-trashy.' She flings the sleeve on the floor and stamps on it.

Then the doorbell pings.

Nobody moves.

But whoever is on the other side has a key, for there's a scraping sound and, a moment later, the door opens and in steps Megan: red lipstick, red high heels, red umbrella. She seems so much bolder and brasher than the Megan Clara remembers from the commune.

'What's going off? Jason told me to come round.' She turns on Mr First Class Finance. 'Whatever it is you're selling, Tricky, she don't want it.'

'Weh-hey, the glammy granny too! I'm up for it!'

'Piss off, parasite!' She pokes him with her umbrella.

This is turning out to be much more fun than Clara had expected. She grabs his other sleeve and gives a tug.

Megan yanks at his belt. 'Get his keks down!'

'Yeah! Three on one! Mind my shirt, it's Ralph Lauren! I'll take the granny first!'

'You mucky shite-gob!' Jason shouts. 'Watch out, Nana!'

He steps back, bends, takes a run, and slams his bullet head hard into Trev's groin. Trev yelps and doubles over in pain.

'Nice one, Jason,' Megan purrs. She winks at Clara. 'The Doncaster kiss.'

Clara smiles nervously.

Then the doorbell pings.

Jason opens the door and Councillor Loxley steps inside, grey-suited and steely. He surveys the scene with gimlet eyes.

'Someone called my office,' he says. 'How can I help?'

Clara meets his eyes for a moment, and gives a little bewildered shrug.

Mr First Class Finance raises his head. 'Dad . . .'

'Stop right there,' says the councillor. 'I'm not your dad. Remember? I warned you . . .'

'Oh, thank you, sir, for coming, sir!' Jackie flings her arms around him. The top button of her blouse pops open.

Then the doorbell pings.

The councillor straightens his tie, Jackie adjusts her top, Megan wraps the belt around her knuckles. Trev stuffs the ripped-off sleeves into his pocket. Clara holds her breath as Jason answers the door.

A massive muscle-gone-to-paunch hulk of a man, complete with tattoos and string vest, is standing on the path. He's pushing a porter's trolley. On the trolley is an enormous gleaming white cooker. Behind the hulk and the cooker is Mr Philpott. He has a bunch of red roses in his hand.

'Fair nymph!'

He steps forward, brandishing the roses at Jackie. He's wearing his brown suit and smells of some sickly sweet perfume which Clara recognises as Zoflora. Jackie buries her face in her hands.

'Jason, what've you been up to?' hisses Megan. 'Go an' make us a cup of tea.'

A smile flits across Jason's face.

'Look here, spud,' barks the councillor, 'it's not wanted. Take it and bugger off.'

'Bugger off, yoursen!' Mr Philpott waves his arms theatrically. 'To a nunnery go! I knew your family when they lived in t' Prospects, Malc Loxley. When you and your cousins nicked all t' lead off of t' chapel roof. And him and his gang of lawless resolutes –' he jabs a finger at Trev '– should've been banged up for that fire. But it were all hushed over.'

'Watch your mouth,' says the councillor.

'What fire?' asks Clara.

'So d'you want this cooker, or what?' The hulk is getting impatient.

'Aye, put it in the kitchen!' orders Mr Philpott.

'No!' shrieks Jackie. 'I don't want it. There's nowt wrong wi' my cooker!'

'Hang on, mate. That's a good cooker.' Mr First Class Finance is assessing it with an entrepreneurial eye. 'What's the spec? How much d'you want for it? Maybe . . .'

Mr Philpott looks suddenly wily. Jackie looks relieved. Megan looks perplexed. The hulk looks hulky. The councillor looks at his watch. Clara looks from the councillor to Mr First Class Finance – yes, there is a definite resemblance. Jason appears carrying a tray with eight cups of tea – hot, strong and sweet.

As she manoeuvres her car off the verge back on to Hawthorn Avenue, she sees in her rear-view mirror that the black four-by-four has already been backed up to the house and Mr Philpott, the hulk, Mr First Class Finance and the councillor are all heaving and shoving the big gleaming cooker into its open hatch. Jackie, Megan and Jason are standing by and watching.

Jason blows her a kiss as she drives off.

It's twilight by the time she heads back towards the M18. The sky is streaked with purple, but the countryside is flat and colourless, spotted with dark bushes and hedges and small red-brick houses where shadows are gathering. The rush-hour traffic has died down, and the evening traffic hasn't started up yet. Where the A6182 crosses the railway line she passes through a scrub-covered dell which is a favourite spot for fly-tipping. Someone has been at it again, she observes, and then she notices that the quantity and bulk of black bin bags that have been dumped look familiar.

She's exhausted and hungry and she could just drive on by and leave them for the wind to blow around, or for someone else to clean up – but she's not that sort of person. Slamming on the brakes, she reverses her car and goes over to investigate. And yes, sure enough, it's the recycling bags from school, which Mr First Class Finance took away.

She opens her boot and rearranges various junk to make room. Behind another box of newspapers awaiting the recycling and tucked under the tyre tools, something green catches her eye. It's her purse – the one she thought Jason had stolen. It must have fallen out of her bag. She checks: her credit cards, the three ten-pound notes, they're all there.

She loads up as many of the bin bags as she can cram into the boot, the passenger seat and back-seat space, and drives back to Sheffield. The rest will have to wait for another day.

SERGE: *Dr Dhaliwal*

Serge couldn't face work on Monday – in fact, he doubts that he will ever be able to face it again – but just to cover himself on Tuesday he signs on with a local GP, a Dr H. Dhaliwal, who turns out to be thin harassed young woman, barely older than him, who questions him in some detail about his accident.

Why didn't he put out his arm to break his fall? Did he black out? He doesn't know.

She confirms that his nose is fractured and listens to his heart in a way he finds vaguely erotic. No one has shown such interest in his body since . . . since . . . Tears mist his eyes.

How did he get home, she asks?

He doesn't want to go into all that, so he tells her he can't remember.

'So you've suffered loss of memory?'

'Totally.'

She diagnoses a moderate concussion, sends him off to the hospital for a raft of tests, orders him to lay off alcohol and to take it easy for a week. She advises him to phone in sick.

'Shall I come and see you again?'

'Only if the symptoms return.'

I am a symptom! My whole life is a symptom! Help me, Dr Dhaliwal!

'Thank you, Doctor.'

She smiles kindly. Actually, she has quite cute dimples.

He's not sure about her concussion diagnosis but, amazingly, when he phones to extend his sick leave ('I'm feeling sort of anxious. And a bit depressed') she doesn't quibble.

He spends the time on his own in his penthouse, watching autumn speed into winter from his window. Brisk clouds race across the sky, and brown leaves appear on his balcony out of nowhere. The evenings are cold. One night, it snows.

By the second week he's beginning to get seriously bored, so he logs on and opens his accounts. In his absence, Dr Black has been doing very nicely. Not only is his cash reserve flush, but SYC has gone through the roof. Serge gasps when he totals up the numbers: he is worth £1.13 million. How did that happen? Pity he sold Edenthorpe Engineering too soon, else it would be even more. Really, this stock trading thing is quite a doddle once you get the hang of it. A peep at Kenporter1601's transactions reveals that he's been selling too. Weird. To look at the transactions, you'd think the two of them had mounted a concerted bear raid to drive the price of Edenthorpe down deliberately – though his role was purely accidental.

His personal finances also seem very healthy. Further investigation discloses a credit to his card account of £10,488.81 from the Poire d'Or restaurant. Nice one. Though a bit late.

The only irritation is a constant tirade of texts and missed calls from Doro, plus a few from Clara and some from an unknown number. He deletes them all. At a time like this, he has to focus his mind on positive thoughts.

He phones the HR department at FATCA to inform them of his progress and is surprised to receive by post, a few days later, a get-well-soon card from his colleagues. There are five signatures. The Hamburger is missing, but Maroushka is there – a curly Cyrillic scrawl in the top right-hand corner. This has the effect of considerably speeding up his recovery.

PART FIVE

Everything Must Go

CLARA: Give 'im no tea

At half past three precisely on Wednesday, Clara zips out of the classroom, straight into her car, and off to Hardwick Avenue.

They're having a family meeting to discuss Oolie's future living arrangements. Mr Clements has called it, Marcus and Doro have reluctantly agreed, and Oolie has insisted that Clara be there.

She notes as she comes through the door that the house has been tidied up. An unfamiliar smell greets her that is floral and slightly sickly – Doro must have been spraying air freshener around.

Oolie greets her with a hug in the hall. 'Hiya, Clarie. 'E's not 'ere yet. Mum says we ent gotter give 'im no tea.'

'No tea? Why?'

'She says she don't want 'im 'angin' around.'

Clara shrugs. Doro seems to be getting more and more peculiar. 'Well, I need a cuppa. I've had a hard day at school.'

She goes into the kitchen to put the kettle on. Oolie follows her.

'Did it come back, that 'amster?' An obscure emotion flits across her face.

This is the second time she's mentioned it.

'Oolie, are you sure it wasn't you that let him out?'

Oolie shakes her head emphatically. 'It worrent me. 'E done it 'imself. Cheeky bugger. 'E nicked the key. I seed 'im.'

'Oolie, you're fibbing! You're winding me up!'

Oolie lowers her eyes sulkily. 'No I in't. Cross me 'eart. Let 'im die. Poker needle in 'is eye.'

Clara has always assumed that Oolie sometimes gets things muddled, but doesn't have the ability to actually invent things. What else has she been inventing?

But before she can pursue this line of enquiry, the doorbell rings and her parents materialise in the hallway. Her mother is wearing a T-shirt that says '*Rectify the anomaly*'. Her father is wearing a tie.

Clara stares. This must be serious.

They seat themselves around the kitchen table.

'Would you like a cup of tea?' Her mother fixes the social worker with a cold eye.

'Mum says you ain't gotter 'ave no tea,' says Oolie.

'No. I'm fine, thanks,' he says.

'Mum says she don't want you 'angin' around,' says Oolie.

'I'll try to be brief, then.' He blinks rapidly as he takes a folder out of his briefcase. 'As you may know, there's going to be a sheltered housing scheme as part of the Greenhill Lees redevelopment plan. There's already a waiting list for places. Now, as you know, I'm very keen to get Oolie-Anna's name down on that waiting list. But I'd like your agreement.'

'And what if we don't agree?' says Doro.

'I think you will,' he says.

Wow! He's quite brave, thinks Clara, to face Doro down like that.

'Tell 'er, Clarie! Tell 'er I wanna have my own flat,' says Oolie. 'I'm fed up of living at home. Cos Dad farts all the time.'

Marcus laughs. 'It's a good enough reason.'

'Who's going to make sure she doesn't eat rubbish?' says Doro. 'Who's going to make sure she takes . . . her medication?'

'What midi-cakes?'

'It's not the end of the world if she sometimes eats a bit of pizza,' Clara chips in.

'We'll put support in,' says Mr Clements. 'We'll monitor things carefully.'

'And Megan'll help,' says Clara. 'Like she said, Oolie'll be more of a presence in her life now than she was in the past.'

'That's not difficult, is it?' Doro retorts.

'You can be involved just as much or as little as you want, Mrs Lerner. It's better to start letting go now, in a planned way, when all the services are in place, than to wait for an emergency . . .'

'He's got a point, Mum,' says Clara. 'You and Marcus are getting elderly, if I may say so.'

She's noticed how tired Marcus looks, and how distracted Doro seems.

'No, we're not!'

'Yes, you are, Mum. It's not going to get any better.'

Doro rolls her eyes. Mr Clements frowns at Clara.

'See it in a positive light. Don't think of it as an imposition. Think of it as a lovely gift to your daughter, Mrs Lerner. The gift of blossoming independence.'

He's obviously been on one of those positive-thinking courses.

'Giff! I wanna giff!' cries Oolie.

'And what if she gets P-R-E-G-N-A-N-T?' Doro spells.

'What's ayan tea?' asks Oolie.

'She's longing for a B-A-B-Y.'

'Look, Mrs Lerner, I know what you're worried about,' says the social worker quietly. 'I went through the case notes, right back to 1994. You know, in the nineties they were finding child abuse all over the place. Since then, we've come to accept more . . . er . . . unconventional living arrangements.'

'That's exactly what I said at the time,' snaps Doro.

'Mm. The other thing I discovered –' he shuffles around in his chair and nods towards Doro almost apologetically '– is that you and Mr Lerner never actually completed the legal adoption process.'

'Because we weren't married! Because we lived in a commune! Because the social worker who interviewed us was a narrow-minded bigot with an obsession about nudity and paedophilia! Probably you are too! What? Don't you shush me!' Her mother turns furiously on poor Marcus, who's had the temerity to raise a finger to his lips.

'I think this is very helpful,' says Mr Clements calmly. 'You need to express your worries.'

'There was a fire! Somebody set the bloody house on fire! Isn't that worry enough?'

'Mum thinks it were me, but it worrent,' Oolie confides to Mr Clements in a loud whisper. 'It were some lads. I seed 'em.'

Doro's cheeks have gone chalky, like an old woman's. Clara feels quite sorry for her.

'I think that's enough,' she intervenes. 'Unless you've got something constructive to say?'

'Why not try it for six months? If after that it isn't working out, you can always go back . . .'

'All right!' Doro sighs, and throws up her hands. 'You've bludgeoned me into submission.' She gets up like a sleepwalker and blunders into the kitchen to put the kettle on.

'Well done,' whispers Clara to Mr Clements.

He shrugs, and smiles. 'D'you think she'll let me have that tea now?'

'I expect so,' says Marcus.

'Dad, you've just farted again,' says Oolie.

Pity about the beard, thinks Clara.

DORO: The fire

Despite the Christmas decorations already drooping between the lamp posts, or maybe because of them, Doncaster town centre looks particularly cheerless on the last Saturday of November, as Doro makes her way along almost empty pavements towards Woolworths, in search of Janey. There are things she needs to ask about the fire, things she needs to clarify. It was so long ago, everyone has forgotten, apart from her, and even her own recollection has become muddied between what she saw, what she inferred, and the things she said at the time, which have become fixed in her memory as a true record of events. Janey's words last time they met are lodged in her mind. 'Wasn't it some lads?'

But Woolworths' windows are plastered with giant 'CLOSING DOWN SALE!' posters, and Janey isn't there. She wanders around the desolate store, between the picked-over counters and posters proclaiming 'BUY NOW WHILE STOCKS LAST!', vaguely remembering having read something about Woolworths going into receivership. It seems incredible that something so apparently permanent, something which has been here since her own childhood, can suddenly disappear just like that.

When she was a little girl, her mother used to take her on Saturday to spend her pocket money on the Woolworths pick-and-mix counter in Norwich. Thirty years later, when they lived in Solidarity Hall, she did the same with Clara and Serge. Serge was one of those kids who always hoarded his sweets, and cried when the other kids tried to steal them. Doro smiles, remembering the tears and squabbles of long ago. Later, he gave up hoarding sweets, and started hoarding other things – snail shells, dried seed heads, pine cones.

Yes, she found the charred remnants of the pine cones in the grate after the fire. Serge must have gathered them in Campsall Woods – there weren't any pine trees near the house. She remembers so vividly, even after fourteen years, driving back from work that day, late because of a hold-up in the town centre. A little girl knocked over by a speeding car. Someone else's tragedy.

She remembers how her heart lurched when she turned into their lane and saw, through the swish of windscreen wipers, a tight little knot of people gawping at the fire engine in front of their house, the great arcs of water playing from the hoses. She remembers the smell of charred wood and scorched paint, the billowing plumes of smoke rising up through the thin useless rain. But why was Serge there? He should have been at school, at the four o'clock chess club. Yet there he was, tears running down his face with raindrops and grey rivulets of ash, jabbering about Oolie and how he'd seen smoke and run all the way to the red telephone box in the village. And she'd looked around for Oolie, thinking she should be back any minute now, and suddenly she'd realised and started to scream, 'Oolie! Where's Oolie?'

They'd broken down the door of the annexe, and pulled her out. She was unconscious, with horrific burns to her arms. Doro had forced herself to be calm, putting her arms around Serge, covering his eyes with her hands. Only when the ambulance arrived did she break down and shout at the idle onlookers blocking its way up the lane. Where had these people come from? She barely knew them. A woman put her arm around her. 'She'll be all right, duck. It's just the smoke.'

Doro shrugged her off angrily. What did she know?

The others drifted back between four and six o'clock – Otto and Star first, then Toussaint and Kollontai, followed by Nick, Moira, Marcus and lastly Chris Howe, who finished work at five thirty. The police took statements from all of them. The absentees were Clara who was away at university, Chris Watt who'd gone to visit her sister in Skelmersdale, and Fred who was in London. The neighbours had melted away. Presumably the police interviewed them too.

They questioned Oolie while she was still in hospital.

'Come on. You can do better than that, sweetheart. Who was there when you came home?' the policewoman coaxed.

Oolie put her hands over her face and started to howl.

'Can't you see, you're just making it worse,' Doro pleaded. 'Why don't you let me talk to her alone?'

The detective was a mother herself. 'I'm sorry, love,' she said. 'It wouldn't stand up in court. I'm just doing my job.'

Doro was sure that Oolie herself was capable of starting a fire by accident, but could she have put the pine cones there and put a match under them? Or was it Serge, home early from school, trying out an experiment or playing a game that had gone dreadfully wrong? Or had someone unknown set out to harm her? Doro shuddered, recalling the incident with the bricks when Oolie was a toddler, wondering why vulnerable people attract such malice.

The minibus driver who'd dropped Oolie off was quizzed.

Why was she there alone at that time? Why had she come home early?

The driver denied he was early; three thirty was the normal dropping-off time. Yes, he'd taken her right up the lane to the house, he said. He thought there was someone at home, because Oolie had waved and disappeared into the house, so the door must have been unlocked.

Had the last person out not locked the door when they left? Or did someone inside the house let her in? Serge?

Serge had called the fire brigade, so he must have been there at the time, or shortly after. Oolie had seen no one when the door from the house slammed, trapping her inside the annexe.

'Have you anything you want to tell me, Serge?' Doro had asked quietly when they were alone together. He was about fifteen at the time.

'Why does everybody think it's me?' he'd yelled, and burst into tears.

She didn't press him any more, but buried the pine-cone fragments in the garden under the broad beans.

The commune with its free-and-easy living arrangements came under scrutiny. The police seemed more concerned about who was sleeping with whom than with how the fire started. Chris Howe confirmed their worst suspicions when he opened the door half naked, and started railing about fascism. Then Social Services got involved and there was talk of taking all the children into care.

The Chrises and their kids decamped one night, without leaving contact details. Jen came and took Otto away, and Nick followed them. Fred stayed in London; he came back one weekend to collect his books and say goodbye. Only Moira and Star, who had nowhere else to go, stayed on in the commune, until they too left at the beginning of 1995. Maybe Doro, Marcus and Serge should have left at the same time. But Oolie was happily settled in a new school and Marcus had become Head of Department at the Institute.

For a while, the four of them rattled around in the huge empty house with its burned-out annexe, charred exposed rafters and sickening stink of smoke that tainted everything. The police investigation dragged on and eventually ground to a halt, with the finger of blame seeming to point at Oolie herself. But Doro still wondered in her heart how Serge's pine cones had ended up in the grate. There were no further clues. A neighbour thought she'd glimpsed a fleeting figure running up the lane, but couldn't give a description or a precise time. Serge running to the phone box, or some bad lad running away?

Despite all the gawping, it seemed nobody had seen anything – or if they had, they weren't saying. In closed communities there's always talk, tittle-tattle, but although they'd tried so hard to be accepted, the commune had never become a part of that subterranean rumour mill, tuned into its gossip networks, subject to its loyalties, secrets and feuds.

But Janey was. Janey must know someone who knew someone who'd lived in Campsall or Norton at the time. Janey must know what had been said, and what was left unsaid.

'Do you know Janey Darkins?' Doro asks a greasy-haired young man on the toy counter, but he just shrugs.

A young woman on cosmetics tells her she's left. 'We're closing down. Everybody's leaving.'

*

Doro wanders blindly out into the dank wintry morning, wondering what to do next. Maybe it's for the best that the questions will never be answered. She sits in a tiny gloomy café, where maybe she would have taken Janey, and drinks bitter charred-tasting coffee from a polystyrene cup, wondering, is it better for Oolie to let the memories lie buried until they finally rot and dissolve away? Or is it better to dig them out and expose them to the bright disinfectant light of day?

There's a whole industry of therapy and counselling and analysis based on the belief that the past must be unearthed and sanitised like a leaking sewer. And there's Time the Healer – with his muddled, murky comfort of forgetting.

Slowly, as if walking has become a great effort, she makes her way back up the empty High Street, with its sprinkling of newly boarded-up fronts, fly-by-night shops selling Christmas tinsel, and shops with closing-down sales. Waiting at the bus stop with her pensioner's bus pass at the ready, she feels the weight of the low grey sky pressing down on her.

What will happen to Oolie now? How could Marcus lie to her for all those years? What is Serge hiding from her?

Everything that has underpinned her life for the last twenty years has been turned upside down in this last month. The allotment, her paradise and sanctuary, is about to be destroyed. Even the city where she lives seems to be disintegrating around her. 'SPECIAL OFFER!', '£1 GREAT VALUE!', 'EVERYTHING MUST GO!' scream the banners.

SERGE: *The Treasury Committee*

Serge decides to walk to work on Monday, rather than catching the tube, to give himself time to prepare mentally for what awaits him. It's a cold, fresh December morning, with a low sun nudging away last night's snow clouds, and melting the traces of snow on the pavements. He says good morning to the shopkeepers opening up their blinds and putting out their pavement signs. He says good morning to the buffed-up office drones sipping a pre-office lungo at the heated tables on the pavement outside Peppe's. He says good morning to the doorman at FATCA and the blonde girls on reception. He says good morning to the four morose guys and one sullen sleepy girl crammed in the lift. He feels good.

The wall of noise as he swings open the doors into the trading hall almost blows him away, after the silence of the last fortnight. But he pulls himself together and smiles. He says good morning to Tootie and Lucie and the Frenchies. The Hamburger's chair is empty. Maroushka is in the glass-walled office, wearing a new black dress with a matching jacket, talking on the phone and swivelling on Timo's old chair. She looks fabulous in black, but older. And her hair's different, pulled back in a tight bun instead of cascading down her shoulders. She catches his eye, wiggles four fingers, then turns away. He hangs his jacket on the back of his chair and switches on his desktop. It takes an age to warm up, upload its fortnight's worth of security scans, configurations, patches and updates, tick-boxes for unintelligible policies, then reboot itself. So he strolls to the glass-walled office and leans in the doorway.

'How's things?'

She finishes her phone call and looks up.

'Everything normal. Welcome back to Securitisation desk, Sergei.'

'I've heard there's a new VP?'

She meets his eye with an uncertain smile, from which the mischievous twelve-year-old grin has only recently been banished.

'He is I.'

A wave of gloom washes over him, blotting out the brightness of the morning. But why does he have this bad feeling? Shouldn't he be pleased for her?

'Congratulations.'

'Thank you, Sergei. Also, you must congratulate me for success of visa application.'

'Congratulations, goddess. So you're not running off back to Zh – . . . to your country any time soon?'

'Here is better money opportunity. Also I am now big Anglo-feel. Queenlizabeth fishanchip cuppa tea Royal Navy Witcliff of Dover. Now I apply for British passport.'

He has never seen her look so misty-eyed before.

'So you don't fancy Brazil?'

'Brazil?' She laughs. 'Why for, Sergei? Primitive persons are inhabiting Brazil. By the way, we are in interesting situation here. Your cooperation will be helpful for new market strategy for Green Shoots. We talk this afternoon.'

She dismisses him with a chair swivel, and picks up the phone again.

'How's things?' he asks the Frenchies, who are looking pissed off and pouty, in an elegant Gallic sort of way. They shrug, their slim shoulders rippling under the classy fabric of their jackets, and reply in low voices, glancing towards the office.

'*C'est un peu emmerdant . . .*'

'*. . . avec mademoiselle. Elle est . . .*'

'*Dites-le. C'est un monstre. Comme la Méduse . . .*'

'Er . . . jellyfish?' He dredges up his holiday French. Of all Maroushka's qualities, jelly-like does not spring to mind.

'Gorgon.'

'Surely she's not *that* bad.'

'You will see.'

'What happened to . . .?' He indicates the empty chair where the Hamburger used to sit.

''E 'as resignated himself.'

''E is lacking the courage.'

'How's things?' he asks Lucie and Tootie.

'Not too bad, actually,' says Lucie. 'There've been a few disappearances, but we keep smiling, don't we?'

'*You* do,' says Tootie through his nose. '*I'm* applying for other jobs.'

'How did it happen – I mean, Maroushka getting the team-leader job? I thought there were more promising candidates . . .'

'Precisely. One minute she's cleaning the office floor, next minute she's sitting in the swivel chair. Makes you wonder, doesn't it?'

'Now you put it that way. But . . .?'

'She either knows something, or she's shagged someone. Can you think of any other explanation?'

He's almost spitting venom, and Serge thinks however bad Maroushka turns out to be, Toby would surely have been worse.

'What about Chicken?'

'He's still his same adorable self. Though nowadays he seems to spend most of his time laying eggs in Downing Street.'

'Really?'

'Apparently he's advising them how to fix the financial crisis.'

'Crumbs.'

'Precisely. And you'd better watch your back, Freebie, because now he's found the new philosopher's stone, he won't need us quants to eliminate risk for him any more.'

'What d'you mean? What stone?'

'Imagine gambling in a casino, Freebie, and everything you win, you keep. And every time you lose, a kind-hearted donkey called Joe Public comes along with a sack of gold and pays off your debt.'

Serge feels a tightness in his throat, like when you try to stop yourself from puking up.

'Unlimited upside?'

'Precisely. He just has to keep the Government on side, by keeping them running scared.' Tootie flings a glance towards the door. 'And speaking of . . .'

Even from where he's standing, Serge can feel the double

displacement of air – puff-puff – as the doors swing open and dis-gorge Chicken into the trading hall. He seems to have grown fatter; for the first time, Serge notices that his belly sticks out over his belt; one of his trouser legs has got hitched in his sock, so you can see the muscular calf tapering to the boot which Serge now clearly sees is built up at the heel. In fact, sideways on, he has the shape of a gro-tesquely elongated chicken.

'Freebie! Good to see you back! How's the nose?' He rests his knuckles on the desk and twists his head round to peer up into Serge's nostril. 'Joachim said you had some digestive problem too. Had to keep dashing off to the loo. You should have said.'

It takes him a moment to work out that Joachim is the Ham-burger.

'Yes, it was a bit embarrassing. But all fine now, thanks, Chief Ken. They gave me the all clear.'

'Good. I'll go and tell Maroushka you're back.'

'There's no need. I've already told her,' Serge blurts.

Chicken's eyes narrow. He leans forward on his knuckles. 'You want to be the sex manager around here, Freebie?'

Is he kidding? Or could this be a promotion? Serge blinks. It sounds good. In fact, it sounds too good to be true. And in the finan-cial world, when things seem too good to be true they usually are.

'Er . . . what does that involve exactly?'

'It means when I want your fucking advice, I'll fucking ask you.' Chicken chortles, showing his teeth.

Serge titters, though Chicken didn't sound like he was joking.

'You've missed a most interesting episode on the markets, Free-bie. New trading conditions. Enhanced prospects for corporate growth. Some might say conflict of interests. But we're confident in our strategy. Maroushka'll fill you in on the details.'

Now he's all smiles again. What the fuck is he talking about?

'You may have heard about my . . . er . . . new involvement?' Chicken continues.

Serge hasn't checked the emails recently. Is there a new woman on the scene? Maroushka? He feels that taste of suppressed vomit again. He's starting to wish he'd stayed at home.

'Treasury. Policy committee.' Chicken's chest seems to puff as he speaks the words. 'We're trying to firm up the Government's commitment to the role of the financial sector in the national economy.'

'Oh, I see.'

'Remind the politicians that what's good for the banks is good for Britain. They've no idea how the financial world thinks. What I keep telling them is, we have to reassure the markets. Show we're capable of fiscal discipline. Chop the public sector down to size. Chop, chop. Otherwise the markets panic. Government bonds get downgraded . . .'

'Downgraded by the . . . er . . . rating agencies?'

'Exactly. Like Greece. Cost of borrowing rises. Public services unaffordable. Riots in the streets. Nasty situation.'

'A great nation brought to its knees by dinner ladies.'

'Ask yourself this, Freebie – why should *you* pay for somebody else's dinner ladies?'

Serge thinks with nostalgia of the thick-armed bosomy dragons who used to dole out gravy and custard from dripping ladles when he was at primary school in Campsall.

'I rather liked –'

'They're not productive, Freebie. Nobody's making money out of them. Think – if it was all in the private sector. Schools. Universities. Prisons. Hospitals. Sheltered housing. Residential homes. Think of the business opportunities.' He's almost panting with excitement, in that glossy bright-eyed Dobermann way. 'Think Russia. End of Communism. Unlimited opportunity. It's our moment, Freebie.

'By the way,' he leans forward quickly and whispers into Serge's ear, 'looks like Edenthorpe Engineering's being bought out. Private equity.'

Before Serge can say anything, he struts off towards the door.

Puff-puff – it swings closed behind him with the same double rush of air, blowing away things that had previously seemed utterly solid, things he'd grown up with, things he thought you could depend on; now they turn out to be just so much flimsy paper. Puff-puff: there goes heavy engineering, now light as thistledown; there go the dragonish dinner ladies. The trouble is, he can't just shrug off the collateral damage, the way the others around him can. The trouble is, Doro and Marcus planted a seed in him of some tough thorny weed that's taken root and prickles inside. He can't feel quite comfortable in these City clothes, however much he likes the style, any more than he could embrace the barmy philosophy of the commune, however much he loves his parents.

Brazil. Focus on Brazil. It's the third way. It's the joker in the pack. It's the escape parachute.

At lunchtime he rations himself to twenty minutes' furtive surfing in the disabled loo. The Edenthorpe Engineering story is worse than he thought – the receiver is in negotiation with a private equity group registered in Luxembourg. The Doncaster plant will be closed and saleable assets sold off. The Barnsley plant will be stripped down to half the workforce. Did he and Chicken bring this about between them? Or did they just set the downward trend for other short-sell investors, who saw the direction of the market and piled in like wolves, bringing the company to the ground? Whoops! Serge feels vaguely sick as he reads, but maybe it's just the smell in the loo.

Brazil. Focus on Brazil. He closes the business page and opens the property-search website – his spending ceiling is higher now – and keys in a few locations. And there it is. Yes! The place of his dreams. A modest single-storey cottage built of wood with thatched gables and deep shuttered windows set back behind a cluster of coconut palms fifty metres from a pristine beach. The concept of 'modest' is relative. It has air conditioning. Four bedrooms, with two ensuites. A private pool. Situated two kilometres down a private road from the nearest village. He opens up the floorplan. He Googles the location. An image comes up of turquoise sea, a silver arc of beach, fringed by dark forested hills. Far out to sea, white-tipped breakers are rolling. He stares. He enlarges the images. He copies and saves the link. He'll print it off when he gets home and leave it on her desk tomorrow.

*

She's back in the glass-walled office, working at the desk that used to belong to Tim the Finn.

He waits for her to summon him in but she keeps her head down, frowning with concentration as she taps away, peering up at her screen from time to time through glasses that keep slipping down her nose – he's never seen her wear glasses before. Even her smell is different – less feral, more floral. He tries to catch her eye, but she's lost in her own garden of algorithms.

It isn't until late afternoon that she finally drops him an email.

No time today. Tomorrow Sergei we must talk. Mx

CLARA: Behind the bookcase

Clara is distracted by the smell in her classroom, which seems to be coming from Jason.

'Is it true that spazzie girl's your sister, miss?'

'Don't call her a spazzie.'

'Why not?'

'Oh, I don't know.'

It's nearly four o'clock, for goodness' sake.

He shuffles away, and she realises now the smell is coming not from him but from the book corner – a bitter, fusty smell that reminds her of Solidarity Hall. She goes over to investigate. Yes, it's definitely stronger here. But everything is ship-shape in the book corner as far as she can see, apart from a heap of little black chippings on the floor like the ones she found under her chair the other day.

Through the window she sees Megan, waiting for Jason by the gate. She waves and Megan waves back. A moment later, the two of them disappear. Then someone else appears in the car park. Someone horribly bearded. Mr Gorst / Alan still looks dishy, but a lot less dishy than before. And here's Miss Historical Postlethwaite wearing a Zhivago-style coat with frog fastenings, and a Peruvian peasant hat with pigtails at the sides. She runs up and slips her hand into his, and he bends and kisses her. Despite the hat. Despite the pigtails. He kisses her.

Tsk. It'll be wedding bells and babies next. Even Ida Blessingman confided last night that she and that serial-killer moustachioed law-yer are getting hitched. No doubt there'll be a massive multilayered cheesecake at the reception. All around her, life is moving on – only she seems stuck in the past, in the secrets of Solidarity Hall.

Before she can decide whether to feel sad for herself or pleased for them, she hears a noise from the book corner – a scraping, rustling sound. She looks. There's nothing there – but the rustling goes on. It seems to be coming from behind the books. The bookcase is as old as the school, and made of oak. Bending her knees, she heaves, and manages to pull one corner of it away from the wall a couple of inches. A wave of stench hits her, and she steps back sharply. Then, holding her breath, she leans forward to look. At first all she sees is a ball of ripped-up paper in the corner of the wall, then she realises the paper is in fact a nest, and curled up in the nest is Horatio, with four tiny babies, each hardly as big as a thumb, all suckling away. She watches, entranced.

Then, because she doesn't trust herself to replace the bookcase without hurting them, she goes to find Mr Philpott.

'So Horatio turned out to be a lass?' Mr Philpott beams.

Between them, they gently ease the bookcase back almost against the wall. Clara takes her empty lunch box out of her bag and flicks out a few crumbs. The responsibility of providing for Horatio and her four little babies fills her with unexpected delight and anxiety. What do they live on? Probably crisps and butty crumbs from the kids' lunches. She wonders about water, until she remembers the plants in their saucers on the window sill.

'Who could be the father of the babies?' she wonders aloud.

'Where there's 'amsters there's mystery.'

She closes the classroom door, turns off the light, and follows him down to the boiler room for a cup of tea before she hits the road to Sheffield.

'Talking about mystery, you mentioned a fire, when we were at Mrs Taylor's the other day. Something to do with the lads in the Prospects.'

'Aye, at Donny Rovers ground, Belle Vue. Back in 1995.'

Mm. Not the same fire.

'Everybody thought it were a gas explosion. Then they discovered the prat who done it left his mobile phone behind at the scene. Ken Richardson, the owner, got put away for four year. Never a dull moment in Donny, duck!'

'Poor old Doncaster Rovers.'

'A defeated joy. But we beat Plymouth Argyle on Saturday.'

They're down in the boiler room now, where it's cosy and clink-ery. Mr Philpott turns up the blaze and puts the kettle on. Outside the window the light is fading, but in here it's a rosy glow.

'Bloke who owns t' Rovers now, Johnny Ryan, he's a plastic sur-geon. Created Melinda Messenger's boobs.'

'But there was a fire, in 1994. At the old Coal Board offices near Askern, where we lived. My little sister got burned. They never dis-covered who started it. Did you ever hear anything?'

'Hm. That's near t' Prospects, in't it? All sorts of villainy goes on down there.' He pours boiling water over two tea bags.

'My sister said it was lads from the Prospects. They set upon her once, when she was little. But she sometimes makes things up.'

'I never 'eard nowt, duck. But they say that's how Malc Loxley got started in 1988, wi' a fire. He was in scrap metal wi' his brother. Doncaster and South Yorkshire Scrap. Saved up enough to put a deposit down on a empty mill near Elsecar. Insured it for half a mil-lion. Watched it burn down.' He fishes out his tea bag, squeezes it with his fingers and tosses it into the boiler, watching it hiss briefly. 'I tell you what, though, you had to be a villain to crawl out of that dump. There were nowt else around 'ere. Milk? Sugar?'

'Just milk.'

'Aye, I wanted to go to college when I were a lad – but they sent me down't pit. Stuck it for eight year. Got injured. Been at school since 1970. Retire next year. Funny how things work out in life.' He picks up his tea again and sips slowly. 'Did you read about that lass who put out a chip fire wi' a pair of giant knickers?'

It's already dark as Clara sets out for home. A few flakes of snow whirl across her windscreen, and she shivers, wishing she'd set out earlier, and not succumbed to the temptation of a cup of tea in the toasty boiler room, and Mr Philpott's stories.

The unresolved mystery of the fire still smoulders in her mind. Was it the lads from the Prospects? Or was it Oolie herself, who'd made up the story to cover her tracks, worried that Doro would never let her move into a home of her own if she found out the truth? It was all so murky and so long ago, maybe they'll never discover what really happened. Maybe it doesn't matter any more.

She lets it drift away like the snowflakes into the night, and muses instead upon the giant knickers, remembering how the commune kids used to giggle to see Doro and Moira's sensible knickers on the washing line. They thought they were so liberated, sleeping around with everybody, like they'd invented the orgasm. Nowadays, girls have to fight for the freedom to say no.

Poor Doro – she'll miss Oolie, when she moves into her own place. Maybe a baby hamster would keep her company. And Oolie might like a hamster when she moves into her new home. That's two of the four taken care of – three, because she'll keep one herself. Mr Philpott, maybe?

Then she worries about the ethics of breaking up this small happy family for human gratification. Perhaps she should just leave them all to live happily ever after behind the bookcase.

No doubt Shakespeare or Wittgenstein will have the answer.

SERGE: *A greyish bra strap*

'We need new philosophy to understand new economic environment, Sergei.'

A dark strand of hair has worked its way free from Maroushka's bun, and she's chewing on it distractedly as she swivels to face him in the narrow glass-walled office. He has to stop himself from reaching out and easing it back into place.

'I thought the housing market recovery was the new philosophy, princess. Green Shoots.'

She's wearing a charcoal-grey skirt, with a creamy silk blouse and a fitted jacket. The severe corporate outfit emphasises her smallness, like a little kid trying to look grown-up.

'Green Shoots is for average investors, Sergei.' Her stockinged feet are crossed on the base of the chair; a pair of black suede platforms is tossed under the desk. 'Now we have new private hedge fund. Will yield great financial benefit in event Green Shoots defaults.' She says it with a little nervous giggle, pulling the strand of hair from her mouth.

'You're selling a product to investors, and at the same time betting it'll fail?'

'Is not against law,' she says, without meeting his eyes.

'No, but –'

'We have possibility of unlimited upside with limited downside.'

From what she's saying, it seems that Green Shoots (of which, she reminds him, he is now the front man) is no more than a vehicle to attract investor interest, packed with mortgages as ticky as time bombs. Its aim is to cash in on a short-term bounce in house prices – technically a 'dead cat bounce' – which she has already calculated will fall again in a few months' time. Meanwhile she has helped Chicken to construct a complex private hedge fund that will reap huge profits if the recession deepens and mortgage foreclosures rise. As she reaches forward to point out the details on a graph on her screen, her bra strap slips down on to her collarbone, greyish against the creamy silk of her blouse.

'Is it . . . er . . . ethical?'

She giggles cutely and her strap slips forward another centimetre.

'Ethics is for average people, Sergei. Not for us.'

Should he tell her her strap's showing? It looks grubby, but strangely sexy.

'In new times average people will be poor, only elite will be rich. Is better to be elite, Sergei.'

If only he could take her by the shoulders and shake her out of this bewitchment of dream-graphs and fantasy numbers that once enthralled him too.

Princess Maroushka!
Hear the song of Serge . . .

If only he could lean forward and ease that grubby bra strap down over her shoulder, to kiss the sharp collarbone and press his mouth on the hungry twelve-year-old lips, which are sucking again on that stray strand of hair. But through the glass, he can see Chicken sauntering down the aisle of the trading hall in their direction, his jacket unbuttoned, his tie loose. A quick expression he can't comprehend flits across Maroushka's face – half a smile, half a wince.

Then a phone rings on her desk.

'Da?' she answers, and rattles off something in her incomprehensible language.

What's she up to now? Though when you think about it, pretty much everything about her is incomprehensible – or maybe he was just too thick to get it.

As he stands up to leave, she raises her head from her call, puts her hand over the mouthpiece and says, 'By the way, Sergei, you also are not very ethical. Chicken knows you been trading on private account.'

Which is kind of obvious by now.

★

At times like this, you need to phone a friend, but the disabled loo is engaged for what seems like an eternity.

When he gets in there, he notices a used condom, slipped down behind the toilet bowl. Somebody's been lucky.

Otto's voice on the phone sounds weightier, less jumpy than before. Fatherhood has given him gravitas.

'Man, there's any number of ways he could hack into your account. What about that memory stick you found? It could have had a rootkit on it. You thought you were spying on him, but he was really spying on you. Heh heh.'

'Shit!'

'Or he could've just cracked your password. All it would take would be for someone to watch your keystrokes as you were logging in.'

'Not possible.'

'Are you sure? People must be walking past your desk all the time.'

'Yes but –'

'But you know, Sergei, I am here only with student visa.'

The words slam into his brain. She was standing right behind him, looking over his shoulder when she said it. She could have noted his fingers on the keyboard. And he was wittering on about the Iranian War. Was it before or after they kissed? He can't remember. Anyway, it doesn't really matter, does it? He feels a cold hand like a touch of death on his heart.

'Yeah, I'll have to think about it. Thanks, Otto. How's Flossie?'

'She's good. She's just learning to smile. Though she usually pukes up afterwards. One day Free Open-Source Software'll win back the world from Microsoft. By the way, I keep getting little parcels from Doro. She's taken up rainbow crocheting. Have you told her yet, about your job? Because Molly said she came up to Cambridge.'

'Not exactly. I'm getting there.'

Though maybe there'll be no need, if Molly has already done it for him. Maybe he'll soon be on his way to Brazil.

'No stress, man. Come and see us again one day.'

'Sure, I will.'

He switches his phone off, noting another missed call from Clara.

CLARA: *Bulldozers on the allotment*

Doro has shut herself in her room and refuses to come out, and Marcus is staying in to give her moral support, so it falls to Clara to take Oolie up to see the start of work on the site of her new home. Oolie can hardly contain her excitement as she hops and slides along on the snow, which is already turning to slush, on their way up to the allotments.

'It's got six bedrooms for residins. And I'm gonner have me own bathroom and toilet. It'll be reyt good. Mr Clemmins showed me t' pictures. And Mum says when I move into me new house I can 'ave a babbie.'

Clara reels, starts to slip, and has to steady herself by grabbing a railing.

'Are you sure she said that?'

'She said mebbe if I'm good. Cos I'm gonner be reyt good.'

'I was thinking you might like a pet hamster to start with.'

'Yeah! I wanna 'amster!'

She squeezes Oolie's hand. Her sister's spontaneous all-inclusive enthusiasm is one of the things she loves most about her.

The allotment is still covered with a thin fall of snow over the vegetable beds and fruit bushes, making it look like a fresh sheet on which anything could be written. There's a bulldozer roaring away, shovelling the earth into mounds and flattening out a central area where the construction site will be. A couple of blokes with shovels are piling the topsoil into the back of a truck which, oddly, has a small SYREC logo on the door. A gang of kids from the Greenhills Estate is hanging around idly and trying to distract the shovellers with remarks such as, 'Hey, mister, can I lend yer shovel?', 'Give us a fag, mister', 'My sister wants to shag you!'

She spots Jason Taylor and Robbie Lewis among them. They hail her arrival as a welcome diversion.

'Hiya, miss!' yells Jason. 'I didn't recognise you with your clothes on!'

'Ha ha.'

'Give us a fag, miss.'

'I don't smoke,' she lies.

At that moment, a Mini pulls up and a young woman in high heels and a pencil skirt gets out, notepad in hand. Then a red hatchback rolls up and discharges a young man with a camera around his neck.

'Is this the Greenhills Allotments site?'

'My sister wants to shag you!', 'Give us a fag!', 'Can I 'ave a go wi' your camera, mister?' the kids chorus.

While the photographer fiddles with his camera, lining up the bulldozer in shot, another car draws up, a black BMW with darkened windows. A fat man in a shell suit gets out of the driver's seat and two men in suits emerge from the back. One is a big beefy man with a shaved head and a tattoo on his scalp; the other is Councillor Malcolm Loxley. The photographer starts snapping. The councillor walks over to the bulldozer, swaps places with the driver, straps the man's safety helmet on and waves at the photographer, the kids and a few other locals who've come out to gawp. The men with the shovels pose with the councillor. The camera clicks away. Then the councillor reverses the bulldozer, revs up and takes a run at a stubborn little fruit tree that is sticking two branches up out of the churned-up snow and mud, yanking it out by the roots, tumbling it over with the debris of a shed, some mangled bean canes and a few old chairs at the edge of the site.

The onlookers clap and cheer. Oolie joins in with gusto. Clara stuffs her hands in her pockets.

He jumps down and shakes hands with onlookers. The notepad lady minces around him in her pointy heels, writing down the words as they tumble from his lips.

'It gives me great pleasure to initiate this resource for the vulnerable disabled folk in our community, alongside a modern retail development for decent, hard-working Doncaster families . . .'

All the while, his eyes are darting around. There is a patter of

347

applause from the crowd. Clara feels her mouth tighten into a cynical smirk. Doro was right to stay away.

'. . . instead of frittering council tax payers' money on politically correct twaddle.'

What's that supposed to mean?

Then, just as quickly as it started, it's all over. The big shaven-headed man standing over by the BMW nods at the man in the shell suit, who comes over and whispers something in the councillor's ear. The councillor waves at the crowd, climbs into the car and is gone. The driver climbs back into the bulldozer and revs up the engine, the shovellers resume their shovelling, the journalists drive off.

As the crowd drifts away, she notices a tall fair-haired young man standing on the far side of the former allotment, beside the truck. Oolie spots him too, and waves with both hands. Mr Clements picks his way around the edge of the site towards them, his feet sinking into soft churned mud.

'They've made a start,' he says. 'Are you excited, Oolie?'

'Yeah. Cos Mum says I can have a babbie when I move in.'

He laughs uneasily.

'Or a hamster,' adds Clara quickly.

'Apparently it's not a council development at all,' he says. 'It's a new private outfit that's running it. South Yorkshire Residential Care. SYREC. They've been awarded several residential contracts around here. This sheltered housing scheme is a new departure for them. I don't know what your mum'll say about that. She has quite strong views, doesn't she?'

'It has been known,' says Clara.

'Am I still gonner 'ave me own toilet?' asks Oolie.

They walk along together towards Hardwick Avenue. The temperature has dropped, and the pavement is treacherous with frozen slush as dusk approaches. Oolie slips, and he grips her hand to steady her. Then Clara, on the other side, takes a slide too. He walks in the middle, both of them hanging on to him.

After a while, he squeezes her hand and says, '*Iron Man*'s back on at the Odeon. It's meant to be quite good.'

'I've already . . .'
She stops herself.
'What's the eyeing man?' Oolie butts in.
'It's a film,' says Clara.
'I like filums! Can I come?'
'No,' says Mr Clements.

SERGE: The ghost rabbit

Serge is deep in thought as he walks home through the half-melted slush down dark empty streets, vaguely recalling the buoyant feeling with which he set out this morning. The age-old human rhythm – one foot before the other – helps him put his thoughts in order as he tries to make sense of today's conversation with Maroushka. She didn't exactly threaten him, but she pointed out, with that funny twelve-year-old grin, that given his role in Green Shoots, and his own off-the-books trading, it would be in his best interests to keep quiet. As if he had any choice in the matter.

He chooses quiet roads and backstreets, where the shops and offices are closed, and treads carefully, because the pavements are treacherous; only the occasional taxi swooshes past him through the dank December night, leaving a scorched taint of diesel on the air long after it has disappeared from view. The cold death-hand is still prodding his heart.

'. . . I am here only with student visa. When study is finish I must go back to Zhytomyr . . .'

His way takes him around the back of Moorgate, across Chiswell Street and up Bunhill Row, where the righteous dead sleep in tidy graves, lightly sheeted with snow. He used to enjoy walking through here sometimes in the daytime – it reminds him a bit of Mill Road cemetery in Cambridge – but at night it seems faintly spooky, or maybe it's just his state of mind that's spooked.

'But Chicken is apply for permanent work visa for me . . .'

She has her visa now. And what did you give him in return, Maroushka?

Her personal betrayal seems more terrible, more deeply appalling than just sleeping with Chicken would have been. Though she probably did that as well.

Suddenly, up ahead near the gate of the graveyard, in the shadows where the trees overhang the railings, a small white shape springs on to the pavement some twenty metres in front of him, and crouches there, looking at him. It's about the same size and shape as a large white rabbit. He stops. He rubs his eyes. His heart is banging like mad. Is it a bad dream?

A lone car sweeps by. The shape doesn't run away, but it trembles slightly. It seems to have just one ear. He starts to walk again, but more slowly now, keeping his eyes fixed on the creature. It doesn't move away, but it sways from side to side; its form seems to change, to swell grotesquely. What the . . . ?

Aah! He stumbles.

A violent wrenching pain shoots through his knee as the full weight of his body twists over the foot which is snared between a pedal and a bicycle wheel on the ground. Some idiot left a bike chained to a railing. As he falls, the white shape leaps at him. He gasps, puts his hands out, and now he sees it's just a carrier bag full of crumpled paper and takeaway scraps that some scumbag chucked away. Shit! His knee is in agony. Why can't people leave bloody pavements clear? It's not a lot to ask, is it?

'You all right, mate?' A small man in a woollen hat has emerged from the Artillery Arms across the road.

'Sure. Fine. I just need a taxi to get home.'

Tears are pouring down his face as the pain takes over, blotting out everything else, and he finds himself sobbing and giggling at the same time on a roller coaster of agony and elation. Everything that was complex before has become beautifully simple, like when you solve a theorem. Like when you're released from a treadmill.

He knows for sure now that he'll never go back to FATCA. A huge wave of floaty lightness lifts him off the pavement, lifts him above the pain, lifts him beyond shame and regret and fear, and carries him curled on the back seat of a black cab to the place he calls home, but which he knows he will soon say goodbye to as well.

By the time he hauls himself into his bed – he takes the lift up, no racing up the stairs this time! – his knee is painfully swollen. He'll have to see Dr Dhaliwal tomorrow.

But before he turns in for the night, there's just one more thing he has to do. He pours himself a glass of Barolo, takes a couple of Ibuprofen and switches on his laptop. He pastes in the URL of the Brazilian property. It's still there, winking at him from behind the palm trees, all $499,000 worth. When he logs into the Dr Black account, he sees his holding has crept up to £1.21 million. He sets up a transfer to his personal account of the whole lot.

The laptop makes a long chuntering noise, like it's grinding its teeth. The screen goes blank. Then, after a few moments, an error message pops up: 'Transaction denied.'

He tries again, for half the amount. 'Transaction denied.'

Shit! He knows the money's in there – he's seen it. Or rather, he's seen big numbers that purport to represent money. Maybe it was all just a mirage, fairy gold, not real money at all. But if he contacts the bank, they're bound to ask questions. Call in the Fraud Squad. His heartbeat kicks up – boom! Boom! Boom!

He tries a third time, for just enough to cover the Brazilian property. The message pops up: 'Transaction denied. Please contact your local branch.'

Ah well.

DORO: *The stimulator*

'Are we gonner see Santa in Oxfam Street?' asks Oolie.

The train is crowded with shoppers heading for London in the pre-Christmas rush, all clutching their bags and gabbling into their phones, but Doro has a more solemn purpose.

'No. We're going to liberate Serge.'

She doesn't mean literally of course, but the way an enchanted dreamer in a fairy tale is freed from a magic spell. The City seems somnolent compared to the festive bustle of the West End. She's printed the map off Google, and she has no trouble finding the tall glass tower where her son is imprisoned.

She enters a high halogen-bright atrium. On one wall there's a motto in ornate gilt letters. AUDACES FORTUNA IUVAT. She dredges up her grammar school Latin. 'The audacious enjoy fortunes.' Too bloody true.

'Can I help you?' asks one of the pretty blonde girls on reception.

'I'm looking for my son, Serge Free.'

'He's called Sausage.' Oolie grins at the girl, who smiles back.

'If you'd just like to take a seat . . .'

Just then, a tall dark-suited man waves his pass and goes through the security gate. Doro grabs Oolie's hand and barges through behind him, waving airily at the receptionist. They follow him into the lift.

'We're looking for Sausage.' Oolie tries her grin again.

'There's a deli on Watling Street,' he replies, unsmiling, and exits on the next floor.

Doro decides against following him and, not knowing which floor to choose, presses the top button. The glass cage whirls them up through floor after floor. Cables hiss and whirr, wind and unwind. Corridors, open-plan offices, men in suits and women in heels flash past.

'Ooh!' gasps Oolie. 'This is reyt good!'

On the top floor, they step out. No one is around. There's a reception desk, but nobody is behind it. Wan light floods in through the glass wall facing them. They're almost on the same level as the clouds. On each side of the lift, a carpeted corridor panelled on one side in glass, on the other in mahogany, gives access to a number of closed mahogany doors. Behind them, the lift doors shut and the lift disappears, summoned from below.

'Where's Sausage?'

'I don't know. Ssh!'

They stand and listen. An intermittent swishing sound, faint but arresting, is coming from behind one of the doors along the corridor.

'Are they shagging?' asks Oolie.

'Could be.'

Whoever it is seems to have phenomenal stamina.

Suddenly, with a clunk and a swoosh, the lift doors open again. Out come a tall blonde woman and a small dumpy boy. The four stand and eye each other.

'Who are you?' says the tall blonde woman to Doro. She's wearing flat pumps and lots of jewellery, which seems to Doro rather vulgar.

'Dorothy Marchmont,' says Doro, feeling not quite confident enough to tell the woman to piss off. 'And who are you?'

'Caroline Porter. Have you seen my husband?'

'I haven't seen anybody up here,' says Doro, deciding not to mention the sound, which has now stopped.

'You wanna see my stimulator?' the boy whispers to Oolie. He has the same Down's syndrome features and gentle, slightly lost expression.

'Yeah, I wanna stimulator!'

'Oolie! No!' snaps Doro. 'I've no idea who your husband is,' she says to the woman. 'I'm looking for my son.' Then, seeing the sad expression in the woman's eyes, she softens her voice. 'How old's your little boy?'

'Not so little. Willy's twenty-four. And your . . . is she your daughter?'

354

They exchange smiles.

'Yes. Oolie-Anna. Twenty-three.'

Oolie and Willy have disappeared, but she can hear their voices somewhere down the corridor.

At that moment, a tiny white rabbit whizzes along the corridor in front of them. Doro rubs her eyes. Then she realises she's not asleep and it's not a white rabbit, it's a white golf ball, moving very fast.

'Willy! Be careful!' yells Caroline. 'He's obsessed with the golf simulator,' she explains.

Ah. Maybe that's what the sound was.

'I think my son works here,' says Doro. 'I've come to find him.'

Caroline nods. 'We employ something like a thousand staff. Is he a trader?'

'I've no idea. I hope not.'

'The traders are on the ninth floor. D'you want me to come with you?'

'Would you?'

'Come on. Let's go.'

'What about . . .?'

'They'll be all right. They can play with the golf simulator. There's nothing much else they can get up to up here.' She presses the call button for the lift.

'What about your husband?' asks Doro, as they glide down to the ninth floor.

'We'll see.'

The hum of noise from the trading floor hits Doro like a wave as the double doors swing open.

'Serge!' she calls.

Gradually, the hubbub subsides. Some eight hundred pairs of eyes are turned on her.

'Serge, I know you're in here! Don't be afraid!'

Silence.

Beside her, Caroline whispers, 'Wow! You've got some voice!'

'Yes, I used to go on demos.'

Why doesn't Serge come forward? There must be a simple

explanation why he hasn't told her before. Maybe he's afraid she'll accuse him of betraying his ideals.

'Serge! It's your mum! You can come home now. All is forgiven!'

The room shivers with a ripple of suppressed hysteria. All over the trading floor, men in suits and a few girls bury their faces in their hands, their shoulders heaving. Even the computer monitors seem to be chuckling, ripples of blue giving way to ripples of red.

'What you want? What for you shouting?'

A fierce dark-haired girl wearing a tight black dress and ridiculous high heels has come in through the swinging doors behind them. She's quite pretty, but too thin, and wearing far too much make-up.

'I'm looking for my son, Serge Free.'

'You mother of Sergei?' The girl throws her a look of barely disguised contempt. 'I thought you are more cultured.'

Suddenly Caroline lunges and grabs the girl by the hair.

'It's you! The Ukrainian whore!'

The girl struggles. 'Let me go! You no understand him! Old abandon wife!'

Caroline goes for her throat.

The girl fights back with knees and fists, dropping her handbag, whose contents spill all over the floor – grotty bits of make-up, a matted hairbrush, crumpled tissues, stained coins. A small square photograph flutters to Doro's feet. She picks it up. It shows two women, arm in arm, smiling at the camera. She recognises the same girl, with shorter hair, wearing a striped jumper; the other woman looks like her but older, with a shapeless grey perm and bad front teeth. Her mother? The girl snatches the photograph out of Doro's hand, scoops up the rest of her scattered possessions and scuttles away, just as the double doors swing open again and a handsome middle-aged man in shirt sleeves approaches them.

Doro had been half expecting to encounter the devil incarnate in the building, but this man looks quite sexy.

'Caroline! Darling! What brings you here?' He kisses his wife's cheek.

His manner is charming, though Doro notes that his shirt is partly hanging out, and his fly is half undone. His smile reminds her of Malcolm Loxley.

'Willy wanted to play golf, so I left him up there. Didn't you see him?' Caroline's face is still flushed.

'I haven't seen anyone. I've been . . . in a meeting. Treasury Committee.'

He waves a wad of papers which Doro notices have a green portcullis logo at the top. So he's running the country too?

Caroline makes a dive to yank his zip up. 'With your Ukrainian whore?'

'What's got into you, Caroline?' he hisses. 'Have you gone mad?'

'Of course I'm bloody mad!' Caroline hisses back.

'Caroline, stop it! You're making an exhibition of yourself!'

Though strangely, the people in the hall are no longer watching their little fracas but seem transfixed by their screens, which are still rippling scarlet.

'You think I care? After you've been exhibiting your cock all over town?'

'Who . . .?'

'This is my friend . . .'

'Doro Marchmont. How do you do?'

'Ken Porter.'

He reaches out a big meaty hand, which Doro notices is slightly sticky.

She seizes the moment. 'I'm looking for my son, Serge Free.'

Why does he wince like that?

Suddenly a howl of sirens fills the hall. The noise bounces off all the hard hot surfaces in a menacing wail: 'Whaaa! Whaaa! Whaaa!' Then the lights go out, the overhead TV screens flicker and go blank, and one by one all the monitors on all the desks, and all the computers, start to close down. With a grand finale of beeps and farewell chimes, the whole system grinds slowly to a halt.

'Fire alarm!' bellows somebody from the back of the hall.

'Bomb scare!' calls somebody else.

Only the watery light from the tall windows lights up the scene of panic as dozens – no, hundreds – of prisoners throw off their shackles and bolt towards the double doors.

'Yes! Liberate yourselves, drones!' cries Doro, as they pour past her, a human flood, rushing down the stairs, because the lifts aren't working, following the emergency lighting along the floor.

'Oh, God! Willy's up there!' Caroline shrieks suddenly.

'And Oolie!'

'Quick! Up the stairs!' Caroline grabs her hand, and fighting against the grey-suited tide they battle up one, two, three . . . six flights of stairs. The husband follows behind.

On the top floor, panting, the three of them stand and listen. All around is eerily calm. No one is there. Eddies of noise drift faintly up from below; the sirens have stopped, but there's still a babble of voices, and it takes Doro a few moments to make out another closer sound, a soft rising and falling susurration that sounds a bit like snoring.

'We need to talk rationally, darling,' the husband says, gripping Caroline by the arm.

Doro notices a mauve vein throbbing on his temple. His left eye is twitching.

'First we need to find the children,' she interrupts.

'Look in the golf simulator.' Caroline points. 'Down there. I'll look in the boardroom.'

Doro has no idea what a golf simulator is, so she pokes her head into several empty offices. At the end of the corridor, a door opens into a room which is completely dark. As she peers into the blackness, a light suddenly flickers on and the far wall of the long narrow room bursts out into a verdant landscape of rolling countryside, a long valley dotted with trees, a stream in the foreground, distant hills. She gasps. In front of the stream in vivid 3D are some lumpy stones and hillocks which, as she approaches, she sees are not hillocks at all, but items of clothing that have been scattered around. Black shoes. Crumpled brown trousers. A pair of white knickers. There's a quiet tck-tck-tck of a machine whirring somewhere nearby. And yes, the rising-falling susurration is coming from in here too, and now it sounds distinctly like snoring.

'Oolie?'

The landscape shudders and bulges, and she realises it's just a hanging sheet on to which the landscape image is projected.

'Oolie? Willy?'

'Randy shaggy bloody goat . . .!' Caroline's shrill voice whips down the corridor.

A moment later, she and the man burst into the room. She is slapping him around the face with what looks like a small wet latex glove, and he's backing away from her, shouting, 'Stop it, Caroline! Please! At least I *used* a bloody condom!'

'Ssh!' whispers Doro. 'Look!'

She pulls aside the hanging cloth, and in the dark space behind it, strangely illuminated now by the shimmering projected landscape, are the two young people, curled up like cherubs in each other's arms.

'Sorry, Dad.' Willy sits up as the light falls on him, stretches, and rubs his stubby hands through his hair. 'I tried to turn it off, but I think I got the wrong switch.'

Oolie opens her eyes, blinks, and a smile creeps over her face. She says in a sleepy voice, 'We're going to have a babbie.'

Far away in the wavering gleaming landscape, a tiny white rabbit races away and pops down a hole.

Epilogue

MARCUS: Ouch!

Ooh-aah! The pain is worse today. This afternoon he'll go up to the hospital to discuss the results of the tests with the consultant, and then, if needs be, he'll have to sit down and talk it through with Doro. Maybe he should have told her before, but why throw her into a panic, when the symptoms are so vague? Generalised tired-ness, a bit of bloating, passing wind rather more than usual (little Oolie spotted that one) and recently this painful constipation. Hope-fully nothing that a dose of good medicine won't cure. With any luck, Doro need never know at all. No, it's not the same as not tell-ing her about Oolie. That was for his benefit, because he couldn't face her accusations, and he's not proud of that. But this is for her sake. The trouble is, she does get into such a flap.

Lucky he managed to keep it under control during the wedding yes-terday, which was quite a jolly low-key affair at the registry office in Doncaster, though Oolie went a bit OTT bouncing around in a blue outfit covered in bows, kissing everybody. And God knows what persuaded Doro to wear that catastrophic hat, which looked more like an implement for steaming vegetables than headgear. Now that she's an Oxfam volunteer she comes back with all kinds of tat, but Serge swears he bought it in a boutique in Shoreditch.

It was good to see Serge and his new partner, a very nice and sensible young woman. Doctor. Indian. Looked like she was pregnant – he didn't like to ask. Apparently they're talking about moving back up to Yorkshire when Serge has finished his PhD. Doro'll be pleased, especially now Clara's gone and Oolie's moved out. Ooh-aah! That pain!

Good to see Otto too, and Molly and their two kids, though God knows why they've given them such ridiculous names. Flossie and Wiki. Whatever next? Toothpick and Nasty? Reminds him of those poor kids Toussaint and Kollontai. Parents should be shot. Kids turned out okay, though, in spite of it. Nick and Jen were there, getting all goo-gooey with the babies. He always thought Nick was a bit Aspergic and Jen was totally mad, but they've somehow re-invented themselves as model suburban grandparents. God knows what Doro ever saw in him.

Star couldn't come – she's been arrested again for some climate disturbance – but Moira was there. She's put on a bit of weight, but she's still gorgeous in the tits department. Funny, he couldn't have said that in those days without risking the wrath of the Femintern. That's what Fred Baxendale called them. He was there too. A bit thin on top. Still wearing the same jumper. On to his nineteenth live-in girlfriend. Or twentieth. Lost count. The jumper, which according to Doro he bought in a Boxing Day sale at John Lewis in 1971, has outlasted them all. God knows what they see in him.

Afterwards, there was a bit of a reception back at Hardwick Avenue, with soya patties, bean salad and lentil bake. For old times' sake, Doro said. Personally, he was never into that lifestyle politics, which he viewed as anti-Marxist. In fact, he used to nip out for an occasional steak to the Little Chef at Adwick. That's another thing he never told Doro. There are only so many lentils a man can eat in his life.

There were some strange people at the reception, who seemed to have turned up uninvited. The caretaker from Clara's school was there, going on about his unweeded garden, with his friend, an elderly Ukrainian engineer, who'd worked at the McCormick tractor works in Wheatley Hall back in 1955, and some of Doro's allotment crowd. There was a wrinkled blonde woman from Askern who sidled up to him in the kitchen and asked whether he remembered sleeping with her during the strike. He nodded and grinned politely, trying to summon an expression of enthusiasm, but he couldn't for the life of him remember. And a woman with pink leggings and a brown poodle, who kept going on about how the Seeing Eye would make him better. She said Serge had told her about his condition. Bloody cheek. Ay-ay-ay!

Shame Clara couldn't come, but she sent a message of love from

Copacabana, where she's gone to set up a school for slum children with that social worker of Oolie's. Doro was distraught when they got together. Apparently she can't stand him, God knows why. Seems a perfectly sound young man, solid working-class background, and Oolie really took to him.

Talking about Oolie, there was all that fuss about her phantom pregnancy. He could have told them nothing would come of it, if anyone had bothered to ask him, as it's well known that Down's syndrome men are generally infertile. Clara gave her a baby hamster instead, before she left, and that seems to have done the trick. And Doro's helping her start a garden at her new place, planting flowers and vegetables and a plum tree. They're still together, Oolie and the young man – in fact, there's talk of him moving in with her. He came up for the wedding with his ghastly mother. She bought Oolie a housewarming present, a little illuminated glass egg timer. Only £280, she said. Saw it in 'How to Spend it'. Poor Doro almost fainted. She and Doro seem to have got quite pally, God knows why. Megan was there too. The three of them got drunk and started sobbing during the reception. It was hideously embarrassing.

Ouch! Enough idle gossip for now. Time's running short, and there are still serious issues to be resolved. As predicted, capitalism is crumbling under the weight of its own contradictions. And it's gratifying to know that they've all made their own contribution to its downfall, Clara with her championing of the children of the oppressed, Doro with her environmental concerns, Oolie by mounting a challenge on the resources of the state and, above all, Serge with his bravura penetration into the heart of the satanic mill, which he succeeded in destabilising temporarily. Entryism at its most daring.

As for him, he still has his major theoretical work to complete, the history of the Autonomist Movement of the seventies culminating in an analysis of how it could pave the way for a post-crash renegotiation of the social contract. Although he's been working on it for seven years, there's much that is still unclear. In fact, it seems to get more unclear as time goes by. Things change so fast. A whole lot hangs on the result of the next general election. Will the world

365

move towards a steadier more regulated form of capitalism? Or will the global financiers be unleashed to push the whole rotten system crashing finally to the ground? There's so much he could contribute. If only he didn't feel so tired all the time.

Ooh-aah! He shifts his weight in the chair, leaning forward to ease the pain. That's better. It's a good thing they've got this wedding out of the way. Doro had her doubts of course, but he persuaded her it could help with adopting Oolie. And as it turns out, it's probably for the best. She's a wonderful woman, sensual, passionate, kind – yes, he's been lucky to share his life with her. And if the result this afternoon goes against him, at least she'll get whatever's left of his pension. Ouch!

Acknowledgements

Many brains have contributed to this book, most of them much better than mine.

I would first like to thank all those who helped me so generously with research into the financial world, especially Peter Morris, without whom I could never have got started, and Robert Deri, Roger Leboff, Roger Johnson, Gareth Jones, Steven Bell, Robert Farrer-Brown and John Scott, who between them advised me about the financial crisis, short selling and naked short selling, spread betting, derivatives and options, the physical layout and organisational structure of investment banks, the roles of quants and traders, pay scales, security procedures, departmental organisation, scams and frauds, rating agencies and the goings-on in the disabled loo. All credit is due to them, and any errors are entirely my own.

I'm grateful to Gary Clemitshaw and Alison Tyldesley for explaining the primary school curriculum. Also to Dorothy Kidd, Sheila Ernst, Dave Feickert, Dave Kent, Max Farrar and others who have reminded, encouraged and informed me about women's liberation and the commune days; any shortcomings in the depiction are wholly down to me.

Many thanks also to those who read through various drafts, offered their comments and weeded out mistakes: Donald Sassoon, Sonia Lewycka, Carl Cramer and Shân Morley Jones. Thanks to Martin and Juliet Pierce for the use of their cosy writing room, and all those cups of tea.

Finally, thanks to my agent Bill Hamilton and my editor Juliet Annan – who between them killed off several minor characters, pruned out weedy subplots and generally sharpened things up – and to the terrific teams at Penguin and Fig Tree who have made the book happen.